"He calls it *CarAlity*; it has a capital 'A' in the middle," explained Calman.

"Of course it does," Winters replied, in his usual sarcastic tone. "How 2005."

CarAlity... A Tribute In New Orleans
by J. Daniel Jones
Copyright © 2016 J. Daniel Jones
First Edition

All rights reserved. This book is protected under the copyright laws of the United States of America. This book may not be copied, reprinted, or otherwise duplicated without written consent of the author or his authorized agents. The use of short quotations, for review purposes only, is permitted.

This is a work of fiction. Names, characters, businesses, places, events and incidents are either the products of the author's imagination or used in a fictitious manner. Any resemblance to actual persons, living or dead, or actual events is purely coincidental.

ISBN: 0998177806
ISBN 13: 9780998177809
Library of Congress Control Number: 2016954869
Pure Entertainment, San Diego, CA

www.CarAlity.com

# Foreword

## September 18, 2016

My name is John Kraman. I'm the Consignment Director for Mecum Auctions, the world's largest collector car auction company. I'm also a TV Commentator and On-Air Analyst for the NBCSN coverage of our auctions.

Over the past 25 years, collector car auctions have become incredibly popular for buying, selling and even just spectating. Many attendees describe the in-person experience at these auctions as the best car show they've ever attended. I like to call it "a car show with a pulse!"

Television has, of course, been a big part in presenting the excitement and action of the auction environment; introducing the myriad variety of cars that, in a typical auction, might span over 100 years of automotive history. The combination of hours-long TV coverage, along with the rapid pace and variety of cars crossing the block, allow for a very concentrated study of both values and general information about the collector car world. Viewers find this combination interesting, entertaining, and even compelling… as do I.

In the summer of 2016, I was invited to preview a novel set in the collector car auction world. The novel also happened to revolve around the specialized environment of automotive television production. It was written by a fellow Motor Press Guild member, albeit one I had never met nor heard of. But, being an avid reader and intrigued by the subject matter, I readily agreed. Within days I received a plain, unassuming, black 3-ring binder. It contained 368 pages with an interesting title, *CarAlity… A Tribute In New Orleans.*

With my immersion in all things related to the collector car auction world, including the TV production aspect, my immediate concern was how accurately a fictional tale would be crafted by someone with a somewhat limited inside knowledge of the auto auction world, or so I assumed. With this in mind, I started reading, with only mild expectations of what was about to unfold.

My first impression was how accurate and believable the characters were, in both their personalities and their various professional roles. While the star of the tale might very well be a certain automobile, I found the individual characters to be introduced and presented so clearly, that I immediately connected with them.

Indeed, it was this character development that was a crucial part of my interest right from the beginning. In addition, the immense amount of intricate behind-the-scenes details are superbly presented; greatly adding to both the realism and my enjoyment.

Finally, the twists and turns, some expected but many not, so drew me into the story that I had difficulty putting it down. Throughout the summer, I was always sad when the corporate jet would land at the auction site, and I had to put *CarAlity* away until the event was over.

Dan has a real gem of a book here. It will not only have a strong appeal to us experienced auction folks, but to anyone who appreciates a great story; superbly crafted and exceptionally well written.

John Kraman
Mecum Auctions
Walworth, WI

# Cast Of Characters
*(In Order Of Appearance)*

1.) **Heinrich Heinzburg** — Consignment seller of a 1940 Mercedes 770k W150 Grosser Tourenwagen.
2.) **Antoine "Andy" Guidry** — Down on his luck TV producer who consigns his 1968 Porsche 911T in the *Muscles On The Mississippi* collector car auction in New Orleans, LA.
3.) **Pat McMillian** — Auction Manager, Collector Car Division, for A-Bear Auctions, New Orleans, LA.
4.) **Jack Calman** — Executive Producer for NGTV, the television production arm of the Neiderland Group.
5.) **Bobby Raston** — An audio genius that specializes in highly complex television field production.
6.) **Mandy & Brandy Fukui**, aka **The Twins** — Gorgeous Eurasian camera operators who take multi-cam field production to a whole different level… almost without realizing it.
7.) **Dean Preston** — PA that recently began working as a free-lance field producer for NGTV.
8.) **J. Roger Winters** — Senior executive at NGTV.
9.) **Herman Adler** — Early 20's college student from Richland Center, WI; ward of **Saul Wittmann**.
10.) **Steve Rampart** — Early 20's college student from Richland Center, WI; former high school football star with chronic knee injury.
11.) **Albert & Nancy Adler** — Herman Adler's parents, now deceased.

12.) **Saul Wittmann** — Wealthy, elderly landowner in Richland Center, WI.
13.) **Sheila Wittmann** — Saul's much younger wife.
14.) **Frank Castleman** — Owner/operator of the Castleman Shell station in Richland Center, WI.
15.) **Shawanda** — Desk Clerk at Best Western Plus, a French Quarter Landmark Hotel.
16.) **Nina Perez** — Jack Calman's administration assistant at NGTV.
17.) **Mason LaCroix** — Counterman at the FedEx Office store next to New Orleans Convention Center. Also, youth minister at the First Free Mission Baptist Church.
18.) **Brian "Cool-B" Simmons** — Senior producer for United A/V, a corporate audio-visual production company.
19.) **Malcolm Walker** — Technical director for United A/V, a corporate audio-visual production company.
20.) **Jack During**, a.k.a. **Jacque Dupis** — A waiter at the Royal Street Oyster House.
21.) **Sandra Melancon** — FOX-15 automotive reporter.
22.) **Joey Banks** — FOX-15 camera operator.
23.) **Grady Peerman** — Owner of Peerman's Peerless Pontiacs, Jackson, MS.
24.) **Alton Briggs** — FOX-15 video editor.
25.) **Preston Moralas** — FOX-15 food reporter.
26.) **Frank LaVere** — FOX-15 news anchor.
27.) **Clarice Courville** — FOX-15 news anchor.
28.) **Stan Niemec** — Owner of SN Auctions and SN Restorations.

29.) **Jay Rollins Broussard** — Pastor of the First Free Mission Baptist Church
30.) **Sheryl Binderhoff** — Librarian at Richland Center, WI.
31.) **Frank McWarren** — Pastor at First Harvest Methodist Church of Richland Center, WI.
32.) **Maurice Schafer** — Retired New Orleans police officer who now provides private security services.
33.) **Dennis Blanchard** — Car wrangler for A-Bear Collector Car Auctions.
34.) **Landry Babineaux** — Car wrangler for A-Bear Collector Car Auctions.
35.) **Joe Fontenot** — New Orleans Police Officer making extra money working security for A-Bear Collector Car Auctions.
36.) **Charlie Bonet** — New Orleans Police Officer making extra money working security for A-Bear Collector Car Auctions.
37.) **Prescott Hébert** — Founder & CEO of A-Bear Auctions, International.
38.) **Jay Bozeman** — Wealthy playboy and car collector from Dallas, TX.
39.) **Mark Hanson** — Wealthy land developer and car collector from St. Paul, Minnesota.
40.) **Dave Givens** — Owner of "Cue The Cars," supplier of specialty and period correct cars to the movie industry.
41.) **Frank Hillman** — A-Bear Auctioneer.
42.) **Marcus, Angie, & Albert Susskind** — Family visiting the HEIL.

# Table of Contents

|  |  |  |
|---|---|---|
|  | Foreword | iii |
| Prologue | Grosser Tourenwagen | 1 |
| Chapter 1 | A Sweet '68 911T | 6 |
| Chapter 2 | '64 442 Tribute | 15 |
| Chapter 3 | Drastic Times | 24 |
| Chapter 4 | Anyone Can Buy New | 34 |
| Chapter 5 | Twin Cams | 40 |
| Chapter 6 | The Pitch | 47 |
| Chapter 7 | Last Minute Consignment | 59 |

| Chapter 8 | Problem Solved · · · · · · · · · · · · · · · · · · · · · · 63 |
|---|---|
| Chapter 9 | Pretty Darn Fast · · · · · · · · · · · · · · · · · · · · · · 71 |
| Chapter 10 | '76 Cosworth Vega · · · · · · · · · · · · · · · · · · · 74 |
| Chapter 11 | The Four Producer Food Groups · · · · · · · · 87 |
| Chapter 12 | It's All About Provenance · · · · · · · · · · · · · · 94 |
| Chapter 13 | CarAlity · · · · · · · · · · · · · · · · · · · · · · · · · · · · · 102 |
| Chapter 14 | Epic · · · · · · · · · · · · · · · · · · · · · · · · · · · · · · · · 112 |
| Chapter 15 | Sieggymobile · · · · · · · · · · · · · · · · · · · · · · · · 126 |
| Chapter 16 | TDF · · · · · · · · · · · · · · · · · · · · · · · · · · · · · · · · 136 |
| Chapter 17 | Just The Assistant · · · · · · · · · · · · · · · · · · · · 144 |
| Chapter 18 | Praise Jesus · · · · · · · · · · · · · · · · · · · · · · · · · 152 |
| Chapter 19 | Double Ewweeuu · · · · · · · · · · · · · · · · · · · · 159 |
| Chapter 20 | 8:27:14 · · · · · · · · · · · · · · · · · · · · · · · · · · · · · 167 |
| Chapter 21 | Partners · · · · · · · · · · · · · · · · · · · · · · · · · · · · 181 |
| Chapter 22 | Gospel According To Saul · · · · · · · · · · · · · 204 |

| | | |
|---|---|---|
| Chapter 23 | Mysterious Ways Indeed | 214 |
| Chapter 24 | Deal Or No Deal | 225 |
| Chapter 25 | VIB | 232 |
| Chapter 26 | Time To Go To Work | 244 |
| Chapter 27 | It's Never Too Late | 253 |
| Chapter 28 | Day Two | 259 |
| Chapter 29 | Phillips | 273 |
| Chapter 30 | Mic Check | 283 |
| Chapter 31 | Not Missing The Big Guys | 293 |
| Chapter 32 | Finalize The Deal | 303 |
| Chapter 33 | Funky Chicken | 309 |
| Chapter 34 | Either Way, I'm Buying | 319 |
| Chapter 35 | It's Convenient | 326 |
| Chapter 36 | This is HUGE | 332 |
| Chapter 37 | Bad Moon Arising | 341 |

| | | |
|---|---|---|
| Chapter 38 | Personal Arrangement | 345 |
| Chapter 39 | Just SOP | 356 |
| Chapter 40 | No Spielberg | 366 |
| Chapter 41 | Live Shot At 10:10 | 373 |
| Chapter 42 | Exactly Like The Storm | 379 |
| Chapter 43 | Let It Shine | 387 |
| Chapter 44 | Big Money, Beautiful Women | 394 |
| Chapter 45 | Minibar Whiskey | 401 |
| Chapter 46 | Make It Two Orders | 404 |
| Chapter 47 | FOX 15 News At 10 | 407 |
| Chapter 48 | Kids | 421 |
| Chapter 49 | Coin Flip | 428 |
| Chapter 50 | I'm No Reporter | 432 |
| Chapter 51 | Discretion | 441 |
| Chapter 52 | Caveat Emptor | 450 |

| | | |
|---|---|---|
| Chapter 53 | Who Dat | 465 |
| Chapter 54 | Not Too Interesting | 471 |
| Chapter 55 | Heinous Hate Incarnate | 482 |
| Chapter 56 | Twice In Two Days | 487 |
| Chapter 57 | Period Correct | 502 |
| Chapter 58 | Mildly Intimidating | 512 |
| Chapter 59 | Very Weird Indeed | 517 |
| Chapter 60 | Long Story | 521 |
| Chapter 61 | None Of My Business | 528 |
| Chapter 62 | It's Showtime | 533 |
| Chapter 63 | Es Ist Hier | 540 |
| Chapter 64 | PROV-E-NANCE | 553 |
| Chapter 65 | If There Are No Questions | 562 |
| Chapter 66 | Make It Three | 572 |
| Chapter 67 | Nowhere Else To Go | 586 |

| Chapter 68 | Something Like That | 592 |
| Epilogue | Who Knew | 607 |
| | About The Author | 615 |

# CarAlity...

## A Tribute In New Orleans

*A Novel By:*

# J. Daniel Jones

*CarAlity… A Tribute In New Orleans*
is dedicated to Cindy, my wonderful wife and the love of my life; always believing in me, and my abilities, despite ample evidence to the contrary.

*Special Thanks:*

John Aronson
*Aronson Associates, Los Angeles, CA*

Bill Coe
*Music & Mix, San Diego, CA*

Christin Grisko
*German Language Guidance*

Thomas Hanson
*Mercedes-Benz Classic Center, Irvine, CA*

Katy Jones
*Cover Illustrations*

William Kent
*Canadian War Museum, Ottawa, ON*

John Kraman
*Mecum Auctions, Inc.*

Will Loomis
*ChromeRunners.com*

Lenny Magill
*Magill's GlockStore, San Diego, CA*

Mecum Auctions, Inc.
*Walworth, WI*

Ryan Moore
*Vaping Technology Consultant*

David Morton
*Mecum Auctions, Inc.*

Jerry Pitt
*The Enthusiast Network, El Segundo, CA*

Susan Ross
*Canadian War Museum, Ottawa, ON*

Vicari Auction Company
*New Orleans, LA*

*First Readers:*
Robert Becker
Bill Coe
Josh "Juice" Jones
Karen Lon

*Second Readers:*
John Kraman
David Morton
Samuel Myers
Mark Sussman
Cindy Tiano
Bonnie Webb

# PROLOGUE

# Grosser Tourenwagen

*Monday – July 31 – 10:42 AM*

> "Everybody's got to have some
> skin in the game."
> — Heinrich Heinzburg

Heinrich Heinzburg literally marched into the mammoth warehouse at the Hamburg docks. He was very much a man on a mission, and was trailed by a massive cloud of billowy white vapor. His ornate vaping device was the largest hand-held unit available, and the most expensive. After two more huge drags, he slipped it into the custom-made black leather sheath mounted to his belt. At first glance, it might easily be mistaken for a small pistol holster. It was basically his only vice.

He had only recently begun drinking the occasional beer, and had always shunned recreational drugs of any type. There was too much to accomplish in life to purposefully cloud his mind. It was both a personal and a family thing.

He paced about the vehicle with a military-flavored demeanor that was finally becoming second nature. He was in his early thirties, six foot two, and visibly muscular, albeit in a wiry sort of way. His straight blond hair was cut in a manner that would have been very stylish in the 1930s, long on top and virtually shaved on the sides. It looked good on him. Actually, everything looked good on him, including the small, very square patch of facial hair directly below his bottom lip. The *soul patch* had a look that was vaguely familiar, if in an uneasy sort of way.

He admired the paint on the black 1940 Mercedes 770k W150 Grosser Tourenwagen. Not because it was polished to a mirror-like gleam, but because it was not. It had a patina of age, but not abuse. It was perfect, and he was all about perfection.

The entire car was covered in a thin, almost gossamer layer of dust. The coating was disturbed here and there by the handling required to get the car to this point in its travels. The steel wheels were body-colored, as was the color ring on the lightly tarnished chrome hubcaps surrounding the three-point star. Delicate cobwebs filled small gaps between the hubcaps and wheels. The spiders that wove those webs had died long before Heinrich was born.

The tires actually held air – for a while anyway – but the deep cracks in the rubber left no doubt as to their age and authenticity. Their airworthiness was not, however, an issue. The entire car rested on multiple jack stands and was secured to a thick wooden platform by heavy-duty tie down straps, cinched as tight as the ratchet mechanisms would allow.

The impossibly long, black convertible top was up, its frame barely visible against the smooth, padded canvas. Although tinted a bit brown by the dust, its structural integrity was obviously responsible for the nearly impeccable condition of the interior.

Inside the car, magnificent leather seats were dry and cracked, yet somehow still inviting. Despite the condition, one could almost feel the luxurious comfort they had once provided and might one day do so again.

Looking like the textbook definition of a *barn find*, Heinzburg was more than pleased with his own personal additions to the car. The two chrome flag holders were mounted to the inside of the huge front fenders. They were just behind the pie-pan sized headlights, which themselves were flanked by four auxiliary driving lights.

Heinzburg smiled as he examined them. He had, at first, debated with himself as to whether to add them. In the end, he had decided the car looked naked without them. Besides, the car had undoubtedly once proudly displayed them. Indeed, despite the recent installation, the flag holders looked as if they had been there since the car rolled off the assembly line. The small red flags were suitably used, but not tattered. Even though they were lying limp against the chrome rods, with just a portion of the center emblem showing, virtually anyone alive today would instantly recognize the simple, yet sinister, swastika.

There was remarkably little else that had needed to be done. The only non-Mercedes item in the car was a pair of seventy-five year old German Army officer gloves lying on the seat, as if the owner had laid them there while he left for a short errand.

Heinzburg had thought briefly about adding a small, suitably aged leather bound copy of *Mein Kampf*, but decided against it.

*Too much is too much*, he reminded himself. He finished the thought with the companion comment; *subtlety is the mark of the master*. They were just two of a number of mottos that were drilled into his family from birth.

To say he was pleased with the presentation would be a gross understatement. Its intricate back-story, supported by the video of the car's discovery, would certainly pass muster. The production had been necessary to accomplish his goal; that being for the car to fully realize its rightful legacy.

His final inspection complete, he motioned to the workers who had been standing by at the ready. They immediately began constructing the shipping container around the car. Time was of the essence, as the ship to New Orleans would most certainly sail on schedule, whether or not his cargo was on it. But it would be, and it would arrive precisely at the proper time and in the proper place. And just in time to be photographed and featured in the LMC.

Heinzburg smiled, remembering the phone call he had finally placed exactly five weeks ago. He had spent months researching the various American auto auction houses. Once he had found A-Bear Auctions, he had immediately known it was the perfect venue. Exactly as he anticipated, the auction manager eagerly agreed to the carefully timed arrival, the LMC promotion, and the unusual financial arrangement. Unusual in that it was decidedly lopsided, to the potential advantage of both the auction house and the manager.

"Everybody's got to have some skin in the game," he muttered in English. He then smiled, thinking the phrase would make a fine addition to the old family mottos. One of the workmen stopped and looked at him quizzically, not understanding the statement and wondering if it was an instruction.

Heinrich smiled, shook his head and said to the workman in perfect German, "It is nothing. Please continue your work."

Finally, the container was completed and moved to the dock. The four top corners were attached to crane lines and the massive box was lifted up and into the hold of the freighter.

He had arranged to be a passenger on the boat, and would accompany his precious cargo until the final port of call. It would be a slow trip, and he was not sure he would like sea travel, but he had nothing else to do. This was the beginning of the culmination of nearly two years of intense planning and fastidious work. Besides, he told himself, he could use the time to further polish this relatively new persona.

He reminded himself that *presentation is everything*. It was yet another of the mottos that had guided his family's endeavors for at least decades, and likely much, much longer.

"Yes, presentation is everything," he said softly in flat, flawless English. He then sighed, shook his head and repeated it again. This time, he infused the English with a heavy German accent and then once more with a much lighter one. He thought about the two versions and tried them both again. It was hard to decide which version he favored. He then shrugged his shoulders, looked up at the ship, and smiled. He would have plenty of time to decide on his accent.

# CHAPTER 1
# A Sweet '68 911T

*Friday – August 18 – 7:33 AM PDT*

> "Now you... you've got soul!"
> — ANTOINE GUIDRY

Even in third gear, revving just barely past two grand, the Porsche sounded incredible. It had always sounded great, but that new exhaust system had transformed the merely great into truly incredible.

The driver smiled as the stoplight in the left turn lane changed to a green arrow. He was half a block from the turn and the lane was empty. Downshifting into second, the engine awoke with a raspy snarl. The wailing sound bounced between the buildings, amplifying and adding rock star reverb to its high-pitched solo. Taking the left turn at just below autocross speed, the driver began tapping furiously on the gate controller clipped to the visor. He kept tapping until he saw the steel gate finally start to roll up.

"Gonna make it!" he cried out loud as his smile grew wider and he made a squealing right turn into the parking garage. He then pushed in the clutch and braked hard at the bottom of the ramp, rapidly slowing to roughly five miles per hour to avoid bottoming out. Neglecting this portion of his favorite maneuver was the reason he was enjoying the new exhaust system on his car... and dreading it on his credit card statement.

Past the dip, and still in second, he let out the clutch and took a hard left. With years of practice, he gave her just enough gas to get her rolling smartly, eased up on the throttle until the revs matched the speed, then slapped the lever into neutral without touching the clutch. He then blipped the throttle twice as he always did. He loved hearing the engine echo through the parking garage.

Still rolling with the car in neutral, he then took a sharp right, braked with authority, and abruptly stopped. He was precisely centered in his reserved parking spot with a huge smile on his face. After a few moments of quiet satisfaction, he got out, locked the Porsche, and paused to look at the brand new Tesla parked next to him.

Standing there, he just shook his head. While the electric vehicle was certainly pretty, it just had no *soul*. He then looked as his beautiful Porsche and took a deep breath through his nose. The smell of the hot, air-cooled engine mingled with slight ticking of the cooling metal to produce a multi-sensory delight. It made her seem almost alive.

He smiled and softly whispered, "Now you... you've got soul!"

An hour later Antoine Guidry, Andy to everyone but his mother, was pacing nervously in his downtown loft.

Even though it was certainly expensive, it wasn't a large place. Even at only five foot ten, it took just a few paces to get from one side to the other. He paused at the window by his desk and saw his reflection superimposed over Market Street.

For sixty-one, he was in reasonably decent shape. It appeared as though he still had most of his hair, when viewed from the front anyway. And despite being at least forty pounds over his ideal weight, he wasn't all butt and belly. He had big muscular shoulders, with matching biceps and strong, sturdy legs. The limbs were kept reasonably toned by semi-regular visits to the downtown 24 Hour Fitness, although at his age it took a whole lot of effort for it to show just a little.

Currently, those broad shoulders were hunched over, the slope matching the frown plastered on his lips. He needed to make a phone call. It was a familiar one, but one he hadn't made in a long time. It was a last ditch effort whose outcome would decide if he was going to continue living in his prewar, converted warehouse condo overlooking the Gas Lamp Quarter of downtown San Diego.

He loved his condo, he loved living downtown, and he loved the gated, covered parking for Max, his pet name for the 1968 Porsche 911T Targa Soft Window. As to Max herself... love wasn't nearly a strong enough word. Guidry absolutely cherished that car. It was one thing, perhaps the only thing, that he owned free and clear.

Not a day went by that Guidry didn't think how lucky he was that he bought her when he did. It was the first auto auction he'd ever attended and the first production he'd worked on as a field producer. This was just before air-cooled 911 prices began their rocket ship ride to *unaffordium.*

Max had been a very late consignment to the SN Auction in Scottsdale. As such, she ended up being the third car on the first day. At that early hour, the smattering of bidders were barely awake, or so it had seemed. When the all-original, incredibly pampered Irish Green Porsche with brown leather upholstery failed to top twelve grand, and he heard the auctioneer announce, "GOING TWICE..." he immediately threw up his paddle. He thought if someone was going to get a steal of a deal, it might as well be him.

Guidry had never intended to actually buy a car. One of his new duties as a field producer was writing voice over copy for the roll-in segments. He had signed up as a bidder simply to experience a little bit of the bidding process first hand, so he could more clearly describe the feeling of being caught up in the moment.

Regardless of his intentions, he did indeed receive a first-person lesson in the concept of auction frenzy. Less than four intense minutes after he first raised his paddle, he was the proud, and significantly less financially liquid owner of a forty-year-old used car, costing him twenty nine thousand dollars. And that was before the auction house commission. After the penalties for early withdrawal, the purchase had left him with just over twelve dollars in his IRA account. Roughly the same amount it still contained.

From that first production of *Bid Battle*, which he often referred to as *The Max Show*, Guidry had gone from being a field producer on the first season, to a two-season stint as a supervising producer, finally ending up as the senior line producer. NGTV executives knew that a majority of *Bid Battle's* success came from Guidry's innate creativity, attention to detail and true love of cars.

The next step was for Guidry to drop his freelance status and become a Neiderland employee, an offer that had been made to him more than once. He was, after all, working more or less full time on Neiderland productions and primarily on *Bid Battle*. But switching to being an actual employee would have resulted in a fairly severe pay cut, at least on a day-rate basis. Of course, being an employee also included benefits such as health care and a matching 401k, but he had bigger plans in mind.

The watershed moment came in 2007 when the current production company for *Bid Battle* had an internal meltdown due to the husband side of the husband/wife partnership having more than a passing interest in his personal assistant. Suddenly the production contract for *Bid Battle* was up for grabs.

Banking on his relationship with NGTV, he founded Pure Entertainment — his own production company — and went heavily into debt for HD cameras and editing gear. With those resources in place, he secured a deal to become the production company of record for *Bid Battle*. The financial part of the deal allowed Guidry to cover the monthly note on the massive equipment loan, albeit just the interest. It also covered his office rent, paid the freelancers, and qualified him for *no money down* loan on his downtown condo.

In 2011 there was talk that *Bid Battle*, whose production values had increased dramatically since Guidry took complete control, would be going into syndication. And, at that year's MIPCOM, there was significant interest in international distribution as well. Not that Guidry would benefit from any of those exciting developments. Even though he produced it, and literally poured his heart and soul into the program, Guidry didn't actually own any part of the show. Not many producers, or production companies, actually did anymore.

In the mid 1990s, the FCC had rescinded long-standing program ownership rules, which had essentially barred broadcast outlets from owning the programs they presented. The new rules literally changed the entire industry. Almost overnight, cable networks, such as HGTV and the Food Network, went from leasing the programs they aired, in a convoluted formula of length of lease and allowable airings, to simply contracting for the production and owning the results outright.

For production companies and independent producers, it was a mixed blessing. Fees for program production went up dramatically, sometimes even quadrupling on the most popular programs. The downside was the even more valuable secondary revenue, in the forms of reruns, foreign distribution, and home video sales, essentially disappeared from their balance sheets.

The exception was programming that had a big media name attached to them, like *Fast Cars & Customs*. Programs like those were either wholly owned by the publishing company, or as a joint venture between the company and the cable network. A sole proprietor production company, like Pure Entertainment, even when lucky enough to get a television production contract, didn't usually own the programs they produced; *usually* being the operative word.

There were a handful of independents that had compelling enough programs that they could make a barter deal with the cable network and retain ownership of the programs. A barter deal was an arrangement where the production company would supply the programming, the network would supply the distribution, and they would share the commercial ad time. If you could swing a deal like this, and manage to sell the advertising time to a national sponsor, you could actually own the program and all the residual rights and income.

That's why, in 2014, Guidry had made a big, life-changing decision. While he wasn't exactly *cash heavy*, he did have that fat line of credit that came with paying substantial bills on time, every time. He also had that sense of programming invincibility that all producers get when something they craft is enjoyed by hundreds of thousands of people a week. Guidry had decided that it was time to produce something that he would own. A sort of personal retirement plan to replace those traditional versions he had never gotten around to re-investing into.

He decided to create an evergreen show, one that wasn't time sensitive and was virtually destined for syndication. He was going to make a program that explored the process of the finding, refurbishing, and restoration of vintage automobiles. The kind of cars people collect, sell at car auctions, and sit home and watch television programs about. While it was not an auction show — he knew firsthand how expensive those had become — it would appeal to the same audience and have even longer legs in the marketplace.

He would go all in, throw the dice and put up all the money for *It's All About The Car*, aka *IAATC*. And, unlike *Bid Battle*, this show would be all his. He would own the domestic, international, home video and Internet rights.

Once he made the decision, he spent an entire year working on putting a full season in the can. He funded the show, his crew, and his personal living expenses off that fat credit line until it was almost depleted. And against all odds, when he was down to the last dollar he could borrow, it had finally paid off. At the 2015 NATPE show, he convinced Redline, a relatively new automotive themed network, to do a barter deal. He immediately put a full court press on some of his past advertising contacts to sign up.

In less than two months, *IAATC* was paying for itself, supporting him and his small group of freelancers, and slowly — very slowly — chipping away at his virtual mountain of debt. At least it had for a while.

*IAATC* was the reason Guidry now had a neatly organized, yet massive stack of bills on one corner of his desk. He stood there, ignoring the stack, his attention focused on two unopened registered letters that were side-by-side and dead center on the desk. One was from Wells Fargo Business Services, the other from the Wells Fargo Mortgage Department. He didn't have to open them. He knew what they contained. His old iPhone 4s was getting sweaty from being clutched in his hand.

Guidry was mentally rehearsing his call to Jack Calman, who was basically the head guy for all the NGTV productions, as well as the executive producer of *Bid Battle*. Calman was someone he had known and worked with for years, although the bridge between them had been burned in a white hot flash of incredible intensity. Calman was also the one person he knew that could solve his financial troubles with a single word.

Guidry took one more look at the registered letter, and then at a slim, dark purple metal tube lying next to it. Screwed into it was a clear plastic cartridge filled with a dark brown, oily substance and topped with a black plastic mouthpiece. Deep in his brain a little itchy voice whispered that he should take just a short hit, not much, just a little, just enough. But instead he silenced the voice, almost angrily, with a quick shake of his head.

Guidry then inhaled deeply, and plastered a smile on his face. For at least the tenth time he reminded himself you can actually hear if someone was smiling. He then tapped Calman's name in his contacts list. He took another deep breath and smiled even wider, waiting for Calman to respond with his legendary greeting, a bright, cheerful, "Yell-ow!"

## CHAPTER 2
# '64 442 Tribute

*Friday – August 18 – 9:33 AM CDT*

"No guts, no glory."
— PAT MCMILLIAN

It was a muggy morning at Café Du Monde. It was almost always muggy at Café Du Monde, situated next to the massive Mississippi river with only a large, earthen levee between them. Since 1862, Café Du Monde had been serving hot beignets and dark roasted café au lait to tourists and locals alike. There is virtually nothing else on the menu.

Pat McMillian was seated at the far end of the open air dining area. He was at a corner table, overlooking Decatur Street and Jackson Square. White, elaborately decorated horse drawn carriages were lined up in front of the Square. The drivers pitched French Quarter tours in heavy Cajun accents to the older strolling tourists who were up early. They also pitched rides back to the hotel to the younger tourists who were obviously up very late.

McMillian wasn't a New Orleans native, or even southern born and bred. He was just about as Yankee as they came, having moved to the Big Easy from Boston just over three years ago.

Although he had quickly embraced the pervasive style and mannerisms of his adopted hometown, the jaunty pork pie and white nubucks could be easily offset by a thick *No R* dialect when, and if, he allowed it to slip out.

He was in his mid-forties, slightly paunchy, with quick darting eyes that seemed to constantly catalog his surroundings in an almost subliminal way. He had inherited his pale skin from the double white whammy of Irish and German heritage, from his father and mother respectively. But while it was still most definitely white, his skin had been somewhat burnished by his three New Orleans summers, the third of which was just now finally beginning to ease its sweaty grasp on the city.

Although at least a couple of months away, fall weather couldn't come fast enough for him. July and August were brutal. New Orleans' humidity and temperatures, both of which were often measured in matching triple digits, weren't easy to get used to. If indeed anyone ever did, regardless of where you grew up.

And though the weather wasn't quite as harsh as just a few short weeks ago, his thin red hair was already damp and plastered in strings against the massive bald spot it endeavored to hide. During the summer, he had tried to convince himself to go *full Picard*, but had yet to muster the courage. As was his habit, McMillian hid his unsightly coiffure beneath a small brimmed hat he selected each morning from his burgeoning collection.

A street musician had set up on the sidewalk. A battered black guitar case was open to reveal the luxurious, thickly padded blue felt lining. It was scattered with a few ones and fives he had placed there to prime the pump. The musician, an old black man with an ancient Martin slung around his neck, was facing the middle of the dining area, about twenty feet from Andy's table.

The guy was actually pretty good, even by New Orleans standards, which were very high standards indeed. The tourists were enthralled by the dexterity of his playing and his obviously polished stage presence. His raspy voice was on key and precisely in time with the complex, bluesy rhythm of his playing.

The locals, hurrying by with their coffee and beignets to go, were more appreciative than mesmerized. Many slowed down just enough to drop a single or two into the case. This was, after all, New Orleans. Music was as woven into the city's fabric as incredible food, bawdy behavior, and hurricanes of both meteorological and mixology variants.

A Vietnamese waitress came by to check on his coffee. The three beignets, puffy square made-to-order donuts piled high with rolling mounds of powdered sugar, were now cold and sat untouched on the plate. There was, however, only a sip or two left in his third cup of the rich, bitter brew, laced with chicory and made palatable by the warm, whole milk that mingled with the coffee in more or less equal proportions.

"Mo coff-eh?" she asked, with her voice rising slightly at the end of the word. Asian accents in this bastion of Louisiana culture always made him smile a bit.

"No thanks," he replied. Three cups were plenty. He gave the waitress a ten-dollar bill and told her to keep the change. He then took a single bite of a cold beignet and frowned as the sugar immediately dusted his shirt. He wondered why he always ordered them as he stood up, frowning at his shirt and brushing himself off with flicks of his fingers. He then finished the beignet with another massive bite, this time leaning over the table to spare his shirt from another powdery onslaught.

He then remembered exactly why he ordered them, as he immediately picked up another one and wolfed it down with the same shirt-saving lean.

He then walked onto the sidewalk and stopped to listen to the blues man for a polite thirty seconds or so. The wizened black man was deep into his rendition of "My Starter Won't Start This Morning" by Lightnin' Hopkins. He was keeping time, and adding a percussive element, by slapping the sole of his worn brown brogue against the sidewalk. McMillian dropped a five-dollar bill into the guitar case and started walking towards the garage where he normally parked whichever car he was currently driving.

Five minutes later he was still nodding his head and singing to himself in a suitably bluesy snarl, "You jest been burnin' bad gasoline…" as he waved at the parking attendant.

"Mornin' Mr. Mac," said the attendant. "You's drivin' the best looking car I's seen today!"

"Jimmy, you say that every time I see you… no matter what I'm driving." replied Pat.

"Dat's 'cuz it always is!"

His car was parked at the entrance to the garage, freshly wiped down with the keys in it. The attendant wasn't going to let anyone near that car. Pat gave him a twenty-dollar bill and walked off without the change, just like he always did.

He was thinking that every job had its perks as he slipped into the seat of his current ride, a deep red, 1964 Cutlass convertible; a 442 *tribute*. Tribute was just another word for fake but this was a good one. So good that it had actually reached the auction block before the whispers of its authenticity, or lack thereof, had burned through the bidding crowd like wildfire.

It had showed beautifully on the auction block, and on the massive hi-def screens that flanked it. But not only did it fall pitifully short of both the pre-auction estimate and the reserve, the bottom feeder bids it did get just added credibility to the derisive mutters of "clone," "tribute," and "damn good... fake" among the serious car collectors.

McMillian was able to subsequently purchase this immaculately restored automobile for less than the price of a CPO Corolla, along with the promise that the non-disclosed modifications of the car wouldn't bar the seller from future auctions. And that he would be allowed to sell subsequent cars under an auction nom de guerre.

McMillian would keep the Cutlass for a year or so, maybe a bit longer, before he put it up for sale on Hemmings. While he would give full disclosure of its tribute status, the main emphasis would be on the immaculate restoration, as well as the heavily breathed on, dual snorkeled, 330ci, Rocket V8. With a factory 10 bolt posi and a 3.42:1 ratio, this sweetheart could literally shred the rear tires, enveloping the car in massive clouds of thick, white smoke. In the muscle car world, this was always a big selling point; actually more like a requirement. A YouTube video link made selling cars like this an easy exercise, which was pretty much the only kind McMillian got.

Prescott Hébert, his boss and owner of A-Bear Auctions, was vaguely aware of McMillian's side dealings. While he didn't exactly approve, he didn't forbid it either. McMillian had brought the Collector Car Division from what seemed a bottomless money pit to a true profit center. And he had done so by the fourth auction and his first anniversary at the helm. For the last two years, he had basically been given carte blanche to run that division of the massive Hébert operation.

His flair for promotion, staging, and dealing with the sellers had made A-Bear auto auctions a *must go* event for people on the hunt for semi-blue chip investments of the four-wheel variety. A-Bear events weren't where you went for a six million dollar Ferrari, but you could certainly spend six figures on rare American iron.

Being able to make a little money from some personal auto dealings was, at least in McMillian's way of thinking, just one of the perks of his position. Now whether the consignment he had just agreed to accept would result in even more of those perks, or a PR nightmare, was still being internally debated.

"Ah well," he said under his breath as he turned the key. The small block came to life with a low, melodic rumbling. "No guts, no glory," he muttered with a smile. "And I'm thinking it's *glory time*."

He tapped the accelerator to release the choke and bring the idle down. He gave it another couple of taps just to savor the sound. The blips echoed through the garage, somewhat tamed but certainly not subdued, by the new Magnaflo dual exhaust system.

McMillian felt that one of the beauties of driver-quality cars was that you didn't have to be afraid to make a few personal choice up-grades. He was awfully fond of that Magnaflo sound, and much preferred it to the more popular Flowmasters. Although being louder and more aggressive, McMillian had always felt Flowmasters had a reverberation somewhat reminiscent of banging on a trashcan. The sound was certainly appropriate for some cars, but not for the luxury muscle he tended to favor.

He turned left onto Decatur Street, gunning it a bit at every shift and smiling at the sound bouncing off the old European style houses. They stood shoulder to shoulder, separated more by their contrasting pastel colors than by actual space. Most were still boarded up, not yet ready to greet the day. French Quarter residents tended to be late risers and McMillian hoped to one day join their ranks.

He headed towards the A-Bear offices in the Warehouse Arts District. He smiled as he checked his watch, noting that he would actually be on time this morning. Or, rather, he wouldn't be more than ten minutes late, which he considered being on time.

McMillian used to come in early, sometimes very early. Not because he wanted to set a good example for his staff, or that he felt the need to accomplish as much as humanly possible every single day. It was because Prescott Hébert had used to come in early; at least he had when McMillian had first been hired. The dapper, bon vivant Hébert was coming to the office less and less frequently these days, which prompted McMillian to take a more *civilized* approach to his own arrivals.

At ten thirty, McMillian was sitting at his desk, surrounded by stacks of papers and photographs of various collector cars. He was typing furiously on his keyboard, slightly hidden by the massive iMac planted in front of him. He noticed a slight movement, leaned over and was surprised to see Hébert looking at him. McMillian waved and Hébert waved back and then walked on. McMillian realized he hadn't seen the old man in the office for at least a couple of weeks.

When Hébert did come to the office, to *make the rounds*, he would arrive about mid-morning and always without advance notice. During those rare occasions, he usually just walked through the building, ensuring that his people were there and working. Unless there was some top-level meeting that needed his personal attention, he would leave shortly thereafter. The spot reserved for the old man's Bentley would be empty well before noon and would certainly remain so for the rest of the day, often the week, and occasionally an entire month. This was especially true during the long summer months.

Company owners always liked to see their employees hard at work, especially their highest paid, salaried employees. Being in that group, McMillian was glad to oblige. At least he would be until he had amassed enough money, and clientele, to start his own auction house.

McMillian thought, was convinced actually, that said time might be coming sooner than later as he watched Hébert walk down the hall to peek in on the Maritime Division's manager. That would, of course, depend on the car being what the German man said it was. He then smiled and continued thinking with a shrug that all it really needed to be was good enough to pass for it.

McMillian then returned to the email he was composing.

"After reviewing the pictures of your '68 restomod Camaro RS/SS," he wrote, "I suggest the following items be addressed. I believe this will ensure the best presentation, and highest bids, in the upcoming *Muscles on the Mississippi* auction." When he finished the list of items, most of which were recommendations to return certain aspects to *factory*, he then hit send and sighed at the remaining list of emails to attend to.

One of the things that constantly amazed McMillian was the number of car enthusiasts, at least those in the restomod world, who truly thought they were an undiscovered Coddington or Foose. Those sellers were routinely shocked when their polished products brought significantly less than a similar model *barn find*. McMillian then stopped, smiled, and double-tapped on a TextEdit icon on his computer desktop.

McMillian added *Barn Find Bonanza* to his list of prospective auction themes. He thought about it, said it out loud a couple of times, and then let the initials roll off his tongue. "BFB," he said softly. "Not bad. Not bad at all."

# CHAPTER 3
# Drastic Times

*Friday – August 18 – 9:26 AM PDT*

> "I don't write to entertain computer nerds,
> porn surfing in their momma's basement."
> — SAMUEL CALMAN

"Yell-ow," said Jack Calman, "this is Jack." He had, of course, looked at the caller ID on his massive new iPhone before he tapped the answer icon. For people close to him, he had classic rock ringtones assigned to their numbers so he could also *hear* who was calling. But even when he knew the caller, he rarely answered with a "Hi Andy," or Bob or Susan or whomever. He felt you could tell a lot about the nature of the call by how they introduced themselves.

"Hi Jack! It's Andy, Andy Guidry. How the heck are you?" came the almost painfully enthusiastic voice piped directly into Jack's ear from his Bluetooth headset. Privately he had to acknowledge that he didn't really like the huge new Apple device, it barely even fit into his pocket. But it was the latest, greatest, and biggest, and Jack did like those aspects... in a lot of things.

Calman was a big guy, in many ways. He had been a desk jockey for most of his thirty plus years at the company and had the physique to prove it. He had also witnessed, and survived, a multitude of changes in the automotive media world. It was a testament to his corporate survival instincts that he was still at Neiderland, despite massive waves of consolidations, re-organizations, and the ever-present layoffs.

Layoffs had become a recurring theme that ran rampant throughout the floundering magazine industry. Staff writers and editors had been laid off by the dozens; summarily removed from the steady employment that many had enjoyed for decades. Of course, the best of them were immediately rehired as freelancers, with, perhaps, even a modest bump in earnings potential. But even if they were one of those lucky ones, it wasn't close to what they had lost in benefits and retirement options.

Still, it wasn't as bad as with the newspapers, whose steady decline in readership left entire bullpens, once glorious in the cacophony of raw sound and frantic activity, now completely silent. The empty desks, lined up like tombstones, would never again be abused by coffee swigging, cigarette smoking, pint bottle nipping journalists hot on the trail of the story du jour.

Samuel Calman — Sammy to the family — was Jack's older brother. He had been one of those journalists. He was a topnotch writer whose love for the craft had literally shaped the career ambitions of his younger bother.

Sammy had worked for the *San Diego Union Tribune* as one of their most fearless, investigative journalists. Decades ago, Jack had told Sammy the Internet was going to indelibly change the media world in general and journalism in particular... especially newspaper journalism. At one family gathering in the early 2000s, Jack told his Luddite brother that he had better start finding a way to market himself independently of the paper. He should start blogging, get a Facebook presence, and begin Tweeting while he still had an audience to build on.

"Yeah, I'll get right on that," Sammy had said, polishing off his second double Jack on the rocks in under twenty minutes, while lighting his next cigarette from the remains of the last. "Just as soon as Twitter starts sending out checks."

He started to laugh, but it became a wheezy cough, from either the whiskey or the Marlboros, or a combination of both. Once recovered, he said with pride, "Little brother, I'm a professional journalist. I write for money. I don't write to entertain computer nerds, porn surfing in their momma's basement."

Calman was pretty sure his brother had known about the cancer at that time but was simply ignoring it. Despite his love of digging out the truth, Sammy likely preferred not to know the details on that particular story.

A few months later he had been let go from the U-T, after twenty-seven years of employment. After a half-hearted three months of trying to learn enough about *new media* to launch a blog, he was found early one morning in the rocks below Point Loma. There was a shattered Jack Daniels bottle not far from his bent and broken body. Thankfully, an early morning kayaker had seen him before the gulls and sand crabs had made too much headway.

Jack had talked to him the day before. The conversation had been brief. Towards the end, their conversations had always been brief. Sammy had complained about his blog, the fact that he had virtually no followers, and his financial situation.

"The savings are running out, little bro," he had said matter-of-factly. "We already refinanced the house again. I may have to do something… well, I just don't know. Something drastic I suppose."

Jack had, as he always did, offered to help out with the money. Sammy had, as he also always did, politely and steadfastly refused.

The fatal fall happened on the anniversary of his parting from the paper. It was also exactly two weeks before his million-dollar, term life policy had run its course. It had saved his family from financial ruin.

Samuel Calman's death had been ruled an accident, caused by carelessness and excessive drinking. Although if you had known Sammy, even a little bit, you at least suspected a different cause.

Jack Calman, on the other hand, was certainly no Luddite. He always embraced new technology, and had done so from the very start of his career. Right out of journalism school he had been lucky enough to land a job with Neiderland Publications, the original name of the Neiderland Group.

Throughout his years with Neiderland, he had held the titles of editor, associate editor, managing editor, and publisher. But it was his current position that he finally felt was the job he was born to do. He was the Senior Media Manager for the entire NGTV division. He was responsible for the implementation, integration, and profitability of all Internet and broadcast based video properties. He truly loved each and every grueling, demanding minute of it; at least every minute that didn't include interaction with the new boss.

In a single day he might be negotiating programming deals with the various cable networks; fielding pitches on new, and now carefully chosen, program concepts; or constructing multi-venue media buys with national advertisers, which was now the norm in most ad buys.

And although Neiderland was dipping their toes into the online video arena, they still had a significant broadcast presence; *FC&C: Bid Battle* being the crown jewel. *Bid Battle* was a property he had personally pitched, developed and guided into its current, highly profitable position in the Neiderland program roster, but only after micromanaging a whole slew of their original *loss leader* programming ventures.

Jack had been one of the early proponents of getting into the television arena. He campaigned hard to jump in with both feet and worked his tail off to try and make a success of the *loss leader* business model. Back in the day, he had even handpicked the original TV crews, always on the lookout for decent camera ops, with moderate day rates, and field producers who knew more about cars than simply selecting *D* and pressing on the pedal.

When he first started running the fledgling broadcast department, it was on a much more hands-on basis. When the number of productions increased to where he was no longer able to actually accompany the crews on every production, he demanded weekly, daily, and sometimes hourly reports from his field producers. Back then he would have up to five production crews in the field, and his cadre of freelance field producers all had his cell number memorized.

Which is why, even though the micro-managing days were long behind him, he wasn't exactly surprised to be receiving a call from Andy Guidry. He hadn't changed his cell number since he got his first Motorola flip phone. And although he hadn't talked to him in well over a year, he could pretty much guess what the call was about.

"Hello Andy. I'm fine. Thanks for asking. And yourself?" asked Jack.

"Great, just great!" replied Andy, just a bit too loud and immediately realizing it.

"So, how's your show going?" Jack asked, just a bit too casually and certainly on purpose. "What's it called? *There's Something About A Car?*"

Jack knew full well what the title of the show was. He also knew, from his contacts at Redline, that it had not been picked up for another season, and likely never would be again. Knowing the network folks the way he did, he also figured he'd known about it well before Andy had.

In just a few years, Redline had evolved into the premiere automotive cable network, with ever increasing production values. Andy's show, being a barter program, just hadn't kept up with that level of production, and likely couldn't. It was the nature of how barter programs were financed.

"*It's All About The Car*," replied Andy, choosing his words carefully. He knew Jack was purposely getting the name wrong. He also figured that Jack knew at least something about his current situation. "It's going great! We're in hiatus for a bit but, truth be told, I'm not at all sure I want to stick with Redline."

"Really?" replied Jack. "You were certainly excited when you first signed with them."

Calman remembered that conversation all too well. It was during a nine p.m. phone call that a slightly inebriated Guidry sprang the news he was leaving *Bid Battle*, as both the producer and the production company. And that he was leaving it immediately; that day, that minute. The problem for Jack was that not only was it less than a week before the next featured auction; it was also that Guidry had poached the best from his usual *Bid Battle* crew to work on his new program, *It's All About The Car*.

"Yeah, I certainly was," said Andy, also remembering his departure conversation with Jack, although perhaps less clearly. "But the ratings aren't what they need to be and I'm still… was still on barter with them. I really need to get a better rate for my ad time and I'm thinking I'll get better numbers at a different network."

"Well, I certainly wish you all the luck in that," replied Jack. "But is that why you're calling me… for network introductions? You do realize you're a competitor?"

Calman didn't have to bring up the fact that beside the crew jumping ship, Guidry had also convinced a few of the larger *Bid Battle* advertisers to become title sponsors of his new program. Their decision had left some rather large, rather expensive gaps in Calman's advertising roster.

"Actually Jack, with this, huh, this reorganization, I find myself with a little extra time on my hands," said Andy. "And to be honest, I really miss working on *Bid Battle*. You know, the thrill of the bid and all. I was hoping you might throw a few producing gigs my way... just until *IAATC* finds a new home."

"Andy," replied Jack, shaking his head a bit, "Again, you're a competitor. We produce shows for a network, just like you. We may not do a traditional barter, but our deal is that we supply most of the advertisers. That's how we retain ownership. We go after a lot of the same advertisers; advertisers with limited budgets that don't support a lot of different shows. Sending you into the field for us is like letting a fox loose in the hen house."

Jack certainly didn't mention that the NGTV distribution structure was about to change.

"OK, Jack," said Andy, with an audible, not quite contrived sigh. "I'll be straight with you. I don't know for sure that *IAATC* will ever be on the air again. I've got a lot of bills to pay that won't go away just because my slot at Redline did."

Andy continued, trying to let just enough desperation show in his voice. "What I'm really hoping is that you'll let me come back to Neiderland, not only as the *Bid Battle* producer, but also as the production company. I've got the brand new 4K Avid system with some great operators. And I'll personally do the offline so you'll know it'll be right. After all, I did develop most of the *Bid Battle* program structure in the first place. And that's when the network started paying us, I mean you, for the show."

"I'm sorry to hear that about your show," Jack replied, "I'm sure something good will happen for you." He didn't feel the need to add that it just wasn't going to happen at NGTV.

"I'm not so sure," said Andy, no longer even trying to keep his actual despair at bay. "I'm in deep and I just don't know what I'll do. I may have to do something... something drastic."

Calman paused and took a breath. Memories of that same phrase washed over him, like waves against Point Loma's rocky oceanfront.

"Andy," said the now somber Jack, "I like you. We all have to do what we think is best and I don't hold your leaving *Bid Battle* against you. But all of the auctions for the rest of the season have been scheduled. The crews are lined up and booked. And we're happy with Burt Blackman. He's a good producer and his company does a great job posting the shows. I really don't have anything to give you. I'm sorry about your program, but business is business."

The dejection in Andy's voice was as thick as room temp 60-weight, "I appreciate that. I know I didn't leave NGTV the right way. Thanks for taking my call."

Jack replied, trying to sound cheerful, "No worries. And of course I'll take your call… anytime. And look, if the right opportunity comes up, I'll try and throw it your way." Jack continued, his voice down an octave, trying hard to sound as sincere as he felt. "Andy, we go way back. And I'm telling you this as a friend. There's no need to do anything drastic. Things will get better, they always do."

"Yeah. Sure," replied Andy. "Well, I guess I'll let you go. Thanks again for taking my call."

"Like I said, anytime," replied Jack. "And really, I'll keep my eyes open for something for you."

"OK. Thanks. Bye," said Andy as he lowered the phone and tapped the call end button. The call was still connected and he had to tap his ancient iPhone a few more times to get the call to actually disconnect.

"Piece of shit," Andy muttered as he tossed the device onto the couch. He sat down and stared out the window for a good thirty minutes. He then sighed, stood up, and snatched up the phone.

"Drastic times call for drastic measures," he muttered as he started tapping on it. Less than a minute later he had found what he was looking for.

He smiled as he thought that, at the very least, he'd get in a few good meals. He picked up the vaping device, took a big drag and held it in as he tapped the number on the phone.

"A-Bear Auctions, Collector Car Division," said the sultry, heavily accented voice on the phone. "How may I hep yew?"

Guidry smiled, remembering when he had that very same accent. It was an accent he could still pull up at will, and often did at parties and such.

"Hello," replied Andy, blowing out a thin stream of vapor and letting a trace of the accent slip into his voice. "This is Antoine Guidry. Is Pat McMillian available?"

"Hold on jest a minute," replied the receptionist, "I'll check."

Fifteen seconds later a jovial voice came onto the line, "Andy, how the heck are you?"

"Hello Pat," replied Andy. "I'm doing fine. Thanks for asking. I'm calling because I see you have a sale coming up and I'd like to put in a car."

"It's kind of late for an entry, but sure, anything for you. I'll get you a good slot," said Pat. "What kind of car?"

Andy took a big sigh and said, "A very sweet, very honest '68 911T." He paused for dramatic effect and added "All factory, a soft window Targa, forest green over brown. She's beautiful and deserves your prime slot. And I'm thinking she deserves the LMC."

# CHAPTER 4
# Anyone Can Buy New

*Friday – August 18 – 6:42 PM PDT*

> "The last three shows, or
> three different gigs?"
> — BOBBY RASTON

Bobby Raston joined the short line at the reception counter of KeyCode Media in Burbank, CA. It was six thirty-six in the evening and, despite being a bit late, he'd been able to park his brand new BMW M4 directly in front of the entrance.

Sam Winfield, the MCA-I volunteer manning the check-ins, brightened as Bobby finally stepped up to the counter. The young man had noticed Raston as soon as he walked in, and how Raston kept looking back at his car.

"Hi Mr. Raston," Sam said with a fawning smile. "Now that's a car!"

"Yeah, it's a car alright," said Bobby with a practiced air of nonchalance. "You gotta drive something." He believed it made your car more of a status symbol if you appeared to take it for granted.

"I've got your name tag right here," said Sam, handing it over and continuing with, "although everybody knows who you are."

Sam was right, at least as far as the audio production world was concerned. Bobby Raston was one of, if not *the* premiere sound guys in the business. If you were in sound, or wanted to be, it paid to know Bobby Raston. Producers took his word as gospel on virtually all aspects of the surprisingly complex task of capturing pristine audio on location. This included sound crew hiring decisions for the labor-intensive reality shows that were now a network staple.

"I wouldn't be so sure about that," replied Bobby, carefully peeling the backing off the nametag.

Raston definitely remembered the young man from the last MCA-I meeting he attended. Sam had come up to him and started jabbering about equipment at a most inopportune time. Raston had been trying to decide which of his opening lines to use as an introduction to the Twins, who had just arrived and were standing alone at the entrance to the room. By the time he had finished his rapid-fire recommendations to Sam, the Twins were no longer alone and his window of opportunity had slammed shut.

"So anyway, I bit the bullet and bought that Sound Devices 688 you recommended," Sam said. "What a SAAAWEET machine!"

"Yeah," Bobby agreed, a bit distractedly, as he attached and then reattached the nametag, wanting it to be perfectly square on the lapel of his new Nordstrom's sport coat. "It's hard to go wrong with a 688. It's an oldie but goodie. Did you get it from Tai or Location Sound?"

Sam looked about the room, grateful that no one else was in line and that he could continue his conversation with Raston. You came to these events for the networking, and this was *networking gold* if you were an aspiring sound guy.

Sam continued, "Location Sound, just like you recommended. Now all I have to do is get some gigs to pay for it!"

"That is always the goal," agreed Bobby, finally deciding the handwritten, stick-on nametag was in the exact, perfect position.

"You had told me you might, uh… well… that you'd recommend me for a reality gig if I upgraded from my old FP-33," said Sam trying hard to sound nonchalant, but not quite succeeding.

Bobby possessed an incredible memory, especially when discussing sound gear. He distinctly remembered that what he told him was that he couldn't possibly recommend him if he didn't have a mixer with a built-in multi-track recorder and time code capabilities, such as a Sound Devices 688. Which was a different statement entirely.

"What's the biggest show you've worked on?" asked Bobby.

"I did the last three gigs on *Pinks*. When they were trying to resurrect it," replied Sam.

"The last three shows, or three different gigs?" asked Bobby. Programs like that, especially on a resurrection budget, often did three or more shows in a day.

"Three separate one-day gigs, three shows a day. They were about two weeks apart," replied Sam. He didn't mention they were also the last paying gigs he'd had, and that was almost two months ago.

Raston knew the program and the producers. He also knew they hired at the low end of scale and weren't too particular. Still, if the kid had also worked the second and third gigs, it meant no insurmountable audio issues had surfaced during post.

"Drag shows are nice gigs, but damn they're loud!" replied Bobby. "I know a producer whose been hired to try and resurrect *Four Wheels TV* for Neiderland. Give me a card and I'll see if there's any room on the sound crew."

Sam produced a print-it-yourself business card like his arm was nitro powered, "Thanks so much Mr. Raston. That would be great!"

Bobby looked at the card, then up at Sam and asked, "You run Letros, right?"

"Of course," Sam replied, "SMQV's." Sam neglected to mention he only had two sets. Of course, he'd be happy to max out his sole remaining credit card to buy a couple more if the gig came through.

Bobby thought for a moment, tapping the edge of the business card on the counter, "OK. I'll reach out to him, give him your info and a little *push*. I believe it's a fourteen-day gig. Can you commit to that?"

Sam blinked a couple of times, thinking how fourteen days at full day rate, plus equipment rentals, would be a financial lifesaver to his rapidly sinking audio career.

"Commit to it? I will wallow in it!" replied Sam, eyes gleaming, his head nodding a bit in excitement. "Can't be enough days for me! This would mean so much. My wife and I were just talking about how…"

Bobby leaned in, again tapping Sam's business card on the counter, and interrupted in what he hoped was a casual tone, "So Sam, are those twin gals here tonight? You know, the camera ops?"

"Oh, you mean Brandy and Mandy?" Sam replied.

Bobby managed to keep the smile on his face, while wanting to scream, "What other smoking hot, twin female camera operators are there?!?!"

Instead he answered in what he hoped was a devil-may-care tone, "Yeah... yeah, I think that's their names. Are they here?"

Sam shook his head, "I haven't seen 'em." He scanned the remaining nametags, and then picked up a printout from the counter.

"Nope," replied Sam, "not on the list. They must not have signed up. It is, after all, a Pro Tools demo. You know camera ops. If it's not about sensors and lenses they couldn't care less."

"Yeah," replied Bobby as he carefully peeled the nametag off his lapel. "I know camera ops."

Bobby folded the tag precisely in half, sticky side in, checking to be sure there was no overlap on the edges. He then laid it on the counter, adjusted it a bit and said, "I just realized I've seen this demo. I think I'll just go home. I'm leaving for a five-day gig early tomorrow and I still have to prep."

"What's the show?" asked Sam.

"The last legs of the La Carrera Panamericana," replied Bobby, obviously ready for this conversation to be over with. "Their audio supervisor got *the revenge* and I've got to go pick up the slack. I recommended him, so I gotta cover for him."

As Bobby turned to walk out, Sam called to him, "Speaking of recommendations, when do you think I might hear about *Four Wheels TV*?"

Bobby kept walking across the small lobby and replied without looking back, "Hard to say. I'll email your info to him. That's all I can do."

Sam watched Bobby get into the new BMW and smiled at the deep, throaty snarl as the BMW rapidly pulled away. Sam continued staring at the empty parking spot, feeling a bit starstruck. He was thinking that when you charge twenty five hundred a day — five times the standard audio op rate — and can work whenever and for whomever you choose, you can certainly afford to drive anything you'd like.

As he began to tidy up the desk, the smile drained from his face. He stared down at Raston's folded up nametag, which was placed on top of his own business card, the top and right side edges precisely squared and matching.

"What a prick!" he said, almost shouting, just as an MCA-I member came rushing through the door, huffing and puffing for air.

"Whew, sure wish that spot had been open when I drove by!" said the guy, leaning on the counter to steady himself as he caught his breath. His bald head was accented by the side hair grown long enough to be pulled into a wispy gray ponytail. The ample girth identified him as most likely being an editor, and certainly not a field guy.

"I had to park three blocks away," he said, still puffing a bit. "Have I missed anything?"

"Nope," said Sam dejectedly as he started to go through the remaining nametags. "Not a thing. It's Ethan right?"

"Yup, Ethan DeBello," he replied with a smile. "So… who's a prick?"

# CHAPTER 5
# Twin Cams

*Tuesday – August 22 – 10:56 AM EDT*

> "The editors are eating up your footage;
> spitting out polished packages faster than
> the producers can schedule them."
> — DEAN PRESTON

Brandy and Mandy Fukui were hot. Actually they were smoking hot, and in more ways than just their looks. It was late morning, in August, and they were standing in the middle of a golf course in Florida.

The Asian-American twins were twenty-eight years old, although they were usually still carded on the rare occasions they went to a bar or ordered a beer with their dinner. They were just over five foot seven with thick straight black hair cut very short, in a feminine hipster sort of way. They tended to dress practically, as befit their occupations, but always with a touch of style.

Today they were wearing shorts; with a tailored fit that while certainly not baggy were also definitely not short-shorts. They were working and they dressed to facilitate that activity, although they would be stunning no matter what their attire.

They both had lightweight camera vests over relatively snug t-shirts. The shirts accented their ample bust lines, but didn't hinder their movements. As was their habit, the clothes would be identically cut, but in different colors. Today Brandy was wearing a Tiffany Blue t-shirt, while Mandy sported one in British Racing Green.

Individually, on the exceedingly rare occasion they worked that way, they were very, very good camera ops. When they worked a set together — when the style, budget, and space called for a crack two-camera team — they were the most sought-after DSLR operators in the business. Said business being reality shows in general, and reality car shows in particular.

The broadcast trend away from scripted shows, with their traditional single camera, multiple take production methods, had made multi-camera production methods de rigueur among show runners.

They usually worked on what they called the FID shows, which in their internal shorthand stood for *faked impossible deadline*. FID shows could only be described as *reality* in the boilerplate prose of a cable network PR staff.

An FID show was where intricate, top-tier car builds happened in a matter of weeks, or even days, versus the months and years that true restorations took. And, of course, *it has to happen on time or all is lost* was the common theme that explained the always frantic work schedules.

It could be an upcoming, *gotta make it or we'll go broke* auto auction. Or it might be some weird bet involving impossibly young, impossibly rich friends willing to pay many times top dollar, but only if it can be delivered to some far off locale and *not one second late or you don't get a penny*. The ridiculousness of the premise didn't really matter to the Twins.

Basically, the Twins paid little attention to the words, and absolutely none to the plot. They simply didn't care. They didn't even pretend to care, and they didn't have to. When show runners saw the results of their efforts, they didn't care that the twins didn't care. They were simply that good at what they did.

In whatever scene they were covering, they had an almost telepathic ability to always be on the *right* shot. When the star made a particularly witty remark, he was on a close-up. When someone pulled out a satchel of cash and started unloading bundles with a *can't turn this down* flourish, they had both the establishing shot and the cut away; perfectly exposed, precisely framed and always in focus.

Savvy field producers quickly came to rely on their uncanny knack to always have the perfect shots for both visual composition and editing flexibility. It made their jobs inherently easier, and so much faster, by not having to sweat the coverage or even block the scene. They loved being able to concentrate on coming up with a story line that, while perhaps not entirely believable, was at least not laughable.

This gave the Twins yet another facet of hotness. They were in so much demand that, unlike most freelance production personnel, they could not only turn down jobs they deemed inconvenient, they could literally pick and choose from the top-of-scale network projects that further cemented their place as emerging industry icons. And they loved to travel.

In the past year they had been home for less than a hundred days. They had worked gigs in twelve states and four different countries. They did incredible work, traveled light, and shared a room. In a whole slew of ways, they were the epitome of a producer's wet dream.

Currently they were standing by their camera rigs, on the fairway of fourteenth hole, waiting to start on yet another roll-in package for the Amelia Island SN Auto Auction. The auction coincided with the Amelia Island Concours d'Elegance. Although they had worked on dozens of auto-themed reality shows, this was the first time they had agreed to do an auto auction gig. They were trying to make the best of the second day, in what they considered an extremely boring five-day gig. The Twins did not like being bored.

"I thought it was going to be cool, working with multi-million dollar cars…" Brandy said to Dean Preston, the twenty-four year old field producer.

Dean, who just four shows prior was a PA, wanted his segments to really stand out. He had assured the staffing producers that booking the Twins to do the roll-in packages on DSLRs, instead of the usual broadcast video cameras, would result in incredible images. So far he had been right, very right. The notes from Burt Blackman, the onsite senior producer, were short and sweet, "Keep it up!"

"… like Ferraris, Duesenbergs, Astons…" continued Mandy, knowing that Dean would turn to her and stopping once he did.

"... and Delahays," finished Brandy, enjoying the way Dean head snapped back to her. It was sort of like watching the crowd at a tennis match. It was an old gag for them, but one that still made them smile... simultaneously.

Mandy continued with, "But it's kinda boring. It's just beauty shots. This would be so easy to shoot single cam."

"Totally," said Brandy, "it's like... why did you need us on this gig?"

Dean, desperate to keep up the enthusiasm, immediately responded with "Are you kidding? You two are incredible! I can't believe how fast you set up your shots, how instinctively each shot blends into the other. The editors are eating up your footage; spitting out polished packages faster than the producers can schedule them. The *Bid Battle* top brass is ecstatic. As I knew they would be!"

"Yeah," said Mandy.

"So," said Brandy.

"It's still boring," said Mandy.

"But yesterday's Dino was kinda..." said Brandy.

"... cute," finished Mandy.

Brandy reached out and gently put a hand on Dean's shoulder, waiting for his head to turn to her, "We mean the car, but you're pretty easy on the eyes yourself."

It never hurt to have yet another field producer clamoring for their time. That's what kept their rate, and reputation, climbing. Beside, men were way easier to manipulate than their cameras, and almost as much fun.

Dean felt his face grow warm. He hoped his blushing might be mistaken as an effect of the strong Florida sunshine. "Ahh, well, uhh, oh, there's the next car," he said as he spotted four SN lot techs, all wearing the prerequisite white cotton gloves, pushing a large pre-war roadster their way.

Leaving the Bugatti on the cart path, the lead tech walked over and peered through the window of the 1961 Ferrari 250 GT Series II Cabriolet parked on the grass. The Twins had just finished shooting the multi-million dollar sports car and it was ready to be returned to holding area. Satisfied the parking brake was off, he reached in and gently pulled the walnut shift knob into neutral. He then called his team over and they pushed it out to the cart path, leaving it pointing in the general direction of the car storage tent.

"Where do you want this one?" asked the lead tech to Dean, gesturing to the massive black, wire rimmed roadster with fender skirts. Dean looked at the twins who were looking at the 1937 Bugatti 57C with a somewhat blasé, yet practiced eye.

Mandy looked up to gauge the position of the sun, frowning that it was getting close to vertical. Brandy tilted her head a bit to get a more offset look at the swooping lines of the front fenders.

Mandy gestured to a spot on the fairway and said, "Put that one over there, with the grill pointing…"

"… this way," finished Brandy, with a finger pointing about six degrees to the right.

They simultaneously picked up their trusty Canon EOS-1D X Mk II DSLRs. They were both in the very mild "video rig" configuration they favored, for both the lightness and the lack of conspicuousness.

That was just another benefit of shooting DSLRs, especially on a gig with semi-pro, non-pro, and even totally unaware talent. People were always less intimidated by, or even ignored, what looked like a high-end still camera but which was actually capable of cinema quality, 4K video.

They walked toward the car as the SN tech finished wiping down the already immaculate vehicle. Without a glance at each other they positioned the cameras at precise angles. With an almost imperceptible, simultaneous nod, they began shooting.

Roughly ten minutes later Mandy and Brandy picked up the rigs, and walked back to stand by Dean, again flanking him on either side.

"Ok," said Brandy.

"We're done," said Mandy.

Dean, still amazed at the swift, fluid concert of motion that comprised the Twins shooting style, asked, "Are you sure, I mean, you're positive you got enough coverage?"

The twins just cocked their heads at him in a gesture that was an unmistakable, if unspoken, "Really?"

"Let's get the next car out here," said Brandy.

"We've probably only got time for one more before the light really sucks," said Mandy.

Dean picked up the walkie-talkie and pushed the transmit button. "This is Dean at video station three. Next car please."

"Already?" came the voice of the tech manager. "You guys are too fast! You're wearing us out! It'll be a few minutes before I have a transport crew available."

Dean, thinking of the last ten minutes spent watching the two professionals bending, stretching, and otherwise contorting their curvaceous bodies, operating the cameras at incredible angles, keyed the mic and replied, "Well, they certainly are fast, but they sure aren't guys."

"So I've heard," came the reply. "Multiple times."

# CHAPTER 6
# The Pitch

*Wednesday – August 23 – 7:12 PM CDT*

"Let me see dat little tang, jes one mo time."
— BLAIR BROUSSARD

Antoine Guidry was tired, and he deserved to be. He had been on the road for three days. He had finished up the long trip from San Diego just a few hours ago with the final taste of what he always referred to as *Porsche pleasure*.

He was extremely lucky he hadn't received a ticket from his weaving in and out of the lower Pontchartrain bridge traffic. He had driven at speeds approaching, and occasionally surpassing, triple digits. It was, after all, his final few hours with his beloved Max and he wanted to enjoy them.

He had been very aggressive in weaving his way through the moderately heavy traffic, blinking away the occasional tear at the thought of trading this marvelous machine for some small pile of money. Especially when said money was already designated for things like overdue mortgage payments, equipment leases, and office utility bills.

He and the Porsche had actually reached Louisiana in two days, two VERY long days, but he had spent the last twenty-four hours visiting family in the rural towns of Ville Platte, Opelousas, Eunice and Mamou. He had eaten gumbo and jambalaya with elderly aunts and drank *ponies* with a myriad of various cousins. Ponies were seven-ounce cans of beer that were peculiar to Louisiana and designed so you could easily finish it before the summer heat had warmed it past optimum drinkability.

As he left each house, in progressively more rural locations, he always smiled at the incongruity of his little green sports car parked next to mud splattered 4x4's and full-sized American sedans. He chuckled at their good-natured ribbing about his little *furrin* car and how unsuited it would be for hunting, fishing, or just south Louisiana life in general. Guidry had always thought that he too was unsuited for south Louisiana life in general.

He had been a bit late leaving the house of his cousin, Blair Broussard, in the aptly named Little Mamou, which, unlike Big Mamou, didn't even have the single stoplight its namesake boasted.

He and Blair were only a few months apart in age. They had grown up together, but followed decidedly different paths. Blair wallowed in the hunting and fishing that was such a huge part of small town Cajun country. As a boy, Guidry had tried it once or twice, but didn't see the attraction. Getting up before dawn to go traipsing through the woods in the cold, wet Louisiana winter just wasn't something he thought of as fun, then or now.

It wasn't that Guidry didn't like shooting. He loved shooting; guns in general and handguns in particular. That was kind of the point. You could go hunting for days and never fire a shot; at least that's how he remembered all of his hunting trips with Blair and his father.

Blair's dad, Orise Broussard, was Guidry's Paran, his godfather in Cajun French. Paran Orise had taken it upon himself to instruct Guidry in those manly pursuits since there was no one else around to shoulder that position.

Guidry's dad was a career Army man that had seemingly always been gone. Guidry eventually understood that his Mom and Dad just didn't get along, and hadn't for quite a while. After all, he would eventually realize, you don't volunteer for three tours in Vietnam when you have a happy home life back in the states.

Andy and Blair, despite being close growing up, always had diametric life goals. Andy wanted to leave small town Louisiana and move to the big city. Blair wanted to leave small town Louisiana and move to the country. Both goals had been achieved.

One thing they had in common while growing up, and likely what kept them as close friends, was an affinity for cannabis. They had been smoking marijuana since they were teenagers, indulging heavily in the ubiquitous swamp weed; low grade pot that ran ten bucks a baggie. They had both continued to indulge in the habit as adults. Guidry had been one of the first to take advantage of the lax guidelines in

California's medical marijuana laws, and had indulged in his habit ever since.

Broussard had been amazed at the vape unit that Guidry had pulled out when sitting on Broussard's back porch. It overlooked ten acres of back yard and was dotted with storage buildings of various sizes. One of the buildings held a surprisingly sophisticated hydroponics operation that supplied Broussard with his own cannabinoid needs... and quite a bit more.

To Broussard, Guidry's vape unit looked almost futuristic, especially when you took a drag and the end of the tube illuminated with a bright blue glow. Broussard had actually scoffed at it, not believing it was really cannabis until the first of some truly huge drags on the mouthpiece began to take effect.

"Dat don't smell like weed and it don't taste like weed," he exclaimed, smacking his lips and shaking his head in disbelief as the concentrated drug invaded his system. Slowly a big smile came over his face and he continued, "but poo yai, it sure do feel like weed."

Visiting with his cousin had taken a bit longer than he had planned, with his cousin repeatedly asking, "Let me see dat little tang, jes one mo time."

Guidry had tried to warn his cousin that vaping could be quite a bit more powerful than smoking, but to no avail. Broussard had taken massive hits, marveling at the lack of a telltale smell, until he could literally barely stand up to give his cousin a goodbye hug.

Guidry, being an experienced vaper, had only taken two small drags during the last two hours he was there. That was still enough to cloud his judgment, and likely both instigated and added to the enjoyment of his blast down the bridge. Which was yet another reason he was very lucky he hadn't been pulled over.

Guidry had checked into the Best Western Plus on the edge of the French Quarter. It was called an historical landmark because at least some of the original building, whatever it had been, was utilized in its conversion. Basically, however, it was all very new, very comfortable, and a very easy four block walk to Bourbon Street.

On his last visit, many years prior, he had stayed in the heart of the French Quarter at the Royal Sonesta on Bourbon. But that was because the A-Bear auction he had been covering was actually being held in the hotel and Neiderland was footing the bill for his suite.

For this visit, he needed more modest accommodations. And besides, it was very noisy on Bourbon Street, regardless of the day or time, and he needed to rest.

After checking in to the hotel, he had driven the Porsche to the A-Bear Auctions office complex in Warehouse Arts District, signed the consignment paperwork, and turned it over to McMillian's team. As a professional courtesy, and a true necessity, it would be thoroughly detailed before the auction began, just a day and a wakeup away.

McMillian had offered to give him a ride back to his hotel and to buy him dinner, which Guidry had gratefully accepted.

He and McMillian were sitting at a corner table at the Royal House Oyster Bar. Although actually established in the aftermath of Hurricane Katrina, the restaurant was bathed in Old New Orleans ambience. Guidry had come here as a child once, when it was Tortorici's. Located next to Brennan's and across from Antoine's, the Royal House had serious culinary heritage to uphold. From the perpetual crowds, and the lines to get in, it was evident it did so quite well.

They had been offered a table in the upstairs Rue Royal dining room, but they had preferred to wait until a table in the tightly packed main room had opened up. They sat just a few feet from the massive antique bar and gigantic mirror that backed it. They were just finishing their third plate of oysters, this one being the Oysters Royale.

They had started off with a dozen raw, and downed them before they had taken more than a few icy sips of the first round of Abita Jockamo I.P.A. beer. They had then downed the beers and ordered another round while waiting for the Oysters Rockefeller. They had a third round of Jockamos with the Oysters Royale.

The waiter came bustling by, noticed the empties and asked, "Another Jockamo gentlemen?"

"Yes," said Andy, "Of course. And we're ready to order dinner."

"No more beer for me," said Pat, "I have to drive home. But I will have a sweet tea with my…" he paused, picked up the menu, gave it a glance and said, "Crawfish Ravioli."

"And I'll have the…" Andy paused and stared thoughtfully at the menu.

The waiter waited patiently, but was scanning the tightly packed room to see a few of his tables also required attention. After a moment he spoke up, "The Taste of New Orleans is very popular. It's a trio dish with Chicken and Andouille Jambalaya, Crawfish Etoufée, and Seafood Gumbo."

Andy smiled and shook his head, "Thanks, but that's all I've been eating for the last twenty four hours!"

He turned to Pat and remarked, "You wouldn't believe how much they get in San Diego for the comfort food I grew up on. It's practically haute cuisine there! Fifteen dollars for a tiny bowl of gumbo, and it's nothing close to what my Aunt Dee can whip up at eighty-five years young and nearly blind."

Andy took another look at the menu, folded it and handed it to the waiter, "I'll have the Shrimp 'n Grits." Turning to Pat he continued, "It's not Cajun food, at least not the Cajun food I grew up on, but it's damn tasty!"

As the waiter was walking to the next table, he called out to him, "And you can bring the beer now!"

Andy turned and smiled at Pat, once again thankful that Pat had offered to buy dinner. Of course, that was before Andy had mentioned that *It's All About The Car* was on hiatus.

"So is it a sweet 911 or a SAA-WEET 911?" asked Andy, a tickle of pain flirting with his heart, threatening to tamp down what he hoped was a persuasive grin.

"Oh, it's sweet all right," replied Pat. "Coming in this close to auction, we won't have time to truly publicize it, but Porsches always sell. And with the stupid prices they're bringing these days, I'm sure we'll both do really well on it."

"I hope so," replied Andy, trying not to sigh. "Do you need any little tidbits on it for the LMC? I can forward you some research on it, as well as a list of exactly what's on this particular car," said Andy as nonchalantly as his desperation would allow. He was referring to the *Last Minute Consignment* email that McMillian had implemented shortly after he first arrived at A-Bear Auctions. Indeed the popularity of the LMC was one of the reasons that Prescott Hébert had such faith in McMillian's management of the auto auctions division.

McMillian had first gotten the idea from watching the Steve Jobs presentation the year the iPhone was introduced. His by then famous, "Oh and there's one more thing," had created such an uproar in the audience, before the product was even introduced, it had planted the seeds for the LMC.

Now, before every auction, McMillian always saved a really interesting offering for his LMC. It was an extremely well crafted email, written from a personal point of view and loaded with both history and high quality photography. It was sent to past and present bidders, a plethora of various car-centric news media outlets, and anyone who had signed up in the Constant Contact capture widget on their website.

It showed up in the subscribers email in-box at precisely twelve ten a.m., central time, two days before the featured car would be offered. At roughly four auctions a year, this would be the eleventh LMC email he had sent. Since he started it, the subscriber list had grown from just under five thousand to the current base of over two hundred and forty thousand subscribers. And it was still growing. The biggest jump had happened when Hemmings' *Sports & Exotic Cars* had described it as *a mailing list worth being on, potential bidder or not.*

Richard Lentinello had mentioned it in his Editors page, praising the "Two, Three, Four & More" LMC that ran just before a Chattanooga auction. That email had described a *last minute consignment* that was comprised of a trio of all original, low mileage Triumph TR Series cars, which the cosigner refused to separate, along with a truly massive stash of NOS parts.

Lentinello, the Triumph guru in the Hemming's editorial roster, was effusive in his praise of the email and its historical accuracy. By the time the fifth LMC had come out, Lentinello had reached out to offer McMillian a position as a monthly columnist.

McMillian had responded that while he was flattered, with his current responsibilities at A-Bear he just didn't have enough time to write a column to the high standards that Hemmings deserved. The real reason was that the journalism side of writing, while certainly having its benefits, just didn't pay enough to interest him.

Regardless of the, "Wow, can you believe what just came in..." tone of the emails, the actual car or — very occasionally — cars that were featured in the emails were often decided on many weeks in advance and purposefully kept out of the advance lot descriptions and printed materials. There would, of course, be an LMC insert, finely printed and suitable for framing, in the bidders catalogs.

LMC offerings were always the last lot to cross the block on the last day of the auction, assuming it was a multi-day event. The timing of the LMC also helped keep the bidders in attendance for the entire auction, which kept the prices up for the later cars.

McMillian, as the sole decision maker in which vehicle was deemed interesting enough to be an LMC subject, had been known to suggest *cash only* donations to his favorite charities to secure the coveted spot. Donations which he would, of course, both gladly and discretely handle for the seller.

"So what do you think, Pat?" asked Andy after a big gulp of his fourth beer of the night. "Couldn't you slip Max into the LMC email somewhere? Maybe as a sidebar?"

The only reason he had timed the trip, to arrive this early, was to try and convince Pat to feature Max in the LMC. He would have preferred to time his arrival as close to the auction as possible. It wasn't that he had anything else to do, it was that his funds were running dangerously short and even just four days in New Orleans wasn't a cheap proposition.

"Sorry." said Pat. "I told you over the phone that I didn't think that was a possibility. Besides, the LMC is already written and scheduled for sending."

"I know," replied Andy, in a tone just this side of pleading. "But that was before you saw her. Now that you see what an incredible car she is, and with the list of factory correct enhancements, I figured maybe you could at least mention her. Just a footnote?"

Guidry was trying hard not to let his desperation show. LMC vehicles always brought a premium, and never failed to get *all the money*. Since he really needed to get all the money, he was determined to plead his case for as long as it took.

McMillian, on the other hand, had been ready for the night to be over the minute he had heard Guidry's response to the obligatory "How's the show going?"

The casual response, a bit too casual, was that while Guidry didn't currently have a media outlet for his show, due to creative conflicts with Redline, he still had contacts at Neiderland. He hinted that he was *in negotiations* for a series of special editions of *Bid Battle*.

"You know vintage Porsches are red hot right now," Andy continued, slurring just a bit and with the unmistakable tones of his Cajun heritage slipping in. "Max would be a great LMC! And..." he lowered his voice as if they might actually be overheard through the din of the dining room, "a *real* LMC, since I just consigned her today."

The media knew that LMCs were more marketing gimmick than true last minute additions, but they still tended to cover it, albeit with a wink and a nod. The LMC was always worth an easy few inches, or minutes, or posts, or whatever it was their particular outlet needed to fill the hungry maw that was the *News*.

McMillian looked at Guidry, wondering if that was indeed desperation in his voice or just a reflection of the beer. Deciding it was a combination, and filing it away for future reference, he replied in a full on, *born on the bayou* accent that was only slightly tinged by his Boston heritage.

"Me, I don't know what you talkin' 'bout," replied Pat, the smile on his lips not quite making it to his calculating eyes. "Dat LMC; mea sha, it's always real!"

Pat leaned over to Andy, lowered his voice and confided, "I'd like to help you, but I can't dilute the LMC, not this one. Wait until you read it tomorrow. It's going to be truly..." Pat paused, searched for the proper word, and with a slow deliberate pronunciation simply said, "historic."

Something in McMillian's voice tickled Guidry's producer instincts. He stared at McMillian as the waiter placed the steaming bowls of food on the table, fragrant with the unmistakable smells of crawfish, shrimp, and copious amounts of spices. The waiter, noting Guidry's nearly finished beer asked, "another Jockamo?"

"No," Guidry replied, not taking his eyes off of McMillian. "Just some water."

When the waiter had left, and they had taken the first spicy bites of their respective dinners, Andy casually asked, "So tell me what makes this LMC so *historic*?"

McMillian paused and decided that whether Guidry learned about it tonight or tomorrow morning didn't really make a difference. And besides, this was a chance to see how the automotive media might react to the announcement, up close and personal. Which was potentially valuable information.

"It all started about five weeks ago," began Pat, "when I got this phone call from Germany."

## CHAPTER 7
# Last Minute Consignment

*Thursday – August 24 – 12:10 AM CDT*

A-Bear Auctions – Collector Car Division
To: (undisclosed recipients)
Reply To: patmac@a-bear.com
Subject: Last Minute Consignment - 1940 Mercedes 770k W150 Grosser Tourenwagen with provenance

Five weeks ago we received a call from Hamburg, Germany. The caller told us he would like to place a very significant car into our upcoming auction. However, due to shipping constraints, he would not be able to get the car to us before Tuesday of this week.

As is our practice, we informed him we would not confirm the listing of a car, such as the one he was describing, without first inspecting it for authenticity.

We also informed him that truly noteworthy cars do much better with significant advance publicity; that two days before a vehicle crosses the block just isn't enough time to generate interest, or even create awareness, among serious collectors.

He informed us that, in this case, he believed we were wrong. He said that, due to extenuating circumstances, he needed to sell this car as soon as possible, and that he believed this car would receive plenty of interest, despite the lack of advance publicity.

He further stated that in addition to its impeccable condition, considering it's been in storage for over seventy years, it possessed a most desirable provenance. He claims this particular Tourenwagen is a previously undiscovered, yet fully documented vehicle that had been dedicated for the exclusive use of Adolph Hitler.

The consigner has assured us he has incontrovertible proof of the automobile's direct ties to the infamous Nazi leader. He stated he will only display this proof at the auction, during its presentation to the bidders. All rights to the provenance will be transferred to the winning bidder along with the car. The reason for this procedure is that he claims these rights are worth as much, or more, than the car itself.

Last Tuesday, the car arrived in New Orleans and was immediately transported to the secure holding facility at our Mardi Gras World auction facility.

Appraisal specialists from the Mercedes Benz Classic Center in Irvine, CA, were brought in to perform an exhaustive, two-day inspection. The experts have determined, and verified in a notarized document, that this vehicle is an unmolested, 1940 770k with period correct German military accessories.

That alone makes this a highly significant automobile, regardless of any verified connections to Adolph Hitler.

This 1940 Mercedes 770k W150 Grosser Tourenwagen, in original condition, will be offered as the last lot of the day, during this Saturday's *Muscles on The Mississippi* auction, at our Mardi Gras World location in New Orleans, Louisiana. The seller's claim to provenance will be publically presented immediately prior to the car being offered for bid.

Under our agreement with the owner, and due to the nature of the provenance, only registered bidders and sellers will be allowed in the hall during the presentation of the provenance. There will be no spectators or media allowed, as well as no recording or Internet streaming of the presentation.

These rules will be strictly enforced, as our agreement with the seller is to forfeit our commission should they not be followed to the letter.

Due to the unique nature of this agreement, as of this morning, all new bidders will be required to post a $5,000,000 (five million U.S. dollars) bidding bond with our bank to be allowed access into the auction. All bonds will be held in escrow for 30 days from the close of the auction. Fraudulent bidder registrations, of any kind, will forfeit their bond to ensure these requirements will be met.

Interested parties should contact us immediately for more information on these new bidder requirements. Telephone bidders, while not being able to view the provenance presentation, are both allowed and welcome to bid on this spectacular automobile. However, new registrations for telephone bidding will also require the posting of the bidder bond.

While we estimate a minimum winning bid of at least $6,000,000 (six million U.S. dollars), with the potential to double or triple that number depending on the provenance, this automobile will be offered at no reserve.

For more information on this, or any of the fine collector cars to be offered at this weekend's auction, please contact:

Patrick McMillian
Collector Car Auctions Manager
A-Bear Auctions
New Orleans, LA

patmac@a-bear.com

(504) 555-2BID

## CHAPTER 8
# Problem Solved

*Thursday – August 24 – 6:00 AM PDT*

> "Who else do you have on tap that's
> got the experience to pull this off?"
> — J. Roger Winters

Jack Calman was already in his office, and had been for hours, when at precisely six a.m. his desk phone rang. Calman glanced at the Caller ID and then snatched it up before the electronic double ring tone had completely died.

He crisply answered, "Yes, sir?" He had been expecting a call from his East Coast crew, but this most certainly wasn't it.

"Have you seen that LMA email put out by A-Bear Auctions?" demanded J. Roger Winters, who was technically Jack's boss's boss but tended to call him directly, and all too often.

"Yes sir, I have. I was just re-reading it," replied Jack. The magazine editor in him blurted out, "And it's LMC, for Last Minute Consignment, not LMA."

"I don't care what it's called," said Winters, his displeasure at being corrected readily apparent. "I only care that we have to cover this! May I assume you're getting a crew down there as we speak?"

"I'm working on that right now," replied Jack. "But we've also got to find a way around this no-media allowed provision. I don't suppose we'll be able to post the bidder bond?"

"Not a chance, bucko," said Winters. "Besides, that's all just PR cow paddies. If you can't handle that nonsense, I've got the wrong man in your position. So, does the wrong man got his heinie planted in that chair?"

"No sir," replied Jack. "I'll figure something out."

"That's what I thought," replied Winters, smugness dripping from his voice. "Now I want you to let me know as soon as Blackman gets there and has a chance to look around. And tell him if he wants to keep working for us, he'll need to come up with some fresh ideas on how to shake things up. This could be just what we need for the ByDemand launch. And if so, we need something more than the boring *pretty car on the block, who's gonna bid what* bull-pucky nonsense."

"Well, that's also a problem," said Jack as he held the phone away from his ear. He knew from experience that the volume from the handset was about to triple.

"And WHAT… is… this… PROBLEM?" shouted Winters.

The legendary TV executive had once been famous for his cursing, so much so that it had often been a source of ridicule in the trade rags. After a particularly humorous piece from *Broadcasting & Cable* went viral, he quit cursing cold turkey. With nowhere else to go, that massive amount of mental energy was channeled into volume whenever he was displeased; a state he tended to be in quite often.

J. Roger Winters had accepted his position in the Neiderland TV operation for the princely sum of $1 per year, plus an exorbitant percentage of stock paired with an incredibly top-heavy bonus structure. Although being one of the founding partners in ESPN, and the original owner of The Speed Channel, he really didn't need money. At his level, money was just a way to keep score, and to keep the ego fires burning.

His yearly bonus, the true bragging meter of his peers, was directly tied to the profits of the NGTV group. No profits meant no bonus; an unacceptable situation to a man used to achieving whatever he set his sights upon.

Winters was determined to transform Neiderland's TV arm into not just a more profitable division, but into an actual network delivered OTT. His plan was to move all of their programming into a premium, subscriber based, online venue. He was staking his reputation on the forthcoming NGTV ByDemand; his reputation being far more valuable to him than mere money. And to do that, he needed fresh programming; shows that created such a buzz that automotive enthusiasts simply had to subscribe.

"The problem is that Blackman is on the Amelia Island show," replied Jack. "They're still in pre-production; shooting and cutting the roll-ins."

"So replace him! Send someone else to Amelia, and get his bohunkus over to New Orleans," demanded Winters.

"I've already tried," said Jack. "I was on the phone with Stan Niemec at six this morning... his time... in Florida."

"You woke up one of our biggest sponsors, and the source of our most popular programming, sucky ratings notwithstanding, to talk about some other auction?" Winters demanded. He never missed an opportunity to remind everyone that their shows needed improvement, at least as far as ratings were concerned.

"Actually, he called me," replied Jack. "He saw the LMC email and thought we might be *interested* in it. He called to remind me that his contract has a *personnel approval* clause."

"He has a WHAT?" demanded Winters.

"A *personnel approval* clause," answered Jack. "There was this set of shows we did in France, before you, huh, before you joined us. We had tried to save money by hiring local crews instead of bringing our own freelancers, but it ended... well it ended rather badly."

"Oh yes, of course! The hood ding on the Duesenberg." said Winters. "Or, if I recall it correctly, what the automotive media *still* refers to as the *Doozy of a Ding*."

Jack thought Winters certainly should recall it since it was one of his Speed Channel announcers that coined the term that seemingly would not die.

"Yes sir, that was it," said Jack.

Even after four years it was a bit of an embarrassment that it had created such a stir, even in the non-automotive media. Of course, it's not everyday a totally original, factory customized Duesenberg, with a ironclad provenance tying it to one of the greatest ex-pat writers in history, left a photo session with a brand new dimple in the hood. The dimple was courtesy of an impatient Italian crew that ignored the standard *never touch the car* edict.

The crew, in a hurry to begin the contractually mandated two-hour lunch break, had taken it upon themselves to open the bonnet for the obligatory engine bay shot. When they opened the driver's side panel, it had smacked into the oversized, but otherwise identical, Duesenberg Flying Lady hood ornament. The beautiful chrome wing tip had been unharmed, save for a bit of paint that was removed with a swipe of a fingernail. The real issue was that it had dented the hood panel, causing a dime-sized paint chip to flake off.

The Italians attempted to pop it out, with moderate success. They then did a little touchup with some nail polish they borrowed from one of the girlfriends that were always hanging around the crew. The color was incredibly close and it actually blended in quite well; well enough to be classified as ten-footer. The Italian crew also hadn't thought it was important enough to tell anyone about it.

The ding had been discovered when the bidding had stalled at four million euro. The current high bidder was casually inspecting the car, while the auctioneer pleaded for just one more bid.

The bidder, a self-important member of the new breed of nouveau riche Russian capitalists, suddenly began pointing at the hood and screaming in highly accented, but certainly understandable English, "Fraud! Dis iz fraud! I retract miz bid!"

The entire auction arena went from an excited buzz to a dead silence.

One of the senior bid spotters, who flanked the edges of the rotating car platform, stepped onto the platform and, in low tones, asked the bidder "To what are you referring, sir?"

The Russian held up the auction catalog, opened to the page detailing the history and provenance of the *one hundred percent original car, unmolested in any way.*

"No vonder he kept saying," gesturing in contempt to the auctioneer, "sold as iz! Luk at dat!" He stood as tall as he possibly could, given his five foot, four stature, and dramatically pointed his finger to within an inch of the damaged area.

The bid spotter had leaned in and examined the area. He gingerly scratched it with his fingernail. He then pulled his hand back, looked closely at his nail, and then up at the auction platform.

The look in his eyes had told Stan Niemec all he needed to know. Besides being the owner of SN Auctions, Neimec also owned SN Classic Car Restorations, a top-tier shop whose work had garnered five Best Of Show awards at the Pebble Beach Concours d'Elegance.

Niemec knew exactly what an undisclosed *repair* meant in a car of that class, and in an auction of this magnitude. He figured it meant about one million euros, and he was right on the money; as he most often was.

The car was removed, the damage assessed, and when it made its second appearance on the block, it sold for two point nine eight million euros. This was despite the assurance of a seamless, undetectable repair by SN's most experienced body man. It is, as the saying goes, only original once.

SN auctions made up the difference to the consigner as a goodwill gesture, and it had made for a great press release. After the auction he had demanded written assurance from NGTV that they would NEVER have a non-vetted crew on one of his productions, regardless of where it was. And that he would have complete approval, or disapproval, over crew management.

"And what did my good friend Stan want to discuss so early in the morning?" asked Winters.

Jack just shook his head at the friend comment. It was well known that Niemec and Winters were far from being friendly.

"He said he just wanted to remind me that we had a contract," said Jack. "He said he had also read the LMC email and that he did not care who was selling what or where. He *mentioned* that if we so much as thought about pulling Blackman from the production, that he would not only refuse to pay for the production side of the contract, but that he would consider his entire Neiderland contract, including print and online, both null and void."

"SHUT THE FRONT DOOR," screamed Winters, "HE THREATENED US WITH NON-PAYMENT AND CANCELLATION?"

"Yes," answered Jack, "and that he would also sue us."

"Okay," said Winters, his voice about 10dB lower, "you need to calm down so we can figure this out."

Jack just shook his head in disbelief, sighed and waited for Winters to continue.

"Let's think this through," said Winters. "Who else do you have on tap that's got the experience to pull this off?"

"We're spread pretty thin these days," said Jack. He was alluding to the massive round of layoffs that Winters had mandated on the first day of his regime.

"But I do know one guy," he continued. "He actually called me a few days ago looking for work. He used to produce for us on *Bid Battle*. He's an independent now, but he was the senior onsite producer for about fifteen shows."

"You mean that Guidry guy? The client poacher?" asked Winters. "The one with the show on Redline."

"Not anymore," replied Jack, "it's been cancelled. But yes, that's the guy."

"Problem solved! Stop talking to me and get him booked. Do whatever it takes, but get him on board with this," said Winters, the decibel level was now at an almost normal level. "And get him on an iron clad, no-compete contract. Which, by the way, is how we do it in real TV. Oh and see what he can think of to spice this up. If that Hitler connection is real, this could be the flagship show we need to launch the network. This could be TV history!"

"Yes sir, I'll get right…" Jack stopped talking, realizing that Winters had already hung up.

Calman picked up his Bluetooth earpiece and pushed a button on the side. The device softly chimed twice and he said clearly, "Call Antoine Guidry… mobile."

"Calling Antoine Guidry… mobile," repeated the voice in the earpiece. After a moment it began to ring.

Calman just stared at his computer screen while he waited for an answer.

# CHAPTER 9
# Pretty Darn Fast

*Thursday – August 24 – 8:16 AM CDT*

> "It's never too early for me."
> — Antoine Guidry

"Who the hell…" Andy muttered groggily as he opened one eye towards his phone on the dresser. In addition to the buzzing noise the phone made as it vibrated against the wooden surface, it was honking at him with a steadily repeating "Ahh Ooo Gaaa."

Andy opened the other eye and turned his head towards the nightstand. He saw that it wasn't exactly early. Even though the room was dark, the clock showed it was after eight. A single pencil-thin shaft of sunlight managed to sneak into the room, past the drawn drapes and their opaque inner curtain. Andy squinted against the brilliant beam with bits of dust floating through it. There was a small stab of pain resonating in his left temple.

He threw the covers off the bed and slowly got up. After stretching, he padded his way over to the phone. He stumbled a bit on his clothes, which lay in a heap where he had peeled them off the night before. He then cursed and hopped a bit when his bare foot stepped on his belt buckle.

Wondering which of the S.O.B. bill collectors would be calling him this time, he froze when he saw the name on the Caller ID. It was Jack Calman.

He shook his head to try and clear the aftermath of the previous night's excess. He credited the *not quite a hangover* to the five beers during dinner and the massive frozen daiquiri he had purchased to sip on while walking through the quarter. After he and McMillian had shook hands and said goodbye, he had spent a couple of hours just wandering around, contemplating their post-dinner conversation, listening to the nightly battle of the bands.

You didn't have to actually go into the bars to listen to the surprisingly good bands that played the French Quarter every night of the week. The music literally blasted through the open doors and windows of the tourist-priced drinking establishments. Whatever kind of music you liked, you could find it in the dozens of bars that lined both sides of the antiquated streets. Although, if you had a hankering for old school New Orleans Jazz you were pretty much limited to Masion Bourbon.

Andy had briefly stopped at the jazz venue, noting that the crowd was awfully sparse and consisted mainly of the elderly and European. These were, perhaps, the last surviving fans of the genre.

He supposed the non-stop vaping had also contributed to his current foggy state of mind. He vaguely remembered giggling like a schoolgirl while passing a beat cop and exhaling a thin plume of vapor. The cannabis vape odor was virtually indistinguishable from e-cigs and other vaping devices, especially outdoors.

He shook his head again, a little more strongly this time, and then tapped answer just before it went to voicemail.

"Jack!" he said with a joviality he certainly didn't feel. "How are you?"

"Hello Antoine," said Jack, "I hope it's not too early for you?"

"Too early?" replied Andy, noting the use of his formal first name and wondering how Jack even knew it. "It's never too early for me. What can I do for you?"

"Well," Jack started, "It's more like what I can do for you. Or, perhaps, what we can do for each other."

Guidry smiled a bit, knowing that the LMC email had gone out this morning. He smiled even bigger remembering the deal he had made with McMillian the night before.

"Okay," said Andy, "so what can we do for each other?"

"How fast can you get to New Orleans?" asked Jack.

"Pretty darn fast," replied Andy. You could hear the smile in his voice when he continued, "I actually happen to be in New Orleans at this very moment."

# CHAPTER 10
# '76 Cosworth Vega

*Thursday – August 24 – 8:57 AM CDT*

> "There's an extra hundred dollars in it if
> you make it here in fifteen minutes."
> — Saul Wittmann

Herman Adler got the text just as he was walking out of his ART175 class at the Richland Center campus of the University of Wisconsin.

"COME 2 HEIL ASAP," he read, his head down as he walked into the hallway. He just sighed, thinking that he really didn't want to miss biology again.

He was tapping out a reply on his phone when he literally bounced off the back of Steve Rampart. Rampart was someone he normally went well out of his way to avoid. Rampart, despite the relatively mild weather was wearing his well-worn letterman jacket with the patches signifying four years of varsity football, track, and basketball.

Herman Adler was just under five foot eight and weighed just over two hundred and forty pounds. His brown hair was extremely curly, almost kinky in texture. He wore moderately thick glasses with gold plated wire rims that were perched atop a somewhat larger than proportional nose.

Steve Rampart was just over six foot three and weighed two hundred and fifty pounds. A pale, pinched face topped his large bulky frame. His cheeks bore deep acne scars, the normal adolescent pimple phase had been magnified tenfold by the enthusiastic use of anabolic steroids during his high school athletic career. It was a career that was abruptly ended just two years ago by a brutal, blindside tackle. He was, for now, able to walk in an almost normal fashion… as long as he was careful to maintain his balance. The subtle yet persistent pain in his right knee was a constant reminder that his chosen profession, one he had assumed was his due since grade school, was simply never going to happen.

"Watch where the fuck you're going, Himey," snarled Steve, carefully turning around so as to keep the weight precisely centered over his ruined knee.

Rampart had been razzing Adler about being Jewish since the fifth grade, despite the fact they both attended the First Harvest Methodist Church of Richland Center. At least they had until Adler no longer felt so inclined.

It was such an old joke by this time that it hardly seemed worth responding to, but Adler did it anyway. It was more out of habit than any true indignation. For what seemed like, and probably was, the hundred thousandth time he replied, "It's Herman, not Himey. And I am not Jewish."

"Yeah, well, whatever you are just watch where the fuck you're going," sneered Steve, "or I might have to punch you in that big-ass schnozzle of yours."

In high school, when Rampart was the king of the hallway, he always had a built-in cheering section. They would all be sporting Richland High letterman jackets, albeit none as badge festooned as Rampart's. Back then, those same old *Jew boy* references would have produced howls of contrived laughter, and murmured repeating of the *slur de jour*.

Now, two years out of high school, Rampart no longer had his sycophant comrades to echo his slurs. His booming voice and ethnic slurs now just caused people to shake their heads and walk more quickly to their next class.

Adler was more bored than outraged. It's not that he didn't remember the humiliation he had felt in those all too often hallway encounters; he most certainly did. He briefly wished, for what was probably the millionth time, that he had connected with the ill-timed swing he had once taken at Rampart.

It was their junior year and enough had been enough. And although he had never actually been in a fistfight, he had seen plenty on TV. Adler had watched a lot of TV. He reared back for a mighty swing, telegraphing his move as surely as if he had yelled, "I'm going to hit you!"

When Rampart took a short step backwards, Adler's swing had only served to spin him around so quickly that he plopped onto his butt. His glasses flew off his face, skidded down the hall, and Adler was immediately plunged into the blurry world to which only the truly nearsighted can relate.

He had always thought it would have been better had Rampart responded in kind; if he had decked him with a mighty right cross or a couple of sharp jabs to his admittedly large nose.

Instead Rampart had just looked down, laughed and said, "Uh oh, watch out for Jew boy. There's a lot of weight behind that swing!" As he walked off with his laughing entourage he made a point to veer to the left and casually step on Adler's glasses.

"Oops," Steve cried out in mock concern, "who left their glasses on the floor?" The laughter only increased as the group meandered down the hall.

Adler wore them the rest of the day, he had no choice if he wanted to see. They were bent and ill fitting; one lens cracked and the other with a deep chip dead center. He had told his parents it happened in gym class and begged them to order two pairs, so he would always have a spare. They replied that money was tight and that he should be more careful. His mother had taken him shopping and helped him pick out the pair he was currently wearing, and likely would be for a very long time to come. They had a sentimental value.

"Much as I'd love to have yet another stimulating conversation with you, I really do need to be going," said Herman, carefully moving out of arms reach before he continued. He knew that Steve couldn't move faster than a slow shuffle these days. As he was walking away he threw a comment over his shoulder, "Say hello to Candy for me." He then turned in mock sympathy, "Oh, I forgot. She went to Milwaukee... like Bill."

The not so subtle jab about Rampart's old girlfriend, the head cheerleader and voted most popular three years running, was still an open wound. Once the extent of his injuries had been realized, and that a pro football career was no longer even a vague possibility, Candice Gorman had dumped Steve in a very public fashion. When Bill Franklin was awarded a football scholarship to UWM, she had applied to the school immediately.

Bill Franklin was a starter in his sophomore year, and Candice Gorman was very photogenic sideline eye candy. It made watching those games on TV more than a bit painful for Steve.

"Fuck you, you fat Jew boy himey bastard!" Steve shouted at the rapidly departing Herman.

"Wow," replied Herman, in mock surprise. "I didn't even know you swung that way, but... who am I to judge?"

There were some snickers, and a couple of outright laughs, from the few students left in the hall as Adler hurried down the stairs. He barely heard Rampart as he stammered out with a bellow, "Oh yeah... well... well... well... just come back here and say that again you chicken shit..." and the rest was lost as the door to the outside closed.

Adler smiled as he walked to his car. Not because of the successful verbal altercation with Rampart, which was a nice change of pace, but because he really loved the way his car looked parked at the curb.

The Firethorn Metallic 1976 Vega was gleaming. The gold wheels were spotless and worked in visual symphony with the gold pin stripes, proudly spelling out Cosworth Twin Cam across the front fenders. The matching Firethorn interior was a bit worn on the driver's side, but the rest of the interior was immaculate. It was almost as if the passenger seats had never been used... which wasn't far from the truth.

He had gotten the car as a junior in high school. His dad, Albert Adler, had known about it since it was new. His boss, Saul Wittmann, knowing that Albert was a bit of a car guy from the immaculate 1970 SS 454 El Camino he drove, had asked his advice on a sporty car for his wife's birthday present. It had been a last ditch effort by old man Wittmann to keep his wife both happy and at home. It didn't work, but then nothing had. At least not the *at home* part.

Sheila Wittmann, an intensely beautiful woman twenty years Saul's junior, had married the older man thinking that copious amounts of money — something neither she nor anyone in her family had ever experienced — would balance with the revulsion she felt every time he touched her.

She had, however, really loved that car. She drove it everywhere, and everyone who saw it knew who was behind the wheel. In the end, it was that instant recognition that proved to be her downfall.

It was a Thursday light, many years ago, that Saul Wittmann had been parked across the road from the Dancing Pony motel. He sat in his truck, staring at the car. Parked directly under the courtyard light, it was like a billboard announcing her blatant infidelity. It was the fourth Thursday in a row that Wittmann had sat in his truck, watching that car. Hurt, humiliation, and anger were taking turns as the predominant mood of the moment.

On that fourth Thursday, anger finally won the battle. He had walked over to the payphone, next to the motel office, and called the Shell station out on the bypass.

The phone was answered on the second ring with a cheerful, "Castleman Shell, how can I help you?"

"Frank," started Saul, "this is Saul Wittmann."

"Hello Mr. Wittmann," replied Frank. "What can I do for you?"

"I need you to come out with your tow truck and pick up my wife's little Chevy," said Saul, the anger making his voice flat and void of inflection.

"Happy to do it," replied Frank, "Is everything all right? I mean I hope there wasn't an accident or anything."

"No accident. Everything's fine. I just need the car picked up at the Dancing Pony motel and brought to my place," said Saul. "I need you to put it in the small barn out behind the house."

"No problem," said Frank. "Did she blow the engine? I hear them Vegas are like that."

"The engine is fine, as far as I know, and I've ceased to care what she blows. Just come out here and get the car. There's an extra hundred dollars in it if you make it here in fifteen minutes."

Saul heard a quick reply, "On my way!" and then a loud click as Frank hung up in a hurry.

One hour later, Wittmann was putting a large lock on the barn door, with the Cosworth Vega inside. It was covered by an old tarp and tucked into the far corner of the building.

He was slinging the last of Sheila's vast wardrobe onto the front lawn when the phone rang. He picked it up and said, "Yes."

"Saul, Honey," came Sheila's voice. "I do believe someone has stolen my car."

"No one stole your car," he replied and waited for the response.

"Then where is it?" Sheila asked, a tinge of fear creeping into her voice.

"That's none of your business anymore," replied Wittmann. "Now listen closely because when I'm finished, I'm going to hang up. I'm going to be gone for the next two hours. Everything I think belongs to you is on the front lawn. Maybe whomever you were fucking tonight will help you come get your shit, or maybe not. I don't give really care. Get it now cause I'm gonna burn whatever's left in the yard when I come back."

He slammed down the phone. He then threw the last load of clothes out into the yard. Wiping away a tear and then shaking his head to clear it, as well as to reset his resolve, he climbed into his truck and went for a drive.

When he came back it was actually more like three hours. All of the clothes were gone and a message was scrawled across the door, "Kiss my ass OLD MAN! As if I would ever let you!"

One year later, the divorce was final. Sheila was now a moderately wealthy woman who had immediately moved to California. She actually did end up in the movies, although not quite according to plan. She had quickly become one of the highest paid porn stars in the business. However, as the steady diet of cocaine and heroin took its toll on her looks and body, the demand for her talents became less frequent and the roles more generic.

Sheila, then known as Savannah Glen, died of a heroin overdose in 1979. It was six days before the neighbors called the police to complain about the odor. Twelve dozen long stemmed roses arrived anonymously at the funeral, where they outnumbered the mourners roughly one hundred and forty to one.

Saul Wittmann never drove, or even touched, the Cosworth Vega that had been put away wet in 1976. During the divorce settlement hearings, knowing how much she loved that car, he simply denied knowing where it was. The judge, whose family had been in the county almost as long as Wittmann's, recognized the tone of Saul's voice. He turned a steely eye toward Sheila and stated more than asked, "You're getting plenty enough without a lot of trouble. Is the whereabouts of this automobile worth putting that in jeopardy?"

Sheila wisely didn't press it and the car remained in that barn for the next thirty-five years. The tarp had kept the pigeon poop off the paint. Multiple generations of farm felines had kept the ever present mice out of the engine bay and passenger compartment; most of them anyway.

In 2013, Albert Adler had knocked briskly on the door to the main house. When the housekeeper answered, Albert asked to speak to Mr. Wittmann. After a brief wait, Saul came to the door. Even in his mid-seventies, he stood up straight and tall. His eyes were clear and he swore he only needed his glasses to read, although his eye doctor would have told a different story.

"Mr. Wittmann," Albert began, "I know it's sort of a sore subject, but I've just got to talk to you about it. My boy just turned sixteen. He's got his driver's license, and he needs a car. Me and him... well, we don't get to spend too much time together, and I was thinking that a father/son project car would kinda help in that area."

Albert stopped, drew in a deep breath and continued, "Is there anyway possible that you might consider selling that Vega in the small barn?"

Saul Wittmann looked at the man who had worked for him for nearly forty years. He slowly nodded his head while the memories of Sheila and the car came flooding back. He hadn't even thought about that car in at least a decade.

"No, Albert," said Saul, after a few moments of mental deliberation. "I don't believe I'd want to sell that car. But if you and your boy can get it running, and drive it out of that barn, I'd be pleased to give it to him as a birthday present."

Albert Adler had never seemed to have enough time to spend with Herman while he was growing up. He worked hard because jobs were sparse in Richland; especially good paying jobs for men who never finished high school. Besides, he didn't know much about the things that interested Herman. Art, history, and that god-awful racket he called music; they really didn't have a lot in common.

But when Herman started taking an interest in cars, at least in the history of cars, they suddenly had a common bond. About a year before Herman was old enough to drive, he had started talking about what he was going to get as his first car.

"It's got to be European, of course, maybe an older Porsche or something Italian…" Herman had announced at the dinner table. "An Alfie maybe? It's really hard to decide."

"So you've been noticing a lot of those All-Pees round town?" chided Albert with a smile on his face. "What with *For Sale – Cheap* signs on them?"

"Well no… I guess. Not really," replied Herman, the little dose of reality had dampened the enthusiasm like spit-covered fingers on a match. "But my first car has just got to be really, really cool."

"Yes Herman, we know," said the slightly exasperated Nancy Adler.

Herman's mother had heard this exact conversation about twenty times too many. And in at least the last ten times she had stated with mock firmness, "Your father has said that he will get you a car, some kind of car, for your birthday. You know it isn't likely you'll be getting some kind of foreign anything." Turning to stare at Albert she would continue with, "Why your daddy lets you go on like this I just don't know!"

Albert would just smile and say, "A boy's gotta dream, honey. A boy's gotta dream. First it's cars, then it's girls; before too long, life is set and dreamin' jest gets you in trouble. A boys gotta dream while dreams can still come true."

Herman's automotive dreams came true the first time his dad had taken him to the barn at old man Wittmann's place. He knew his dad had worked for Wittmann, but then a lot of dads in this town worked for Wittmann.

They drove right past the house and stopped in front of the barn. The door was open and a shaft of the early morning sun pierced through the door. As Herman and Albert climbed out of the El Camino, Herman was peering into the barn. The sunlight was falling just short of an old tarp covering what was quite obviously a small car.

Herman turned to his Dad and asked in a halting, tentative tone, "Is that… my car?"

Albert smiled and said "Yep, that's your car. And it's foreign… just like you wanted. Kinda foreign anyways."

When they had pulled the tarp off the car, Herman stopped and took a step back. The Vega was on three flat tires, and the last one was only half full. There was a huge stain in the dirt under the engine of the car and despite the tarp, the windows were a bit murky, kinda like cataracts on an old dog.

"It's beautiful," he said, and he meant it. "But what's foreign about a Vega?"

Albert had a big smile on his face as he said, "Let's pop the hood and I'll show ya!"

As Herman looked at the Cosworth Twin-Cam 16-valve, fuel injected engine. His mouth opened, as if he was going to say something but it took a couple of gulps before he could stammer out a "Wow. That, huh, that looks, huh… wow."

Two hours later, Saul Wittmann was watching from the door of the barn. Herman and Albert were so busy examining the car, talking about what would be required to resurrect the car, that they didn't even notice him. The excitement in both their voices was deeply moving to the old man.

The was a broad smile on Wittmann's face, but his eyes were a bit moist at seeing that little car again. That car had been like a little bump on your head. A bump that, every once in a great while, you'd re-discover. You scratch it, and worry it, and before too long you've ripped it off and it becomes too sensitive to touch. Then it heals and you forget all about it. At least you do until you find it again.

When he had first put the car into the barn, he would occasionally come up with some sort of plan on what to do with it. Burn it, crush it, donate it, sell it; whenever he thought he had figured out what to do with it, it somehow had never seemed *right*.

Now, after all these years, seeing the excitement in the boy's face and hearing the pride in Albert's voice as he explained exactly what it would take to resurrect the car... he knew this was *right*.

One year later, he was standing at the rear of the funeral hall, looking at the back of Herman's head. Herman's head was high, but his shoulders shook from the sobbing as he sat directly in front of the two caskets.

Wittmann slowly nodded his head. He had made a decision. And he knew this one was also *right*.

# CHAPTER 11
# The Four Producer Food Groups

*Thursday – August 24 – 9:18 AM CDT*

> "But we want to do something different, more than just a standard *Bid Battle* format."
> — JACK CALMAN

Andy Guidry was sitting at Café Du Monde nursing his second large café au lait. He idly watched the little black birds hopping about searching for crumbs. They wouldn't get any from Andy. His order of beignets was long and completely gone. The plate had been cleaned of the powered sugar via repeated swipes with a spit-moistened index finger. He would have ordered another plate but funds were getting tight. Nearly two fifty for three donuts was a bit taxing on his limited budget. It would be better spent on a muffuletta from Central Grocery later in the day.

The open-air café was reasonably empty at this time of the day. The early breakfast crowds of both locals and tourists were already fed and on their way. Currently, the tables were sparsely occupied and what customers were there shared the *barely slept through the hangover* look that Guidry wore.

He was contemplating the phone call he had with Calman just forty minutes ago. He thought he had played it pretty well, especially considering his barely wakened, semi-sober state, and that he had been bereft of his customary massive daily dose of caffeine.

"Andy," Jack had asked him, a bit suspiciously, "how is it you happen to be in New Orleans? And does it have anything to do with the A-Bear email this morning?"

"Sort of," replied Andy, "although I haven't actually read it yet. Still, I'll bet it's about a certain Mercedes 770 with some interesting provenance. I also know a few other details that I'll bet aren't in that email. Which is why I was going to call you. This is going to make for some great TV, for someone, and I'm just the guy to produce it. Which I assume is why you beat me to the punch."

Calman had paused for a moment. He had been caught off-guard by Guidry already being in New Orleans, as well as his reference to *other details*. If Guidry was anything, he was a good field producer, always able to find a storyline amidst the chaos of a live event.

"So, what are you thinking about on this?" asked Jack.

"You called me first," answered Andy, "what's on your mind?"

"Well, first off it's awfully hard to believe that an unknown Hitler car has somehow surfaced and is being auctioned off with less than two days notice. AND that it's happening in an A-Bear auction," said Jack. He continued in what he hoped was a casual tone. "But we were thinking that it *might* be worth fielding a crew to cover it."

"Interesting," replied Andy in an agreeable tone. "But why are you calling me? I thought using me was like… umm, how did you put it? Oh yes, it was like letting a fox loose in the hen house."

Jack was thinking that you had to give the man credit. He had a hell of a memory and that's why his shows always flowed so well.

"Ok, I'll put my cards on the table," said Jack. "IF we decide to cover this, and that decision hasn't actually been made, we'd normally send Blackman to supervise the production. But since he's tied up on an SN auction in Florida, we're just… well, we're exploring available options before we make a decision."

"And I'm the option?" asked Andy.

"Well, you're one of them," replied Jack, "if you're available, and we can come to a deal. Which brings me back to my original question of why you're in New Orleans. If you're already working on this for someone else, we can stop talking now."

"Why I'm here is my business," said Andy. "But I'm not covering the auction for anyone else, at least not yet. No deals have been… consummated. Although it is pretty darn intriguing, don't you think? And I do happen to have an *in* that no other producer will have."

"What sort of *in*?" asked Jack.

"Like I said, I haven't actually read the LMC email, but as I understand it, no media will be allowed in the room while the provenance is being presented. And that provenance is the only thing that authenticates the car," said Andy.

Andy continued, choosing his words carefully. He had to let just enough information slip to suggest the insider status he was trying to portray. "I happen to be in sort of a loophole that allows me to be there during the auction, and the presentation with, perhaps, a small crew. And my presence, and mine alone, would still be in accordance with the rather involved, penalty heavy contract that A-Bear Auctions has with a Mr. Heinrich Heinzburg."

"I assume this Heinzburg is the consigner," said Jack.

"That is correct," answered Andy.

"Ok," said Jack, with a short pause for effect before he continued. "So if you haven't read the email, how do you know so many details about it?"

"I had dinner with my old friend Pat McMillian last night," said Andy. "It just sort of came up in the conversation, although that was likely why he insisted on our dining together. He wanted to get my opinion on how best to document, and monetize, their involvement with the selling of such an historically important car; what with the short lead time until the auction. And, of course, whether they might persuade me to become involved with it. He was actually quite adamant."

Guidry waited to hear if Calman was going to make a comment. When he didn't, Guidry thought it was time to set the hook. He didn't even notice he was smiling.

"He wanted to know what kind of ideas I might have on making this into a documentary," Andy paused for effect and then continued, "something that would sell as, say, a History Channel special."

Calman thought a moment, trying to decide just how much actual truth was leaking into this conversation.

"Andy, let's cut the crap. I'll be straight with you, so you be straight with me," said Jack in a confidential, yet congenial tone. "We are very interested in doing a show on this. But we want to do something different, more than just a standard *Bid Battle* format. For one thing, there's no way we could put enough resources in place fast enough for that kind of program. Another reason is… well, the rest of the event just isn't that interesting. It is, after all, just an A-Bear auction."

"Okay, fair enough," said Andy. "So what did you have in mind?"

"That's what I'm being straight about. We don't really know," said Jack. "Something that's out of the box; not the usual auction coverage. Perhaps something that, as you mentioned, might be more documentary than episodic? What were you thinking as far as format?"

"Well," said Andy, "I've actually thought of a few different ways to cover this, but I've got one idea that I think is going to be frigging incredible, groundbreaking actually. The logistics would be tough as hell, but I think I can pull it off. If I were given the right resources."

His coming up with a format to fit the circumstances had actually had been a topic of conversation the night before, and an overall logistics deal had been struck. It was, however, more of a personal arrangement with McMillian than an official one with A-Bear Auctions.

Guidry had been mulling it over during his post-dinner French Quarter wandering, but he really hadn't, as of yet, come up with even one solid concept; must less one that was *frigging groundbreaking*. But he also didn't get to where he was by not being confident in his producing abilities. He wasn't a half-bad negotiator either.

"So pitch me." Jack replied. His patience with this game was starting to run thin.

Guidry smiled, hearing the brass tacks starting to poke through in Calman's voice.

"Well, I don't know," said Andy. "I was going to talk with Pat before I called you, but you were too fast for me. I don't know where he is on this. He might already be reaching out to his network contacts, and I think my involvement is going to be a big part of his pitch. It's really hard to say. It is kinda early."

"You're right. It's early. There's almost a whole twenty-four hours before the auction begins," said Jack, sarcasm dripping from his voice. The tone then immediately changed to one which signaled the end of the conversation, "Listen, I can find someone else. Remember, it was you that called me looking for work; ANY kind of work. I said I'd call you if something came up; something I could give you so you wouldn't have to take drastic measures. So I did, because I'm a man of my word."

Andy's smile faded a bit, thinking it was too late to avoid that. The drastic measure had already been taken. Time to concentrate on the matter at hand.

"Jack, I appreciate that... and you," said Andy. "You gave me my start and I'll always owe you. I can deal with Pat. They just want the PR and they want it on the air. If someone else will pay the cost of producing it, I sure they'll go with it. I can make it happen."

Andy paused, waiting for a reply. Not getting one, he took a deep breath and continued, "Listen... honestly... you're going to love my new concept on auction coverage. And this is the perfect situation to apply it. It is a true perfect storm of production elements that will make the show irresistible. I promise you, this is ratings gold. And it's not a one-time shot. This concept has legs. It could go mainstream."

There was at least five seconds of silence, which seemed like fifty, before Jack spoke, "OK. So again, pitch me."

"I'm almost finished with the outline," said Andy, hoping the relief in his voice wasn't too glaring. "Give me two hours to polish it, and I'll call you with the details. And I promise you're going to love it."

"OK. Two hours," replied Jack. "That would be eight twenty-seven my time, ten twenty-seven New Orleans time. You call me."

Andy had stared at the "call ended" message on his phone, laid it on the nightstand and slowly began to get dressed.

That was when he had decided to walk down to Café du Monde and get filled up on the producer's four basic food groups... sugar, fat, carbs and caffeine.

Enjoying the somewhat cool, mid-morning humidity of the open-air cafe, he started to rally his thoughts as the much needed caffeine jolt finally started kicking in.

Guidry took mental stock of the situation. He needed to come up with an incredible groundbreaking format, as well as the logistics on how to pull it off, on an auction that was starting in less than a day. Taking out his phone, he checked the time and calculated that he now had just over an hour to do it.

He took a deep breath, smiled, and asked himself what he was going to do with the rest of the time.

# CHAPTER 12
# It's All About Provenance

*Thursday – August 24 – 9:26 AM CDT*

> "But I have no doubt that it will be sufficient for the bidding to be... enthusiastic."
> — Heinrich Heinzburg

"Do you mind if I vape?" asked Heinrich Heinzburg as he settled into the leather armchair opposite Pat McMillian's desk.

Pat just shrugged and said, "Suit yourself."

McMillian had seen plenty of vapers. It was the latest hip thing at the clubs. Despite what he read about its supposedly more healthful attributes, he wasn't fond of the massive clouds of exhaled vapor that some of the more industrial models could produce.

Just a few weeks ago he had witnessed a *Vape Duel* between two smoke shop employees down on Canal Street. Though it was more publicity stunt than actual competition, the massive clouds of white vapor were impressive until one realized that the thick rolls of mist indicated air that was previously inside the participants.

Although intellectually, McMillian realized it was only a visual indicator of what happens to air naturally, it was still a bit disturbing. After watching a bit, he had taken a wide arc to avoid the clouds and continued on his way.

"Excellent," replied Heinrich. "I am quite addicted to it," he said as he removed the ornate device from its small holster.

"That's quite a unit," stated Pat as Heinrich powered it up and took a slow, strong drag on the massive chrome nipple. He then tilted his head back and released a huge stream of white vapor towards the ceiling. The air conditioning return vent in Pat's office did an admirable job in removing the vapor. It reminded McMillian of the airflow testing tunnels where technicians would introduce plumes of smoke to see how the air was streaming over the various parts of a car.

"Danke," said Heinrich, holding up the device and admiring it. "It is the best, in my opinion, although I do not believe it is available in the United States." After another deep drag on the nipple and the accompanying exhale, Heinrich continued, "I find the practice both relaxing and stimulating. It is a most pleasant paradox."

McMillian gave a brief flicker of a smile and then picked up a folder on his desk. It was time to get down to business.

"The report from the Mercedes Benz Classic Center is quite conclusive," started Pat. "As far as the car itself, it is most definitely everything you have claimed it to be. It is now only the provenance of it having been a car actually used by Hitler that is in question. Are we still sticking to the pre-arranged timetable?"

"As we discussed, I will publicly present that provenance immediately prior to the bidding. I believe it will have the most impact at that moment. The bidders will find the provenance quite, uhh," Heinrich paused for a moment, as if searching for the proper word, and then continued, "quite intense and very valuable... in and of itself."

"So you have stated, repeatedly," replied Pat, "and I am looking forward to seeing it." Pat paused for a moment and then continued, "The, ah, the outcome of our agreement will be contingent upon its intensity and, of course, its verifiability."

"It is what it is," said Heinrich with a shrug, smiling at his use of the American idiom. "It will be up to the bidders to accept or discount the provenance as I have no other proof of the car's validity. But I have no doubt that it will be sufficient for the bidding to be... enthusiastic."

"It will need to be," said Pat. "And I must compliment you on your English."

"Thank you," replied Heinrich, "I have studied hard to bring my English to this level. It will be necessary for a proper presentation."

"And, considering the circumstances, the accent won't hurt either. I am very much looking forward to your presentation," said Pat.

"So," Heinrich continued, gesturing to the folder with M-B Classic Center stamped on the front. "With the independent verification now in hand, may I assume the last impediment to our arrangement has been removed?"

"Yes," replied Pat. "I have begun the necessary financial arrangements and they should be completed within the hour. This is, however, a very peculiar way to auction a car. You would likely stand to make far more money with our more traditional arrangement and fund disbursement procedures."

Heinrich's eyes narrowed as he spoke "Mr. McMillian, we made this arrangement weeks ago. I have invested quite a bit of resources in upholding my side of this bargain. My terms are simple, and have not changed from the start of our negotiations. Nor will they."

Pat quickly replied with what he hoped was an assuring manner, "And we intend on honoring this agreement to the letter! Why would we not? A-Bear will make far more money in this arrangement than in a normal consignment." Pat paused a bit and continued, "But as this arrangement is out of the ordinary, we don't necessarily want it to be public knowledge, due to its… complexity"

"I believe the arrangement to be quite simple," said Heinrich, staring directly into Pat's eyes. "I would like to make three million, seven hundred and fifty thousand U.S. dollars from the auction of my car. When it sells, I want any and all funds up to that three million, seven hundred and fifty thousand U.S. dollars immediately transferred to my bank account in the Cayman Islands. Again, it is to be transferred IMMEDIATELY upon the sale. There will be independent representatives from our respective banks, as well as independent legal counsel to confirm the transaction takes place as agreed." Heinrich was talking slowly, as if to be sure that each detail was completely understood.

"Any and all funds above the three point seven five million is the A-Bear commission, nothing less and nothing more," Heinrich continued. "It is up to A-Bear to pre-verify that the buyer has the financial ability to consummate the deal, as the funds will be transferred from a verified, fully funded escrow account set up by A-Bear Auctions. The transfer is NOT contingent upon the purchaser's payment."

Heinzburg stopped and took another mighty drag on the vaping device, blowing the vapor to the ceiling in a mighty expulsion. He paused to watch as the return vent once again whisked it away.

He then looked back at Pat and continued, "That was our deal from the beginning and it has not changed. It is now time for you to provide verification that the funds are now available and being held in escrow under this arrangement. And, also, that your bankers are both aware of, and are fully prepared to execute those terms. Is this, or is this not, how you understand our agreement?"

Pat smiled and replied, "Herr Heinzburg, we have no intention of trying to modify this arrangement. A-Bear Auctions stands to make many times what our normal commission would be. Depending on your provenance, this car could easily bring two or three times your financial requirement. Perhaps even a great deal more. That is why they call it an auction," Pat paused and looked at his stainless steel Rolex Explorer. He thought that by Monday, he might well be in the market for that solid gold vintage Daytona he'd seen at Adler's on Canal Street.

"In exactly one hour we have our meeting with the bank, and our respective lawyers, to ensure that all arrangements are to your satisfaction," Pat said. He then lowered his voice and leaned over his desk, "And as to our arrangement?"

"Yes, our arrangement is already in place," Heinrich replied. "Assuming the car brings me the full three point seven five million, immediately upon receipt of the funds to my bank, a *donation* of two hundred and fifty thousand U.S. dollars will be transferred into your Cayman Island account.

Heinzburg paused, enjoying the greed that glittered in McMillian's eyes before he continued. "However, to continue being clear about our arrangements, any amount less than the three point seven five, will be deducted from your donation. And, if the sale amount is three point five million or less, this donation is no longer… financially feasible and this portion of the agreement is no longer valid. Is this how you understand our *additional* arrangement?"

"Yes," replied Pat, with a nod and a smile. "That is exactly how I understand it."

"Good. It is most convenient that we do our offshore banking at the same establishment," continued Heinrich. "My banker, who also happens to be your banker, will be available after the meeting to confirm he has received the necessary instructions from me, and that he should consider this a binding contract between us."

Heinzburg thought, and not for the first time, that regardless of the contracts, agreements, and attending bankers and lawyers, it was this donation, and only this donation, that would ensure the immediate transfer of the auction proceeds.

Satisfied, Pat leaned back and resumed his normal tone of voice. Looking Heinrich directly in the eye he said, "And now, the provenance. I believe we are at the agreed upon stage of our arrangement where you are to show me the provenance that ties this car, irrefutably is the word I believe you used, to Adolph Hitler."

Heinrich, staring back at Pat in an unwavering gaze replied, "Yes, it is."

"Good. I am anxious to see it. When all is said and done," said Pat, "the successful outcome of this endeavor will certainly depend on it. In this world, my world, it's all about provenance."

Heinzburg was actually a bit excited. He had been waiting for this moment for months and was anxious to finally witness someone viewing the video for the first time.

"You are correct in both statements," Heinrich stood up with his valise in hand and continued, "I assume you have the required equipment, as discussed?"

Thirty-two minutes later, McMillian was in the A-Bear conference room staring at the Blu-ray player menu on the widescreen TV. It had defaulted to that screen once the video was over. His lips were slightly open, still shocked at what he just saw. He had only to press a button on the remote to replay the video but had decided that once was enough; actually, more than enough.

"And you have the original film for this?" he asked. He swallowed, and then continued, choosing his words carefully, "I mean here with you, in New Orleans."

"Ja, I mean, Yes I do." Heinrich said as he stood up and walked to the player. He ejected the disk and returned to his chair, snapping it into the generic album case. He then continued, "As I told you, the film was transferred directly to my hard drive from a Lasergraphics Film Scanner in my presence.

The scanner was set up using the first fifty feet of the film for the optical pin registration. At that point I had the technician restart the transfer and leave the room. After the film was scanned, I personally encoded the digitized film file onto this Blu-ray disk."

Heinrich reached into the black leather bag at his feet and pulled out a G-Force hard drive and an old, yet seemingly lightly used 16mm film can. He placed them both on the table, the can on top of the hard drive, and then carefully laid the Blu-ray case on top of them both.

"These," stated Heinrich, "are the only copies of this film in the world."

Pat swallowed, looked at his watch and then stood up, "Then let's get to that meeting. At our lawyers rates, we don't want to be late."

Heinrich smiled at Pat, "With the amount of money we will both be making, a lawyer's hourly rate is somewhat inconsequential."

Pat smiled and replied, "Perhaps, but five hundred dollars an hour is five hundred dollars an hour and there are two of them. And remember, the car isn't sold yet." Pat stood and opened the blinds that had shielded the conference room from the hallway windows. He then unlocked and opened the door, "Shall we?"

"Quite," replied Heinrich with a sharp click of his heels.

Heinzburg thought the heel clicking might have been a bit too theatrical, but then shrugged it off. Besides, he kind of liked it. At this point, it almost felt natural.

# CHAPTER 13
# CarAlity

*Thursday – August 24 – 9:37 AM PDT*

> "By the time you call him tomorrow morning, he'll be in way over his head."
> — J. Roger Winters

"Yes sir?" asked Jack Calman, snatching up the desk phone before the second ring finished.

"Get me up to speed on that New Orleans Nazi car," demanded Winters. He was not known to waste time with pleasantries so Jack followed suit.

"Guidry's on board, and he's in New Orleans now," started Jack, knowing what was coming next and not relishing the tail end of this discussion. Still, he had done what he was instructed to do.

"Nice," replied Winters. "Fast work. So what about the *spice*? What's going to make this show different from all the other boring auction shows we produce on a monotonous basis? What's going to make this the perfect launch vehicle for our new online network?"

"Guidry had a pretty good idea on that," replied Jack, wondering how this had turned into that. "He says he's going to tackle this as a reality show."

"A reality show!" blurted Winters. "What's so gosh darned good about that? When's he going to find the time to outline segments, set-up scenarios, find the right people who can come off as *real*? There's no time for that nonsense and only an idiot would green-light that!"

"It's not a reality show like a regular reality show, it's a reality show like *Candid Camera*, where the people in it don't actually know they're in it," said Jack. "He says it will be *real* reality."

The phone was eerily silent for a couple of beats.

"I like it," said Winters. His voice was at an almost normal level, which was positively contemplative for him. "How's he going to pull it off? What's the work flow?"

"As you may have read in the Last Minute Consignment email," explained Jack, "the only audience allowed during the presentation of the provenance will be registered buyers and sellers, no media allowed."

"Big deal," interrupted Winters, "so he registers as a buyer."

"Well, as it states in the LMC, at this point you can only register with the auction house by posting a five million dollar *bidder bond* with their bank," said Jack. "I had Nina call, and even if we post the bond, we will forfeit the money if it is revealed we are there solely as media. The *reveal* being that we do a show on the auction. That would make it a VERY expensive program."

"Fiddlesticks," muttered Winters, "So, how are we getting around that with this reality show concept?"

"Guidry was already registered with A-Bear, and said he has been for nearly a week," replied Jack.

"Big doodie, so he's registered," replied an increasing impatient Winters. "What difference does that make? I thought you said it was no media allowed."

"He's not registered as media," replied Jack. "He says he's there selling a car."

"What kind of car?" asked Winters.

"He didn't want to go into it any further," replied Jack, "other than it will be sold the same day as the Tourenwagen."

"Well that was serendipitous," replied Winters. "But what good is it? I don't want a blog post. I want a TV show! How's he going to get a crew in there?"

"We're pulling Mandy and Brandy off the SN shoot," explained Jack. "They will pose as bidder companions at the auction. Granted, they will be photo obsessive companions, with state of the art DSLRs, but it's positively stereotypical for Asians to have nice cameras and be using the crap out of them. Especially at an event like this."

Jack took a deep breath. So far this was going better than he thought. Of course he had yet to hit the sticky part yet. "He, I mean, we expect that many of the last minute bidders, those able to post a five million dollar bond in this short a time frame, might also have companions that accompany them to New Orleans. The Twins will just blend in, at least as much as they ever do."

Calman was merely reciting the plan and parameters that Guidry had pitched to him. All the questions Winters was asking were questions he had asked Guidry. He thought it wise to answer them to Winters in the first person, as if he had been part of the planning stage.

"But isn't Guidry known by all the big fish bidders, and the auction house?" asked Winters. "How about that snake that runs A-Bear? I mean the auto auction manager, not the owner. Is he in on this?"

"Supposedly, yes. McMillian is on board as it doesn't exactly violate his agreement with the seller, what with him being able to prove Guidry was registered as a seller days before the LMC went out. Knowing McMillian, I would assume there is a substantial fee involved with this arrangement as well. As far as avoiding recognition, Guidry will be using a proxy to attend the auction in his place, which although isn't exactly usual in an auction on the A-Bear level, also isn't against the rules," replied Jack. "And that proxy will be the one to enjoy the Twin's companionship during the auction. He'll be running audio with the Twins on camera. That is, basically, the crew."

"Who's the proxy?" asked Winters.

"He says he's going to get Bobby Raston," replied Jack. "And that only Raston could pull this off, audio wise."

"RASTON," blurted Winters, almost choking on the word. "On a podunk two camera shoot! What's the budget on this? How the hell will we ever repurpose the footage to make up for Raston and the Twins day rates... much less whatever day rate Guidry is charging!"

Winters' paused and then, with a sudden realization, continued, "Hold on a gosh darned minute. Having the credentials to get into the auction, with a crew, must have made Guidry think he was pretty flippin' valuable! What's he soaking us for?"

"Well…" started Jack. This was where it was going to get loud. But Winters had told him to get it done; to do whatever it took. So he had.

"Guidry isn't working for us as a contractor," started Jack, using the current *term du jour* for freelancer. "He's pre-licensing the show to us with, actually, pretty decent terms. US terrestrial and cable rights, unlimited airings for three years, with an option…"

"LICENSING THE SHOW TO US!" screamed Winters, carefully enunciating each word despite the volume. "WHO THE SAM HILL DOES HE THINK HE IS?"

Jack held the phone away from his ear. Winters was so loud that Jack imagined he could actually feel the handset vibrating. The pause after the question made Jack think the question was more than just rhetorical. He put the phone back on his ear to answer just in time to be blasted.

"I CAN'T FLIPPING BELIEVE YOU WOULD AGREE TO THIS!" screamed Winters. "IN CASE YOU DON'T HAVE A CALENDAR HANDY, THIS ISN'T 1995!"

Jack took a deep breath. He knew it was better to get it all out so he could ride the anger wave all at once, and hopefully not get pulled under by the rip current. Jack couldn't help but smile at his mental beach metaphors. You can take the boy out of California; you can't take the California out of the boy.

Jack took a deep breath and began, "It's actually being licensed to us as a pilot. As I was saying, we have the exclusive option to pick up the series. He calls it *CarAlity*; it has a capital A in the middle."

"Of course it does," Winters replied in his usual sarcastic tone. "How 2005."

"Anyway," continued Jack, "We'll have the option to place a thirteen episode order."

Jack held out the phone to avoid the audio blast but it didn't come. Indeed with the handset at arms length, he barely heard that Winters had begun to speak. He quickly pulled the phone to his ear.

"...could be very interesting. I'm starting to like the concept, the show concept anyway. The name sucks," said Winters. "What are the terms?"

"The pilot is pretty steep, he wants a hundred for it, but with the thirteen show order, subsequent shows drop to sixty grand each... plus any location fees and actual travel expenses."

"But this contract is just for the pilot?" confirmed Winters. "There is only a first right of refusal for the series?"

"Yes," said Jack, "That is correct. He did want a non-pick up penalty fee of twenty-five grand if we buy the pilot but decline to pick up the series, but I negotiated him out of that."

"Negotiated how?" asked Winters, "What did you give up?"

"Nothing really," replied Jack, "He agreed to wave the penalty fee if we would do an immediate money transfer into his bank account for fifty thousand dollars... as a deposit against the pilot fee. If we don't like the finished pilot, we can decline the program and not pay the remaining fifty. That way we both have skin in the game. I was just about to submit the forms to accounting so it would be in his bank before the end of the day. He was pretty adamant that it happen before close of business today."

"Really..." muttered Winters, at a somewhat normal volume. For him it was positively a whisper of contemplation. "Didn't you tell me his Redline show was on hiatus?"

"Well, that's how he's putting it," replied Jack. "My contacts say it's more cancelled than on hiatus, but yes, that is correct."

"And he was adamant about the money being wired today," asked Winters, "before the close of business." It was more a musing statement than a question.

Jack answered it anyway, "Yes, he insisted."

"Was there any mention of the deal being off if the money was not in his account by COB?" asked Winters.

"Well, not exactly. It's a verbal agreement," replied Jack. "But like I said, he gave up the non-pick up penalty fee in exchange for the immediate deposit and I agreed to it. You told me to get it done. I got it done."

"Hold off on transferring the money, but have it ready to go… and I mean immediately ready to go," instructed Winters. "And don't take any more calls from Guidry today," Winters ended the sentence with an evil little chuckle.

Winters then continued with his instructions, "We'll make him sweat it out before you return his calls tomorrow. Tell him you're sorry you couldn't return his calls, but that something happened to your phone. Then tell him you don't know what happened to the transfer, that you left strict orders that it was to happen and that you'll check into it immediately."

"I'm not sure I understand why we're…" said Jack, who then immediately held the handset away as the screaming started.

"I DON'T GIVE A FLYING FLIPPER NIPPER WHAT YOU UNDERSTAND!" yelled Winters. But then his voice immediately dropped to a more reasonable level as he continued in the tone one takes when explaining complex matters to a somewhat addled individual.

"Here's how we're working this. We make him wait because he obviously needs the money, and he needs it quick," explained Winters. "With this kind of production schedule, he'll be committing funds that he thinks are, or soon will be, in the bank. By the time you call him tomorrow morning, he'll be in way over his head," Winters paused to chortle again. He was obviously enjoying this.

"So after your first call tomorrow, let him stew for about ten minutes or so. Then call him back and say the reason the funds didn't transfer is that upper management has declined the offer… as it stands," explained Winters. "Tell him we will agree to the financial terms, in full, but that if we decide to buy it, we get full rights to the pilot. No license fiddle faddle, I'm talking a TOTAL buyout for both the show AND the concept. He'll counter with giving us a twenty-five percent equity share, we counter with seventy-five percent. If you have to, settle on a fifty-fifty deal, but not a percentage point less. Got it?"

"Yes sir, I've got it, but I don't know if he will go for that," replied Jack, "He was pretty adamant about his terms, and I did already agree to them."

"Anything in writing?" asked Winters.

"No," said Jack, "but I gave him my word."

"Screw your word, this is business," replied Winters. "Throw him a bone and say that we'll agree to the twenty five grand non-pick up penalty. But also tell him that you've been royally chewed out for doing this deal verbally. Tell him the new deal absolutely has to be in writing to proceed. Then get the contract drawn and fax it to his hotel. Tell him to sign it, have it notarized, and return it.

Then, and only then, transfer the money, but do it immediately. Have it ready so that the minute you see the fax, the money will pop into his account." Winters paused and actually gave a low chuckle. "That'll show him who's in the driver's seat."

Jack sighed. Over thirty years of his word being his bond, just got tossed in the trash like a used snot rag. "So," he asked Winters, "what if he doesn't agree to it?"

"He will," replied an obviously smug Winters. He truly enjoyed using money as his primary weapon in this war called the TV business. "There's a reason he wanted the money immediately and we use that to our advantage. We've just got to give him enough rope and he'll do the rest. Any more issues I need to deal with?"

Jack took a deep breath, thought about his alimony payment, the mortgage on a house he no longer lived in, two kids in college, and his sixty-four deuce and a quarter convertible that was in the middle of being transformed into a very expensive, incredibly kick-ass lowrider.

"No sir," he replied, "I don't believe there is."

"Good," said Winters briskly, "keep me in the loop on this."

"Will do," said Jack, speaking into the now dead handset. He looked at it for a moment and then placed it onto its cradle.

He picked up the money request form he'd had Nina fill out. There was a big red "Urgent" stamped on it. He sighed and placed in on the stack of papers on the edge of the desk. He looked at the clock on his computer screen, slowly shook his head in resignation, and hit the intercom button on the phone.

"Nina, I believe I will be going home now," Jack slowly said to Nina Perez, his assistant of nearly fifteen years. If he was in the office, she was in the office... no matter what he did to dissuade her from matching his schedule.

Nina replied in a concerned voice, "Are you OK?"

"No," replied Jack. "Not exactly OK, but don't worry. I'll be fine. I'll see you tomorrow."

"Did you get the paperwork to accounting for the money transfer?" asked Nina.

"No, we're putting a hold on that," said Jack. "But we'll likely need to do it first thing tomorrow."

"But you said it had to get done today," Nina said in a quizzical tone.

"I know what I said," sighed Jack, "but the urgency has been... subjugated."

"Sub-ja-gated," repeated Nina, precisely enunciating each syllable. She then asked Jack, "What should I tell Mr. Guidry about the transfer, if he calls?"

"Oh, he'll call," replied Jack in a rueful voice. "Tell him it's been... tell him you don't know why it hasn't been transferred. Tell him you filled out the paperwork yourself and that it should have already gone through."

"Will do," replied the ever-efficient Nina.

"Thank you," said Jack, "I'll be out of touch for the rest of the day." As he left the building, he picked up his phone, held down the power button and swiped it to off.

# CHAPTER 14
# Epic

*Thursday – August 24 – 10:02 AM PDT*

> "But wait... there's more!"
> — ANTOINE GUIDRY

"Holy Christ, my fucking feet hurt," said Bobby Raston to no one in particular. He lived alone, very much alone, and traveled way too much for pets. Raston was forty-two years old, a stout two hundred and forty-one pounds, and stood five foot four at best... in his heels. All of his shoes were custom made with lifts that, depending on the style, added an extra inch or two.

He had just wheeled in a custom made case that looked both very industrial and very well used. The black aluminum sides were scratched and dented, but obviously thick enough to take the abuse. On top was a black Cordura suitcase with latches that secured it to the case. Just behind it was a heavy duty, telescoping handle. The suitcase had a similar amount of wear and looked pretty much like it was made to be there, although Bobby had actually designed and built the attachment system.

Raston left the cases in the foyer and walked downstairs into the huge living room. It had an expansive view of the valley and, at the very edge of it, the Pacific Ocean. He plopped onto the couch and kicked off his shoes. He sat there rubbing his feet, muttering for at least the thousandth time, "There's way too many fucking stairs in this house."

Raston had bought the tri-level house mainly because of its proximity to John Wayne airport. He had also, of course, justified the price by imagining all the women who would be enthralled with the luxurious house jutting out into the valley, supported by huge metal stanchions.

The front door of the house was on the street level. To the left of it was a driveway that led into a generous, almost fastidiously neat two-car garage. On the left was where he kept his Chevy Bolt EV. It was equipped with every available option and its 220V charging station was expertly installed on the wall next to it. The Bolt was his daily driver and had plenty of range to get him to all his usual destinations, the most frequent of which was the airport.

The other bay held the new BMW M4, but that one didn't leave the garage very often. It was what Raston called his chick magnet, although it didn't seem to be working as well as the salesman had assured him it would. When he had the time, he would likely trade it in on something with, hopefully, more attraction.

From the front door, or from a side door inside the garage, you came to a small landing foyer that faced a wide marble and steel stairway that led down to the second floor.

The second floor contained a chef-quality kitchen to the right and a sprawling living room to the left. The living room had floor-to-ceiling glass walls and sliding doors that led to the expansive, full-length balcony. The living room was tastefully furnished with overstuffed, overpriced leather furniture, arranged more to enjoy the view than facilitate conversation. There was a Steinway grand piano in the far corner. To the left, halfway down the staircase and above the living room, was the formal dining platform. On the marble floor was an Oriental rug, and on the rug was a hideously expensive fifteen-foot, black lacquer table that matched the piano's finish. The back wall of the dining area was a custom built cabinet that was split through the middle with a four-foot tall saltwater aquarium running the length of the dining area.

Down yet another staircase, on the third floor, were the bedrooms. The master suite, complete with massive Jacuzzi tub, steam shower, walk-in closet, and dressing room, was separated from the two guest rooms by a custom-designed home theater.

The theater area featured four leather recliners, with integral cup holders, arranged in pairs. The rear pair was on a short platform to allow an unobstructed view of the Sony XBR-85X950B 85 inch 4k Ultra High Definition TV. The stunning monitor seemed to float in thin air, a foot or so in front of bunched up black velvet curtains that formed a small cove around it.

Surrounding the recliners, and attached to the circular track suspended from the ceiling, spindly aluminum arms held seven precisely arranged, angled, and aimed Genelec 8130A speakers. The Genelec SE7261A DSP Subwoofer was positioned proudly in view, directly under the huge Sony monitor.

Raston had acquired the speaker system from a friend whose recording studio had gone into the red and thus had needed some quick cash to keep the doors open. Raston knew the guy was hurting, so when his friend had tried to put the squeeze on Raston for a loan, he responded by waving cash in front of his face in a low-ball offer for the speakers. He got them for what amounted to pennies on the dollar.

With a single tap on an iPad, the black velvet curtains would enclose the area, small lights would softly illuminate the chairs, and the rear surround speakers would descend from the track to position themselves behind the chairs. Another tap on the iPad and the massive Sony video monitor and a Pioneer Elite SC-89 A/V receiver would turn on simultaneously. Through a custom designed UI, you would then choose your entertainment feed. A viewing experience way better than any theater, would immediately envelop the lucky viewers.

Raston had thought that four and a half million for the exclusive property was money well spent or, rather, well invested. Upon closing, he had visions of the extreme difficulty he would have in deciding which beautiful starlet he would allow to accompany him home, after the obligatory wrap party for the rare occasion he worked on a scripted show or feature.

Since his purchase of the house, there had been an even dozen such wrap parties, but he had always come home alone. He really did need to work on that.

Even at a day rate of twenty-five hundred dollars a day, and often working twenty to twenty-five days a month, Raston lived a far more extravagant lifestyle than his audio income would support. Truth be known, and not many people did know, ENG audio was more avocation than vocation. To Raston, it was more like a game. He truly enjoyed figuring out solutions to the increasingly difficult task of getting pristine audio under the harshest and most intricate working environments.

So while his ego demanded that he be at the highest pay rate the market would support, he actually gave the producers and show runners a great value for the money. He was not only incredibly skilled, but by booking him, producers had access to a plethora of highly specialized microphones, transmitters, and recorders. And this was no off-the-shelf gear that could be bought with mere money.

Raston had been a child prodigy in the field of RF engineering. He graduated from the University of Colorado in Boulder, earning a Master's degree with honors exactly three days after his eighteenth birthday. When you're an overweight, underage uber-nerd, what else do you do but study?

He currently held six patents on RF technology that were intrinsic to the highest priced offerings by LetroSonics, Zaxcomm, Sennheiser, and Sony. The royalty payments alone would allow him to afford whatever house he wanted, drive whatever car he'd like, and eat at whatever restaurant was the current rave of the LA food critics.

Raston worked because there was something special about obtaining what the masses took for granted; really great audio in a reality situation. Sure, he worked on feature films, but with multiple takes, numerous setups, and *all the time in the world*; that style of production wasn't really much of a challenge. And what really motivated him was the challenge.

It was also that way with women. With the resources at his command, regardless of his looks and mild OCD personality, there was no reason he should ever be lacking in female companionship. But normal women didn't interest Raston. He only went after stunningly beautiful women. And the more they refused his interest, the more interested he became.

More than one wrap party afterglow, in Raston's mind anyway, had been later tinged with the delivery of a restraining order. It was not because Raston was violent, because he most certainly was not. It was because he was persistent or, rather, VERY persistent. Plus, he didn't seem to get the subtle signals that most people received and processed on an almost subliminal level.

At the present time, however, Raston was simply exhausted.

He had just returned from five days covering the La Carrera Panamericana, the *gentlemen's race* that ran through the Mexican interior. This year it had started at Huatulco and ended up in Zacatecas. The final festivities included the traditional donkey march through the steep hills of the colonial town.

The crowd was entertained by a ten-piece mariachi band and fueled by a dozen or so teenagers handing out small cups and holding plates overflowing with fresh cut lime wedges. The cups were tied to ribbons to hang them around your neck. You wore them that way so they'd be handy when the older boys came by with huge glass jugs of Mescal. That had been just over twenty-four hours ago and he thought he could still taste the raw liquor on the back of his tongue.

It had been a grueling, last minute assignment. This gig had overlapped with another by a single day, and so he had told the producers he wasn't available. He had convinced them to hire Matt Mitchell, one of the few audio supervisors he trusted with some of his more specialized RF and monitoring gear. Two days into the shoot, Matt had contracted a monumental case of Montezuma's Revenge and had to drop out. Since he had recommended the guy, as well as the three other audio techs, the producers called him in a panic. Despite having been back in LA for only one day, he had agreed to drop everything and take over. He did, after all, have a reputation to maintain.

The Carrera production was structured so that the audio supervisor and the three audio techs supported the three two-man camera crews that covered forty-two race teams. That might seem like a lot of teams to cover with three crews and, in actuality, it was. At least it was in the beginning of the race.

Despite being a gentlemen's race, or perhaps because of it, within the first few days the team count would usually whittle itself down to around a dozen or so, due mainly to catastrophic mechanical errors but with just enough spectacular accidents thrown in to spice up the show.

Bobby was happy that, for once, he didn't actually lose any gear. And, he added as an afterthought, that no one had died.

Competition style reality shows were notorious for losing the small intricate microphone and transmitter systems that Raston relied upon. Costing thousands of dollars each, and with hours of intricate modifications on every unit, losing even a few during a production could rack up the expenses and, more importantly to Bobby, the time it took to modify them to his purposes.

Production companies who did those sorts of shows would actually rearrange their schedules to accommodate Raston's services whenever possible. Those who enjoyed his services on the really large, really rugged productions were used to a final bill that would often included tens of thousands of dollars for lost, or otherwise damaged mics and transmitters. It was a cost of doing business, and the final results were always worth the cost, and more.

Raston took another deep breath and sighed. As much as he loved the work, with the two back-to-back shoots, it had been nearly two weeks of fourteen-hour days, capped with four-hour parties every night. At forty-two he wasn't exactly old, but he certainly wasn't young. And he wasn't exactly in the best physical condition but, then again, he never had been.

"I'm going to have to turn one of the guest bedrooms into a workout room," he muttered to himself, twisting his lower back with a hand on his hip. He belonged to three of the most exclusive gyms in LA, but he never actually went. By the third club he joined, he had decided they were highly overrated as prime hook-up spots and had subsequently lost interest.

The thought of exercising was quickly displaced by the question of what he was going to eat for dinner that night. Bobby believed it was never too early to think about dinner. He was actually an excellent cook, nearly chef quality, and food was one of his passions. He had once read that women loved men who could cook. So he'd spent nearly a year taking classes at the LeCordon Bleu on Sunset to perfect that skill.

Tonight, however, the massive kitchen, with its industrial level appliances artfully blended into the modern décor, would remain both cold and dark. This was, after all, LA. Or pretty darn close to it. If you were willing to pay the price, you could have almost anything, from almost anywhere, delivered to your door.

Bobby smiled as he began his mental dinner selection routine. He would start the process by first deciding on a general area of the world. Then he would decide on the country and finally on a specific region. He had just about decided on something eastern European when his cell phone rang.

"Fuck," said Bobby in a tired whisper. "What now?"

Raston looked at the phone, saw the Caller ID, and seriously contemplated letting it go to voice mail. He then took a deep breath, sighed and hit answer.

"Raston here," he said into the phone.

"Hey Bobby, glad I caught ya. How's it going?" said Antoine Guidry, a bit too quickly and with just a little too much enthusiasm.

"Who's this?" asked Bobby, knowing exactly who it was.

"It's Andy, Andy Guidry," replied Andy, also knowing Bobby knew exactly who it was.

Guidry and Raston had worked together more than a few times when Raston was just starting out. They weren't what you'd call close, but they had a decent working relationship. At least Guidry didn't owe him money, as did half the other independent producers Raston knew.

"Hello Andy," replied Bobby. "What can I do for you? Make it brief, I just got in on an three-leg flight from Mexico, doing the Carrera," Bobby paused for effect and continued. "Didn't we work on that race together, what, ten or twelve years ago?"

"Yeah we did," replied Andy, "fun times."

Guidry had begged Jack Calman to let him cover the race back in the day, when Neiderland was just getting into the TV world and didn't yet have a direction for their programming. This meant they hadn't yet found what the viewers would watch and the advertisers would pay for; or at least partially pay for.

Back when Guidry covered it, it had been a low budget experiment in paid programming on Speed. Now it was a big yearly show that FOX Sports spent a ton of money on to ensure stellar production values.

"Yeah. Fun," replied Bobby. "Listen, I'm pretty beat. I really did just get in. So, why are you calling?"

"For more fun!" said Andy, hoping the tone of his voice was more excitement than desperation. "I'm calling to give you the sweetest gig ever. And I am not exaggerating in the slightest when I tell you this is history making."

"OK," replied Bobby, "I'll give you five minutes. Where, what, and when?"

Guidry remembered Raston's brusque manner and tried not to let it shake him. He really needed Raston on this. He was the only audio guy he knew that could pull off the production he had pitched to Jack Calman. Since Calman had bit, Guidry had to get Raston.

"Bobby, that's just one of the things I like about you," Andy replied. "You like it quick and to the point."

"Yes, I do," replied Bobby. "So let's make it four minutes. Where, what, and when?"

"New Orleans, auto auction, and PDQ." said Andy.

"Out of the question," said Bobby. "But thanks for calling."

"But wait… there's more!" cried Andy in his best TV huckster voice. "Listen Bobby, I know we haven't worked together much in the last few years…"

"Actually, not at all in the last six years, ten months and," Bobby paused for just a split second and then finished with, "twelve days." He wasn't being sarcastic; he just had a head for figures and liked being accurate. Bobby continued, "But regardless, I've had one day off in the last fourteen. I'm still hung over from the Carrera's final award ceremony. And I don't do auto auctions."

"Sounds like fun to me! And yeah, I know you don't *usually* do auto auctions, but this isn't like any car auction that you've ever done, or seen, or been a part of. I'm doing an auto auction program that's never been done before, and I'm not even sure it can be done," Andy was now in his element. He was pitching, and he was good at it, whether it was to a network suit or reluctant talent, he had a gift for making his enthusiasm more than a bit contagious.

"It's only one real work day, with an additional day for practice and prep, not that you need it," said Andy, the flattery subtle, but there. "It's going to be an extremely small crew and the logistics are extremely challenging. The audio is going to be the most difficult part of the whole production and I'm not even sure it can be done. But I do know if anyone could pull it off, it would be Bobby Raston."

"Ok, I'm barely semi-interested," replied Raston, not even fighting the urge to yawn. "But, what do you mean by PDQ?" asked Raston.

"I mean today. There's a United Airlines flight leaving John Wayne for Louis Armstrong at twelve fifteen. It's only one stop and about three and a half hours total. That's probably the best if you can make it cause it gets into New Orleans around five thirty. There's also a Delta flight leaving LAX at one forty-five, but it's five and a half hours and two stops. But that one doesn't get in until nearly nine, New Orleans time, and I'd sure like you here earlier than that. But I understand, the early one might be hard to make. So just take your pick and I'll take it from there," said Andy.

"Andy," said Bobby in a patient, tired voice. "I haven't heard from you in years and you call up wanting me to drop everything and fly out with less than two hours notice? It's just not going to happen."

"I think it will," replied Andy.

"And what makes you think so," asked Bobby, a little intrigued by the confidence in Andy's voice. "And do you even know what my day rate is now?"

"Yes, I know your day rate. Everybody knows your day rate. And I think you're going to do this gig because I know you, and what gets your motor running. This is the first ever, true reality car show. It will be epic! It will be revolutionary! And it takes place at an auto auction that will make history, and one that only my crew will be allowed access into."

Raston sat up a little straighter. He did a very quick, yet incredibly accurate mental inventory of the audio kit still standing in the foyer. Three transmitters were toast, but that left seventeen packed and ready to go. Five of the subminiature,

Raston-modified Countryman mics had been mangled, and two had snapped cords, but he had plenty of spares in the gear locker. There were only two minor repairs needed for the rest of the gear, which he could do in less than twenty minutes and almost anywhere. His personal invention, the RigMaster, was in pristine shape and just needed to be charged.

From the pause in the conversation, Andy knew he had Bobby thinking about it. Now was the time to pull the trump card. "And I've got a camera crew you're going to love working with."

"Yeah, I'm sure. But you do have my attention," said Raston, "What is so revolutionary, so *epic* about this production? What makes this historic? And why would I care who the camera guys are? We're down to two minutes."

As Guidry pitched the concept, Raston sat up straighter. He forgot about the pain in his feet and the rumble in his belly. And when Guidry played his ace in the hole, Raston was hooked.

"Okay," Bobby replied, "I'll do the gig and I'll take the John Wayne flight. Five large is the rate, with an extra five bills for equipment prep on such short notice. I like the concept, but it's only going to work if this is indeed historic."

"It is truly historic and, with you on board, the production will be truly epic," said Andy, the smile in his voice finally matching the broad grin on his face. "Do you get the Last Minute Consignment emails from A-Bear Auctions."

"No," replied Bobby as he stood up, wincing a bit but otherwise ignoring the pain in his feet. "Why do you ask?"

"That's where the historic factor comes in. I'll forward it to you along with the hotel address," replied Andy. "Is your email still the same?"

"AudioGod@audiogod.com." said Bobby as he slowly walked up the stairs to retrieve the suitcase. "Why would I change it?"

"No reason," said Andy, "no reason at all. Rent a car at Louis Armstrong and I'll meet you at the hotel. I'll reimburse you."

"Yes, you will," agreed Bobby and then hung up without another word. He trotted up the stairs with renewed energy and unlatched the suitcase from the audio gearbox. He then hurried down the two flights of stairs and into the bedroom where he dumped out the dirty clothes and began filling the case with fresh ones. "This place really does have too many fucking stairs," he muttered. But there was the beginning of a smile on his face.

"This might very well be epic," he thought as the expression turning more leer than smile and his eyebrows actually wagged. "In more ways than one."

# CHAPTER 15
# Sieggymobile

*Thursday – August 24 – 11:37 PM CDT*

> "We can't go above that amount
> or we'll need to sell the house and
> perhaps even the HEIL."
> — Saul Wittmann

Herman Adler stopped the Cosworth Vega in front of a large red steel building out on State Highway Zz, about a mile north of US 14.

As usual, the only other vehicle was the old man's white, four-wheel drive F150. As long as Adler had known, or known of, Saul Wittmann, the man had always driven a white, four-wheel drive F150. He'd lost count of how many the old man had owned over the years. The old man had likely lost count as well.

The only thing that separated the generic building from a thousand others that dotted the vast Wisconsin countryside was a small glassed-in front entry hall and the huge sign mounted directly above it.

The glass in the entry hall was covered inside with heavy brown paper that was showing its age. The sign above the hall was also covered, this covering being a tightly bound, heavy canvas tarp. Because it was so tightly bound, and very weathered, if you looked closely, and the light was right, you could easily make out the embossed letters that the tarp covered; *H*, *E*, *I*, and *L*.

Herman climbed out of the car and walked towards the building. He wondered if it was that the Wi-Fi needed rebooting; there was some obscure marking on an artifact that surely meant... something; or it was yet another new arrangement that he needed an opinion on; an opinion that was required immediately. Basically when it came to the HEIL, everything was an immediate need.

Adler sighed with a resigned half smile. Saul Wittmann was not only his legal guardian, or at least he had been until he had turned eighteen, Wittmann was more like family. And family was one thing he was definitely short on.

His mom and dad died the night the El Camino left the road and found the only tree in a thousand yards. It wrapped the front end around it and slammed the huge engine into the tiny, two-person passenger compartment. The police had told him that at the speed they were going, they were likely dead before the engine joined them.

Both of his parents had been only children, and his grandparents had also died early. His grandma, on his mother's side, had been the last to pass when he was twelve.

Saul Wittmann took him into his home and treated him well. If not like a son, then certainly like a favored nephew.

Anything Adler had needed, or wanted, he got. And he was both grateful and appreciative. But, as Herman unlocked the front double door and stepped inside, he was wondering just how much longer he could handle this.

Adler walked past the counter, flanked by the empty glass displays, and into the massive main room. As he passed the life size, photorealistic wax model he instinctively gave it a quick salute and muttered "Yo Sieggy."

The model was impressive and had literally ignited Wittmann's obsession, although at the time Adler hadn't realized how deep it would burn. When passing the wax figure, he'd often shake his head, ruing the day it had arrived.

He had been a senior that year and had come home at his usual time. He noticed the huge packing crate in the yard and wondered what the old man had bought this time. A lot of time, a lot of money, and a fascination with online auction sites had meant newly opened packing crates in the yard were not an unusual after-school sight.

At the time, Adler had thought it most resembled a coffin with arms.

He had walked into the house and was stunned by an incredibly realistic wax model of Adolph Hitler in an elaborate, totally authentic, military uniform. His face was smiling underneath the short polished brim of his tall crowned cap. The hat was covered in braid and topped with an ornate emblem of an eagle clutching a swastika shield. This was obviously when things were going well for old Adolph. He looked happy, proud, and confident.

His body was twisted slightly to the right, with his head even more so. His right arm was stretched out in an arrow straight salute, with his left arm by his side and bent at the elbow. His fingers were curled, so as to grasp whatever it was he was built to lean against.

"Nice statue of 'ol Adolph," Herman told Saul Wittmann, who was sitting in a nook, just off the dining room, in front of a massive computer screen.

"Are you going to put him in the front yard with an iron ring in that left hand?" Herman had asked with a smile, "Kinda like those old lawn jockeys you used to have?"

"Shut your mouth boy," Saul muttered, barely looking up from the screen. "Hitler was a good man, a great man; he was just a bit misunderstood." Saul turned from the screen and told Herman, with all sincerity, "I've been doing a lot of research on this, and if it wasn't for the Jewsmedia and..." he turned to peer at the screen through those glasses he still *only needed for reading*. He read carefully, his lips moving silently as he practiced the pronunciation, and then turned back to Herman and continued, "and the Judaized Intelligentsia that holo-hoaxed the entire world into believing differently, he would be honored for his efforts in saving the white race from the extinction plans of the transnational Zionist Occupation Government."

Adler nodded slowly. Last year it had been that the U.S. Government was being controlled by aliens, who had set up headquarters in Area Fifty One. That's where they had converted the buildings into environmentally sealed structures with a methane atmosphere.

Alder didn't think that Wittmann was exactly senile, but he also didn't think he was entirely sane. But then again, he likely never really had been. Adler also felt a bit guilty since it was at his insistence that the two hundred-year-old farmhouse even had an Internet connection.

Ever since it had been installed, he had dutifully listened to, and feigned both belief and interest in, a proliferation of conspiracy theories, dubious medical advice, and *too good to be true* investment offers which had always turned out to be a most accurate description.

Little did Adler know that on the fateful day old Adolph joined the household, Pro-Nazi Zionist conspiracy theories would settle into Saul Wittmann like a voracious tapeworm. And, like a tapeworm, would begin sucking the very life out of him.

It was mere weeks before the artifact collection began to outgrow the family house, even with its numerous barns and storage sheds. That's when the HEIL was born.

The summer after Adler graduated high school, Wittmann had contracted with General Steel to construct the HEIL. The name, he had proudly told him, "stands for the *Hitler Education and Ideology Library*."

Since then, the old man had spent untold amounts of money, collecting everything he could get his hands on that had been connected with Adolph Hitler, the Third Reich, Germany in general, and Nazi Germany in particular. The rear of the building did indeed house a library of sorts. Wittmann had filled aisles of expensive oak bookshelves with books, ledgers, documents, and loose paperwork of all kinds. It all looked very neat and orderly. But, because he could not speak German, there was no true organization to the vast collection.

The majority of the building was used to display photographs, stand-alone exhibits, and dioramas seeking to depict the various stages of Hitler's life.

Topics included Hitler's boyhood; his Army service during World War One; the rise of the Nazi party during the Weimer period; and the successful annexation of Poland and the other *lost states*. Even the fall of Berlin, detailing the heroic ending of the Führer's life on his own terms, was depicted in what Saul had named *The Hall Of Truth*.

All of the items in the collection were authentic. Wittmann had been adamant that there would be no fakes or reproductions to soil the image of the Der Führer.

"I'm in the office," shouted Saul, as Herman walked into the building. "Hurry, you're not going to believe this!"

Adler walked to the side of the building that contained a small two-room office. The sign above the door, which was always wide open, stated it was the World Headquarters of the International Society for the Abolition of the Zionist Occupation Government.

Adler walked through the front door, through the reception area and into the back office, with a Director sign on the also always open door. Wittmann sat in front of a huge iMac with a 5K Retina display.

"This," he said to Herman, while pointing at the screen with his boney finger, "is what will make the collection complete. It is…" the old man paused and looked up at Herman to complete the statement with dramatic conviction dripping off the word, "destiny."

Herman leaned over and looked at the screen, "What's a Last Minute Consignment?"

"Some bullshit promotional email from an auto auction house in New Orleans," replied Saul, turning his attention back to the screen. "From what I understand, it's used to promote a late entry into whatever the current auction is. But that's not the point." Saul stood up and gestured to Herman to sit down.

"Read the email," Saul commanded as Herman sat in front of the screen. As Herman read, he knew why Saul was so excited. They had long known that old *Sieggy*, as Herman referred to the mannequin, was originally designed to be standing in a car, left hand clutching the windshield and right hand saluting the admiring throng.

"It's short for Sieg Heil," Herman had informed Saul when he first started using the Sieggy nickname. Wittmann wasn't fond of it. He considered it disrespectful and kept insisting that Herman use the proper title, *Der Führer*. It was Adler's secret pleasure to occasionally *let it slip* when he was talking about the pride of the old man's collection.

"Wow," said Herman. "That looks like Sieggy's car." He knew this because behind the mannequin there was a huge photograph of Hitler in the exact same pose, in the exact same car, saluting a sea of admiring white faces. "Too bad it's going to cost so much."

"You mean Der Führer's car, but yes," said Saul Wittmann slowly and methodically, with the hint of a German accent that inexplicably crept into his voice whenever he was at the library. "It is too bad, but not insurmountable."

Adler knew that tone. He knew something was up. And he knew he wasn't going to like it because, well, because he had never liked it before.

"What's on your mind, Saul?" Herman asked cautiously.

"I think the estimate is inflated," replied Saul, "I believe with the inevitable protestation, and the also inevitable sycophantic coverage in the Jewsmedia, that many of the serious car collectors will be adverse to bidding too highly. If, indeed, they come to bid at all."

Wittmann stood and walked to the outer office and stared out the doorway to the Hitler mannequin. It was his first acquisition and the pride of his library. Currently, the left hand, clearly meant for the windshield of a magnificent touring car, was clutching a short chrome bar that had been machined, threaded in the middle, and screwed into a heavy chrome mic stand.

"Mit de Grosser Tourenwagen," Saul said, with a heavier accent than Herman had ever heard, "Vee vill be able to finally open zee library and pay proper homage to zee greatest man who ever lived."

"Huh... right, whatever" replied Herman. "But there's still a matter of a five million dollar bond just to be allowed to bid on it; and the auction starts tomorrow."

"I have already wired the money into the auction house escrow account," said Wittmann.

"You what?" exclaimed Herman. "Where the hell did you get five million in cash?"

"I had it, mostly," said Saul. "The bank was willing to put up the rest of the money against my real estate holdings."

"You mean the house and this... this property?" replied Herman, knowing that the old man had been selling off his once vast acreage of farmland, on a more or less regular basis, for quite some time. He had needed to fund his ability to pay whatever it took to obtain his Nazi treasures, as well as free up the time to manage it.

"Yes, but it will be worth it," he said, pausing slightly as he thought about the assets he had just transferred to the bank. "We just need to get the car for four million or less. I had that much in cash and liquid assets available. We can't go above that amount or we'll need to sell the house and perhaps even the HEIL."

"Four MILLION dollars!" exclaimed Herman, "You'd spend four million on an old car that doesn't even run and may, or MAY NOT, have been a Sieggymobile?"

The old man turned and shot Herman a look that told him to tread carefully.

Herman continued, "I mean one of Der Führer's staff cars?"

Saul returned to looking out the door and at the mannequin. "I would spend all I had, all that was needed. But I cannot spend more than four million and keep the library. And without the library, there would not be a proper, suitably respectful place to display these priceless artifacts."

"So you're going to this auction, all the way down in New Orleans," asked Herman, "just hoping that the estimate is wrong and that it won't go for more than four mil?"

"Nein," replied Saul, "Vee are going to zee auction, and vee will make sure that purchasing this car will be distasteful for the other buyers. I am hopeful it will go for much less than four million dollars. There iz, after all, no reserve."

"Wait a minute, did you say WE are going?" asked Herman, "And WE are somehow going to try to keep the price under four million? And just how are WE going to do that?"

Saul slowly turned from the doorway and looked at Herman, nodding his head with a coy smile and a twinkle in his eye that Herman hadn't seen in a long time. "We can talk about it on the way to the house. We've got to start packing and planning. We leave in two hours. I've already made the arrangements."

Adler just sighed and didn't even mention that he had classes tomorrow. He knew it didn't matter.

Almost marching, Wittmann strode out the door and towards the front of the building. Adler stared at the old man as he stopped in front of the mannequin, turned to it, clicked his heels together, saluted and shouted "Sieg Heil!" It was a loud, powerful voice that belied its origin.

Wittmann then turned and walked towards the entrance. He stopped and turned back to Herman and shouted out, "Turn out the lights and set the alarm! Come on boy, we've got a car to buy!"

Adler sighed and started out after him. Wittmann had already walked outside when Adler passed the mannequin; so he just flipped it off and muttered his usual parting phrase, "Fuck you, Sieggy."

He then went to the control panel behind the counter. He turned off the lights and set the alarm, typing N-A-Z-I into the keypad. The alarm pad started to beep as he turned and walked towards the door, keys in hand.

He stopped at the door, took a deep breath and said, "This is really going to suck," and then walked out to join the old man.

# CHAPTER 16
# TDF

*Thursday – August 24 – 5:47 PM CDT*

> "Did I mention I'm getting an Escalade?"
> — BOBBY RASTON

Bobby Raston walked off the jetway and into Louis Armstrong International Airport. He had a smile on his face. It was more than just looking forward to the shoot. Being a sound guy, he kinda liked flying into an airport actually named for a musician.

He had been able to keep both the metal gear case as well as the suitcase with him. Even though they were attached to each other, and exactly the right size for a carry on, you were technically only allowed 1 bag, regardless of size. He could often schmooze his way into keeping both by buttering up the gate attendant and getting onto the plane as a pre-boarder.

Of course it was a lot easier if there were first class seats available. He belonged to four different frequent flyer programs and each had copious amounts of mileage on each of them. If there were seats available, he normally got upgraded to the front of the plane.

On this flight, there had been no first class seats available or, apparently, even an aisle or window. What Antoine Guidry had considered *taking care of it* resulted in Raston spending the first, and longest leg of the flight in coach, and in a middle seat.

From John Wayne to George Bush Intercontinental, he had been wedged between a fat, sulky teenage girl, who never once removed her ear buds, and an elderly Hispanic man, who seemed enthralled by the whole experience. The man had studied the airplane exit card, as instructed, while the attendant explained the safety features. He had also been totally delighted by the free coffee later in the flight. He managed to slosh more than a few drops of hot black liquid onto Raston's designer jeans as he fumbled for the cup the attendant passed to him.

The man had tried to engage Raston in conversation, but he had quickly followed the girl's lead. Raston pulled out his iPad mini, chose a video from his huge collection, and plugged in a well-worn pair of Bose noise cancelling headphones. Raston watched a lot of movies on planes. It was his favorite way to pass the time unless, of course, there was an attractive female traveling companion to chat up, or at least try to.

Houston to New Orleans had been a much nicer flight. He had been able to secure a first class seat, but the guy sitting next to him wasn't anybody special so he watched an episode of *The Walking Dead*.

As he strolled into the New Orleans airport, he took an immediate left. He briefly looked up at the signage to confirm that he was on the way to the rental car counters. He had been to this airport many times before and knew his way around. But he'd been to many airports, many times before, and he believed in double-checking.

It was also his normal habit to pre-book the car when he made reservations. He liked just taking the shuttle directly to the rental car lot, climbing in and leaving. But with the last minute preparations, there simply wasn't enough time.

The packing, checking the gear, and making a couple of minor repairs took far longer than he thought it would. He was actually surprised when his phone alarm had gone off and it was time to leave for the airport. Raston had barely gotten there in time to check in and go through security. And with the amount of electronic gear he carried, going through security was never just a walk-through.

Still, today was a travel day. He had plenty of time to go to the rental car counters, see which company had what cars, and drive into New Orleans to meet Andy at the hotel.

As he was approaching the counters he was mentally planning the rest of the evening. There would be a talk about the workflow since he knew Guidry knew nothing about his RigMaster audio device. Then they could decide on a call time and grab some dinner; which would hopefully include a little quality time with the camera ops.

Since all of the counters had signs indicating that cars were available, he walked up to the Budget counter. He tended to be frugal, even when he was going to be reimbursed.

"How kin I hep you, sir?" asked the young black woman at the counter, her accent clearly giving away her New Orleans heritage, or at least a southern Louisiana one.

"I'm going to need a car for four days, counting today," said Raston. "A small SUV, a hybrid if you're got one."

"We don't have 'enny hi-brids, but I have a nice Hyundai Santa Fe or a Ford Edge," she said with a smile. "Have you rented from us before?"

"More times than I can count," replied Raston. "Let me get you my," he paused to glance at the placard on the counter. "My RapidRez number."

He pulled out his iPhone and quickly found it. But as he looked up from the phone to the agent, he caught a glimpse of female perfection out of the corner of his eye. His head whipped to the side as if it were on a gimbal. It was the Twins, THE TWINS, walking towards the automatic doorway that led to the taxis.

They were both dressed in skinny jeans, with matching tops, one cream and the other sky blue. The tops hugged their supple curves, accenting their achingly perfect breasts. The form fitting jeans did the same for the lower half of their bodies.

They were each pulling small, wheeled carry-on bags and had large, identical backpacks slung across their shoulders. These had the benefit of making their breasts jut out a bit further than normal. There wasn't a male head within eyesight that wasn't following their progress through the airport.

Without a word to the counter attendant, Raston grabbed the handle of his gear and rushed off to catch up to the Twins. He walked out of the door and was assaulted by the hot humid air that was a late August afternoon, New Orleans style. He could tell by the faces of the crowd, both male and female, that the Twins had turned left. He did the same. They were in the cab line when Raston caught up to them.

"Helllloooo ladies," said Bobby with a huge smile on his face. They simultaneously turned to face him, with a resigned look on their face. They had already been hit on twice since leaving the plane, although those pilots had been kind of cute, as opposed to the short rotund guy who was currently leering at them.

Bobby stuck out his hand; desperately trying to keep his eyes on their faces, he said, "I'm Bobby Raston. I'm running audio on this shoot."

The Twins had, of course, heard of Raston. Everyone in the business had heard of Raston. But they had never worked with him before or even met him, although he looked somewhat familiar.

"Hi Bobby," said Brandy, taking his hand in a surprisingly firm grip. "I'm Brandy Fukui…" she said letting his hand go just in time for her sister to latch onto it with an even firmer grip.

"And I'm Mandy Fukui. We've heard a lot about you," she said, dropping his hand and turning her head to indicate her sister. She turned back just in time to catch Bobby staring at her breasts.

"And if even half of it is accurate…" started Mandy.

"…this will be an interesting shoot," finished Brandy with a knowing smile.

Raston didn't quite know how to take that comment, but he plunged ahead.

"Listen, there's no need to take a cab, I'm going to pick up my, huh, my Escalade. Ride with me over to the Buuggg… huh, I mean the Hertz lot. We'll pick up the car and you can ride with me to the hotel," Bobby said in a rapid-fire voice, which he hoped was both friendly and convincing. "It'll give us time to talk about the shoot. I'll explain how your cameras tie into my gear and how we keep everything in sync, even with starts and stops. I've got plenty of room. Did I mention I'm getting an Escalade?"

The girls looked at each other, looked at Bobby, and then back at each other. An almost imperceptible head gesture was all they needed.

"That's so kind of you..." said Brandy.

"...but we're already here, and it's almost our turn for the cab." continued Mandy.

"We worked all day and then barely caught this flight," said Brandy.

"We're really ready to get to the hotel," finished Mandy.

"Besides..." started Brandy.

"...it's just audio," finished Mandy.

"What's to know?" asked Brandy. If you knew Brandy, you knew the slight smile meant she was teasing him.

"Just audio?" replied a suddenly indignant Bobby. "In a reality show audio is the... huh... the..."

"I think it's a great idea!" said Dean Preston, holding out his hand to Bobby. He had been standing next to the Twins the entire time, but Bobby hadn't even noticed him. Raston took the young man's hand, gave a limp halfhearted shake and then dropped it.

"Hi, I'm Dean Preston. I'm a P Aaaa," he started, but his voice trailed off and he began again, "I mean, I'm a field producer, independent, but mostly for Neiderland. I think it's a great idea to ride along with you to the hotel. I've heard you have very interesting ways to set up reality show audio and I am dying to learn more."

Bobby looked at the tall, slim, handsome young man. He normally didn't like to be around guys like that as it only accented his short, stocky build. Everybody might love Costello, but Abbot got the girls, he would say... to himself... all too often.

"And you're on this shoot?" asked Bobby.

"Yep," replied Dean with an honest, open grin. "And damn glad to be here!"

"I'm hoping this really will be," he paused a bit to remember what he had been told by Mr. Guidry when he was offered the gig. "Epic, that's the word. I'm looking forward to an epic shoot."

"Yeah," muttered Bobby, "epic. So I heard."

Guidry had *neglected* to tell him there was going to be another guy on the shoot. "It'll be you and the Twins, working together like peas in a pod," was how Andy had put it. That's literally what had sealed the deal.

Mandy looked at Brandy. They shrugged their shoulders and said together, "OK."

Dean smiled at Bobby and said, "Then it's decided. We'll ride with you."

Bobby plastered a somewhat less than sincere smile on his face and said, "I'll just dash back to the rental counter and meet you over there, at the Hertz bus. Shouldn't take ten minutes."

The Twins just nodded, but Dean replied, in an excited tone, "GREAT! Oh, and uhhh," he paused and smiled before yelling out, "SHOTGUN!"

'Yeah," said Bobby with a smile that started and ended with his lips, "Great. I'll be back in ten."

As Raston walked back to the doors leading into the airport, Dean turned to the Twins and said excitedly, "That guy is a bona fide audio genius. I can't wait to work with him!"

"Yeah," said Mandy with a sigh, remembering the eyes that darted to her breasts the moment he thought she wasn't looking.

"Us, too," said Brandy echoing the sigh.

They looked at each other, shrugged and started off towards the rental car shuttles. Preston followed, unable to keep from joining with the crowd in staring at the perfect pair of buttocks, swaying together in symphonic unison.

Dean was thinking that *epic* might not be a strong enough word.

## CHAPTER 17
# Just The Assistant

*Thursday – August 24 – 6:51 PM CDT*

> "Jack, we were supposed to be
> playing straight with each other."
> — ANTOINE GUIDRY

"I'm sorry Mr. Guidry, but it's still being denied," said the plump, curvaceous young lady at the front desk of the Best Western Plus, French Quarter Landmark Hotel. Her mocha colored skin contrasted with the brilliant white teeth, framing a practiced smile that said she'd seen this before. She handed the debit card back to Andy, who took it with a bit of a scowl.

"I'm terribly sorry," replied Andy Guidry, sincerity dripping from his voice. "I'll call my bank immediately and see what the issue is." He looked at the brass nametag she was wearing on her uniform blazer. "Shawanda, can you please keep these rooms on hold for just a couple more hours? The funds transfer is absolutely going to happen today."

They had already tried to use Guidry's sole remaining credit card, but it had been denied as well. While waiting for the deposit to be transferred into his bank account, he'd used that credit card to buy the plane tickets for the crew. He was now substantially over his limit and Guidry knew better than to call and ask for another increase. He had already done that before he left San Diego, and he'd had to literally beg a customer service manager to get even a modest bump in the maxed-out credit line.

Shawanda smiled at him again, peered at the flat screen monitor, tapped a few keys and replied, "Well, I'm not supposed to hold any rooms unless they are secured by a valid credit or debit card. But we're not completely sold out, and since you're already a guest…"

"Thank you! Thank you so much!" interrupted Andy, "I'll get this matter taken care of immediately. I'll call you the minute I hear from my bank."

Shawanda picked up where she had left off, "Since you're already a guest I can hold the rooms, but I'm afraid your guests won't be able to actually check in until the debit card is able to clear the hold."

"Yes," replied Andy, "I understand. Thank you so much, that won't be a problem." As he turned to walk away, already pulling out his cell phone, Shawanda stopped him.

"Mr. Guidry," she said. Andy turned back to the desk.

"Yes?" he replied in a hesitant voice.

"Your room is secured with that card as well," she told him. "Since we now both know that the card won't… uh, won't *clear* any longer."

"I totally understand your concern," Andy said, leaning in over the desk, and trying desperately to turn on the charm.

"The funds will be in this bank account before the end of the day, west coast time. I'm sure of it, there's just been some minor mix-up with a money transfer. There'll be more than enough to cover my rooms, and the rooms of my guests, with as big a hold as you deem necessary."

Shawanda looked at him, head cocked slightly, eyes a bit narrowed as she contemplated his predicament. She then made a decision, "Ok, Mr. Guidry. I suppose that will work. But I get off at nine, and since this is a *special* circumstance you'll need to take care of this issue before then, at least for your room, or you'll need to make other arrangements."

"Absolutely," replied Andy, still smiling but itching to get out of the lobby and call that SOB Jack Calman. "I understand. I'm going to take care of this immediately, and it will be settled WAY before nine."

"Very good, Mr. Guidry," said Shawanda, "When you come back to take care of this, please ask for me. I'll need to handle this personally."

"I certainly will," replied Andy. "You've been more than kind. And I will mention it to your manager."

Shawanda's eyebrows perked up a bit as she quickly said, "No, please don't do that. I'm overstepping my authority a bit and this arrangement needs to be between you and me, and you and me only."

"Again, you are too kind," replied Andy, realizing that Shawanda was definitely going out on a limb for him. "And I understand completely. I'll see you by nine, or sooner."

"That would be good," she replied, looking over his shoulder at the young couple that had walked up behind Andy. Dismissing him with another huge, brilliant white smile, she then addressed the couple, "And how can I help you?"

Guidry had his cell phone out and was calling Calman before he even left the lobby. As he walked into the courtyard, the call immediately went to voice mail... again.

"Fuck," exclaimed Guidry, a bit too loud as he ended the call. A young couple, sitting at a table, gave him a dirty look. The pre-teen kids, splashing in the pool, were obviously theirs.

"Sorry," mouthed Guidry to the couple, and then immediately walked out of the courtyard and into the attached parking garage.

Guidry took a huge breath and stood at the edge of the parking lot.

He knew he needed to calm down. He closed his eyes, took nine more deep breaths, and began to argue with the little voice in his head that insisted it was a good time for a quick vape or two. After a couple more mental nudgings, the little voice won.

Guidry took the slim, vaping pen from his pocket and inhaled deeply. He blew out the thin stream of vapor. Even though he couldn't feel it yet, the mere act of vaping calmed him, so he did it again. As the cannabinoids began to take the edge off his jagged nerves, he redialed Calman's number. As expected, the phone immediately went to voice mail.

"Hi, this is Jack," said the recorded voice. "If you only want me to call you back, just hang up and I will. Otherwise, leave a message."

"Hi Jack, Andy again." said Andy, hoping his voice didn't betray his concern or the cannabis, "Sorry to keep bugging you, but that transfer we agreed would happen today still hasn't made it to my bank. I really need to know what's going on with this."

Andy paused for a second, took another deep breath, lowered his voice and continued, "Jack, we were supposed to be playing straight with each other. Let's not quit now. Call me back."

Guidry hung up and noticed the time. Raston had already landed. So had the Twins, along with that PA Calman had insisted he also hire.

"Why do I need a PA, and at that rate?" he had complained to Jack during their earlier negotiations.

"He's a field producer, not a PA," Jack had said, "at least he's not a PA anymore. I'd feel much better about the production, and our investment, if there was at least one more person on the crew. I've been doing this a long time and I know how screwed up things can get if you don't have enough people. And besides, do you know what you call a producer without a PA?"

"A PA," replied Andy. It was not only an old joke, but it was one he had told Jack when they first started working together, mainly to get him to supply him with a PA on those early, shoestring budget Neiderland shoots. The necessity of a PA was a bit less apparent when it was Andy paying the day rate.

Doing some mental calculations on the landing times, and the distance from the airport, he thought to himself. "They should be almost here."

Suddenly a thought came to Guidry, "Damn, I should have told them to meet up and ride in together in Raston's rental car," he thought. He began wondering how much the cab ride from the airport was going to eat into his severely dwindling cash on hand.

"Damn, damn, damn! I can't think of everything," Guidry muttered out loud. "Maybe I do need a production assistant, or a field producer, or whatever the hell he is."

The term assistant suddenly triggered an idea. Guidry scrolled through the contacts app on his phone, found the number he was looking for and tapped it. He was happy to hear the phone ring a few times instead of going directly into voice mail mode.

"This is Nina," said the voice on the phone.

"Hi Nina," said Andy, trying hard not to be too exuberant, or depressed. "This is Andy, huh, Antoine Guidry. I've been trying to call Jack for the last few hours, but I keep getting sent to voice mail so I thought maybe his phone was dead. Is he in?"

"Hello Mr. Guidry," replied Nina. She liked formalities. "Mr. Calman is not available at this time. And I'm sorry, but I wouldn't know if there are any issues with his phone."

Andy stood up a little straighter and tried to keep the alarm out of his voice. "Nina, is there anything wrong, I mean wrong with this deal?" Andy knew that Nina was privy to the smallest detail on any and all deals that Calman was in charge of.

"Not that I'm aware of," Nina replied. "But I am, after all, just his assistant."

"Yeah, right" said Andy. "Anyway, Jack was supposed to get a wire transfer into my account before the end of business today, and that deadline is getting pretty close on the west coast. I was actually expecting it to be in my account by early this afternoon. I've been checking all day and it's not there. That's why I've been trying to call Jack, and that's why I'm calling you. Do you know anything about the deposit?"

"Yes, I do," she replied. "I personally filled out the request for accounting. Although why it hasn't happened yet, I don't exactly know. As Mr. Calman was leaving, he did say that if you called, I was to tell you that he would call you tomorrow morning."

"WHAT!" screamed Andy. "As he was LEAVING! He knew this wasn't going to happen and he didn't call me! This is UNACCPETABLE! WE HAVE A DEAL!"

"I don't know what to tell you Mr. Guidry," replied Nina. Her tone clearly indicated that she wasn't used to being screamed at, and would not put up with it again. "Again, Mr. Calman told me, to tell you, that he will call you tomorrow. That is all I can tell you about this matter. Is there anything else I can do for you?"

"No," said Andy, struggling to keep his voice under control. "No, I guess not."

"Very good," replied Nina, "Goodbye. Oh, and Mr. Guidry do you have the main phone number for our office."

"Huh, yes I do," said Andy.

"Good," said Nina, "then please don't call me on my mobile unless it is absolutely necessary. It doesn't look proper for me to be on a cell call during business hours."

"All right, sure," said Andy in barely more than a mumble, "won't happen again." The depression setting in was now very apparent in his voice.

"Excellent," replied Nina. "Mr. Guidry…"

"Yeah?" murmured Andy in what was almost a whisper.

"I'm sure this will all work out," Nina said. "Mr. Calman is a good man. If he told you he'd wire the money, and it didn't get done, there's likely a very good reason. I'm sure it will all be cleared up very soon. I'll personally remind him to call you the very moment he steps into the office."

"OK," said Andy, trying to wrap his head around the news. "Thanks."

"Have a good day Mr. Guidry," said Nina as she hung up. She looked through the big picture window that framed Calman's empty office. She shrugged and went back to work. She was after all, as she had told the man, *just the assistant.*

After Guidry hung up he tried calling Jack one last time. He got the voice mail and immediately hung up just as a new Escalade drove up into the parking area. Guidry immediately recognized Raston as the driver but wondered who was in the passenger seat. He shrugged, put a big grin on his face and walked out to greet them.

## CHAPTER 18
# Praise Jesus

*Thursday – August 24 – 6:57 PM CDT*

> "I'll have 'em all ready to pick up by tomorrow morning, no rush charge, if you tell me what this *Hitler Car* thing is all about."
> — Mason LaCroix

"We'll have four of the 'Hitler Cars For Hitler Lovers!' four of the 'Hate Hitler — Hate His Car!!' and six of the 'No Bids for Hitler Hate!!!'" said Saul Wittmann to the counter clerk.

The young man had a vanilla cream complexion, with burnt orange freckles splattered across his high cheekbones and wide flat nose. They were in the FedEx Office store directly across the street from the Ernest Morial Convention Center. The convention center itself was directly in front of, although catty-cornered and across the railroad tracks, from Mardi Gras World.

Less than two hours ago Saul and Herman had arrived in New Orleans and rented the Chevy Impala. They tossed their luggage in the trunk, drove through downtown New Orleans, past the convention center, and finally stopped directly in front of the Mardi Gras World building at 1380 Port Of New Orleans Place. Herman wished he had insisted on that bathroom break he'd suggested before they left the rental car lot.

The huge Mardi Gras World building blocked the view, but not the smell, of the wide, brown Mississippi River, nearing the end of its twenty-three hundred mile journey. The site had no doubt been the location for countless warehouses, docks, and assorted shipyard buildings over the last few hundred years. Now, however, a large non-descript warehouse, typical of port cities in southern climates, occupied the location.

The front of the building was corrugated sheeting that went thirty feet straight up. The only architectural break in the vast slab of white was a six-foot tall band of olive brown that covered the facade that was added to hide the air conditioning equipment. The only ornamentation on the building was a huge *Mardi Gras World* in ten-foot tall block letters. On the other side of a twenty-foot tall receiving door were the words *Blaine Kern Studios* in identical lettering.

Past the end of the long warehouse was the River City Complex, the building where A-Bear auto auctions actually took place. It was a large white building with a peaked roof that sloped down towards the front of the long building. The main entrance jutted out from the building at least twenty feet high and was itself sporting a peaked roofline that sloped down to either side. There was even a small cupola that dotted the roof just behind the main entrance.

The gate leading to the River City Complex was open, albeit with a guard sitting on a stool beside it. The large man, at least three hundred and fifty pounds, had skin so black it seemed to suck in the waning rays of the New Orleans sunlight. It made it hard to actually see his facial features.

Once Herman had told him they would be attending the auction, and were just finding their way around, the big man broke into a smile and said he'd be happy to help them.

"Dat dere's the entrance to the Bayou Room. The one under de cupola." he had explained, pointing in the general direction of the River City Complex. "Dat's where dey's have de parties so the folks can thinks dey's at a planation." He stopped, smiled and continued with, "course it's all air conditioned and dey ain't gots no bugs."

"Is that where the auction is held?" Herman had asked the man.

"No, sir" the man said. "De auctions is in de same building, but in da big hall right next to it, on de utter side from us."

The big man stopped, pulled a sky-blue bandana from the right front pocket of his dark blue Dickey pants. He took off his cap, wiped his face and continued, "It's a sight when da cars show up. Dey's all drive down Race Street, dat's this street here, and cross de tracks into the backside of de complex. Dey gets checked in at the entrance and then deys drive to da utter side, facing da river."

The guard stopped talking, wiped his face one more time, put his cap back on and stuffed the bandana back into his pocket. "Dat's like de best damn car show you ever seen, right on de river. Feel like youse almost under da bridge."

Nice as he had been, he wouldn't let them actually drive down to the building, citing that they were preparing for the auction and no visitors were allowed. "Dat's why I's here today. Dey only needs guards when da auction's goin' on. There'll be a lot mo guards around tomorrow and da day after dat." He paused and leaned in, "When all de cars is here, dats a lotta money just sittin' round. So where ya'lls from?"

After a couple more minutes of polite banter, and a couple of recommendations on *foods youse just gots to try while youse here*, the guard was able to direct them to the FedEx Office store, which seemed to be the first step in Wittmann's master plan, and where they were now.

"So when can I pick up the signs?" Saul asked the young man at the counter after he had completed his order. His engraved plastic tag indicated his name was Mason.

"Normal time would be tomorrow before noon," Mason LaCroix told Saul. "We're kinda slow right now. So if you want to pay rush charges, they can prob'ly be ready 'fore we close. That's at nine tonight. I'd say anytime after eight thirty or so."

"So if I end up needing more signs, can they be done in two or three hours?" Saul asked him.

"Yas sir, if you want to pay the rush charges," Mason replied, "but it ain't cheap."

Saul cocked his head for just under two seconds and replied, "I'll pay the rush charge on this set of fourteen, but we won't be back today. We'll just pick these up tomorrow morning on our way to the auction. What time do you open?"

Mason nodded and said, "Seven thirty, on the dot. I won't be here, but yer order will."

"Ok, that's fine," replied Saul. "And make another set... no, make that two more sets of fourteen signs to be ready by noon. And they'll all have handles, right?"

"Oh, yeah," replied Mason. "We've got plenty of handles."

"So what's the damage?" asked Saul as he pulled out his wallet.

"Let's see," said Mason, peering at the computer screen, "Dat's fourteen signs times... what is it, three sets, with one set on rush," Mason stopped and looked around the nearly empty store. "Tell you what. I'll have 'em all ready to pick up by tomorrow morning, no rush charge, if you tell me what this *Hitler Car* thing is all about."

Saul smiled for a second, and then lowered his eyebrows, wiped the smile from his lips, and began speaking. The tirade started off in a low, serious tone but slowly rose to a fervent pitch.

He started off with rhetoric about Hitler as the most evil, demonic, insane, racist son-of-a-bitch that ever walked the earth. He segued into the *supposed* Hitler car that was going to be auctioned off on Saturday. He eloquently, yet plainly stated that the entire concept of this car being somehow more valuable because of a *connection to Hitler* was an affront to decent, God-fearing people. He closed with the firm conviction that anyone who would even bid on the demon limousine are themselves evil and racist and should be both chastised and hated by God and every, single one of his righteous servants.

Wittmann paused in his tirade, then leaned forward and looked directly into Mason's eyes. He then spoke in a low, commanding voice, "I'm going to give these signs to God-fearing people so that the righteous can show their indignation at the crass monetization of this abomination of an automobile!"

"Wow," murmured the mesmerized Mason.

Herman was also a bit dazed, and truly amazed at how convincing Wittmann was. Especially considering he was spouting the exact polar opposite of the types of rants and raves he had been hearing for the last couple of years.

"Sir," Mason replied, "What can I, and the youth group at my church, do to help you in this?"

Saul smiled at Mason and then stole a glance at Herman. Saul's smile got even wider when he saw the incredulous look on Herman's face. He turned back to Mason and said, "Bless you son! You obviously know Jesus as your personal savior. You decide how many people you think will rally to this righteous cause, add that many signs to the order, and then just tack it onto my bill."

Mason smiled back at Saul and said, "Sir, dat's gonna be a LOT of signs!"

Saul looked at Herman and nodded his head towards him in a *that's how it's done* gesture. He then turned to Mason and replied, "That's exactly what I was hoping to hear. I could tell you were a man of the faith when I walked in the door. Jesus always brings us together when he has need of our services."

Saul then handed him a credit card and continued, "Now let's get this bill tallied up and get moving on those signs."

Mason had just started to punch numbers into his keyboard when he stopped and looked down at the credit card. He studied it briefly, then looked up and said, "Brother Saul, I think we's gonna to need some flyers to pass out. To explain this to the other people, jest like you explained it to me."

Saul nodded his head and turned to Herman, "Did you hear that? *WE* are going to need some flyers. You're the college boy. Sit down at that computer and start typing. We don't have much time and we've got a lot of things to do."

"But you isn't gonna do it alone," said Mason, his voice rising in excitement. "Because help is on the way! Praise Jesus, help is on the way!"

# CHAPTER 19
# Double Ewweeuu

*Thursday – August 24 – 7:07 PM CDT*

> "Drinking on the streets is practically
> a lifestyle in New Orleans."
> — Antoine Guidry

Andy, Bobby, Brandy, Mandy, and Dean were walking through the French Quarter, taking in the sights, with Andy acting as their tour guide.

He had been pleasantly surprised to see his entire crew in the huge Escalade. With the issues at the front desk, having them all arrive at the same time was a good thing. A really good thing, as it was much easier to stall them all at the same time.

After introductions were made in the parking garage, he told them their rooms weren't quite ready, "New-Ahhh-Lens moves at a mo leisurely pace den utter big cities," Andy had said in the thick Cajun accent from his boyhood, much to the delight of Dean and the Twins.

"Just park the car and we'll walk down to the Quarter for a couple of drinks and some food," he had told them with a smile, reverting back to his normal speech pattern. "Then I can fill you all in on the show concept."

Guidry told them they would start out their tour at Lafitte's Blacksmith Shop Bar, the oldest continually operating bar in America. It was only a three-block walk from the hotel and, at Bourbon and St. Philip, it was pretty much dead center of the French Quarter.

The Twins were snapping photos and shooting video at the old houses that lined the street, some were still shuttered up and all were painted in various shades of faded pastel. The varying colors seemed to be the only thing that separated one house from the other, as they stood butted up next to each other.

Guidry had led the way, explaining that the houses were very European in their construction, with many of them having elaborate courtyards that belied their plain exterior. "You can buy a mansion in the Garden district for what one of these would set you back," Andy told them. "The reason most of them are closed up is that many of these are city homes for the wealthy, and not occupied for months at a time."

The Twins just looked at each other, nodded their heads, shrugged and continued shooting.

At Lafitte's, they each had a Voodoo daiquiri from one of the four daiquiri machines that, along with the digital jukebox, stood out in stark contrast compared to the ancient bar, bar back, walls and the two inch thick wood plank tables. Raston had tried to defer from the icy cold, intensely sweet slushy concoction, but Guidry wouldn't hear of it.

"Frozen daiquiris are as much a part of the New Orleans experience as crawfish, boudin, and oysters on the half shell," Andy had said as he brought the big Styrofoam cups to the table. He now had less than three hundred dollars in his pocket, but figured that was plenty enough to get them into the right mood to explain the situation.

His plan was to get them excited about being in New Orleans, enthusiastic about the CarAlity concept, and then understanding about his current lack of funds... in that order.

When a young tourist type played a Jay-Z song on the jukebox, Andy stood up and announced, "Time to go! Next stop, Royal Street Oyster House."

"But what about our drinks?" asked Dean. "We just got them."

"Bring 'em with you," replied Andy, taking a long draw on the straw. "Drinking on the streets is practically a lifestyle in New Orleans."

Bobby was walking next to Andy, listening to his stories of the various world-class restaurants that dotted the French Quarter, most located just off Bourbon on the many side streets. Andy told them about Bananas Foster during brunch at Brennans, Muffulettas for a late lunch at Central Grocery, dinners at K-Paul's and NOLA, and Oysters Rockefeller virtually anywhere there was a menu and a table.

"If you can't find a meal to love here," said Andy, "then you just don't love food."

"So where are we heading?" asked Bobby, the nearly empty Voodoo daiquiri cup clutched in his hand. His mood had improved substantially.

"We're going to the Royal Street Oyster House," replied Andy. "I had dinner there with Pat McMillian, the head of auto auctions for A-Bear, just yesterday. That's where I made the deal that will give us complete access before and during the auction, and exclusive access during the Hitler Car bidding."

"So what's this about a automotive reality show?" asked Dean. "Mr. Calman said it was unlike any other show in the reality genre. How is it different? What's the production workflow?"

Dean had been dividing his time between listening to Andy and keeping an eye on the Twins, who were basically a *two gal parade*, drawing appreciative looks and low murmurs from tourists and locals alike. If the Twins even noticed the attention, they didn't care. Men staring at them was a normal part of life. Their cameras never left their hands as their nearly full Voodoo Daiquiris had been summarily deposited in the first trashcan they had passed.

Guidry stopped outside the Maison Bourbon Jazz Club, whose sign proudly stated it was "Dedicated to the Preservation of Jazz," and waited for the Twins to catch up. Inside the club, a couple of guys were moving mic stands and rearranging stools while another was replacing a head on one of the toms.

"This show is more an entirely new concept than just another a show within the reality genre," replied Andy with a much bigger smile than he actually felt. As he continued the Twins caught up to them. Andy noticed the raw hunger in Bobby's eyes as he looked at them and knew it had nothing to do with food. He congratulated himself on his earlier negotiation tactics without missing a beat in his narration.

"It's a concept I've been working on for…" Andy paused for dramatic effect, "gosh, it sure seems like a long time." He smiled and thought ruefully that it had must have been almost twelve hours by now. Andy continued, "The elevator pitch is *Candid Camera* in a high stakes auto auction."

"But who are the featured players?" asked Dean, "Who will drive the show?"

"I'll explain more when we're off the street," replied Andy as he watched a slim young lady dressed in a black tux, and sporting a very convincing handlebar mustache, parade down the middle of Bourbon. She was leading her very muscular, very bearded "bride," who was in a billowy white wedding dress. She was leading him via a gold plated, heavy chain dog leash clipped to a two inch wide, spiked leather collar fastened around his neck.

Guidry smiled as he saw the incredulous look that passed between Dean and Bobby, as well as the simultaneous look of delight that splashed across the Twin's faces as they brought their cameras up and the shutters started clicking.

"Now that's something you don't see everyday," said Bobby, watching the bridal show as it continued down the middle of the street.

Andy laughed and replied, "That depends on where you are! The French Quarter was the bastion of debauchery nearly two hundred years before Las Vegas was even a dot on a map."

Dean turned to Andy, smiled and said, "Wow, if these streets could talk…"

Mandy looked up at the sign on the club and turned to Andy, "So why the 'Preservation of Jazz?'" she asked.

"I thought New Orleans was all about jazz," said Brandy.

"Wasn't it like, *born* here?" asked Mandy.

Andy nodded his head and did a somewhat theatrical sigh, "Ah yes, New Orleans… the birthplace of jazz. Unfortunately, or fortunately for the local economy, this is one of the few places in the Quarter, and certainly on Bourbon, that you can sit down and listen to actual, old school jazz."

Andy started walking, but slowly as he continued playing tour guide. As the street and sidewalks were getting more crowded, the rest of the group stayed closer to Andy.

They were heading into the middle of the nightclub cluster, whose open windows, and opening acts, were filling the street with rock, rap, and a smattering of late 70's disco. Even this early, the bars were moderately full of customers, drinks in hand and smiles on their faces.

"Bourbon Street is a massive adult playground, and these bars give the customers what they want, which isn't *old school* jazz," said Andy. "I do know of a couple of really good, old fashioned blues bars that will occasionally do a nice rendition of the old jazz standards. You haven't heard real music until you hear a seventy-year-old black guy on a slide guitar with a harmonica back, belting out *When the Saints Go Marching In*."

"Wow," said Dean, "that sounds amazing!"

"Maybe we'll go there after we discuss the show, and down a few dozen!" said Andy, still keeping his jovial face on. He was beginning to worry about just how he was going to sell his crew on the concept and explain his current lack of funding. He was trying hard to convince himself that Jack would come through with the deposit, although his talk with Nina had made that increasingly hard to believe. He checked his watch, seeing that it was still relatively early on the west coast. He decided he'd try

Calman's mobile one more time before he got to that part of the discussion.

"What about the hotel?" asked Bobby. "Don't we need to check in? I'd imagine hotel rooms are going to be in short supply with the auction and all."

Andy smiled and replied, "The folks that had planned to be here for the auction, have already made their reservations. The people who are flying in to bid on the Hitler Car, and able to post the five million dollar bond, aren't likely to be staying at the Best Western!" Andy plastered on a huge smile and continued, "Besides, the rooms are on hold. We'll be fine. Let's get some cold brews, a few dozen oysters on the half-shell, and celebrate. This will be the game changer in reality programming, and we're *da players* who's gonna do it!'"

Dean looked at Bobby with a friendly, conspiratorial look and echoed, "Game changer?"

Bobby shrugged and replied, "That's what the man said."

Mandy looked at Brandy with a somewhat concerned look on her face, "Oysters… on the half-shell?"

Brandy also shrugged and replied, "That's what the man said."

The Twins looked at each other, wrinkled their noses and said "Ewweeuu."

Andy smiled, a very real, very big one this time, and said, "You're gonna love it, I promise. And if you don't want oysters, you can always have some 'gator!"

"Double Ewweeuu!" exclaimed the Twins and they all laughed as they continued down the street.

"To the Royal Street Oyster House," said Andy with a theatrical flourish, pointing his finger in that general direction.

As Andy turned to lead the group through the thickening crowd, and the increasing waves of music that were flooding the street, his smile faded, but just a bit.

He was hoping that if anyone could pull this off, that it would be him. He didn't have a lot of options.

# CHAPTER 20
# 8:27:14

*Thursday – August 24 – 7:12 PM CDT*

> "You will then eject the disk
> and hand it back to me."
> — HEINRICH HEINZBURG

Brian *Cool-B* Simmons and Malcolm Walker had finished hooking up the last of the camera feeds a couple of hours ago. Brian, the show producer on this gig, had worked on literally hundreds of shows in his seventeen years with United A/V. United was one of, if not the, largest audio-visual production companies in the United States.

From rather humble beginnings in the mid-eighties, corporate AV had become a multi-billion dollar business. In the early days, the majority of jobs tended to be audio support with a single camera IMAG set-up, which was short for image magnification. The single camera feed the presenter's image onto large screens flanking the stage and was considered state-of-the-art back in the day. A lot had changed from those days.

Before the dot-com bubble had popped, it wasn't unusual for larger clients to demand huge multi-camera extravaganzas. These productions were orchestrated by top-dollar talent in mobile control rooms hauled about by semi-trucks; control rooms stuffed with enough technology to broadcast a prime-time football game.

During this heyday of video excess, Simmons had seen, and worked, them all.

The real big spenders, the companies that had really pushed the envelope in the corporate AV world, had been the multi-level marketing groups, followed closely by the large tech companies. Brian had worked on gigs that filled huge auditoriums to capacity, and entire sports stadiums to the brim.

Simmons took his job seriously. It was basically live TV, where he had first started his career, but for a smaller audience, and one that was in very close proximity. And it was one that paid far more than any local TV position would ever match. Simmons was a perfectionist and proud that his shows were flawless… at least from a technical point of view.

The closest he had ever come to blowing a gig was when he had lost his voice during a particularly brutal gig at the old RCA Dome in Indianapolis. It had been in the late nineties, on a job for a MLM company that sold miraculous magnetic healing devices, as well as the promise of untold riches if you could only develop a deep enough downline. A common theme in that genre of business endeavors.

Not being able to speak above a low croaking whisper had made calling the cameras, and the dozens of video roll-ins, a painful challenge, but he had pulled it off. To this day he blamed the dome for the speech loss, with its pressurized interior holding up a couple of hundred tons of fiberglass roof. It certainly wasn't his penchant for working back-to-back twenty-hour days and celebrating each day's brief respite by drinking copious amounts of Knob Creek whisky, two ounces at a time, with exactly three fresh ice cubes per drink.

Brian had cemented his rep, and earned his nickname, at a 2002 show in Seattle. The CEO of yet another MLM opportunity was in the midst of the usual over-the-top presentation.

Deep into his pitch on the "incontrovertible evidence of the longevity enhancing qualities of fossilized plants, concentrated and fused on a molecular level into our proprietary blend of nutraceuticals..." he had simply stopped mid-sentence. He slowly lowered his arm, which had been pointed ramrod straight at the audience, until it hung loosely at his side.

Simmons was calling the show less than fifty yards away, behind the stage in the Video Village.

He knew something was up and rapidly called out, *"Ready on 3, take it."*

The video on the sixty-foot screens flanking the stage, as well as the dozens of smaller ones throughout the convention floor, switched to camera three, tightly framed on the bottle of the companies flagship product, just in time to see it start to slip from his grasp.

*"Ready 2..."* Brian instructed the TD and in the same breath, *"take 2."*

The scene on the gigantic screen changed to a full body shot as the bottle left the man's fingers and hit the stage with a thud and a small bounce.

*"ECU on his face camera 4..."* Brian called for a close-up on the side camera almost before the man had started turning towards it. *"Hurry 4,"* said Brian into the Telex headset mic, *"READY-4-TAKE-4"* was almost one word as the man's suddenly ashen face filled the screens. He looked down at the plastic bottle rolling away from him. He looked back up at the audience, gave a little smile, and opened his mouth as if to speak.

*"Going back to 2... a little wider 2..."* said Brian. *"Hold it, hold it."*

As the presenter started to waver Brian called out, *"Take 2."*

The screens changed back to the wide shot as thousands of people stared at them, transfixed as the presenter, impeccably clad in his Armani suit, with sky blue shirt and contrasting white collar, keeled over like a toppled tree. He was dead before he hit the floor. An ear-shattering thump accented the fall as his *Madonna mic* hit the floor a millisecond before his head. The reverb from the sound washed over the stunned audience.

*"Ready logo,"* Brian now in a much softer tone, *"I said ready logo,"* he repeated as he stood up and reached over to tap the Still Store operator on the shoulder. The operator hurriedly switched from the bottle graphic, with bullet points, to the company's logo, mainly used for pre-show audience walk-ins and walk-outs.

*"Take logo,"* said Brian. Having just now noticed he was standing, he slowly sat back down in his chair and rested his arms on the small directors table in the center of the darkened control area.

His crew was momentarily stunned and silently stared at the dozens of different sized screens that added to the low, back stage illumination. The entire convention floor also sat in silence. It lasted for just under three seconds before bedlam erupted.

A much younger Malcolm Walker, a slim young black man in his mid-twenties, had been the guy at the Still Store. As his favorite music video at the time was *Fantastic Voyage*, Walker had inadvertently christened him with the nickname that had stuck ever since. It was a conversation starter then and required even more explanation now, given that Simmons was a redneck-looking white guy, obviously past sixty, all of five foot eight and certainly every bit of two hundred and fifty pounds.

On that day Malcolm had turned from the Still Store and simply said, "That was pure Coolio Mr. B. You are a total ice cube, an absolute Cool-B!"

Brian had looked up at him, without the faintest idea of who, or what a Coolio was, and nodded his head.

"Thanks," he replied in a voice that was uncharacteristically low. "I think."

As backstage erupted with people running around and shouting for paramedics, the rear doors flew open causing light to flood into the backstage area. The operators remained at their stations. The hipper among them nodded their heads, murmuring phrases, like "I'm just chillin'; like Cool-B."

Walker had latched onto Simmons as a mentor, and Simmons had appreciated someone with a work ethic that almost matched his own. The young black man, *straight outta Compton,* and the middle-aged white guy from 'Bama had become a sought after team; working all the big gigs for United A/V.

However, during the last twenty years or so, the massive increase in computer power had been slowly transforming high-end corporate AV production. Long gone were the days of setting up literally tons of broadcast switchers, tape decks, routers, still stores and chyrons, as well as staffing it with a ten-man Video Village crew.

For a seven-camera show like *A-Bear's - Muscles On The Mississippi*, once the lighting was done, and the cables were run, the entire operation pared down a mere five people, including camera operators.

Front of house and on the floor were two RF-equipped roving cam operators and the jib op. Hanging from the rigging, were three Sony BRC-H900 robotic cams, two on the sides and one in the middle. All three were remotely controlled by Malcolm from the Video Village.

The small, ultra high-definition cameras, with incredibly sharp and powerful zoom lenses, were mounted on gimbal heads with motorized bases. Each camera was controlled through a single RM-IP10 remote controller, and up to sixteen synchronized camera moves could be pre-programmed into the device. The robotic cameras were far smoother, and a lot faster, at panning, tilting and zooming than any camera operated by a mere human.

For this show, and others of its size, Walker also ran audio, also thanks to the digital revolution. On this show he was running a Mackie DL1608; a digital mixer with an iPad control surface.

By simply removing the iPad he could walk all around the room, remotely controlling the mixer, so he could easily set levels and pre-program the mixes for the various audio requirements of the show. From the iPad, he could precisely shape the sound through the built in reverbs, compressors, gates, delays, and a thirty-one band EQ. He could then *snap shot* each setup for instant recall during the actual event.

Regardless of the incredible advances in presentation technology that Simmons had witnessed during his thirty plus years in the business, one thing always remained a source of deep personal pride. It was something that no mere machine or app could ensure. It was that there would be no screw-ups, no delays, and no technical issues on one of his shows.

Simmons made a point of being highly organized. Every show, no matter how small, had a ring binder devoted to it. He called it the *bible* and it basically never left his side. In it were call sheets, schedules, the locations of things like power panels and exits, and the all-important *rundown*. The rundown was the who, what, where, and when; a minute-by-minute outline of was supposed to happen on stage.

Simmons didn't like surprises. Last minute changes were inevitable, and being able to roll with them was part of the job, so anything that could be pre-planned, pre-programmed, buttoned down, and secured most certainly was. At least it was on one of his shows.

That's why when Pat McMillian finally walked into Video Village with a tall young man dressed in all black, European cut clothing, carrying a Blu-ray disk case in his hand, Cool-B's eyes brightened as he stood up and smiled.

"Hello, Mr. McMillian," said Brian. "Is that the..." he paused, picked up the bible and flipped the page. Adjusting his head angle to accommodate his progressive bi-focals he looked at page twenty-seven of the rundown, looked up and said, "the day two, LMC Provenance roll-in?"

"You got it, Cool-B," replied Pat. This was the fifth show Pat had done with Brian and he liked using the nickname he had overheard the crew call him.

"There are actually two videos to be played. Chapter One is an introduction and Chapter Two is the provenance," explained Pat. "Before the car rolls onto the block, we want to cut the house lights and run the intro. Then as the intro ends, a spotlight will appear and hit the car. Once the applause dies down, house lights come up and we introduce the owner. The owner will give a short talk. We'll begin preliminary bidding until the interest starts to die, then we'll run Chapter Two on his cue."

Simmons looked at Walker, gave him a single nod and handed him the bible already open to the proper page. Walker nodded back, indicating he understood the directions, and started scribbling in the show notes.

Pat continued, "This is Mr. Heinzburg, the owner of the *featured* car."

"You mean the, huh," said Brian.

"The 1940 Mercedes Tourenwagen," Malcolm chimed in, reading it from the bible.

"Right," said Brian. "Pleased to meet you. I've been waiting for the disk," he said holding out his hand to Heinzburg.

Heinzburg ignored the outstretched hand and instead clicked his heels together with a short, crisp single nod of his head. He was beginning to like this new affectation. "Zee pleasure is mine, sir." Heinrich said as Brian pulled back his unshaken hand, just a bit perturbed.

"Please be aware that this disk is the only one in existence," said Heinzburg, "and it is vital that it be played at the precise time, and in the precise order, during the auction process."

"Yes sir," replied Brian, "that's my job. We'll take good care of it and make sure the videos play perfectly, exactly on cue. Now if I could have the disk?"

"As I said, this is the only disk in existence," said Heinrich, still making no sign of handing it over. "The information on it is embargoed until it is played at the auction. I am only here to make sure the disk will play properly. We shall play as much of Chapter One as your technicians require to check for proper color and audio. Then we shall play the first twenty-two seconds of Chapter Two, no more than that. You will then eject the disk and hand it back to me."

Heinzburg paused, looked at Brian to be sure he was listening, looked over at Malcolm to see he was still taking notes, and then continued with his instructions. "I will deliver the disk to you exactly five minutes before the automobile is auctioned. You will need to be ready to play Chapter One as soon as you cut the lights. I will call for Chapter Two by introducing it to the audience as Das Provenance." Heinzburg stopped, smiled a bit and asked, "Are we clear on these procedures?"

"I'm clear on the run-down," replied Brian, "but that's not how we normally do things with source material. We like to have everything we need, in hand and ready to go, for the entire show. It's just our SOP, our standard operating procedure."

Brian gave Heinrich a reassuring *been there, done that* smile because he had. Back in the bad old days of tape to tape editing, it wasn't unusual for a *happy face* video to be delivered to the Video Village mere minutes, if not seconds, before it was due to be played. Brian had never liked that. "We always take great care of client materials," he said. "Besides, nowadays we don't even really need…"

"In this case," interrupted Heinrich, "that will not be possible." He mirrored the smile on Brian's face, minus the sincerity. "I will retain possession of this disk. You will not see it again until I deliver it precisely five minutes before the..." as impossible as it might seem, Heinrich seemed to stand just a little bit straighter and more rigid as he continued, "the bidding begins on the 1940 Mercedes 770k W150 Grosser Tourenwagen. You must incorporate this into your *S, O, P*."

Simmons nodded a bit as he looked at Heinzburg. He then glanced over at Walker, who was quietly observing from a seat in front of the equipment rack. Simmons nodded his head and shrugged. He then turned back to Heinzburg.

"Ok," said Brian slowly, "that's not a problem." Brian's Alabama drawl started to get far more pronounced than normal. "Utter den dat, we'll jest due what we due. May I have dat disk now, Hair Heinzburg?"

Without a word Heinrich handed over the album case to Brian who turned, handed it to Malcolm and said, his accent back to being vestigial, "You heard what the man said. SOP with his instructions." Malcolm nodded and inserted the disk into a rack-mounted device, waited for it to load, tapped a few keys on the keyboard, looked at the screen and said *"Roll-in Ready on 4."*

*"Roll Chapter 1, take 4,"* instructed Brian. Most of the video monitors displayed an opening shot of an impossibly beautiful mountain scene, including the forty-inch source and program monitors. Heinzburg's voice came from the audio monitors as the video began dissolving between various beauty shots.

"Austria. Perhaps the most beautiful location in the world. Home to majestic mountains, gorgeous glens, raging rivers, lipid lakes and… foreboding forests, Austria is an Aryan paradise. Austria is also the home of two rather notable residences of Herr Adolph Hitler. Perhaps the most famous is this, the Kehisteinhaus, also known as 'The Eagles Nest.' Many are under the impression that this was De Führer primary residence. It certainly seemed …"

"I believe that's enough," said Heinrich. "Your equipment seems to be compatible."

*"Cut Chapter One,"* said Brian. *"Ready Chapter Two."*

Malcolm complied with a couple of taps on the control panel and replied, *"Chapter Two ready."*

*"Roll Chapter Two to the first,"* he paused and turned to Heinrich with a smile, asking the question, although he certainly remembered the instructions, "the first twenty-two seconds?"

Heinzburg nodded his head and replied, "Yes, that is correct."

"Got it," said Brian who turned back to Malcolm, *"Roll Chapter Two to twenty-two seconds in."*

Brian paused and said to Malcolm in a low voice, "Remember, SOP on the source."

"Roger that, Cool-B," replied Malcolm. His voice was barely above a mumble while he still looking at his control panel. "SOP all the way and in progress." He then called out, *"Rolling Chapter Two to twenty-two seconds in."*

The video began to play what looked to be an old black and white film clip, obviously unedited as evidenced by the light leak artifacts in the beginning.

"No audio," stated Malcolm, looking over at the meters on the Mackie.

"Correct," confirmed Heinrich. "There is no audio at this point. There is audio in the second half of the video. Get ready to pause the disk, naaa"

The motion on the screen stopped before Heinzburg could finish the word.

"That's twenty-two seconds," announced Malcolm, "to the frame." Malcolm looked up and asked, "Can we play a portion with the audio so I can set a level?"

"That will not be necessary, nor allowed," replied Heinrich. "The audio is set to the same level as in Chapter One."

"I told you these guys were good," said a cheerful Pat to Heinrich. "Satisfied?"

"Humpth," snorted an appreciative Heinrich, "they certainly are as accurate as you assured me. I suppose we should play it again while standing in front of the stage, to ensure it is playing properly on the audience screens."

"No need," said Brian. "Put Cam One on screen, tighten up to the IMAG. Let's play the first thirty seconds of Chapter One and then replay the opening twenty-two seconds of Chapter Two."

"Roger that," replied Malcolm. With two taps on the controller, and a slight manipulation of the joystick, the main program monitor displayed a shot of the stage's right side screen. Three more taps on the keyboard in front of him and the video started again. Chapter One played, followed immediately by Chapter Two, each pausing at the precise, pre-programmed spot.

"Satisfied?" asked Pat.

"Yes," replied Heinrich, "Quite satisfied." Heinrich turned to Brian and, as he held out his hand, his left eyebrow rose just a bit.

Brian continued to smile and look at Heinrich while he said, "Malcolm, the disk please."

Malcolm checked the computer screen, nodded almost imperceptibly and ejected the disk. He put it back in the album case and handed it to Brian, who handed it to Heinrich.

"Excellent," said Pat. "You guys are the best."

Pat made a gesture to the exit at the rear of the room. "Shall we?" he asked Heinrich and the two men left.

Brian sat for a minute and looked at the camera monitors. Once the two men had left backstage, he asked, "Malcolm, what's our SOP on disk-based source material?"

"We transfer all elements, at native resolutions, into redundant Doremi video servers for format conversion and show insertions. We then keep the disks in case of server failure; to allow playback from the back-up Blu-ray player if necessary," replied Malcolm with a smile.

"And did we follow our SOP... as modified by the client?" asked Brian.

"You bet, Cool-B," replied Malcolm with a big smile, "The content is on the servers and we gave him back the disk." Malcolm then leaned over to read the display panel, "Chapter One is exactly seven minutes, to the frame. Chapter Two is eight minutes, twenty-seven seconds, and fourteen frames." Malcolm paused for a moment and then asked, "I don't know about you Cool-B, but I'm wondering what so damn special about the rest of that video?"

Simmons didn't answer right away as he watched the camera monitors. Heinrich and McMillian were in the hall, standing in front of the stage. McMillian was gesturing to an area to the side of the stage, obviously explaining something. They watched quietly as McMillian obviously finished his explanation and the two men exited the hall through large glass double doors.

"There's only one way to find out," replied Brian as he turned to Malcolm, "Here's how I see it. We're gonna see it anyway and you know how I hate surprises on my shows. Plus, since the client indicated there was audio in Chapter Two, we're only doing our job to play the full video so we can pre-set those levels. Clients have been known to be wrong about things like audio levels, which could severely impact the integrity of the show."

"So, we're going to watch it," stated Malcolm.

"Yup," replied Brian. "I don't think we have a choice."

Malcolm just smiled at the rationalizing. He tapped a button on the video switcher, and brought up the Doremi onto the program monitor. The video was still frozen at exactly twenty-two seconds.

"From the top," instructed Brian.

Malcolm tapped a key on the keyboard and the video started playing from the beginning. Eight minutes, twenty-seven seconds and fourteen frames later they were staring at the last frame of the video frozen on the screen.

"Holy shit," said Malcolm.

"Yep," replied Brian. "You can say that again."

"Holy shit," repeated Malcolm.

They then turned to look at each other. Neither of them laughed.

# CHAPTER 21
# Partners

*Thursday – August 24 – 7:26 PM CDT*

> "But in a best case scenario, you get to make *CarAlity*, it hits, and you own seventy five percent of the entire series... after expenses plus fifteen."
> — BOBBY RASTON

Jack During, aka *I am Jacque Dupis, and I shall be pleased to be your waiter for the evening*, scanned his tables from the corner of the Rue Royal room. This upstairs room was in stark contrast to the much more crowded, infinitely more rustic, oyster bar and main dining area of the Royal Street Oyster House. These tables actually had space around them, and were draped with white tablecloths. Although it was officially the private party room, it was opened whenever the main dining area had to start turning people away.

Despite the relative opulence, tourists usually preferred the downstairs dining area even if they had to wait. It was more boisterous, more in line with the stereotypical New Orleans Oyster Bar. It was normally the locals, out with their families or with business associates, who actually requested to *go upstairs*.

Jack considered himself a student of human nature, and liked to amuse himself by trying to guess the circumstances of his guests.

At the far corner, next to an open set of the tall double doors lining two outer walls, was a fat man, just over middle aged, dining with an equally fat young woman at the cusp of her twenties.

They were obviously, to Jack anyway, a father and daughter dining together, but not in celebration. They had serious matters to discuss, and were doing it during dinner, at a neutral location.

In the center of the room, three tables had been pushed together to accommodate a party of eight. It was a family that included an elderly woman, three teenagers, an attractive young lady in her early twenties and her also attractive companion. Mom and Dad were seated at each end of the table. They were obviously celebrating the elderly woman's birthday. The *birthday girl* was smiling broadly and seated at the center table, flanked by two of the teenagers.

But to Jack, it was the two tables pushed together at the far corner of the room that were the most intriguing. The five people were an interesting group, although they would have been far less interesting if not for the truly stunning twin gals that had accompanied the three men. The room burble, a mish mash of low conversation from the various diners, had literally paused en masse, when Jack had led the group from the stairs, through the dining room, and to their tables.

Jack smiled a bit, noticing that the fat guy at the double doors was having problems keeping on top of whatever sensitive topic he was discussing. His eyes flitted to the Twins every time his daughter's eyes dropped to look at her food, or simply to avoid looking at her dad.

Yes, the women were stunning, but not in an overtly glamorous sort of way. They wore very little make up, if any, and they were dressed in casual, but well fitted clothing that showed every curve of their lithe bodies.

The men enjoying the company of the stunning young ladies were an odd assortment. They were obviously more business associates than friends. The body language between them suggested that they weren't very comfortable in each other's company just yet. Although the obvious host of the evening, seated at the head of the table and facing the center of the dining room, was certainly trying to create a sense of camaraderie.

He was obviously the one who was footing the bill, and it was of some concern to him. Jack noticed how his eyes flitted from the menu descriptions to the cost and then defocused as he made mental calculations. As each round of drinks and appetizers arrived, the mental arithmetic was further tallied.

Jack surmised that this was a guy who was going to pay cash and that the supply was far from unlimited.

The young guy seated next to the host had been asking him questions, which seemed to require elaborate explanations. The short round guy in his forties was seated between the stunning women and was obviously enjoying the experience. As opposed to the host, this guy was bucks up. From the Breitling on his wrist, to the Lauren on his back, to the handmade shoes; this guy wore his money casually, but on display for those who knew what to look for.

The table had been through the entire oyster menu, from the initial two dozen raw, to orders of Oysters Maque Choux, Rockefeller, Royal, and Chargrilled. The also had two orders of Oyster Puff Pastries and an order of Oyster Beignets. The table was on the fourth round of beers, although both the women and the rich guy had stopped at two, with only the host and the young guy opting in for the rounds three and four.

Jack had also been tallying up the bill and hoped there would be enough left in the guys pocket for a decent tip.

The low sound of fresh sobbing alerted Jack that his father/daughter diners needed some attention. The man was gesturing to him as the daughter buried her face in her hands; he was making the universal scribbling pantomime that said he needed his check, and quickly.

Jack nodded to the man and hurried over to deliver the bill. As he passed the table of five, the host made a gesture to him for another round of beer, and this time the women and the rich guy also nodded their heads in agreement. Jack nodded and smiled to show he understood and hurried off to attend to the other table.

"So basically we are a mobile *Candid Camera* team without the gag," Andy explained to his guests. "We find the big fish, the know-it-alls, the characters. We get them to do the hosting, and to tell us, and the audience, about the hero cars. If they're the seller, we get them to brag about the car, make predictions, and capture their pleasure, or pain, as the gavel goes down."

Andy drained his beer and looked around for the waiter. He saw he was attending to another table, so he shrugged and continued.

"If they're a buyer, then why?" asked Andy. His passion and conviction pumped up both his energy and his diction. He scanned the faces of his crew and slowly continued with a dramatic flair, "It could be for an investment. That's OK, especially if the guy can really explain why the car is an investment. A lot of people will like that. With the proper graphics, some archive footage, it would make a good segment. It could even be a great segment!"

Andy paused, and then leaned into the table and glanced around the room. It was like he was imparting the wisdom of the ages and he didn't want the grandma gathering to steal it.

"But what if it's a car just like a car they once had, a car they had once shared a lifetime of memories with their then future wife. A wife who had recently died."

The Twins and Preston were getting into the narrative and leaned in a little closer, as if to hear him better. Bobby Raston did the opposite, leaning a bit back in his chair to ease the pressure. That last Oyster Puff Pastry was more filling than it looked. He also had a more pragmatic look on his face, as if deciding if this little bit of common drama would be believable in what he was beginning to think was a pretty good concept.

"What if it's someone who's not a pro that's selling a car? A car that a young man asked his Mom to order for him so it'd be there when he got home?" said Andy, taking shallow breaths as if being overcome by the story. He glanced down briefly and then slowly raised his head and continued, "What if he finally made it home, but in a body bag. What if he had been killed with only six days and a wakeup left on his Vietnam tour?"

Andy smiled a bit as he noticed Raston finally lean in, even if just a little bit. There was now a genuine look of interest on the audio man's face.

"What if the seller, an elderly woman in an wheelchair, stops mid-sentence in her story, lost in thought. And we cut to an over the shoulder shot to see her staring at the 1968 Chevelle SS 396 Convertible with the L89, 375 horsepower engine. It's Matador Red, with white hockey stick stripes and a white top. Black bucket interior with red carpet, AM/FM 8-Track, and, of course, a 4-speed with Positraction. We then cut back to her face, and there are tears rolling down her cheeks."

Andy paused as Jack brought them the round of beers. He then started to pick up the picked over plates, but Andy stopped him with a pleasant, "Could you give us a moment on that?"

"Mai oui," replied Jack, "May I get anything else started for you in the kitchen?"

"No," replied Andy, "Just the check please."

As Jacque left to get the bill, Andy took a sip of his beer, set it down, looked at the group with a big smile and continued his story.

"And what if Mom, who now needs the money so she can get into a decent nursing home, refused to let the car be auctioned off in its garage find condition. What if she insisted that it be completely detailed? So clean and shiny it looks as if it just rolled in from 1968; straight off a dealer's showroom floor."

Andy paused, took another sip of his beer, and continued with a big smile on his face, "And what if the last shot we see, before the car rolls onto the block, is a big close-up of Mom's face as she speaks?"

Andy let his eyes go down to stare at his hands folded in front of him. After a dramatic pause, he lifted his gaze, swept the table and continued in a slow, halting voice, "I just couldn't let the last memory of my boy leave me with it all dusty and dirty. He was a good boy. He always kept his room clean. I know that's how he'd of kept his car."

Andy looked at everyone at the table, staring at him, wondering what he would say next. Andy broke out into a smile, leaned in and said, "And that's when the audience tears would start."

The Twins smiled at each other and tapped the upper parts of their hands together in clapping gesture.

Dean said, "Well, of course that would be a hell of a story, but it's made up. That's just not real life, and aren't we talking about a show that deals in real life?"

"Every one of those examples are real stories," replied Andy. "Story segments I've produced for *It's All About The Car*. And those were just in the last two years. Those stories are out there. They happen every single day. They just need to be captured."

Dean and the Twins looked at each other, nodded their heads and turned back to Andy as he continued, "But something happens when you set them down in front of the camera. I mean you can get the story, but it's just not the same as the first time you talk to them. When they are telling you the story for the first time, it's more open, more real. And that's what we're going to capture. There's a story, hell there's a dozen stories at every decent auction and this will be a whole new way to tell them. That's what we are here to do, to capture the *real reality* in the fascinating world of cars, the *CarAlity!*"

The Twins looked at each other quizzically. Dean got a thoughtful look on his face. Bobby just laughed out loud.

"*CarAlity*," Bobby snorted, once he finished laughing. "What kind of name is that?"

"I don't know," chimed in Dean, "it's kinda catchy, but I guess it's kinda cutesy too."

Mandy and Brandy both picked up their beers in a toast.

"We like it," said Brandy.

"This will be fun," said Mandy.

"To *CarAlity*," they both said, in unison, as they lifted their beers.

"Yeah," said Dean raising his beer. "To *CarAlity*."

Andy already had his beer in the air. He turned to look at Bobby, saw his dubious expression and said, "It'll grow on ya!"

Mandy and Brandy both turned to Bobby and leaned into him just a little closer than they needed to. Mandy, to his right, nudged him just a little with her left elbow and said, "Come on, Bobby. Don't be like that."

Brandy, to his left, leaned in even closer. As she gracefully draped her arm around his shoulders, her breast lightly brushed against him, "This is going to be very… interesting."

The subtle gesture had a galvanizing effect on Bobby Raston, as his eyebrows arched and he seemed to sit up straighter.

Andy could see the wheels turning in Bobby's brain and knew it was more than just the proximity to Twins that had him thinking. But before he could address it, Dean piped up.

"So far, I'm loving the concept, but the audio is going to be a killer," said Dean, his eyes bright and alert although his speech was a bit slurred. "Long lenses can take care of the video, but how will we get decent audio if we don't have a staged area, like they did on that… huh, *Cameras Candid* show?"

"*Candid Camera*," replied Andy, "and yes, audio will be the biggest challenge in this whole workflow." Andy stopped, looked at his nearly empty glass, shrugged and picked it up anyway, and held it high. "And that is why I requested... nay, I demanded, the superlative services of the one man who can pull this off; the premier audio guru of our time, Mr. Bobby Raston."

Bobby smiled at the statement. It was certainly true. As Andy had been describing the production workflow, Bobby had been recognizing, and mentally solving, the audio issues.

"Okay then. With the gals' camera work, and Mr. Raston's incredible audio," said Dean, "then I think this could work."

"For what it's worth, I think it's a great idea," said Bobby. "But it's going to be a lot more effort for the same rate of pay."

Andy smiled and replied, "Bobby, that's why you get what you get for a day rate. There's nobody that could pull this off but you. I don't have the slightest idea of how you're going to do it, but I know you will."

Bobby acknowledged the compliment with a little roll of his eyes that said he'd heard it all before. "Yes, that's true. But really, you'd need a team our size for each subject you want to cover. And we are the only team, are we not?"

"Yes, we are the one and only team," replied Andy. "But for this pilot program, we are only covering one car, the Hitler car, and we are going to cover the crap out of it."

"That email you forwarded to me said there would be no media allowed into the auction," said Bobby. "It said to even get in, you need to post a five million dollar bond that would be forfeited if you were discovered to be media."

Bobby paused and gestured about the room and continued, "This is a nice restaurant, and the oysters were superb, but we are staying at a Best Western. No offense, but do you have five million to burn on getting *CarAlity* footage of the actual auction? And without the *CarAlity* viewpoint, doesn't that leave the premise flat?"

"Actually," replied Andy with a smile, "What the email said was that to gain access AFTER that date, you had to post the bond. I already had access, I am a registered seller in this auction and have been since last week."

"Ok, so you can get into the auction while still playing by the rules," replied Bobby. "How does that help us? We'd need the entire crew in the room."

"As a registered seller, I was able to add three additional co-owners of my car, to help in the decision making. I didn't plan on Dean at the time, but I think I've got an even better idea for him."

"Okay, fair enough, but what *decision making*?" asked Dean. "What's to decide? It's an auction."

"One thing might be whether to lift the reserve or not," replied Andy, "but that doesn't really matter. What matters is that I will have the additional badges to get our crew into the actual auction. We will be the only camera crew smack dab in middle of the auction of the decade."

"What about the AV crew working the event?" asked Dean. "They use United A/V and those guys are good. I know, I used to work for them before I started getting broadcast work with Neiderland. Could we also get their footage?"

"I have already contracted for the broadcast rights to the ISO and mix feeds from United A/V," replied Andy, nodding his head and thinking that perhaps Jack was right about needing the kid. "Unfortunately, or rather, fortunately for us, the A-Bear contract with the Hitler Car seller has some very peculiar provisions to protect the provenance. Basically, during the presentation of the provenance all the cameras will be pointed at the floor with the operators standing at least five feet from them. And that includes the PTZ remote cams."

"So we're going to be the only camera crew able to shoot the actual provenance," asked Dean.

Andy leaned in and said in a low whisper, "Actually, we won't be able to shoot the provenance as I happen to know it's a video. But I've figured out a way to grab it when it's played just prior to the bidding; supposedly for the first time to an audience. We'll need to get clearance from the buyer after the auction, but I don't anticipate that to be a huge problem. The buyer will likely want all the publicity he can get. What's more important is that we get to capture what no one else will have; the reactions during the video's first public showing. Reactions from the crowd, from the auction staff, and from the seller; supposedly, a very interesting character."

"What's on the video?" asked Dean.

"That, I don't know," replied Andy.

"But you sure seem to know a lot about this whole screwball set-up," stated Bobby; his eyes narrowed a bit as he studied Andy.

"I do," replied Andy, "and it cost me." Andy paused and shook his head, and continued "Or it will."

"What do you mean, 'it will?'" asked Bobby.

Andy sighed and looked at his phone. He saw there were no calls, texts, or emails from Jack or anyone at Neiderland.

"I have an in with Pat McMillian, A-Bear's Auto Auction manager," explained Andy. "For a *donation* of ten thousand dollars we will get the exclusive broadcast and Internet rights to all the AV crew footage, as long as we credit A-Bear Auctions for its use. Since the LMC letter hadn't gone out yet, he took and approved my verbal request for the extra badges. He's throwing in those extra co-owner credentials as part of the ten grand arrangement."

Raston was now paying very close attention, to both the words and Guidry's body language.

"The only caveat is we can't shoot any of the provenance video off the I-Mag screens," said Andy. "McMillian, and his lawyer, believe that will keep them within the confines of the special consigner agreement A-Bear has with the seller."

"Andy, I like your style," stated Bobby, "But didn't you say '*or it will?*' Does that mean you haven't paid the man? Your whole shoot concept rests on getting the footage rights and crew access. What if he changes his mind?" asked Bobby, "Or someone makes him a better offer?"

Andy began to speak and then quit as Jack walked up with the check.

"I hope you found the food satisfactory," murmured Jack, "and that I was of service."

Andy picked up the check, took a look at it, did some mental calculations and smiled. He pulled out a cheap, magnetic money clip, pried out all the cash, and dropped it on the small tray.

Giving Jack a big smile, he picked up the tray and stated loudly, "Jacque, the food was trés bien, as was the service." Andy made a formal gesture of handing the waiter the small tray loaded with bills of various denominations and said, "Merci."

Jacque took the tray, and with a quick glance, figured it was enough to cover the tab with an almost decent tip. He bowed his head just a bit and replied, "You are too kind. Please come again and bring your delightful companions with you."

"I have no doubt we shall be back," replied Andy who then turned back to the crew as Jack walked away.

Andy took a deep breath and sighed, as if making up his mind. "The reason I have not given McMillian the money is very simple. I do not have it." Andy stopped, sighed again and continued. "I have a deal with Neiderland for the advance licensing of this show. I have given them very liberal terms in exchange for a very quick advance."

Andy stopped and took a big swallow from his beer. He felt an intense need to vape, but then he always did when he was drinking and in a stressful situation. Which, he thought, lately seemed to be most of the time. He took a deep breath and continued.

"Our agreement was that the money would be wired into my account by the end of business today, Pacific Daylight Time." Andy checked his phone, tapped into an app and shook his head. "That was about thirty minutes ago and the money is most definitely not in my account. I've tried to call Jack Calman multiple times, but I just get an immediate transfer to voice mail."

"Mr. Calman has his phone turned off?" asked Dean, as if this simple fact deserved to be national news.

"So it would seem," said Andy. Now was the difficult part. "The money I just gave the waiter was all the cash I had left. My credit cards are maxed, and my debit card is tapped."

Andy paused and gave a rueful smile, "So yes, if Neiderland doesn't come through on our agreement, then the entire project is basically down the tubes. Not only can't I pay your day rates, I can't even check you into the hotel." Andy looked at his watch and continued, "And not that it matters now, but the reservations are going to expire in about thirty minutes."

Andy gave what he hoped was a winning smile. "I'm afraid, at the very least, that you'll all have to put up your personal credit cards for your hotel rooms tonight. Hopefully, I'll get the money into my bank account by tomorrow and I'll be able to cover the bill before we check out."

Mandy and Brandy looked at each other, rolled their eyes and shrugged.

Dean, however, immediately spoke up, "How much are these rooms? I only have a debit card and my account isn't exactly overflowing. Broadcast may be more fun, but it doesn't pay nearly as well as corporate video."

"Well," replied Andy, "if we get back before the reservations expire, we'll get the *reserved it a week ago* rate of one fifty a night. I don't know what it will be if the reservation expires."

"How much is Neiderland supposed to front you? Are you sure it's a licensing deal? That's pretty unusual these days. If so, what are the license terms?" Bobby asked.

"Well," started Andy, "It is definitely a licensing deal. But the financial details are proprietary infor…"

Bobby held up his hand, palm facing Andy in the universal stop gesture. He turned his chair slightly and curled his index finger at Jack twice, signaling him to come over.

"Yes sir," asked Jack, who had hurried to the table, as if magnetically drawn to the Breitling Chrono-Matic 49, in eighteen karat rose gold, that was loosely fastened to Bobby's wrist.

"My friend and I forgot it was my turn to buy dinner," Bobby said, pulling out a black American Express Card and handing it to Jack. "Please bring my friend his cash, and put the bill on this. And add an extra fifty dollars, on top of this tip, for the trouble; as well as your superlative service this evening."

"Of course, sir," replied Jack, taking the card while bowing and backing up at the same time.

"So here's the deal," said Bobby, staring directly at Andy. "I figure they are giving you forty, maybe fifty thousand as an advance against what… one hundred twenty for unlimited US license rights to this program. Maybe it's a five year term…"

"Three," interjected Andy.

"Three is good," said Bobby as he continued. "Out of that forty k…"

"It's fifty," said Andy.

"Out of that fifty," said Bobby and continued, "you were going to pay this Pat guy his ten, fund the rest of us at our day rates and expenses and then pay for post. Which wasn't going to leave you with much left over, at least until you got the rest of the money for the first show. But I'll bet you have some sort of deal for more of these *CarAlity* shows, assuming that the first one is the hit you're pitching it will be."

"Actually," said Andy, now speaking directly to Bobby as if the others at the table didn't even exist. "My total fee for the pilot is a hundred grand, which includes concept and creative. The fifty large is the deposit and they only pay the remainder after it's done and if they decide to pick it up on a three-year license agreement. They also have first right of refusal for another thirteen *CarAlity* shows at a forty percent discount per show, if they contract for the entire series."

Raston nodded at the deal. It wasn't bad. Actually, it was damn good. He hadn't dealt with Neiderland in a long time. They simply wouldn't pay his day rate. But he had dealt with that asshole J. Rogers Winters, whom he had heard was now kicking ass at Neiderland. Holding up a deposit, on a done deal with a deadline, was definitely a classic Winters move.

"How much can you trust this McMillian guy?" asked Bobby.

"I've heard, from people who know, he's like an honest politician," said Andy with a smile. "Once he's bought, he stays bought."

Bobby thought for a moment and then started to speak, "Ok, here's the deal. I'll fund this entire project from here on out, but all of my out-of-pocket, plus fifteen percent, comes off the top of the first check from Neiderland, or whomever we sell it to if they end up bailing. For my funding, I get twenty-five percent of this program's revenue stream, both domestic and foreign, in perpetuity. I also own five percent of any succeeding programs or the twenty-five percent if I choose to work those as well."

"And why," asked Andy, "would I take such a offer? My deal with Neiderland is solid, other than the little missing deposit issue, and I own it all."

"You'll take the deal, " replied Bobby, "because tomorrow is Friday, the first day of the auction. We might be covering only one car, but we'll need to cover the crap out of it. We'll need to hit the ground running if we're actually going to pull this off. Now, excuse me for a moment and think about that."

Bobby looked around to find Jack, saw him and motioned him over.

"Jack," Bobby started as he came over.

"It's Jacque, sir," said the waiter.

"Yeah," said Bobby with a smile, "I'm sure it is. Anyway…" Bobby motioned for Jacque to lean down and whispered to him. Jacque smiled, nodded, and scurried away.

"Plus," said Bobby returning his attention to Andy, "I can guarantee you that as long as you are desperate for their money, Neiderland is going to string you along. The deal is too good, on your side anyway, and they will change it. They just need you to get in deep enough that you'll settle for whatever deal they offer as long as you get some cash. And you're at that point now. Stick with them on this, and you won't own any of this show."

Andy was nodding his head because Bobby was making a lot of sense.

"Take my deal and your money worries are over," said Bobby. "And we get started with *CarAlity*, episode one, bright and early, first thing in the morning," explained Bobby, who then paused and continued in a low, soothing tone. "Listen, I'm taking all the risk that this will even work as a network-quality show. Oh, and speaking of which, I'll also need some editing input, at least as far as the sound design is concerned. Anyway, if worst comes to worst, all you are out is your time. But in a best case scenario, you get to make *CarAlity*, it hits, and you own seventy five percent of the entire series… after expenses plus fifteen."

Raston noticed the waiter hovering near the kitchen, looking at him expectantly. He subtly shook his head at him and turned back to Guidry.

"And," Bobby continued, "when Jack Calman tells you some bullshit about having to revisit the deal, and he will, you're in a position to tell him to take it or leave it, as is," said Bobby with a big smile. "And, at that point, if they do come back, they'll be ready to take it."

"So what about us?" asked Mandy.

"What do we get out of this?" asked Brandy.

Amazingly, Bobby had been so engrossed in the negotiations that he had almost forgotten about the two beauties mere inches from his elbows.

"Yeah," agreed Dean, with a hopeful tone in his voice. "What about us?"

"Nothing changes for you," said Bobby. "Except I'm covering your day rates as part of the deal so you'll definitely get paid. Which is more than you had before."

The Twins looked at each other and communicated wordlessly, through subtle head gestures and facial expressions. They then nodded and Brandy began.

"The only way you're going to pull this off is with us," said Brandy.

"Since we were contracted under false pretenses, we feel we deserve not only our day rate." continued Mandy.

"But that we should also get a percentage of the program," said Brandy.

"And the series," finished Mandy who continued with, "we think ten percent each is fair."

"It's not coming out of my cut," replied Bobby, with what he hoped was an endearing smile that flitted from twin to twin, "so it's not my call."

"It's two days work," replied Andy, "at your day rate, that is not a ten percent deal. How about you each forgo your day rates, we still pick up your expenses, and you split ten percent; making it five percent each?

"We forgo our day rate, and each get seven point five," said Mandy.

"But we get the same deal on any further programs in the series that we work on," continued Brandy.

"With first right of refusal and an extra five percent, total, to serve as DP," countered Mandy.

"When we go to bigger crews," added Brandy.

"And we will need to go to bigger crews," finished Mandy.

Andy thought about it for a moment, and then looked over at Bobby who simply said, "It's your call. I'll pay their day rate anyway, to keep our deal intact, but if you want to trade some of your share of the pie and keep the cash, it's fine with me."

"Uh," started Dean, "so where do I fit in on this?"

Andy, Bobby, and the Twins all stopped and looked at Dean.

"Well Dean," said Andy somewhat condescendingly, "you get your day rate. What else would the PA get?"

"First of all," said Dean, "I'm a field producer, and this is going to get complicated. You're going to need me. Secondly, uh, secondly, well…"

The Twins looked at Dean. They liked Dean. Sure, they had caught him staring at their assets often enough, but what guy, or gal for that matter, didn't. He was sweet, and he respected their abilities.

"Dean, Dean, Dean, Dean, Dean," repeated Andy as if speaking to a particularly dense child who was trying to get away with something. "That's just not how it…"

"Dean needs in," interrupted Mandy.

"Or we're out," said Brandy.

Andy looked at them incredulously, and then looked at Bobby who shrugged and said, "Again, it's not my call but we really need the Twins."

Andy sighed and said to Bobby, "Same deal? You pay his day rate, plus fifteen, against the show budget and I get the money?"

Bobby nodded.

"Ok," Andy said to Dean. "Two percent, no day rate, with the same deal for future shows."

"Five percent with no money," countered Dean, "or three percent with half my rate."

Andy smiled and replied, "I'm going to regret this, but I need the money. I'll do four percent with no money, with the same on future shows IF I decide to use you. But no guarantee, or first right of refusal, until after the first season."

"Deal," said Dean with a smile and holding out his hand. "I don't need a guarantee on future work because you're going to find that I'm a handy guy to have around."

"Ok then, it's a deal," replied Andy, shaking Dean's hand.

Andy then stood up and held out his hand to the Twins, who each stood up in turn, shook it and said, "Deal."

Andy then turned to Bobby, held out his hand and stated, "I believe this will either be the best or worst production deal I have ever made with anyone. Deal?" he asked.

"Deal," Bobby replied as he stood up and shook Andy's hand. "And it's likely to be both."

Never taking his eyes off of Andy, Bobby then raised his hand and curled two fingers together in a *bring it on* gesture.

On cue, Jack, who had been standing to the side and at the ready, popped the cork on a bottle of Dom Perignon Metamorphosis Brut. Another waiter started removing the dirty dishes still on the table while a third waiter started passing out flutes.

Jacque poured a bit of the wine into Bobby's glass for his approval, but Bobby said, "I'm sure it's fine. Fill 'em up while the bubbles are still working."

While the rest of the glasses were being filled, Bobby turned to Andy and said, "Just so you know, this bottle is on me and is NOT a *CarAlity* expense. I figured we would have a reason to celebrate."

As Jacque filled Mandy's glass, she looked at Bobby and asked, "You know what?"

Brandy finished it for her, "You're kinda cute."

As Bobby blushed, Mandy reached out and ran a finger along his cheek, "Make that real cute."

Andy lifted his glass and said, "To *CarAlity*, the new gold standard in automotive programming."

They all said in unison, "To *CarAlity*," and then sipped at the expensive wine,

"Wow," said Dean, "that's good stuff!"

"I still don't know about that name," said Bobby.

"It'll grow on ya," replied Andy with a smile.

One more glass each finished the bottle and they were finally ready to leave. The beer and wine combined to made them all a bit unsteady as they walked down the narrow staircase, and out onto Bourbon Street.

"I'm starting to feel really good about this," said Andy as they stepped off the curb and into the crowd. "Let's go to Pat O'Brien's for a Hurricane nightcap."

"Let's go to the hotel, check in, and get a good nights sleep," countered Bobby. "It's going to be an early call."

"Oh yeah," said Andy, "I forgot about the hotel. That better at least be the first stop."

"First and last," said Bobby a bit more sternly. "I've got money in this now, and I expect a wide awake and rested crew. Besides, now that I've got an idea of the production workflow, I've got to do some modifications to my audio gear."

"You're right, partner," said Andy as he started leading the way to the hotel, patting his vape pen to assure himself he still had it. "Let's go hit the hay and get some sleep. Breakfast starts at seven in the hotel lobby and it's pretty good. I'll meet you there."

Andy stopped, tugged on Bobby arm and semi-whispered, "Can you take care of my room against the show budget? With, of course, your fifteen percent surcharge."

Bobby just looked at Andy, wondering if he'd bitten off more than he wanted to chew. Suddenly the Twins each grabbed one of Bobby's arms and pulled him close to them. A soft, perfect breast snuggled next to each of his shoulders.

"Come on Bobby, we don't want to lose the hotel room," said Mandy as they got him moving again, and quite a bit faster.

"That's right," said Brandy. "It would be no fun for us to all sleep in the car!"

Raston wasn't quite sure he agreed with that statement, but he looked back to Guidry and nodded his agreement that he would also pay for his room. After all, a few hundred here or there wasn't exactly an issue to him.

Bobby then laughed and began walking even faster, pulling the Twins along with him.

Dean, not particularly liking the Twin's newfound affection for the short, round rich guy, hurried to catch up.

Andy watched them as they snaked their way through the crowd, getting ahead of him with every step. He then pulled out his vape pen, took a deep drag, and blew it out in a thin, white stream. Despite the copious amount of alcohol, he almost immediately felt the fuzzy calm of cannabis entering his system.

Andy was smiling broadly, thinking the evening had sure turned out better than he initially thought it would. He used his free hand to pat the wad of bills in his pocket. He then took one more big hit on the vape pen, held it for a moment and then blew it out.

"Hey, partners" Andy called out, as he slipped the pen back into his pocket. "Wait up. I'm the old man here!"

"Then hurry up, old-timer," yelled Mandy.

"We need to get this man to the hotel A. S. A. P!" yelled Brandy with a laugh, as they pulled Bobby along with him.

Bobby Raston reveled in the envious stares from the people in the streets, especially those close enough to hear Brandy. They clearly thought, at that particular moment, that he was the luckiest guy in New Orleans.

With a huge smile on his face, he decided that he most likely was.

## CHAPTER 22

# Gospel According To Saul

*Friday – August 25 – 8:07 AM CDT*

> "You are here to cast a shining light on the minions that would glorify his filthy name!"
> — Saul Wittmann

"Holy shit," said Herman Adler as he finally turned onto Henderson, towards Race Street and the entrance to Mardi Gras World. Traffic had been much heavier today, with literally dozens of classic and modified muscle cars interspersed with more modern vehicles; all headed to the auction site.

Both the grassy median and the pedestrian walkway on right side of the street were packed with young people, ranging from early teens to mid twenties. There were also a fair number of older people interspersed among them. There were at least two hundred, maybe more, and it seemed as though every single one of them was waving a sign. While there were certainly a good number of professionally printed versions from the FedEx Office store, the rest had been homemade, or in this case, church-made.

Some of the handmade signs bore the same slogans that Wittmann had ordered the day before. Others bore different slogans, but along the same lines.

"Hitler Car is a Hateful Car," "No bids are good bids for Hitler Car," "Adolph + Automobile = Abomination" and Herman Adler's personal favorite, "Adolph was an A Hole, don't B 1 2."

Walking down the line of cars was Mason LaCroix, the counterman from the FedEx Office store. He was holding a large stack of papers, stopping at each car, speaking briefly to the occupants, handing them one of the full color flyers that Herman had written and laid out the day before.

In addition to Wittmann's fiery rhetoric, it featured swastika graphics and photos of a Grosser Tourenwagen, with Hitler standing in it. A little Photoshop manipulation had transformed the salute into an outstretched hand, with a stack of hundred dollar bills in it. Herman Adler never ceased to be amazed what you could find, and do, for free on the Internet.

When Mason came to the Impala and bent down to speak, his face broke out into a huge smile.

"Brother Saul, Brother Herman, praise Jesus it's a glorious day!" he replied, crouching down so he could look directly into the car.

"The signs we made at the shop didn't go very far, so we had to make our own," he said with a smile. "When I told my youth group about this travesty, they all wanted to help spread the word!"

He stopped, looked at the huge group of protesters, and turned back to Herman and Saul and continued, "And I guess a bunch of them brought friends. Some even brought they's parents and grandparents. Fighting Satan is everybody's job!"

"Praise Jesus," proclaimed Saul from the passenger seat, "Praise Jesus and all you've done in his glorious name!"

"Brother Saul," said Mason, "I know you're on your way into the den of evil to spread the good word against bidding on that accursed car, but could you say a few words to your soldiers in the fight?"

Saul looked at Herman and said, "Keep driving, I'll catch up." He then climbed out of the car and stood tall and proud, like an ancient oak that seems at one with time.

Mason shouted out, "Brothers and Sisters, this is Brother Saul. He's the man who alerted me, and us, to the evil that is taking place in our fair city."

Almost immediately, the crowd quieted down. They were used to being preached to. The cars, however, continued their slow march down Henderson to Race Street, directly across from the big Mardi Gras World warehouse entrance.

Saul scanned the crowd; their attention made him stand up even straighter. The early morning sun was hot on his head, promising to be far more brutal before the day was done. Saul took a deep breath, almost tasting the river in the still, humid air.

Mason continued his introduction, speaking loud and clear with an almost musical cadence, "The selling of the cursed Nazi car, right here on the banks of the mighty Mississippi, might have gone unnoticed by me... and you... were it not for this man. Praise Jesus, praise Jesus!"

A lone voice shouted out from the median, about half way down Henderson, "Amen, Brother Mason, Amen."

Then the rest of the crowd broke out into a flurry of "Amen," "Praise Jesus," "Praise God," and "Hallelujah."

Mason held up his hand and, in a few seconds, the crowd was one again quiet. "Brother Saul will now say a few words before he goes into the lion's den to fight this evil head on."

Herman Adler just shook his head as the car in front of him, a '69 AMC Hurst SC/Rambler, rumbled ahead one more car length towards the gate. At this rate, he'd be at the gate in about five minutes.

"And I will park. And I will leave that old coot," he muttered to himself. He knew he wouldn't, but he smiled at the thought of the old man having to talk his way into the venue while Herman had his bidder credentials tucked into his pocket, right next to his own.

"Brothers and sisters," said Wittmann, addressing the crowd in a loud, steady voice. "Fighting evil can be a lonely job. Not everyone is up to it."

"Bless you, Brother Saul," shouted a middle-aged woman, standing next to her son.

"Thank you Sister," said Saul, "And yes, I have been blessed. Lord almighty, I have been blessed with you, and you, and you, and all of you!" Saul had pointed at the middle-aged woman, then at a tall gangly young man dressed in basketball gear, and finally at a very thin young girl whose very dark skin was in stark contrast to her lemon yellow sundress. She was holding a sign almost as tall as she was, blazoned with a crossed-out swastika.

Saul then had made a sweeping gesture at the crowd, "And I thank God for each and every one of you who has come out to confront Satan. You are here to cast a shining light on the minions that would glorify his filthy name! Glorify it by spending their ill-gotten lucre for a vehicle utilized solely for evil by the devil incarnate himself, Adolph Hitler!"

The crowd was hushed; the signs almost unconsciously lowered a bit as they hung on Saul's words.

"Now, not all of the people attending this auction, intending to bid on this car, realize the evil of their way. Not all of them understand that Satan himself is behind the false prophet of... well, of profit. Making a profit from an association with evil is tantamount to supporting evil, to glorifying evil! Does God want us to glorify evil?"

"NO!" shouted the crowd.

"Does God want an inanimate object to be considered more valuable because it was used for evil?"

"NO!" replied the crowd.

"Does God want the sale of this car to illustrate, to the entire world, that evil association does not make something worth more money, but less?"

"YES!" replied the crowd. A few "Praise Jesus" and "Amens" punctuated the affirmations.

"We will show the world that evil anywhere, in any shape, and in any form, does not add to an object's secular value, but detracts from it." Saul was truly in the moment, wondering why he never thought of doing this before. He was bathing in the power of crowd manipulation. "We will shine God's holy light on those that would profit from evil, and those that would supply that profit. Praise the Lord!"

"PRAISE THE LORD!" shouted the crowd.

"PRAISE JESUS!" yelled Saul.

"PRAISE JESUS!" responded the crowd.

"Amen, brothers and sisters, AMEN," replied Saul. He looked around and saw that Herman was only two cars from the gate guard.

"Thank you for hearing God's word today," said Saul. He lost his rigid upright stance, and started to hunch over just a bit, visibly letting his age show through. "I thought I would have to fight this fight alone. Then God led me to Brother Mason, who led me to you."

Saul reached out and placed his hand on Mason's shoulder and smiled and nodded at him before continuing, "It's time for me to go into the den of Satan and face that evil head on. To praise Jesus, in all his glory, and let potential bidders know of the shadow that Satan has cast upon their eyes. To help them cast aside that shadow and see the error of their intentions."

"Amen, Brother Saul, Amen," boomed a distant voice from behind Saul. As the crowd echoed the phrase, Saul turned and saw the shout had come from the gate guard, who was standing there seemingly mesmerized. The guard was standing next to a Maroon metal flaked, '52 Hornet that was even lower than the original *step down design* had dictated. So low that the paperwork an elderly white arm was waving out the window was barely higher than his stomach. The guard did a little start, noticed the papers, and then bend down and spoke into the car window.

Saul couldn't help but smile.

"Brothers and sisters, we must stay the course," said Saul, speaking loudly but no longer shouting. "The Devil's limousine will not be sold until tomorrow night. Some of the misguided that would buy this car will not even come to New Orleans until tomorrow. Some will come in private jets, perhaps most, and they will be chauffeured into this facility by fancy cars."

Saul paused and slowly scanned the crowd, "It is imperative that each and every one of you be here to greet them. For many, it will be the first time their eyes are opened to the unwitting abomination in which they have come to participate. In that revelation, you are truly doing God's work and he will reward you for it."

"AMEN," shouted Mason.

"AMEN," shouted the crowd.

Saul looked at the crowd and nodded his head. He opened his mouth, as if to continue speaking, but then just closed it. He then put his palms together, as if in prayer, and bowed his head until his lips touched the two forefingers of his hands. He was that way for at least five seconds, the silence from the crowd accentuating the normal traffic and dock sounds. Saul then lifted his head, turned to Mason, held him by his shoulders, and then hugged him. The crowd broke the silence by unleashing a mighty cheer.

As Saul started walking towards his car, which was next in line at the gate, the crowd started chanting; "No bids for Hitler Hate. No bids for Hitler Hate. No bids for Hitler Hate. No bids for Hitler Hate."

As Saul got into the passenger side, Herman was looking at him with a mixture of amazement, disbelief, and a touch of horror. He noticed the car at the gate was still stopped at the guard, who was gesturing down Race Street, obviously explaining how to get into the auction car holding area. Herman put the car in Park, and turned to Wittmann.

"So, I thought the plan was that we were going to rally the New Orleans Jewish population?" asked Herman. "And, not that I was looking forward to it, but I thought I was going to be the one to do the rallying, due to my — let's see, how did you put it on the plane — oh, yes, due to my Jew-boy appearance. I also thought it was me that would be passing out signs, trying to sway the crowd, while you were the guy who swoops in to pick up the car for a song because everyone else was too overwhelmed by the protests, or too afraid of the publicity."

"Well," replied Wittmann slowly, shedding the Brother Saul persona he had so easily assumed, "plans change. This," he said, gesturing to the crowd, "was a gift to our cause." Wittmann went pensive for a moment, "Perhaps a gift from…"

"Excuse me, Brother Saul," said the massive gate guard, with an equally massive smile, who had walked back to the car. Herman hadn't noticed that the car in front of them had left and was driving down Race Street, towards the auction building, the low burble of its Flow Masters reverbing off the warehouse walls.

The guard had walked back to them and was bending at the waist, looking into the passenger window, "Does you remember me from yesterday?"

"I certainly do," replied Saul. "You were kind enough to direct me to the FedEx Office where I met Mason LaCroix. If not for you, none of this would be happening."

The guard was taken a back a bit, raised up and looked at the protesters waving their signs and Mason walking down the cars, handing out flyers to those that would take them. He then saw that three different news vans from WVUE, WDSU, and WGNO had taken a short cut around the back of the convention center and were now parked and starting to set up cameras. Their respective reporters had already started to mingle among the crowd, with a couple of the people pointing to the Impala.

"Less jest keep dat to ourselves," replied the guard. "Does you have your auction credentials?"

"Yes, we do," replied Herman, pulling them from his pocket, and spreading them apart so the guard could see both badges.

"Looks like youse about to be on de news," said the guard.

"Really!" said Saul, looking at where the guard was gesturing. He started to reach for the door handle and said, "Maybe I should go and…"

"You know," said Herman thoughtfully, "there are basically two full days until the Tourenwagen crosses the block, today and tomorrow, and they are called *investigative* reporters."

Wittmann sighed and said to Herman, "Yes, you're right." To the guard he said, "I'm not looking to be in the media just for doing God's work. I'd like to get into the auction house before the news finds me. Where do we park?"

"Bless you, Brother Saul," said the guard, "I knows you was a good man when I's talked to you yesterday. Let's me see your badges again."

As Herman held them up, the guard got a puzzled look on his face. He then said, "Youse in the VIB parking, down next to the auction house." Their credentials, and VIB parking passes, had been waiting for Saul at their hotel. It was a perk he received by virtue of his five million dollar bidder bond.

"That's the good parking, down next to the auction hall. If you don't minds me axing, how'd you get dem passes?" said the puzzled guard.

"The Lord works in mysterious ways," replied Wittmann.

"Yeah," muttered Herman, "real mysterious."

The guard stood up as Herman put the car in drive. As the Impala pulled away, the guard heard Herman asking Saul, "OK, so I guessing now you're going to want me to do the bidding. Well let me tell you, I've got half a mind…"

The guard looked puzzled for a moment, then just shook his head as a '68 Torino GT pulled up. Raising his voice a bit to compensate for the lumpy rumble of the 428 Cobra Jet, he asked, "And how may I hep yew?"

# CHAPTER 23
# Mysterious Ways Indeed

*Friday – August 25 – 8:42 AM CDT*

> "Regardless of our financial arrangement,
> this is still my gig, my crew, my decisions."
> — ANTOINE GUIDRY

"Did you get it?" asked Andy Guidry as the Twins climbed back into the Escalade, settling into the second row of captain chairs.

"Yes," said Mandy.

"Of course," said Brandy.

They looked at each other like Andy had asked them if they remembered to breathe.

"What about audio?" Andy asked Dean.

"Amazing!" replied Dean, who had wormed his way between the Twins and plopped down on the rear bench seat. "It was just amazing," he repeated as he stared at the Sennheiser 816 location rig that Bobby had handed him just minutes earlier. Bobby just smiled and nodded his head. He was sure it was.

No more than twenty minutes earlier, they had turned onto Henderson from Tchoupitoulas Street. They had immediately seen the crowd, holding up the signs and occasionally waving at some of the classic cars waiting their turn to get to the gate.

Almost instinctively, the crew had sprung into action. Bobby put the big SUV into park and hit a button that activated the power lift gate. As it started to open, Bobby slid out from behind the wheel and walked to the back to get to his audio kit.

The Twins had also needed no instruction. They each grabbed their 5Ds and monopods, and popped out of the vehicle. They were shooting establishing shots almost before the doors closed.

At the rear of the vehicle, Bobby had removed a long, black Sennheiser 816 shotgun mic from a custom made holster along the side of his "go kit." It was housed in a low-profile wind blimp, much thinner than normal and covered in a trimmed down version of the traditional "dead cat" wind diffuser. The fuzzy material was colored black rather than the more usual gray.

In the original design he had covered the slender blimp in thin, black acoustic foam. A scary incident in Italy, where a near-sighted Polizia had perceived it as a gun barrel, had made Raston go for a more traditional setup. It was now more recognizable as audio gear, but not as blatant as a stock configuration.

Attached to the blimp was a pistol grip handle, which could be screwed onto a boom pole. However, the weight and length of the mic made that an unwieldy set up, and Bobby had other rigs for that sort of duty. Bobby had designed this rig expressly for handheld audio capture.

Because of the extreme directionality and sensitivity, the Sennheiser 816 had been a sitcom audio staple for the last forty years. Countless soundmen had supported their families by manning massive audio booms, hundreds of pounds of steel and aluminum designed solely to support that light, slender tube that swooped and swiveled above the actor's heads. They no longer made them, but unlike cameras, which seemed to start depreciating the moment you opened the box, vintage audio gear just seemed to get better, and more valuable, with age.

Raston's 816 was, of course, more than a bit modified. He had virtually eliminated the propensity for this type of mic to also pick up audio directly from the rear. There was also a small bracket that ran perpendicular to the blimp, swivel mounted between the handle and the blimp base.

On the bracket was a small wireless transmitter that worked across a wide range of frequencies. You could swing out the bracket, adjust the transmitter, and then swing it back under the blimp to keep it out the way. It secured itself under the blimp with a positive *click*.

Raston preferred using the *outlaw freqs* that had been snatched from the general public by the FCC back in the early teens. It was supposedly to dedicate them to ambulance and other first responder requirements, but in actuality they had been pretty much unused ever since.

The wireless transmitter was connected to the long slender mic inside. In addition to a standard Bluetooth signal for operator monitoring, it transmitted an HDX-compounded, high-frequency signal to a small, touchscreen device about the size of an iPhone 8 Plus, albeit about three hundred percent thicker, which was still plenty thin. This remarkable device, his RigMaster, was legendary, in a very literal sense. Only people that worked with Bobby, or for him, ever got to even see it. Those that had been lucky enough to see it in action, or actually handle it, spoke of the RigMaster with outright awe.

He could have easily sold the advanced technology to any of the big boys for a few million... or more. Sound Devices had been after him for years just to license it to them, but Bobby no longer needed money. He liked the fact that the RigMaster was his, and his alone.

Another reason for its exclusivity was that he had been in a number of serious conversations, with seriously beautiful women, who wondered why he was lounging on a chair, staring into his mobile, while they were shooting a scene. No mere royalty payment was worth giving up this surefire conversation starter.

During the audio run down, before they left the hotel that morning, he had attached small wireless receivers to each of the Twins cameras. Bobby had modified the Shure LensHopper mini shotguns so that they also received a wireless signal from the RigMaster.

The left audio channel on the DSLR was always fed timecode. It was generated by, and transmitted from, the RigMaster. Via a switch on the LensHopper base, the right channel could either record the ambient audio from the

LensHopper mic or a mix from any, or all, of the sixteen channels the RigMaster could receive and record.

Bobby was standing by the lift gate, powering up the RigMaster and routing the Sennheiser signal to record track one, while Dean stood next to him, watching the process.

"Can I run audio?" he asked, obviously excited.

"This is pretty complicated," replied Raston. "I should probably get this and let you drive the car."

"Hey, I'm not here as the driver," said Dean. "You gave us a rundown on the audio configurations last night and again this morning. This looks like a good time for me to start getting a feel for it."

Bobby was shaking his head, thinking that he had already set it up to monitor the audio through the RigMaster and he didn't have time to dig out a Bluetooth monitor for Dean. Then he looked up and saw the Twins were already a hundred yards down the road.

He had quickly weighed the options. He could run to catch up with the Twins, and arrive all out of breath and sweaty. That was definitely not a good look for him. Or he could give Dean the Senny and RigMaster and see how he does.

He had given Dean the mic and the RigMaster, and simply said, "That is worth more than you will make in your entire lifetime. Don't drop it."

Dean smiled at Bobby and said, "Me drop something? I still have my iPhone 5s from high school, and it's pristine!"

With that he turned and started loping after the girls in a gait that seemed somehow both leisurely and extremely quick.

Bobby turned to go back to the drivers' seat but then stopped, turned back to his go-case and unlocked a middle drawer. He pulled out one of six personally modified, Bluetooth earpiece devices. He then closed the drawer, pushed a button to close the tailgate, and walked back to the front of the Escalade. He waved an apology at the people behind him and climbed back into the driver's seat. He then moved up the two cars lengths that had cleared in the time it took to swing the crew into action. He could configure the Bluetooth devices while they were waiting in line.

Twelve minutes later the Escalade had almost gotten to Convention Center Boulevard when the crew had climbed back into the vehicle.

"Just amazing," continued Dean, looking at the audio rig in his hands. "The pickup and fidelity is incredible. It's, it's…"

"It's high tech with a vintage heart," finished Bobby, nodding with a self-satisfied smirk. "It's very organic."

"Yeah, yeah, yeah, I'm sure it's great," said a somewhat distracted Andy, looking at his phone to check who was calling. He tapped the button to send the call to voice mail. It was the third time that morning and he supposed he'd have to answer it eventually. He shrugged and then stuffed it into his pocket and asked, "So, what the hell was going on up there? We couldn't really hear it from here."

"I don't know," replied Brandy.

"Lots of people, holding lots of signs. It looked really great in an high compression shot, shooting down the line and racking the focus," said Mandy.

"The old guy was cool too. I got a wicked close-up when he was hugging the black kid," said Brandy.

"Maybe some kinda preacher?" finished Mandy.

"Well I could hear it perfectly," said Dean. "From what I could gather, the young guy with the papers arranged for all these people to protest against the Hitler car. And he found out about it from the old guy, but I'm not quite sure where he comes into the picture."

"Wow," said Andy, "this is already starting out great and the actual Hitler car auction isn't until tomorrow evening." Andy thought for a second and he said, "Ok, we've got some time before we even get to the parking lot."

Andy reached into his shirt pocket and pulled out a pair of eyeglasses with fashionably clunky frames and thick temple arms. As he put them on his face, he asked Bobby, "These things ready?"

"Of course," replied Bobby. "Remember that the side pickups aren't nearly as sensitive, or as detailed, as the front facing hyper-cardioids embedded in the temple arms."

"Yes, yes, I know," said Andy. "We all went over this stuff last night, multiple times." Andy wanted to add *instead of having Hurricanes* but thought better of it.

"My best audio will be directly facing the subject no further than one point five meters away." Andy continued, reciting Bobby's late night tutorial. "It will be less in a noisy environment. The side mics are mainly useful in half-meter distances, to monitor audio that is happening directly next to me. Perfect for eavesdropping in a relatively crowded environment and great for opening up the mix during post."

Andy turned to the back seat and said, "OK, you get out first and get into position. I'll get out and go talk to the paper-passing kid and see what I can find out."

"Looks like you're going to have to wait your turn," said Dean, nodding towards the scene outside the front windshield.

Andy turned and saw that not only was Mason being interviewed by one news crew, but another was waiting in line.

The cameraman on the third crew was shooting B-roll of the crowd, while an extremely attractive reporter was talking to the gate guard. A Sennheiser MD 46, complete with mic flag and butt-plug, was held down by her side. While she was obviously just getting information, it seemed to intrigue her.

She held up a hand to the guard, as if to say 'Wait just a moment,' and called for her cameraman.

Andy opened his mouth to speak, but Bobby beat him to it.

"Dean," said Raston in clipped commanding tones. "Give me the RigMaster and put this into your ear," he said, handing Dean the Bluetooth earpiece he had just finished configuring. "We want to know why a news crew wants to interview a gate guard."

The Twins were out of their respective doors almost before Bobby had finished speaking. Dean was close behind, inserting the earpiece and then silently mouthing the word, "Wow" as he, once again, gained *super hearing* from the mic feed.

As they hustled away, Andy took off the glasses and turned to Bobby and slowly said, "Regardless of our financial arrangement, this is still my gig, my crew, my decisions. I say what we do, and do not cover; as well as how and for how long."

Bobby just looked at him, knowing that Andy was right. There could, and should, only be one person in charge. That's just how it worked. Every gig needed a vision, and the stronger the vision the more chance the production had of turning out either really good or really bad. It was that middle ground that most productions inhabited, and why most shows sucked.

Bobby smiled and said, "Sure thing, Andy. You're absolutely right. You let me know if I'm stepping on your toes, and I'll be happy to back off."

Andy's mouth opened just a bit as the surprise caused his eyebrows to lower and put a quizzical look on his face.

Bobby smiled, thinking that's the kind of response that gets them every time.

Bobby held up the RigMaster and asked, "So do you want to hear what's going on?"

Andy cocked his head a bit and asked, "Can we?"

Bobby tapped on the huge screen in the middle of the Escalade's dashboard. He enabled the discovery mode, tapped in a device key, and suddenly they were surrounded by amazingly clear audio of the gate guard being interviewed as he checked credentials and directed the traffic.

"So the man responsible for all of this, for all of these people protesting the auction of the Hitler Car, had VIP parking?" Andy heard the reporter ask. "Parking you had been told was ONLY for consignment cars, auction officials, and what was described to you as *preferred guests*?"

"Huh," replied the gate guard, "actually it be called VIB parkin'. Dat stands fo Very Impotent *Bidder*."

Andy and Bobby looked at each other, quizzical smiles breaking out across their faces.

"The plot thickens," murmured Andy.

"Since I find it hard to believe a two-year-old Impala is going to be auctioned," the reporter continued. "Is it safe to assume that the elderly gentlemen, who was just speaking to this impressive crowd, either works for the auction or is one of the preferred guests," the reporter was slipping facts into the question with a practiced ease.

She continued the question with "Guests, whom we have recently discovered, have each posted a five million dollar bidder bond just to get into the actual Hitler Car auction tomorrow evening?"

The big gate guard stopped abruptly, stood straight and blinked a couple of times in surprise. He looked at the reporter, then into the camera, then back at the reporter, and started to speak.

"I's don't know nothin' 'bout any bidder bond," he said. "But I's don't think dat Brother Saul is going to be doing any bidding on de Devils limo."

"How do you know that?" asked the reporter. "Did he say that to you?"

"Nope," replied the big man. "He only sayed one thing. He sayed de Lord works in mysterious ways. And I's cain't talk to you no mo 'cause traffic is backin' up and I's gots a job to do."

The gate guard turned to take care of the next car in line. The Twins and Dean turned to look at the Escalade from their respective positions. Andy waved for them to return to the vehicle and said to Bobby, "Too bad we don't have walkie talkies."

Raston rolled his eyes at him and replied, "We've got better. I'll set up comms before we start shooting inside."

"Which reminds me," said Andy, "I'm going to need to, huh, obtain the extra passes before we can all get in."

Bobby pretended not to understand him, pausing just enough until the rear doors opened. Dean scrambled through to the rear seat as the Twins climbed in after him.

"Oh," said Bobby. "You need the money. Open the glove box."

Andy did and saw a thick envelope. He pulled it out and saw a thick stack of bills with a business card separating the main stack from a much thinner one. He held the open envelope up to Bobby with a questioning look on his face.

"The main stack is the ten grand. Take out the smaller stack and stick it in your pocket. That's another twenty eight hundred and fifty-five dollars," said Bobby. "Having been a *donor* in lots of different situations, I have found there are sometimes excellent buys on added benefits, providing you have the cash. But it's best if it seems that's the last of it. Hence the odd amount."

Andy nodded his head in appreciation, thinking that he was beginning to like his new business arrangement. He pocketed the money, smiled and said, "Ok, as soon as we park in the main lot, I'll hop on that little shuttle and go meet my man at the auction office. While I'm gone Dean can use these glasses and milk the ringleader kid for info once the TV stations have finished with him. Let's be ready to go as soon as I get back with the passes."

"Unless I'm able to mic the room, all I really need is right here," Bobby said, holding up the RigMaster. "But I'll bring a few stashable transmitters just in case I see an opportunity. We'll be ready to roll when you get back."

"And we're always mobile," said Brandy.

"Ask anyone," said Mandy.

"That's true," said Dean. He then put on the glasses and, with a big smile, asked the Twins, "How do I look?"

"Like a dork," teased Mandy.

"But a cute one," assured Brandy as she patted his shoulder.

They all laughed a bit, and then Andy said, "Look at us! Less than two hours on the job and we're already a team. Ok, it's our turn."

As the Escalade pulled up to the gate guard, and Andy leaned out the window to talk to him, Dean was looking around at the huge crowd of protesters and thinking about what the guard had said. "Mysterious ways," he whispered to himself. "Mysterious ways, indeed."

## CHAPTER 24
# Deal Or No Deal

*Friday – August 25 – 6:47 AM PDT*

> "He probably pitched us both on the show, and now he's giving it to them!"
> — J. ROGER WINTERS

"Hi, this is Andy from *It's All About The Car*. If you just want me to call you back, hang up. I always return missed calls. If you need to leave a message, here's the beep."

"Hey, Andy! Jack Calman here." Jack spoke into the phone with a cheerfulness he rarely felt while in the office this early. "Sorry about missing your call yesterday. My phone was off! Yes, MY phone. Go figure! Guess I should have wondered why I wasn't getting any calls!"

Jack did a halfhearted laugh, decided it sounded dumb, and continued in a more serious tone. "Look, I know you're busy, or you would have answered one of my other calls, but we're ready to get this deal done and get the money to you.

Like I said in my first message, we just have to modify it a bit. The suits came unglued at the deal I made and insist on a few changes. I think it's still a deal you can live with and the important thing is to get you the money. Call me back. Let's..."

The phone cut him off in mid-sentence, "If you'd like to send this message, just hang up. If you'd like to delete this message and recor..."

Jack tapped the end call icon and set his phone down onto his desk.

He had come in at six a.m., anticipating the frantic phone call, or calls, from Andy Guidry. He didn't like going back on the deal, but he did like his job... or, rather, he had liked it. And, regardless of recent change, he certainly still needed it.

Nina had left a beautifully handwritten note on his desk. Of course, all of her notes were beautifully handwritten.

"Mr. Guidry called, as you thought he would," Jack read in the efficient, yet beautifully cursive penmanship. Although the notepaper had only a simple 'From The Desk Of Nina Perez' across the top, each line was perfectly equidistant from the other, as if they were on ruled paper.

Jack continued reading, "He was concerned about the transfer of funds not being completed yesterday. He asked that you return his call, concerning this matter, at your earliest convenience."

"Yep, I'm sure he did," muttered Jack. What concerned him weren't all the phone calls, texts, and voice mail messages from yesterday. It was the absence of communications this morning. Jack had fully expected there would be at least four or five calls from this morning alone, but although he had six messages on his office phone, none were from Guidry.

Jack sat back and took the last cold sip from his fourth cup of coffee that morning. He resisted the urge to call Andy just one more time. It was getting close to nine a.m. in New Orleans, and the lack of communication would normally mean that Andy had either pulled the plug on the gig, which wasn't very likely for a number of reasons, or that he no longer needed Neiderland backing. That also seemed unlikely, but Andy was a good producer with a decent track record and one hell of a salesman.

Jack was going through likely scenarios. When the money hadn't arrived, Andy had done something, but what?

Suddenly an idea came to him, and it was an obvious one. Maybe he had pitched Redline and they had bit. There was going to be a serious *oh shit* moment with Winters if that's what happened.

As if on cue, his desk phone rang. Calman looked down and saw that it was precisely seven a.m. and the caller was J. Roger Winters.

"Double crap," muttered Jack as he snatched up the phone and said, "Yes, sir?"

"Are we all set on this *CarAlity* thing?" demanded Winters, continuing before he heard the answer. "Did we settle on the fifty/fifty or were you able to squeeze him down?"

"Actually," replied Jack, "I haven't been able to talk to him yet."

"WHAT?" shouted Winters. Jack heard a big expulsion of breath as Winters obviously tried to calm down. Winters continued in a lower tone, obviously trying not to sound too aggravated, "So, exactly why haven't you talked to him yet? Wasn't the plan to contact him early this morning, get him to sign over the rights, and send him the money to seal the deal?"

"Yes, sir," replied Jack, "that was the plan."

"OK," replied Winters, in a slow deliberate tone, enunciating each word carefully as if speaking to someone who wasn't entirely fluent with the language. "Then why, exactly, did we not follow the plan?"

"We did," replied Jack. "It was Guidry that didn't follow the plan."

"What the heck in beejeebers are you talking about?" asked Winters, still not shouting but at least 6dB higher in volume than a normal person.

"Guidry called multiple times yesterday," explained Jack, "mainly to my mobile, which I didn't answer. He also called and talked to Nina."

"Of course,' said Winters, condescendingly. "We knew that would happen when we pulled the rug out from under him. But what about this morning? Why haven't you called him?"

"I have called him," replied Jack, "multiple times. I've left messages, but no response. At least not yet."

"Hummm," mused Winters. He lived for this cat and mouse game of program negotiations. At least he did as long as he was the cat.

"For some reason, he really needed the money yesterday. But now, in less than eighteen hours, something has changed." Winters was more thinking out loud than actually discussing the situation with Jack.

"How about Redline? Do you think he could have pitched it to them in this short of... DAG NAB IT!" he screamed,

"That's it! He was playing us against each other. He probably pitched us both on the show, and now he's giving it to them!"

"I thought of that," replied Jack, "but it doesn't seem possible. Redline is a big corporation. I can't believe they could move as fast as we can, at least not in getting the money out there. I know for a fact there would have been a lot more paperwork before they could give up that kind of cash."

"Well, something has happened and I want to know what it is!" exclaimed Winters. "Is the money all set and ready to transfer?

"Yes, sir," replied Jack.

"Then keep calling him until he answers," instructed Winters, "and I mean that literally. Keep calling, OVER AND OVER AND OVER, until he ANSWERS!"

"Yes sir," replied Jack, sighing just a bit.

"If you don't hear from him by ten a.m., I expect you to be on a plane to New Orleans," said Winters. "If you do hear from him, impress upon him that WE HAD A DEAL. This is not a DEAL OR NO DEAL conversation! Remind him that we have the first right of refusal and we expect him to keep his part of the bargain."

"But we are changing the deal," said Jack. "If we change the terms, he can just refuse and go with… go with whatever."

"Does he know we're changing the deal?" demanded Winters. "Is that why he's not responding?"

"I don't think so," replied Jack, "I've only left messages. I may have mentioned a few *changes* in one message, but nothing specific."

"Then this doesn't make sense," said Winters. "But whatever it is, I don't like it. Keep calling and keep me in the loop. And get on a plane if you can't get ahold of him," said Winters. "Oh, and call the Twins or that kid you told me about. Maybe they know why Guidry isn't answering."

"That's a good idea," replied Jack, and it was. He wondered why he hadn't thought of it and then chalked it up to too many late nights and early mornings.

"YES, IT IS," said Winters, "And, of course, I'M the only one who can come up with them. Here's another one. Have you texted him yet?"

"Actually sir, I was…" the click of the phone hanging up cut Jack short. He sat for a moment, and then looked out his office window at Nina, who had arrived at precisely six-thirty. How she knew when he came in early, he'd never quite figured out, but he'd never complained about it. Nina made almost as much in overtime as in regular hours, but Calman never complained about that either.

"Nina," he called out, "check on the earliest flights out of LAX to New Orleans."

"Yes, sir," she replied, looking at her computer screen where the available flights were displayed in the Orbitz window. "There are two non-stops this morning. The first is at nine ten, which would be cutting it close. The next one is at eleven fifty-five."

Jack didn't even wonder how she had that information at her fingertips. He had gotten used to her efficiency and come to just accept its almost supernatural qualities. He looked at the pile of papers on his desk, and then at the calendar on his screen.

"Thanks," he replied. "Book me on the eleven fifty-five. Can you get me the number for that kid, the field producer you told me to recommend to Guidry? The one that was working with the Twins in Florida."

"His name is Dean Preston," she reminded him. "I'll send the number to your phone so you'll have it."

Before she had finished her sentence, his phone played the cash register sound he had programmed for incoming emails. It was from Nina and had a vCard attached. He clicked on the card and it added Dean's address, phone number, and a brief bio into his Contacts folder.

Jack paused, smiled, and wondered just how even more horrible his life would be without her.

He sighed and decided he'd shoot Guidry a quick text before he called the kid, but only because he wanted to be able to say he'd done so if Winters asked him. Calman didn't believe in texting when the situation needed good old-fashioned conversation. And if ever there were a situation that needed live negotiation, this was it.

# CHAPTER 25
# VIB

*Friday – August 25 – 9:36 AM CDT*

> "Andy, this is Sandra Melancon,
> a reporter for the local FOX
> affiliate, WFNO Channel 15."
> — Pat McMillian

"That is a most adequate job of displaying her," announced Heinrich Heinzburg, as he strolled around the short platform that supported the Tourenwagen. "Most adequate." His shirt was stark white, starched into crisp angles with a glossy surface and open at the collar. Everything else was black, from the highly polished dress boots, to the tailored slacks, to an expensive looking lightweight jacket with subdued tactical styling cues.

Pat McMillian was looking at Heinzburg's ramrod posture and the way he walked. He literally strutted around the car with his hands clasped behind his back. McMillian was wondering if the militaristic mannerisms were genuine or some sort of elaborate ruse; mere window dressing to support the selling of the car. For the hundredth time since he'd seen the video, he wondered if this wild story could actually be true. And for the hundredth time he told himself that it didn't really matter. It was going to make a lot of money for everyone concerned, and he was very concerned.

McMillian was dressed in a grey, pressed-cotton suit, accented with a heavy silk, navy blue tie. His French cuffs sported thick gold cufflinks in the shape of classic car steering wheels. He had a small collection of these and today he was wearing '64 GTOs.

"I'm glad you approve," said Pat. "It is a very important automobile and deserves to be presented as such."

The rest of the auction cars were parked in the huge expanse of concrete just south of the Mardi Gras World River City Complex. There were roughly two hundred and fifty cars parked in nice orderly rows, with a little more room between them than normal. It was mainly an assortment of restored and custom muscle, with a small scattering of decent quality European and British sporting machines. Basically, it was a gearhead's wet dream. There was also a smaller parking area to the side of the show cars; reserved for executive staff and the VIB cars.

The more valuable auction cars were displayed under an industrial quality, semi-permanent awning. The awning ran along the side of the building and was erected relatively close to it. This was to allow maximum utilization of the expansive concrete pad between the River City Complex and the high tensile wire fence. The nautical style fence was the only thing that separated the massive, embossed concrete pad from the mighty Mississippi river. The view was made even more spectacular, especially to car people, by the sight of the two massive bridges suspended over the river. Their arc was almost as flat as the river and the land that held it at bay.

The 1940 Mercedes 770k W150 Grosser Tourenwagen was situated in the place of honor, all by itself under a smaller version of the large awning. The car was dead center to allow for plenty of walking room around the entire car. The short platform was protected by a ring of barrier stands, connected together by their webbing on which were printed, "Do Not Enter." There were also "Do Not Touch" signs at all four corners. To further emphasize the seriousness of the request, two large, uniformed policemen were stationed at the front and the rear of the car. They were smiling, nodding, exchanging pleasantries, but noticeably keeping their eyes on the twenty or so people who were looking at the car, and stealing glances at Heinrich as he strutted through his inspection.

This awning placement held the pole position in the auction hierarchy. Situated directly south of the main entrance on the river front side, the huge black convertible was displayed at a forty-five degree angle to the building. Everyone going in and out of that entrance was exposed to every angle of the impressive vehicle. And it was certainly impressive.

Even though it wasn't polished to a mirror gleam, like the restored and custom cars waiting their turn on the block, it was certainly presentable. There was some surface rust on the bright work, but it didn't look too pitted. The paint and convertible top were covered in a gossamer layer of talcum-like dust, which a persistent breeze off the river was trying remove with some measure of success.

The front and rear doors were hinged in the middle so that the front doors open "suicide" style while the back opened in the more normal configuration. The front passenger door and rear driver's side door were both open to show off the nearly perfect interior.

The car was supported by six jack stands. There was one on each corner and in the middle of the long frame on each side. The tires, with severely cracked and hardened rubber, just barely touched the platform, and were actually filled with air. Although whether they would hold the weight of the massive car seemed rather doubtful.

At each of the riverside awning posts was a large tripod easel, secured by bungee cords to heavy sandbags between their legs. They each displayed identical signs mounted onto thick foamcore.

"Der Führer's Automobil" was blazoned across the top of the sign. Underneath the title was a large photo of The Eagle's Nest chalet. Next to the photo, in a bold sans serif font, formatted as if from a newspaper article, was a brief description of the setting.

> **The Kehisteninhaus, or the Eagle's Nest, was a gift to Adolph Hitler to celebrate his 50th birthday. It is believed that this automobile was part of that gift, and was to be dedicated to Hitler's private use during his stays at the Eagle's Nest.**
>
> **However, due to a variety of circumstances, Herr Hitler rarely utilized this magnificent residence; some historians say he visited it fewer than 10 times.**

Under the photo of the Eagle's Nest was another taken from the front entrance of the Berghof. Neville Chamberlain is climbing the steps to meet with Adolph Hitler. Next to this photo was more identically formatted text.

> **Since it was Herr Hitler's preference to receive diplomats and dignitaries at his private residence, it is believed that this vehicle was subsequently transferred to the Berghof compound in the early months of 1941. In addition to Herr Hitler's transportation needs throughout the compound, its primary duty was to pick up and deliver distinguished visitors to Herr Hitler's home.**
>
> **Due to its relatively small operational area, the use of this car was extremely limited, but there is ample photo and cinemagraphic documentation of his use of this car during his visits.**

A row of large detail shots of the car, both exterior and interior, filled the middle of the poster with more text underneath them.

> **For these reasons, this car is believed to be the lowest mileage example of a 1940 Mercedes 770k W150 Grosser Tourenwagen known to exist, with less than 1,800 kilometers recorded on the odometer.**
>
> **This car will be presented to interested bidders as the closing auction item at approximately 5:30 p.m., Saturday. At that time, additional**

**provenance supporting this cars authenticity will be revealed to prospective bidders.**

**Auction Estimate:
$3,750,000.00 to $6,000,000.00**

As Heinrich walked over to Pat he slid the large, ornate vaping device out of the black leather holster clipped to his belt. He hit a button on the side of the device and drew deeply on the thick chrome mouthpiece. He exhaled a relatively small cloud of vapor and looked at the device with a mixture of puzzlement and displeasure. He studied the LCD readout, rapidly pressed some buttons on the side of the device and took another deep drag. This time the cloud was bigger, and more dense, but Heinrich still shook his head as he again studied the device.

"Problems?" asked Pat.

"It is nothing serious," replied Heinrich, "I need to rebuild the atomizer. I shall visit one of your vaping establishments this evening. Do you have a recommendation?"

"Unfortunately, I don't, huh, indulge in vaping, but I see it around a lot," replied Pat, "I'm sure there are some *establishments* within a few blocks of your hotel. Just ask the concierge."

"Danke," replied Heinrich, still making adjustments. He held the button down and took a mighty hit from the device. Thick, white fog streamed from Heinrich's upturned mouth and danced across the car, as well as across the few dozen people now crowding around it. A few of the men who had been enveloped in the fog turned and shot Heinrich a few menacing looks.

"Looks like it's working fine now," said Pat. He noticed the looks but didn't figure on any Cajun/Kaiser clashes, at least not as long as he had the off-duty policemen on his payroll and they knew who was signing the paycheck.

"Did you happen to, huh, to notice the demonstrators outside the grounds?" Pat asked Heinrich.

"Ja, I did," replied Heinrich, slipping his vape mod back into its holster and looking at Pat. He continued with a small sardonic grin on his face. "It was interesting. Were you responsible?"

"No," Pat quickly replied, "of course not." Pat looked at Heinrich trying to decide if he looked pissed off or merely amused. "I don't know who rallied them, but it's not like the auction is a secret. I guess we have to expect some, huh, some interest."

"It is good," replied Heinrich, "it adds validity."

"Yeah," replied Pat. "I supposed that's one way to look at it."

Pat then noticed Sandra Melancon, a petite, fortyish TV reporter with a small waist, pert breasts, and a delicate café au lait complexion framed by a mane of auburn hair. She was walking towards them, mic in hand. Her camera operator was carrying a big broadcast video camera on a heavy tripod. He had to struggle a bit to keep up. They had obviously left their van at the Race and Henderson exit and walked there. He made a mental note to talk to the auction gate guard before this turned into a media circus.

"Or, maybe not," he thought as he saw Heinzburg's reaction to the reporter.

"I see we are attracting some interest," he said, his fingers caressing the leather holster, but not removing the vaping mod. "That is good, as long as it supports our efforts."

"Then you don't mind if we let the media in today?" asked Pat.

"Not if it is within reason," replied Heinrich. "I will leave that to your discretion. As long as there are no media in the room tomorrow, I can see nothing but good from as much advance publicity as we can garner."

"An enlightened viewpoint," replied Pat. "Let me introduce you to the reporter, I'm sure you'll agree she can be very easy on the eyes."

"Quite easy," replied Heinrich, "but I have somewhat of an aversion to the media." He smiled at Pat and continued, "An aversion I would wager you don't share? Anyway, I am satisfied with the security and the rest of the day doesn't interest me." Heinrich's fingers were impatiently tapping on the leather holster. "I believe I shall go to my hotel room and make preparations for tomorrow."

Sandra Melancon walked up to them, said "Good morning, Pat," and then firmly shook McMillian's hand. That out of the way, she turned to the tall, handsome young man standing next to him. It didn't take much reporter's intuition to know that this was the owner of the *Der Führer's Automobil.*

"Hello," she said, holding out her hand to Heinrich, "I'm Sandra Melancon, from FOX 15."

Heinrich clicked his heels, took her hand, and slowly turned and lifted it. His back was ramrod straight as he leaned down and softly brushed his lips against it. As he released her hand, he looked into her eyes with a mischievous grin and replied, "And I, unfortunately, am late for an appointment. If you would please excuse me." He dropped her hand and walked briskly towards the auction hall entrance.

Sandra turned to Pat and asked, "And that would be the owner of the Hitler Car?"

"Well," replied Pat, "I'm not exactly at liberty to say, at least not at this time. But I can answer any questions you might have about the actual car."

Sandra gave a sigh, turned to her camera op and asked, "Joey, where do you want him?"

"In the shade of the awning, so the light is the same as on the car," replied Joey Banks, a veteran news camera operator. Banks had been in the business a long time. He was young enough to have missed the old Bell & Howell Filmo days… but not by much.

Five minutes later, Sandra called out "Cut," shook Pat's hand, and suggested they might need to go out for drinks again someday soon. Especially if there were a reason to celebrate, such as her getting an exclusive interview with the mysterious Hitler Car owner.

While Pat was pretending to be contemplating some way to make that happen, he saw Andy Guidry burst out of the doors. He abruptly stopped when he saw the car. After a few seconds of staring, he shook his head a bit and started scanning the crowd. He then saw Pat and started over towards him.

As Andy walked up to them, Pat smiled and said, "Sandra, may I present Andy Guidry. He's an old associate of mine who happens to be in sort of the same business as you. Andy, this is Sandra Melancon, a reporter for the local FOX affiliate, WFNO Channel 15."

"Pleased to meet you Mr. Guidry," said Sandra, shaking Andy's hand. "What part of this business are you in?"

"I used to be the senior producer for *Bid Battle*, but now I produce a cable TV show on classic car restoration," replied Andy, a bit too quickly. "It's called *It's All About The Car*."

"What network?" asked Sandra.

"It's on," Andy paused, "Well, it's on hiatus for now, but we were on Redline."

"And if your show is on hiatus, what brings you to the Big Easy and this auction?" asked Sandra, her reporter instincts tingling just a bit. "Anything to do with *Bid Battle*?"

"Actually," Pat jumped in, answering for Andy, "he's selling a car at the auction. He has consigned a beautiful '68 911T Targa that will be sold tomorrow just before the noon break."

"Soft window or glass?" asked Sandra.

Andy paused for a minute, took a second look at the attractive reporter, and answered, "Soft window, but the plastic is pristine. I live in San Diego, so it was almost always down. Are you a Porsche fan?"

"Well, I'm a car fan in general," she replied. "That's why the auctions are my beat, but I have a little Porsche myself, a 914/6."

"Nice," replied Andy, "what year?"

"It's a '72, but it's not exactly stock," Sandra replied. "It's set up for autocross."

"I've always liked those..." Andy stopped midsentence as his phone made a buzzing sound in his pocket. He held up a finger, pulled it out and saw it was from Calman. In addition to the six missed calls, and two voice mails, Calman was now texting him... and had done so twice in the last half-hour.

"Need to talk. Ready to wire money. Please call ASAP!" read Andy. The text message was displayed on the front of his iPhone so he swiped the screen to make it go away.

"It was a pleasure meeting you," Andy said to Sandra, "but I'm kinda on a mission here."

He turned to Pat and said, "We've got some business to attend to, and time is flying by. Let's get this done."

Pat nodded and turned to Sandra and said, "Please excuse me, and I *will* work on that interview request for you." He then turned to Andy and said, "Let's go to the office. I have the documents you requested. I assume that your, huh, that your *paperwork* is in order."

"Of course," said Andy. He turned to Sandra and said, "I'd love to talk Porsche with you sometime. Perhaps you'll be here tomorrow?"

"If it's still news, I'll still be here," she replied. As the two men turned to leave, Sandra glanced over at Joey, who was shooting B-roll of the big, black Mercedes. She strolled over to check it out.

"Now that's a car," she said admiringly, and started scanning the crowd to see if she could spot anybody that looked like they belonged in the social strata that could bid on it.

On the other side of the car was the old guy who had been rallying the crowd. He was with a short, kinky-haired kid who was paying far more attention to her than the car, but not in the way she was used to. The kid was looking at her in more apprehension than appreciation.

Then she remembered her conversation with the River Complex gate guard. He had told her that all of the high roller bidders would have a small VIB sticker on their credentials badge, indicating the wearer was a Very Important Bidder. She smiled when she saw that both the old guy and the kid had that sticker on their badges.

The smell of a story made her nostrils flare as she walked over to introduce herself.

# CHAPTER 26
# Time To Go To Work

*Friday – August 25 – 10:12 AM CDT*

> "Nice as they may be, you won't find some Restomod GTO Judge parked next to a pre-war Bugatti T-57."
> — ANTOINE GUIDRY

"OK," gasped Andy as he climbed into the driver's seat of the Escalade. He had run over from the shuttle stop. He was thinking he really needed to start going to the gym more often, and to do more cardio when he did.

Bobby was sitting in the passenger seat with the RigMaster in his lap. The Twins were seated in the middle row bucket seats, their video rigs at their sides. Dean was in the third row bench seat.

"I've got the badges." Andy handed out three Bidder badges to Bobby, Mandy, and Brandy. Each had their names on them but with identical bidder numbers. "These are all tied to my bidder account, so no buying any cars."

Bobby looked at him with a raised eyebrow, and Andy quickly added, "Well, no buying any cars that you don't want to pay for." Turning his attention to the Twins he continued, "Don't even bid for the fun of it, because that can get real expensive, real fast. I know."

Andy then held out a roll of cash. "And you were right, here's two grand. For only eight hundred and eighty five dollars, which was" Andy made quotations marks with his fingers and continued, "'all the money I had,' I was able to get an *A-Bear A/V Crew* badge for Dean. If anyone asks, he's a new hire who needs some field experience. No one will think twice about him poking around backstage and such."

"Nice," said Bobby, "but keep the cash until this is over. Cash is like grease when things get sticky. We'll bill what you use against the cost of production."

"Let's split it," said Andy, as he started to count the hundreds. "You're going to be on the front lines and you might need some grease as well."

Bobby looked at him and smiled, "Keep it all, I've got plenty."

Andy stopped counting, looked at the cash, nodded a bit, and then looked at Bobby.

"So far this whole partner thing doesn't suck nearly as much as I thought it would," he said with a smile and then stuffed the money back into his pocket.

"There are ups and downs in everything," replied Bobby. "So let's go over the work flow one more time, just so we're all clear. And how does it change now that Dean has access?"

"That's a good question," replied Andy. "But I'm not sure it changes that much, at least not today. I got the badge because I thought it would come in handy for tomorrow when Dean was going to use my badge and I'd stay out here to monitor the audio. You never know when whoever's in the car might need access to the auction."

Andy paused, trying to sort things out in his mind. The vape hit he took on the way back wasn't helping in that regard. "Anyway, so today we stick with the original plan. I'll do the *interviews* with the folks outside, by the car. You'll run audio on that snazzy gadget of yours while the Twins shoot. Dean will stay in the car and monitor the audio so he gets a good handle on the types of questions, and the style I want, for tomorrow… when the big fish arrive."

"That's when I take over the interviews, because most of the really high rollers will already know you," replied an enthusiastic Dean.

"Yes, correct," replied Andy. "Now the badges I got for you guys," continued Andy, directing the statement at Bobby and the Twins, "have those little VIB stickers on them. Those will let us park at the facility, in a little area next to the auction vehicles. I got McMillian to give us those in case the RF doesn't travel as far as Bobby thinks it will."

Bobby sat up a little straighter and slowly said, "If I say you'll be able to monitor outdoor audio from here, then you'll be able too."

"And I believe you, but it never hurts to have a back-up, just in case," replied Andy. "Besides, if we did park that close, especially tomorrow, then the audio from inside the auction house could be monitored."

"I didn't say that," said Bobby. "I said the signal would be 'monitor quality' at up to one hundred yards, in the open. I haven't been in the building, so I don't know how much signal, if any, will punch through."

"Exactly," replied Andy, "So now we have the option to park in the closer lot if we need to."

Bobby nodded and said, "Ok, closer is always better. Why not just park there now?"

"For today at least," said Andy "I don't want to call attention to the car by having someone camping out in it. If the audio carries this far…"

"It'll carry." Bobby interrupted him.

"Then we'll stay here," said Andy. "I've got something in mind for tomorrow."

Andy looked at his watch. It was a mid-seventies Rolex DateJust with a Jubilee band and Thunderbird bezel. It was something else he was on the verge of selling; at least he had been before last night. Andy shook his head at the time and continued, "Anyway, I'll do the interviewing today. We won't worry about releases unless there's something really great. The entire area is posted with signs warning people that video recording is in progress." Andy was speaking from experience now; three years working for *Bid Battle* meant he had nearly fifty shows under his belt in almost identical settings.

Andy continued, "Most people think it's for the security cameras, but they mainly put them up for blanket clearance of the crowd shots during the auction. For the most part, that will hold up for our purposes."

"I've always wondered about that," said Dean. "Couldn't someone just claim they didn't see the sign?"

"It's also in the seller/bidder agreement they signed," replied Andy. "But I like that you're thinking about that stuff. Anyway, because we're not the news, if something is really great, we'll want rock-solid releases just in case. Did you download that release app I told you to get?"

"Yup," replied Dean.

"Good, and everyone else?" asked Andy.

The Twins looked up from making minute adjustments to their 5Ds, shrugged and nodded. They didn't do releases, but they also didn't argue unless it was worth it.

Bobby replied, "I didn't mention it last night, but I was an early investor in *Release It*. It was already on my device."

Andy took a deep breath and opened his mouth, as if to speak, and then just shook his head and smiled. He let out the breath, took a more normal one and spoke, "Anyway, today is more of a practice run for the big day tomorrow. A few of the big bidders might come in today, but the guys that can buy the Hitler car won't be very interested in the rest of these cars. Nice as they may be, you won't find some Restomod GTO Judge parked next to a pre-war Bugatti T-57."

Andy stopped, smiled and continued with, "Remind me to tell you about a show I once worked on that had a customized Duesenberg get a little ding in the…"

Bobby cut him short, "I'm sure we've all heard about the *Doozy of a Ding*; let's get to work. Basically today is a B-roll and practice day. We find the angles, dial in the freq's, set levels, maybe even ID some potential bit players." Bobby stopped and smiled, as though he couldn't help himself. "And, of course, get into character."

Andy was a little perturbed at Bobby jumping in on his pre-pro meeting, but then he smiled as well. "Tell me this *undercover production* isn't going to be fun?"

The Twins looked up with big smiles on their faces.

"It is going to be a challenge," said Mandy. "And we…"

Brandy stepped into the pause and finished "We LOVE a challenge!"

Dean spoke up from the back, "Yes indeed, it's going to be quite a challenge, shooting a two-camera interview without the subject knowing he's being interviewed, or shot!"

"Not that," said Brandy. "The real challenge is…"

At that both Mandy and Brandy reached towards the front passenger seat. Mandy, seated behind the Bobby, snaked her arm between the window and the seat. Brandy, seated behind Andy, reaching in from between the front seats. As their fingers lightly caressed Bobby's ears he immediately stiffened. It was as if their fingertips carried an electrical charge.

With their fingertips dancing their way from his ears to his neck, and down to his shoulders, they spoke together in low, harmonic, sultry voices, "The real challenge is being Bobby's bit-ches."

The car went silent for just a second. Andy immediately opened his mouth, but couldn't think of something to say.

Then the Twins started laughing, which ignited the car. As the peels of laughter died down, Bobby's eyebrows were still raised in that look of adrenalin-fueled surprise; the position they had assumed when the Twins first touched him. It truly was a moment that would be indelibly burned into his memory.

"Hard as that may be," said Andy, still chuckling a bit. "We must soldier on." Andy held out his hand to Dean, who looked at him with a puzzled expression.

"The glasses," explained Andy.

"Oh," said Dean, "You can forget you have them on."

He handed them over to Andy, who put them on, smiled ruefully and replied, "I can only hope."

"Ok," said Bobby, "Pop the hatch and I'll get the comms. For myself and the Twins, we'll use my iPod comms with earbuds. Andy, I assume, would rather use the earpiece. We'll switch it to push-to-talk, but you'll only need to do so to communicate with Dean or the Twins. I'll be hearing you through the glasses' mics as I monitor the feed.

"And there's no way we're going to run out of storage on the cameras or that, huh," Andy paused trying to remember the name.

"RigMaster," Dean chimed in. "It's a RigMaster."

"Yeah," said Andy, "The RigMaster. There's no way you'll run out of storage on that thing? You're running four tracks just from the glasses."

Bobby just shook his head, smiled, and started to lecture, "First of all, even though we're recording at 24 bit, 96kHz, audio takes far less storage space than video, which I could also record, but perhaps not continuously as I tend to do with audio. Secondly, it records to micro SD cards, and I use sixty-four gigabyte, Samsung UHS-1 Class 10 cards. Even at that relatively high audio sample rate, I use just over one gigabyte per hour, per track; one point oh three six eight to be exact. Running four channels is roughly four gigs per hour which, rounding down for safety and taking into account that I don't like to fill cards to capacity, means we can easily record fifteen hours... continuously. Even if I were recording on all sixteen available channels, I could record at least three point five hours. And that's recording continuously, and on one card. I have six cards with me, so I'm pretty sure I will not *run out of storage*."

Andy just smiled, not wanting to even comment on Bobby's little lesson, and simply asked, "Mandy, Brandy?"

The Twins looked into the pockets on the front of the cute little denim vests they had worn in lieu of their normal Domke shooter vests.

"We're set," Brandy said simply.

They used SanDisk Extreme Pro, 128GB CFast cards. The media was roughly the size of a small matchbook, and not a whole lot thicker, and the little card wallets they each carried each held six cards. At their normal shooting rate of 29.97 fps, in the ALL-I intraframe compression, they got well over two hours of video per card.

"We've got plenty," echoed Mandy.

"Batteries?" asked Andy. The Twins just rolled their eyes.

"How about lenses?" Andy continued.

Brandy patted her camera lens like it was an old friend and replied, "28 to 300, f three five to five six."

Mandy continued with, "Image stabilized with ultrasonic focus motors."

Brandy finished with, "We're set."

"OK, then. There's the shuttle. I'll sit in front, you guys sit in back. We'll do a quick mic, err, glasses and comm check on the ride. Dean, call my cell if reception goes to shit." Andy then held up his hand at Bobby, as the audio man opened his mouth to speak.

"I know, I know, nothing will go wrong. Look, it's nothing personal. It's just my job to be prepared for the stuff that won't go wrong. Now let's do this."

As the four reached down to open their doors, Dean spoke up from the back, "This is so great! It's like being a secret agent, without having to worry about being shot."

All four stopped, with their hands still on the door handles.

"Yeah…" said Andy.

"Let's hope…" said Bobby.

"What do you mean?" asked Dean.

The Twins just looked at each other, shrugged and opened their doors.

It was time to go to work.

# CHAPTER 27
# It's Never Too Late

*Friday – August 25 – 10:14 AM CDT*

> "She lives for stuff like this."
> — Herman Adler

"That was a bad idea," said Herman Adler. "That was a REALLY bad idea."

"Son, victory doesn't favor the timid," replied Saul Wittmann. "If we want to discourage people from bidding on this car, so we can bring it to its rightful home, then we need to spread that point of view any way we can."

Herman had dragged him from the shade of the Tourenwagen awning as soon as the interview was over. He pulled him over to a deserted spot along the building, between the Tourenwagen and the larger awning that shaded the other featured cars. Saul Wittmann was watching the reporter.

Melancon was looking around, gauging the time/value ratio of interviewing anyone else. He saw her look at him and then mention something to the old camera guy. He picked up his camera and they turned to go into the auction hall. After a couple of steps, she turned back to Saul, gave him a small wave and a dazzling smile, and then continued into the building.

"That's an attractive woman," said Wittmann, "real attractive."

"Yeah," agreed Herman, "It goes with the job. Look, it's one thing having an army of religious idiots packing the road. They don't know who you really are, and don't really care. They live for opportunities to picket in the name of Jesus. But she is a TV reporter. She lives for stuff like this. Did it ever even cross your mind that she's probably googling you right now?"

"So?" replied Wittmann, a bit offset by Herman's tone. It wasn't like the boy to be so disrespectful. "So, she'll find out I'm a farmer and business man from Wisconsin."

"Yeah, a farmer and business man from Wisconsin that had the money to put five million dollars into a bidder escrow account just to get into a car auction. And did so just so he could come to preach, literally PREACH against people wanting to buy the very car he paid that much money to be able to bid on. You shouldn't have let the camera guy shoot your badge, and we shouldn't have these stupid VIB stickers on them."

"So I'm a successful farmer and business man, so I do want to put down five million dollars as a deposit, a deposit I'll get back, just to be able to come down here and persuade people against buying that car," explained Wittmann. "That just makes for a better story. Better stories get wider publicity.

Wider publicity means more people to protest and keep the price down. I still don't see a downside to this."

"What about more publicity means more people who might want to bid on the car?" asked a sarcastic Herman, nodding his head like he'd just announced *checkmate*.

"Anyone who would, and could bid on this car, already knows about it. While you were snoozing on the plane, I was doing my research. There's just not that many people who would buy a car like this, and the ones that can… well, that's one of the things they live for and they already know about it."

Wittmann paused for a bit and nodded his head a bit before continuing. "Local TV coverage will only expose the auction to more of those fine folks outside the gate, whom you referred to as religious idiots. And speaking of which, I expect never to hear that term again."

"And what," said Herman, with the air of a player laying down the winning hand after matching the last reckless raise, "if in their background check of the mysterious, well-landed country gentlemen — a hitherto unknown born-again preacher — what if they discover you are also the sole owner and curator of the HEIL?"

"The HEIL is not even open," replied Wittmann in a much more subdued tone, realizing that might indeed pose a problem.

"And you think that just because you have a tarp over the sign that people don't know what you've been doing out there? Just the sheer number of deliveries to the HEIL would keep everyone in town talking, if it wasn't such old news," Herman paused, thinking that was done is done, and what will be will be.

At this point Herman figured there really was no sense in pointing out that half the county knew that *crazy old Wittmann* was building a Nazi shrine out in the farmland. Folks in rural Wisconsin were, by a massive majority, white Anglo-Saxon Protestants who tended to mind their own business.

Now if a big-time reporter showed up in a news van, asking some questions and promising to put them on TV? Well, that might pose a problem, but it would also take a fair bit of initiative. Hopefully, the reporter they just talked too was more fluff than fire.

"Well, let's not worry about that now," said Herman. "They'd have to move pretty fast, and even though it's FOX, it's local FOX. But if we do get the car..."

"You mean WHEN we get the car," interrupted Saul, glancing over at the Tourenwagen. The crowd around it was getting heavier as more bidders, sellers and guests had started to arrive and flock to the car that was creating such a ruckus.

"OK, WHEN we get the car they will be doing some serious follow-up. It's my name on the badge, but it won't take long to figure out that I'm your registered guest."

"Co-bidder," corrected Saul, "You needed to have the authorization to bid against the escrow deposit"

"OK, co-bidder, whatever, anyway," replied Herman. "When they find out that the winner of the auction was the co-bidder of the guy that came down to tell anyone who would listen what a sin — and I do believe I heard you refer to bidding as an actual *SIN* — what a sin it is to even bid on this car, well then there is going to be some in-depth investigative reporting."

"And what a story it's going to make," agreed Wittmann. "The publicity will be priceless," he said as he broke into a huge grin that showed off his yellowed, but sturdy looking teeth. "Literally priceless. The HEIL will become world famous in the blink of an eye."

Saul Wittmann looked away from the car and looked at Herman. His gaze was steady, as was his voice when he spoke, "We are doing nothing illegal, either here or with the HEIL. This is America and we have every right to do business. We can advertise and otherwise seek to influence public opinion. As long as we don't outright lie to people, then there is nothing illegal about this."

Saul paused and took a deep breath, and nodded his head with conviction. He looked back at the Tourenwagen, the upper half of the car peeking out over the heads of the crowd around it. He continued speaking, but it was more to himself than to Herman, "The Tourenwagen belongs in the HEIL. Whatever we must do to make that happen, we simply must do."

Herman looked at Saul. The old man was in obvious car lust and was staring hungrily at the old Mercedes. He then looked over to the massive ribbon of water as a snippet of song from the oldies station popped into his mind, something about a *bad moon arising* with *trouble on the way*.

He was trying to remember the band's name when Saul announced, "All right then, enough of this yakking. Let's go get the signs out of the car and start passing them out."

Herman put a concerned look on his face, "I'm thinking that if I'm going to be the surprise bidder, maybe I shouldn't be seen handing out Hitler Car signs."

Saul smiled and said, "What better way for you to be a surprise bidder, than as someone who was handing out signs to discourage the bidding. And anyway, it's too late to change the course. We've got to follow the path as it presents itself." Saul stopped and took another look at the massive automobile. He took a big breath and let it out with a sigh.

"It's just like if you fell into that river," continued Saul, turning to Herman and nodding at the massive Mississippi, "Once you're in it, you can't swim against it. You've just got to go with the flow. And we are in it, and in deep."

Herman just nodded his head and looked over at the great blue-brown ribbon of water that silently flowed with unimaginable volume and irresistible power. He then turned and started walking towards the car to help pass out the signs.

"I really should have learned to swim," he thought. "Too bad it's just a little too late."

# CHAPTER 28
# Day Two

*Friday – August 25 – 3:56 PM CDT*

> "I gotta be there when my
> Goat crosses the block."
> — GRADY PEERMAN

"Yeah, it's a nice car and all, but it's got no bidness at this auction," said Grady Peerman. He then looked down at the ground like he was looking for a place to spit. Like most car people, he was more than willing to give his opinion on anything automotive.

Just a minute before, Andy had seen the semi-scowl on the weatherworn face of the man as he walked up to the Tourenwagen. Once the auction had started, the crowds around the big Mercedes had thinned quite a bit, with the majority of the people inside where the bidding action was taking place.

He had held up his auction catalog to cover his mouth, and alerted both Bobby and the Twins with a quick "We've got one. Roll cameras, roll sound."

The small Bluetooth receiver in his left ear almost immediately came back with "Speed" from Bobby and "Rolling" from the Twins. As he had walked over to the guy he took a quick glance around and saw that one of the Twins was standing next to Bobby at the front of the car, on the building side, where she could shoot Andy and his next "subject" through the empty area created by the barricade webbing. The other Twin had moved around to the same position, but at the rear of the car so she could get the reverse angle.

The Manfrotto monopods attached to their cameras had small, stabilizing legs that could be deployed with a twist and a tug on the bottom. Once in place, the monopod was actually able to stand on its own. Although not nearly as sturdy as a real tripod, they were certainly sturdy enough for their purposes. Both of the Twins had their monopods in that configuration so they could position the camera, and record video, without seeming to be actually operating them. A light hand on the shaft allowed the twins to pan or tilt just enough to keep the framing decent.

Indeed, they both seemed to be preoccupied with conversations. A casual glance would never give an indication that they were recording an interview some thirty feet distant. The Twin next to Bobby was talking to him and Andy could see that he was thoroughly enjoying the attention, yet still occasionally glancing down at the RigMaster he held in his hand.

The Twin at the rear of the car was being chatted up by one of the off-duty policeman guarding the car. He was close enough to have been able to see she was recording, if he could have torn his eyes from her to glance at the LCD screen on the back of the camera. There wasn't much chance of that happening.

"What makes you say this car's got no business being at this auction Mr., uh…" Andy peering down at the man's bidder badge and continuing with, "Mr. Peerman?"

"Well, I'll tell ya," replied Peerman. "I've been doing car auctions for over forty years. I've seen them go from just a way to buy used cars that the dealers didn't want on their lots to what 'cha see today. The days are gone where you'd find a five bills Vee Dub next to a five large LTD next to a fifteen k Porsche. Auctions have become specialized. An A-Bear auction is all 'bout vintage muscle, custom cars, and restomods. That's what people come here to buy and sell."

Peerman looked over at the Tourenwagen, shook his head and turned back to Andy with a smirk on his face and continued, "Does that look like a restomod to you?"

Andy looked over to the big Mercedes, squinted a bit, then looked back at Peerman and replied, "Well, I guess that depends on what a *restomod* is?"

Peerman's face suddenly brightened a bit and a smile deepened the wrinkles on his face. Like all car guys, he enjoyed sharing his knowledge.

"A restomod is a car that's been restored to *better than factory* specs, with an occasional upgrade here and there to make it more *drive-able*," stated Peerman with an authoritative air.

"It really is the best of both worlds," he continued. "You git the swagger of an old-school ride, with the comfort and reliability of a modern car. Take the '64 GTO I'm selling this afternoon," Peerman stopped, looked at his watch and continued, "Which is coming up in jest about thirty two minutes, in case you're interested. From the outside it looks like any other '64 GTO convertible, well a Day Two anyway. But the mechanicals are pure twenty first century."

Andy put a somewhat confused look on his face and asked, "What's a *Day Two*?"

Peerman smiled, checked his watch, and then continued, "Well, I can't stand here jabbering too long. I gotta be there when my Goat crosses the block. But a Day Two refers to the type of things a young man would do to his new muscle car, basically the day after he bought it. Crager mags, jack up the back, slap on some traction bars; basically all the goofy stuff kids used to think was cool back in the day. And, I guess, that some of us still do."

"So all the mechanicals are modern, like new brakes and stuff?" asked Andy. He was trying hard to look like he was fascinated with all this new knowledge.

"Yeah," replied Peerman with a condescending shake of the head. "Stuff like four piston Brembos all around, Bilstein shocks, Hotchkis suspension, Eaton posi-diff, Tremec TKO tranny, and an Anniversary Edition 427 GM Hi-Po crate engine."

Andy was now truly impressed and replied in awestruck voice, "The ZL1 Tribute engine?"

"Exactly," said Peerman whose smile abruptly changed to a look of puzzlement. "How come you know about the ZL1 and not what a restomod is?"

"Huh, well, huh," stammered Andy. "I think I saw it on a Facebook post, or a Tweet or something. I think 'cause it's so expensive." He paused a bit, not having to do much acting to come across like he was searching for an answer.

"You know it could have been on *Fast 'n Loud* or that *Counting Cars* show," replied Andy. Seeing the old man's puzzlement fade from his face he decided to continue down that road. "That's why I was confused with what a restomod was. I thought all cars were restored using new motors and stuff."

"Well, it used be that way," replied Peerman. "Nowadays, the big buzz is about originality."

"Really?" replied Andy. He was thrilled at this interview, thinking that this guy was money in the bank! The trick was to keep him talking in long enough sound bites.

"Absolutely," said Peerman. "Take my GTO," he stopped suddenly and took another look at his watch. Peerman then cocked his head a bit to better listen to the auction banter that was taking place just through the doors. Satisfied that there were still a number of cars to be sold before his came up, he continued, "Take my GTO. It's a beautiful car with lots of creature comforts to go with the drivetrain. It's got Classic Auto Air; eight-speaker stereo with a thousand watts and Bluetooth; brand new interior from the carpet to the top, with Dynamat. And it's got an incredible paint job that, by itself, cost three times what the car sold for new. It will likely bring anywhere from sixty-five to eighty-five when the gavel drops."

Andy tried hard, but was a bit unsuccessful in keeping his face straight as he asked, "Sixty five... hundred?"

Peerman looked at him like he had just crossed the line. His eyes squinted a bit and he looked at Andy like he was almost sure he was being *messed* with.

"Thousand," Peerman replied. And this time he did spit, letting loose with a mighty wad that splattered onto the concrete. His eyes narrowing a bit, he continued, "Now if it was a factory correct, entirely original 1964 Pontiac GTO with the all the right options — things like Tri-Power, 4-speed, 3.90 rear with Safe-T-Track, factory tach — well then, if such a car was to be auctioned today, you'd easily be into six figures. Heck, I'd be a bidder on that."

Peerman stopped talking. He looked at Andy, and then scanned the crowd, stopping briefly at each of the Twins. Each was nonchalantly holding onto a monopod. And on each monopod was a very professional looking camera pointed at him. He looked back at Andy, cocked his head and asked, "What's going on here? Are you shooting me?"

Andy put on what he hoped was a winning smile and gave just a little laugh before he said out loud, "OK, cut cameras." Turning to Peerman he continued with, "I do believe you caught us Mr. Peerman. Do you remember the show, *Candid Camera*?"

Peerman started to smile and replied, "Yep, I sure enough do. Used to be one of my favorites when I was a kid."

Andy continued, "And have you ever seen the show, *It's All About The Car*?"

"Yeah, I think so," replied Peerman. "The one about people finding and restoring cars. I think it was on Redline, but I haven't seen a new one in a while. It was a bit slow, but the cars were nice. My favorite car show is *Bid Battle*. Why?"

Andy had to force the smile a bit, the response about *IAATC* hurt a bit, but he continued, "We're a production team for the company that does *Bid Battle*. We're starting on a new reality show, sort of a *CarAlity* show. It will be sort of a cross between *Bid Battle* and *Candid Camera*, and you were great!"

"And you filmed me without my permission?" asked Peerman in a monotone.

Andy was having a hard time reading the expression on the man's face, so he just shrugged and continued. "Well, that's kinda the point of the show. But when you came into the venue there were signs all over that you might be video recorded for broadcast purposes. It was also in the registration form you filled out. But just to make sure the producers don't have any questions about using your incredible explanations about restomods and the value of originality, could I get you to sign a release?"

Peerman pursed his lips a bit and nodded his head as if thinking.

As he waited for the man to speak, Andy was thinking that this could easily go bad. He hadn't thought about what to do if they were outed as a crew.

"If I'm on the show, you'd have to ID me, right?" Peerman asked.

"Yes," Andy replied, "but we could just use your last initial. It wouldn't have to be your full name."

"I'll sign a release under one condition," stated Peerman.

"What's that?" asked Andy. He was thinking to himself that this is where he was going to appreciate Bobby telling me to keep the cash. This interview was golden and worth paying for.

"When you ID me, you need to ID my full name and the name of my shop, Peerman's Peerless Pontiacs. Oh, and that we're in Jackson, Mississippi."

Andy broke out into a broad grin and replied, "That would be a pleasure!"

"Oh," added Peerman, "and I'm sure you'd do this but you'll have to put in some video of my GTO as it crosses the block. And get a shot of the engine if you can. That's twenty-three grand of V-8 go power with all the pretty stuff on it."

Andy smiled and held out his phone with the ReleaseMe app already launched. He scanned the QR code on Peerman's badge to load his contact info into a new release form. Handing the phone over to Peerman, he said "You can read it but it basically says that we can use your interview in any way, shape or form and forever. Standard stuff. Just sign it with your fingernail on the line with the X."

"Fair enough," said Peerman, scrawling an indelible scribble across the screen. He then looked up at Andy and asked, "Can I get a picture with the camera gals? They're never going believe this at the shop. Not 'til the show comes out anyway."

Andy thought a bit, figured *why not*, and motioned to the girls to come over, although he knew they could hear the conversation. While they walked over he said to Peerman, "Mr. Peerman, I'm hoping we can we keep this our little secret? It wouldn't be much of a hidden camera show if everyone knew where the cameras were."

Peerman looked at the two beautiful women walking towards him, the identical cameras emphasizing the Twins' own virtually indistinguishable features.

"Good luck with that," he said with a smile and spit again. "But no one will hear it from me. Besides, I'm outta here as soon as my car sells. It's going to be a circus here tomorrow."

He handed Andy his LG smartphone to take the picture with. As the Twins arrived they smiled at him and positioned themselves on either side.

Andy took a couple of shots with Peerman's phone and then said, "Let me take one with my phone. We might be able to use this in a credit roll or something."

Andy dug out his phone and noticed that it had been nearly two hours since Jack had tried to call, text, or email. He was thinking that now would probably be a good time to call him back. He owed him that much anyway.

As Peerman walked away from them and towards the auction entrance, Andy told the Twins, "I've got to take a break and call Jack Calman." He then gestured for Bobby to join them, but kept talking since he knew Bobby could hear him.

"We've gotten six really good interviews, a couple of duds that may have a few usable sound bites, plus that weird woman who kept spouting *No Bid for Hitler Hate* and all that other crap that was on those signs outside," said Andy, who paused a bit to collect his thoughts and then continued. "But we've got to be more careful. With Peerman, that makes three times we've been busted today."

Andy paused and looked at the Twins, standing with their monopod mounted DSLR rigs. He was thinking that if you took away the stunning good looks, and the twin factor, they basically looked very *production crew*.

"Anyway," Andy continued, "We should get a bit of a crowd coming out to see the Hitler car before they leave, so we'll see if we can pick up a couple more interviews. For now, let's get some B-roll of the auction action and make sure we cover Peerman's GTO. And make sure to get a shot of that engine."

Andy thought for a bit more and then continued, "We'll likely need a lot of C/Us of people looking shocked and such if you can get it. But keep the background tight and compressed so it will cut with the stuff we shoot tomorrow."

The Twins looked at each other and shrugged. Instructing them on how to shoot B-roll was like telling them how to breathe; or how to be beautiful.

"What about me?" asked a somewhat crackly, yet certainly understandable Dean.

"By the way, you were right," said Andy to Bobby as he arrived and stood next to Mandy. "The distance was no problem."

Bobby also shrugged. He was used to being right.

"Dean, if you think you've gotten a feel for it," said Andy, "you can come on down to the auction. I think we'll let you do a few interviews to practice up for tomorrow."

"On my way," said Dean immediately.

"Good," replied Andy. He took off the hidden mic glasses and slipped them into his pocket. Putting his hand over them, and leaning over to Bobby, he said in a low voice, "Cut my audio while I call Calman."

Bobby brought up the RigMaster and tapped the screen a few times, stopped and looked at it, pulled on a menu and tapped it again. "Done," he said, "now I'm the only one who can hear you… partner."

Andy opened his mouth, as if to speak, then stopped, closed it and nodded his head. "Ok, I'll try to find someplace quiet so I can put it on speaker phone."

"No need," replied Bobby. "Just pair the Bluetooth headset to your phone. The RF transmitter will still operate so I'll be able to hear both sides of the conversation. I'll patch it to a track on the RigMaster. It might be useful to have a recording of this conversation."

"You know," said Andy with a smile, "your day rate is seeming more and more like a bargain."

Bobby just shrugged and smiled. He'd heard that line before.

Andy tapped onto his iPhone, enabled Bluetooth pairing, and connected the phone to the earpiece. "This might take a bit. I'll find you guys later."

Guidry then walked away from the Tourenwagen and towards the waters edge. While walking he tapped on Calman's number, fully expecting it to answer before the second ring.

When he reached the river, the phone was on the fifth ring and Calman's voice mail message started playing.

"That's odd," said Andy out loud, more to himself than to Bobby. "It's almost two thirty there and from all the calls he made earlier, I'd expect him to pick up immediately."

"Maybe he's talking to that dickhead Winters," replied Bobby through the earpiece.

"Yeah," said Andy, "maybe so."

He stood in muggy air, with the sun beating down on him, enjoying the sight of the river. In the distance he noticed a paddle wheeler, probably a relatively new tourist boat but looking like a real time capsule. It was making slow, almost imperceptible progress towards him. He saw a small puff of white above the boat and milliseconds later heard the sound of a steam whistle.

This was his heritage. He felt at home here, like he belonged. He reveled in the feeling for a minute and then shook it off.

"Ok, I'll try him again in a bit," said Andy. "You guys doing all right in there?"

"Oh yeah," replied Bobby, his smile showing through his voice. "Some of the bidders are even looking at the cars instead of the Twins."

"I'll bet," said Andy. "Let me know when Dean gets there so I can give him the glasses and headset." Almost subconsciously he patted his pocket where he had his vape pen, like a man does when he's afraid of losing something precious. "I'm going to take a quick look at the car corral and see what's coming up for auction tomorrow."

"Will do," said Bobby.

Andy pulled out the vape pen and took a semi-deep drag off the mouthpiece. This cartridge was filled with cannabis oil from the Train Wreck strain, a sativa/indica hybrid. Andy thought it leaned more on the indica side; certainly a pronounced body buzz, but leaving his head clear enough to think. Or so he liked to tell himself.

He started walking towards the rows of cars. He knew where he was going. He had spotted the location almost as soon as he had walked in. He walked straight over to Max and stood there looking at his soon to be ex-911T.

"I sure wish I didn't have to sell you," he muttered sadly.

"Then don't," came Bobby voice in his ear.

"Yeah," replied Andy a bit angry at forgetting he was mic'd, sort of anyway. "That's easy for you to say. Some of us aren't swimming in money."

"Seems to me that your circumstances have changed a bit since you first decided to auction the Porsche," replied Bobby. "Why sell her?"

"I signed a contract and turned over the title," said a rueful Andy. "She's gonna be sold."

"Couldn't you just buy her?" asked Bobby.

"Well," replied Andy, thinking about that possibility. "I suppose I could. I would just owe the auction house the buyer's premium. But depending on what it sells for, that could be expensive." He didn't continue with that just because Bobby was funding the production, it didn't mean he was any less cash deprived on a personal basis.

"Oh, well," said Bobby, "your car, your money, your decision. Dean just walked up."

"Ok," said Andy, "Oh, and the audio sounds pretty damn good for being this far away and from inside the auction hall."

"Yeah," replied Bobby, "I figured it would. I just don't promise something I'm not one hundred percent sure of."

Andy took another, smaller hit off his vape pen, blew out a thin stream and said, "I'm going to try calling Jack again. If he still doesn't answer, I'll meet you inside."

Even standing in the noisy and crowded auction hall, Bobby could hear the quick sucking sounds of Andy on the vape pen. While part of his brain was congratulating himself on the noise-cancelling circuitry he had incorporated into the RigMaster, the other part was running scenarios as to how Andy's vaping habit might affect his new business venture. He then heard Andy say, "Still not answering. I'm coming in."

"Ok," he replied, "we're at the..."

"I'll find you," Andy said, as he slipped the pen back into his pocket.

A few minutes later, as Guidry walked into the room, he looked for heads turned away from the stage. Following their gaze he immediately found where Bobby and the Twins were. Bobby was staring at the RigMaster; one Twin was pointing her camera at the stage, while the other pointed hers at the audience. Dean was standing behind them, observing their methods and appreciating their curves.

"You know partner," said Andy into the Bluetooth transmitter, "For the next shoot, a couple of fat, old geezer camera guys would certainly be less conspicuous."

"But not nearly as nice to work with," replied Bobby, "but anytime you want to grab a camera…"

Andy smiled and ruefully thought that he'd set himself up for that little stinger, although it wasn't far from the truth. He hoped to never find out if he still had it in him to make a living as a camera op.

He then began to wonder what he might do about the Twins for tomorrow, when the really big crowd, and the really big fish would be there. His fingers briefly touched the vape pen in his pocket and he decided he'd have to think about it later; when he was able to get into his *enhanced creativity* mode.

# CHAPTER 29
# Phillips

*Friday – August 25 – 4:14 PM CDT*

> "The whole thing is weird, but this *is*
> America and that *is* private property."
> — ALTON BRIGGS

"Let's sneak the B-roll in a little sooner... start at the word *these*," Sandra Melancon said to her editor.

They were just finishing the cutting of a promo that would be used to tease the story during the six o'clock newscast. Sandra thought that since she still had a little time, she might dig a little deeper and see if she couldn't expand the story a bit for the ten-thirty edition.

Alton Briggs, Ton to his friends, had been a news editor for almost forty years. He cut his teeth in the days of tape-to-tape, three quarter inch, U-Matic editing. He remembered being amused by the old guys and their tales of souping film and actually cutting it to edit the story for broadcast. That's why they still call the editing process *cutting*. Now he was one of the old guy's telling tales about the old days of A/B rolls, time base correctors, sync generators, offline, online, CMX, ADO, LTC and VITC.

Briggs could remember when you actually had to make copies from the source tapes so you could have a dissolve between scenes. And when reporters actually looked at their footage before they came into the edit bay.

Digital video and non-linear editing had truly transformed the entire industry, and it had happened incredibly fast.

Used by everyone from the top echelon of A-List Hollywood editors to the wedding video guys, non-linear editing was so ubiquitous that anything else was considered stone age technology. Nobody even digitized their footage anymore. At least when the video was still recorded on tape, you could watch it play as the computers sucked it up and thereby get a feel for the edit.

Now everything was shot on memory cards of various flavors. You basically plug it in, transfer the files, and you're ready to edit. Any type of special effect, from dissolves to picture-in-picture to the once revolutionary *page turn*, is just a matter of dropping an icon on a timeline. The possibilities for a final product were virtually endless, but to most professional editors, the most elegant edit was still the one the old news guys had been limited to, the *cut*. A well-placed cut — an abrupt change to a different angle or point of view — was the hallmark of the true editing professional. Despite all the limitless editing effects now available, the cut was still the only editing technique that, when done properly, was truly seamless and invisible to the average viewer.

Melancon had been in the business for over twenty years and could read the writing on the wall. She knew that when the old-timers like Briggs were gone, reporters would be editing their own stories. In some of the fledgling, *Internet Only* news departments, reporters were already shooting, reporting, and editing their own stories. She truly hoped to retire before it came to that for her, but not because she didn't have the necessary knowledge. It was that she believed that collaboration between professionals made for a better product.

She not only knew the mechanics of importing, editing, and exporting in the correct formats and data rates, she had also studied the art of editing. Of how skillfully woven images not only enhance, but actually *sell the story*, convincing the audience of its veracity. And she knew that Briggs was a true editing artist and always tried to work with him.

Briggs also liked working with her. She was certainly easy on the eyes, but mainly it was because she respected the craft, stayed in the bay when he wanted her to and left him alone with a piece when he didn't. This was one of the times he wanted her input to help sell the story.

Earlier they had edited the short teaser roll-in for the four and five p.m. newscasts, as well as the longer two-minute piece. The two-minute cut would be the roll-in on the live shot scheduled for the five thirty newscast. Long gone were the days of three hour-long newscasts per day, airing at six, six, and ten, with a half-hour slot at noon. News departments were expensive and program directors were scheduling big blocks of news time to try and amortize that investment; on paper anyway.

During the week, WFNO Morning News started at four thirty a.m. and went until nine. "FOX 15 News at Noon" was the only single hour news program on the schedule. Early evening news started at five p.m. and stretched until seven, although it changed its name from "FOX 15 News at 5," to

"FOX 15 News at 5:30," to "FOX 15 News at 6," at the appropriate intervals. The late news started at nine p.m., changed to "FOX 15 News at 10," and ended at eleven'ish, often pushing the start times for the late night sitcom and drama re-runs from the exact top or bottom of the hour. Someone in programming once tried explaining to Briggs exactly why they did that, but it wasn't his shift, he wasn't normally up that late, and there was the fact that he didn't really care.

But just because they had over eight and a half hours of news to fill every day, didn't mean they actually had over eight and a half hours of news content. Like every other news organization, from network to local, they just repeated the same stories over and over again, stories beginning as *Breaking*, progressing to being *Updates,* until it became a *Who Cares Anymore* recap if they need to fill some time.

This *Hitler Car Auction* story that Melancon was working on had some legs. Barring any huge, breaking news story to push it out of the way, it would see air at least a couple of times on the early evening newscasts. If she wasn't sent out on another story between now and when she officially clocked out for the day, she'd do a little digging into the background of this Wittmann character.

Her late news story would be more about Wittmann, and the controversy he was creating, than the actual Hitler Car itself.

"Play the promo clip for the ten thirty news while I read the anchor VO copy," Sandra instructed Ton. He appreciated that Sandra wanted to see how the clip would flow under the live VO. Most of the younger reporters didn't know to do this, and couldn't care less if they did.

"Ok, in three, two, one..." said Ton as he tapped the K key on the keyboard and the video began to play on the computer screen as a green vertical bar scrubbed along the multi-layered timeline.

The video started with a low, relatively tight, rolling camera shot. The camera op had shot it sitting on the floor of the van, with the side door open, while Melancon had driven it parallel to the protesters and their signs. The shot then cut to the Hitler car with a few dozen people around it. The next shot was from an old photo pulled from the Internet. It started with a relatively close shot of Hitler riding in what seemed to be an identical car, giving his infamous stiff-armed salute, and pulling out to reveal a crowd of what seemed like millions. It then cut to a shot of Wittmann preaching to the crowd, cut to a reverse shot of the crowd listening, and then finally to a shot of Wittmann talking on camera with a handheld mic, sporting a FOX 15 flag, in front of his face.

While the edited clip was playing, Sandra read the VO copy, "Big controversy today at Mardi Gras World, the site of the third annual A-Bear's "Muscles On The Mississippi" classic car auction. A last minute addition to the auction line up, billed as a car that was actually used by Adolph Hitler, is causing these angry people to let their feelings known. This man is at the center of the demonstrations, but is also registered as an actual bidder and has paid five million dollars for the privilege to do so. We find out why in this FOX 15 exclusive at...

"Then they tag it," said Sandra to Ton, "depending on where it is in the story line up."

"There's more to this than that old guy is letting on," said Ton. "And why would anyone care that much?" Ton grabbed the mouse and clicked on the timeline to the rolling crowd shot. "Half of these kids couldn't tell you who Hitler was if you stopped them on the street and showed them that picture."

"Exactly," agreed Sandra. "And this old guy shows up out of Nowhere, Wisconsin, with no contacts or prior planning, and in less than twenty-four hours pulls off this kind of demonstration. And he's not even a real preacher, just some farmer guy. But a farmer guy with enough scratch to post a five million dollar bidder bond at the drop of a hat. Which, by the way, I also find very odd. This no press allowed, high-security auction, five mill bidder bond to protect some sort of mystery provenance… this is just too weird not to have a great story buried in there somewhere."

"Well," replied Ton, "I don't know if it's EMMY® material, but it's pretty good. And the old guy was pretty sharp for his age. Actually pretty sharp for any age."

"Yeah, he was sharp but those answers seemed too…" Sandra paused, searching for the right word, "too *pat*. Like they were practiced a bit too much."

"Yep," said Ton. "There's more of a story there, but Wisconsin's a bit out of our *core news market*." Ton made quotation marks with his fingers as he repeated the mantra of their current news director.

"That's true. But the actual auction is taking place here in NOLA, and that is our *core news market*." She also made the gesture signifying quotation marks. "Remember that intern Blake Fontenot? Remember how he ended up getting a reporter gig up that way?"

Briggs looked at her and gave a shrug that clearly said he neither remembered nor cared.

"Well, he did," Sandra continued. "I texted him to call me. I'm going to see what he might know, or can find out about this guy."

Depending on the response the actual story got from its early evening news debut, and the follow up on the late news, she would likely be covering it again tomorrow. A little background info on Wittmann might come in handy, allowing her to freshen up the story.

"I still can't believe I can't actually attend the auction," Sandra complained to Ton as she watched him set up the timeline to export the finished video file to the news server.

"Yeah, that is sorta weird," replied Ton. "The whole thing is weird, but this *is* America and that *is* private property. If they aren't breaking the law, then they have the right to say who can, and cannot, attend their event. And charge whatever they'd like for the privilege."

Briggs was a Tea Party Libertarian, whose views would have been more at home at FOX network than the south Louisiana affiliate. But he had seniority and, if he wanted to, a pension he could start tapping tomorrow. He didn't bother to hide his political views.

"I've been covering car stories for a long time and I guarantee there is something big here," said Sandra. "I just don't know if I have the time to figure it out before the story dies."

Ton just shrugged and said, "Oh, well. If it dies, there's always another one."

Sandra just sat and thought a bit, "This one's different. This could easily be picked up by network and go national. Anyway, I've got a live shot on location at six forty, so I've gotta go prep."

Her phone buzzed repeatedly to signify that an actual call was coming it, a rarity in this age of texting, email, and Facebook alerts. She looked at it and said, "There's Blake now. Good work, Ton. I'll see you later with update material, if I get any."

Sandra stood up, tapped the phone and, as she walked out of the edit bay, said "Blake, how are you? It's so good of you to call me back. Listen, I've got this story I'm working on..."

As the door closed, Briggs turned back to the computer screen, saved the project, and proceeded to call up the next story to be edited. This one was by the food reporter whom Ton thought came across a lot more gay on-camera than he was in real life.

Briggs was thinking how in news these days, everyone had to have their *hook* to stand out. In general, and in line with his Libertarian leanings, he didn't really care about gay people, one way or the other. But he had been around long enough to remember when reporters were mostly men, and they acted like it. News was certainly different then, not as *socially aware*. Not necessarily better, or necessarily worse, just different.

"It's an Étouffée that is simply TDF," said Preston Moralas, the thin, handsome, well-dressed man on the screen. He was, of course, wearing his signature oversized bow tie. Ton had been working on the piece for about an hour. He watched it once more and then moved the close-up clip of the dish twenty-three frames earlier in the timeline, cutting back to an exterior shot exactly at the words "AND where you'd least expect it!"

"That was easy," he thought as he named and exported the file and called up his on-screen editing to-do list. He saw that Sandra had booked a session during the last two hours of his shift. "Well, aren't we confident we'll have something new," he muttered just as Preston Moralas came into the bay waving one of the old P-2 video recording cards the station still used.

"More B-roll for the Kajun Kitchen story. They gave us an extra thirty seconds in the ten o'clock so I went and got more interviews."

"Great," said Ton in a tone you would recognize as sarcastic only if you knew him very well. "I was thinking it was way too short."

"You would not believe the food at this little hole in the wall!" said the always-enthusiastic Preston. "And the entire wait staff could be snatched up and dropped on stage as Chippendales! They are almost as delicious as the food!"

Briggs thought to himself that perhaps he was wrong; perhaps Moralas was every bit as gay in person as he was on-camera.

"It's good TV," replied Preston, "Actually it's GREAT TV, and I've got a hook at the end that's going to positively kill. I smell EMMY® number ten right here."

"So where do you want these interviews in the timeline," asked Ton.

"Who knows?" said Preston with a wave of his hand. "You're the editor." He handed the P-2 card to Ton and said, "I'll be back in an hour."

As the door closed, Ton mumbled, "Can't wait." He proceeded to import the footage into a bin and continued under his breath, "Can't wait to retire and be done with this."

He then thought that what he really couldn't wait to see was whether Melancon came up with more dirt on the Hitler Car auction. He shook his head thinking it was a shame that he'd only get to see the impressive automobile in the edit bay.

Seeing that he had a few more minutes until the Kajun Kitchen files were finished transferring, Briggs double clicked the icon for the full-length story that would run during the five thirty newscast. It had a series of artful cuts showing various close-ups of the car. Suddenly, he noticed something that made him stop the video. Unlike the science fiction shows of only a decade or so ago, with today's high definition video you actually could zoom in and still maintain a fair amount of detail.

Briggs enlarged the frame and peered closely at it. He then put a marker on the timeline, named it Phillip, and saved the project. With a sigh, he noticed the Kajun Kitchen interviews had finished transferring and it was time to start looking at the clips.

The first interview was with a lesbian couple celebrating their anniversary. "Now there's a surprise," Ton muttered. He then cocked his head a bit and thought that if he split the clip here, and left the audio rolling, it really would help the flow as he cut to a wide pan of the dining area.

He dropped the clip into the timeline, made the edit and played it back. He couldn't help but smile at how well it fit and then moved on to the rest of the interviews.

# CHAPTER 30
# Mic Check

*Friday – August 25 – 5:22 PM CDT*

> "I think they're going to get everyone
> all worked up and then announce
> that it is, at best, a tribute car."
> — Wrought Iron IPA guy

"Hey, Mr. Big Time. I guess you're too important to come say *Hi* to your old buddies?" Dean smiled at the text.

His phone showed it was from Malcolm, who must be working this gig. He glanced up at the ceiling, located which of the PTZ cameras was pointing at him, gave it a big smile, and then shot it the bird. The car wranglers were having a bit of a problem bringing the next car onto the block, so Malcolm must have seen him while scanning the crowd for B-roll with the robotic cameras.

A few seconds later his phone buzzed with another text, "Oh, so that's how you treat the people who taught you everything you know... what little that is."

Dean's thumbs flew over the screen as he texted back, "I thought this was an important show that needed top-drawer talent. Obviously I was mistaken. Is Cool-B on the gig?"

"Yup, you know it," came the reply. "Come on back when you have a chance. And bring those lovely ladies with you."

"Will do," texted Dean, "There's only a few more cars left to sell. I'll come back after it's over."

"Good idea," texted Malcolm, "We wouldn't want a repeat of that HP gig."

"Push one wrong button and you're scarred for life!" texted Dean.

"As it should be," came the reply. "See you in a bit. Don't forget the ladies!"

Dean put his phone back into his pocket and looked up to see Andy walking towards him with a bit of a scowl on his face. "I assume that's an urgent matter that just can't wait until you're off my clock?"

Dean replied, just a bit hesitantly, "Well technically it's OUR clock, to a degree anyway, and no it's not *urgent*, but it could be important. That text was from the AD on the AV crew. Some of my old buddies are working this show. They were inviting me and, huh, well, Mandy, Brandy, and me back to the Video Village. It couldn't hurt to get a little heads up on what they're supposed to be doing during the Hitler Car auction. Since we get access to their feeds, knowing exactly what they can and can't cover will help us fill in the gaps during the actual auction."

Andy nodded in appreciation and thought that Jack had been right. The kid was a good field producer and he was already glad he'd hired him.

"Good work," Andy said to Dean. "When are you going to meet them, and why do they want you to bring Mandy and Brandy?"

Dean, Bobby, Mandy and Brandy all looked at Andy like he was a four year old asking why the sky was blue.

"Oh, yeah, right," muttered Andy. "When are you going?"

"After the last car," replied Dean. "These shows tend to run pretty fat on tech and slim on crew. We don't want to distract them until the auction is wrapped. And *some* of us can be *very* distracting."

"Ok," said Andy, looking around the room and cocking his head a bit from one side to the next. He turned to Bobby and asked, "Are you sure we're going to get decent audio in here? It sounds pretty *live*."

The room was enormous, and very *live* indeed. It seemed to be the size of a football field, with highly polished concrete floors. The floors were laid with wide industrial carpet runners to aid in directing foot traffic, but audio reflections had plenty of open concrete to bounce on, seemingly amplified and made into a white noise by the reverb.

The huge room was open to the roof, with the peak in the ceiling some forty feet above the floor. There was a huge lighting grid hanging from the ceiling, some twenty feet above and centered over the front of the seating area. The back edge of the grid ended at the back of the stage. Hanging from the grid was the lighting for the stage. In addition to the standard fixed fixtures, there were a number sophisticated lighting instruments that could remotely sweep the room. They were able to swivel three hundred and sixty degrees, as well as adjust both the size and the color of the spotlights they produced.

Currently, the hall felt more like a party than an auction. The announcer patter still filled the room, but it danced atop the blanket of room noise like a great lead guitar in a mediocre six-piece band. Most of the chairs, a few hundred padded folding models, were empty. They were lined up like tombstones facing the stage, sporadically populated by small groups of bidders.

This late on the first day, the more exciting cars had been sold. So unless you were interested in a particular car, or seeking to lowball almost anything because of the shallow bidding pool, you were back at the bars while they were still open and free to registered bidders.

Large Mardi Gras props also helped tame the room reverb. They were strategically placed around the room, positioned to show off their size yet not hamper the flow of people. Easily the most impressive were the massive caricature heads; expanded 3-D cartoons depicting all manner of people and animals. Each were mounted on rolling stands and were big enough for two people to stand inside without touching.

Raston had removed his Bose QuietComfort noise cancelling headphones and was also listening to the room.

"The ambient will certainly be there, but the temple mics in the glasses are super cardioid. As long as they're pointed at the subject, we'll be fine." Bobby looked up at the lighting truss and then at the speaker arrays mounted high on both sides of the stage. "Ideally, I would tap into the AV system and also get a feed from it," Bobby paused and continued, "But since that's not likely to happen, I could just hang a lav with a high pressure diaphragm in front of one of the arrays."

"Tapping into house sound shouldn't be an issue," said Dean. "Especially if we're doing it after the show goes dark."

"Oh sure," said Bobby. "I guess you're thinking we just show up, ask to tap into the board and they'll say *No problem, you want a line or mic out?*"

"Yeah," replied Dean, "That is pretty much what I think. First of all, I know the guys running the show. I've been on dozens of shows with them. Second, if there's some *resistance* I believe Andy can just get this…" Dean paused for just a beat to remember the name and then continued, "this Mr. McMillian to give the OK. I am, after all," he held up his badge, "on the crew."

"Yeah, yeah, yeah," said an impatient Andy, "tapping into the board isn't going to be an issue. I'll get Pat to introduce us and authorize whatever we want, but I don't see why we need to record it separately. When they're bidding, the house cameras will be all over it. And, again, we have access to that footage with its audio. I'm more worried about pre and post bidding audio, and getting some decent room ambience for the mix. That's what we're going to need."

"Then as long as there is no operator error, we'll be fine with audio from the glasses," said Bobby in a resolute tone.

"Good, we'll be counting on it," replied Andy. "We've got a few more cars left before they start shutting down. Let's roll a few on the remaining bidders and then some at the bar area. Then we'll know for sure."

He looked over at the Twins and said, "This would be a good time to find some angles. Try to be…" he stopped and looked at them, feeling the seed of an idea start to germinate. "Try to be inconspicuous."

Both Twins both lowered their chins and gave him a look that clearly communicated that it wasn't their fault men were pigs.

"Yeah," said Mandy.

"Right," said Brandy.

Dean snickered a bit until Andy fished the glasses out of his pocket and handed them to him. "You're up," he said, "Let's see what you can do."

Dean put the glasses on his face, broke into a smile and started looking around. His gaze settled on three guys in their late fifties.

One was holding an auction catalog and showing something to the rest of the group. Another was pointing to his watch, and gesturing to the auction stage. The third guy wasn't paying much attention to the conversation and was just looking at the stage, watching the current car being auctioned.

The stage consisted of a low platform for the cars with a much taller, draped platform behind it. Perched on the upper platform were the auctioneer and his helpers, surveying the room like judges in an inquisition. Flanking the auctioneer's platform were dual twenty-five foot, Hi-Def screens. Currently, one was showing various beauty shots of the car while the other showed stats on the car and the current bid.

Each of the three men had a beer in their hand; watch man and catalog guy each had a Bud and the guy watching the auction clutched a Wrought Iron IPA.

"That looks like a story in the making," said Dean, nodding his head towards the group.

The Twins quickly looked around, each one's gaze locking onto a particular spot in the hall.

"We'll be ready to roll in three," said Mandy as they both walked off to their respective destinations.

Dean watched them walk away and then turned to Andy and Bobby with a huge grin on his face. "Can you believe we get paid for this?" he asked. He took a deep breath, transformed the grin into a more congenial smile and said, "Mic check?"

"Audio's good," replied Bobby.

"Then let's see what these gentlemen have to say about the auction in general, and a certain Hitlermobile in particular," said Andy and strolled off to towards the group.

"I like the kid," said Bobby.

"Me too," replied Andy. "I think he's going to work out fine."

"We'll know soon enough," said Bobby as he tapped a few commands into the RigMaster.

In their earpieces, Andy and Bobby both heard an almost simultaneous "Rolling one, rolling two" from the Twins.

Andy looked at Bobby and mouthed the question, "Which is which?"

Bobby just shrugged and mouthed back, "Who knows?" and then said out loud, "Speed."

"Gentlemen," they heard in their earpieces as Dean walked up to the group and asked, "Are you guys waiting for the Boss 302?"

"Maybe," replied the guy holding the catalog, "who wants to know?"

"I'm Dean. I'm with the video crew," Dean held up his badge. "When the bidders get a little sparse, we like to try and get an idea on who might be bidding on what. It's easier for us to set the camera angles for the IMAG and such."

"Wouldn't it be easier to shoot the bidders when there's not as many people," the watch pointer asked.

"You would think, and it sorta is, but with more people it's actually easier to cover up not knowing who's bidding," replied Dean. "Plus, we don't like to be panning across a bunch of empty seats. Doesn't look good for the auction company."

The men looked at each other and shrugged.

"Yeah," started one of the men, "we're gonna bid on the Boss."

"Beautiful ride," said Dean. "Who's going to get it?"

"We'll flip it," replied the catalog holder. "We own a little shop over in Natchez that specializes in classic muscle."

Twenty yards away, Bobby and Andy sat in a couple of chairs in the deserted back half of the seating area.

"Not bad," said Andy. "The audio swells a bit, but that's to be expected. He can't be looking at all of them at the same time.

"I'll be mixing in some of the omni pickups on the sides of the glasses during post," said Bobby. "Add a little compression to the temple mics and it'll be more than acceptable."

"Well, it's more than acceptable now," replied Andy. "After Dean finishes with these guys, we'll do a test at the bar and see how it does in a crowd."

"A Hitler car!" Dean's pretty convincing exclamation grabbed their attention and they both stopped talking and paid attention to the remote conversation. "A Hitler car right outside the doors?"

"Yup, that's what they say anyway," said the watch guy.

"Wow," said Dean in mock astonishment. "They never tell us anything. A real Hitler car right here in New Orleans."

"I don't believe it," said the catalog guy. "It's too weird, too rushed, and this nonsense 'bout the provenance not being revealed until the actual auction…"

"I think it's all theatrics," said the Wrought Iron IPA guy, taking a deep pull on the Abita brew. "I think they're going to get everyone all worked up and then announce that it is, at best, a tribute car. At least as far as the Hitler connection is concerned."

"Really," said Dean, "why do you think it's a… a… did you say *tribute*?"

"Son," replied Mr. Wrought Iron, "let me tell you a little bit about the classic car auction business and how you spot a fake."

"You don't know it's a fake," interrupted the watch guy. "You barely looked at it."

"I didn't have to," replied Mr. Wrought Iron, "Real or fake, we're not bidding on it, and I don't care how it looks. It's just too weird to be real."

"I don't know," said the guy with the catalog. "Remember that Mecum auction in Mobile? The one with the '70 442 with the W30 package. We didn't bid on that because you kept saying *If it's not in the description it's not…*"

Andy pressed his earpiece and asked, "Are we good on video?"

One Twin was at the side of the stage, looking at her nails, while her monopod mounted camera just *happened* to be pointing at Dean. The other Twin was at the back of the stage, just feet from the car she was pretending to photograph, but with the powerful zoom lens in the 300mm position.

Both Twins nodded just a bit to indicate that they had the shots.

"Keep rolling," Andy transmitted to the crew. "Dean, you're doing great."

"Thanks!" came Dean's reply, almost immediately and interrupting the catalog guy's story.

"Thanks for what?" he asked, with a puzzled look on his face.

Dean quickly replied while pointing to his earphone, "Someone in the control room said I did a great job hooking up the monitors. I'm sorry… you were saying?"

"Well, then *this* SOB," continued Mr. Catalog pointing to Wrought Iron guy and laughing, "decided we needed to run the VIN before we could bid. Who the hell could run a…"

Andy looked at Bobby, gave him a big smile and mouthed the word "Gold."

Bobby just nodded his head and smiled back.

As he sat there, looking at the levels on the RigMaster, Bobby was starting to think that the *CarAlity* name was starting to fit, and it was starting to grow on him. He glanced over at Andy, who was listening intently to his audio monitor, and wondered if he had registered the web domain yet?

He brought up the 4G web browser that was also built into the RigMaster. Less than thirty seconds later he tapped *Buy Now* and it was done. Andy turned to him with a smile and a big thumbs up. Bobby returned the gestures and swiped the screen to bring back the audio controls.

Bobby was a very firm believer in protecting his investments.

## CHAPTER 31
# Not Missing The Big Guys

*Friday – August 25 – 5:47 PM CDT*

> "Yeah, I was thinking we need to tone down their whole *production crew* vibe, but I'm not quite sure how."
> — Antoine Guidry

Pat McMillian did a double take at the caller ID that popped up on his phone. He tapped the answer icon and said, "Jack Calman, it's been a while. It's been a long while. How the heck are you?"

"I'm fine, Pat. Thanks for asking," replied Jack.

"What can I do for you?" asked Pat.

"Are you at the auction site?" asked Jack.

"Of course! Where else would I be?" laughed Pat. "Auction days are fourteen hours long... if you're lucky. But you know that."

"Yes, I certainly do," replied Jack. He wasn't laughing, but you could hear the smile in his voice. "So, what you can do for me is to tell your gate guard to let me in."

"What?" replied Pat, "You're here? In New Orleans?"

"Yup," answered Jack, "and I'd like to come and talk with you if I can... especially if Andy Guidry is still onsite. I've tried calling all morning but he wouldn't pick up."

"Well, I don't know if Andy is still onsite, but he's been here most of the day and I haven't see him leave," replied Pat, his mind racing to try and come up with some reasons why the great Jack Calman would be here, in New Orleans, and unannounced. The few times he had met him before, he had known about it days, if not weeks in advance.

"Let me talk to the guard and I'll tell him to let you in," said Pat.

There was a bit of muffled discussion on the other end and then Jack came back on the line. "The guard says you told him to only take direct calls from you, on the walkie talkies. He said you told him you didn't want any *media assholes* trying to scam their way onto the grounds."

Pat laughed, a bit self-consciously, and replied "Well, that is sorta what I told him, but I meant some of the less *legit* media... huh, media representatives."

Earlier in the day, after Sandra had bluffed her way in, Pat had told all the guards, "Nobody gets into this auction without a legitimate auction badge or my verbal approval. And that approval will be from me, in person, or on our walkie talkies. A Press Pass is not an open ticket to this event for any media asshole who thinks the rules don't apply to them."

"I'll take care of it," Pat continued, "Which gate are you at?"

Pat heard a little mumbling and then Jack came back and said, "The Race Street entrance."

Pat picked up his walkie talkie and said, "This is McMillian to the Race Street gate."

The reply was immediate, "Hello Mr. Mac. This is Clovis at the Race Street gate."

"Clovis," said Pat, "Please allow Mr. Calman entrance into the auction site."

"Ok, sir," replied the guard. "I hope I didn't offend him, but I was jest repeating yers instructions."

"No worries," said Pat, rolling his eyes a bit. "Tell Mr. Calman I'm in the auction office to the right of the stage."

"Yas sir, I will," replied the guard.

Pat looked at his watch and counted off thirty seconds and picked up the walkie talkie.

"McMillian to Clovis," he said as he keyed the mic button.

"Yas sir?" came the immediate reply.

"Is Mr. Calman on his way here?" Pat asked.

"Yas sir," replied Clovis, "He started walking as soon as he heard where you was."

"Good," said Pat. "Now listen closely, and not only you, but everyone that's on this channel. Again, unless you hear differently, from me and only me, Jack Calman, or anyone else who shows up without a badge, is NOT allowed into the auction tomorrow. Period. Everyone got that?"

Four different voices came back, one at a time.

"Yes sir."

"Understood."

"Got it"

"Ten-four, sir. I'll make sure of it."

The last was from Maurice Schafer, who ONLY went by his last name. Schafer was a retired New Orleans policeman whom Pat always hired as a sort of independent security coordinator.

This was apart from the security team he hired through Commodore Security Services. McMillian liked having Schafer around during auctions. Schafer had been *persuaded* by the NOPD to take early retirement but, as part of the deal, he retained the right to carry a gun, either openly or concealed, as he had during his twelve years on the job. Although at six foot six, and a hard three hundred pounds, he had never had to use it. Or so he claimed.

As a freelance guard, McMillian paid him roughly ten times as much as the CSS guards. The hefty day rate was how McMillian made sure of where the big man's allegiance lay; an allegiance he had proven was highly valuable more than a few times during some *special assignments*. Schafer had also brokered the off-duty cops that had been hired to guard the Hitler Car.

"Hello Pat," said Jack Calman as he walked into the auction office, "It's good to see you."

Calman and McMillian had a bit of a strained relationship. A-Bear's auto auctions had been an occasional featured event on *Bid Battle*, but they had been summarily dropped from the schedule last season.

McMillian, like all auction managers, had been given advance notice of which cars the field producers were considering for auction highlight segments. It had been rumored, but not officially proven, that although McMillian had virtually nothing to do with the cars selected, he used his advance knowledge to solicit *donations* for *arranging* for featured spots in the television program.

At the time it had been easier to just drop A-Bear from the schedule than to pursue any further course of action. They did, out of courtesy, explain the reason for the exclusion to Prescott Hébert, the owner of A-Bear Auctions.

That had been a big source of embarrassment to McMillian. Indeed, it put his continued employment at A-Bear into dire straits. But McMillian promised that with or without the *Bid Battle* exposure, revenues would continue to climb, and he staked his job on fulfilling that promise. Since the revenues did continue to climb, and Hébert was a man of his word, McMillian was still there. But ever since the incident, there had been an air of cool formality between McMillian and Hébert that had never warmed up, and likely never would.

"And it's good to see you!" said an overtly jovial Pat. "Andy didn't tell me the big guy would be coming in for the show. If he had, I would have tried to get you a pass into the Tourenwagen auction. Unfortunately, my hands are sort of tied on that one."

Calman just smiled, nodded, thinking that McMillian was just as slimy as ever.

"Yeah," said Jack, "This Hit… this Tourenwagen is making quite a splash. Your marketing on this car was really gutsy, but it seems to be working. How many of the big boys ponied up that five mill bidder bond?"

Pat thought a moment, trying to decide if there was any benefit in keeping that number a secret. He couldn't think of any so he replied, "We got three so far. Bozeman from Dallas, Hanson from Minnesota, and Givens, that movie car guy from LA. Isn't he a buddy of yours?"

"An acquaintance," replied Jack. "Those are some heavy hitters. If you can convince them this really is a car used by Hitler, you'll likely blow past that five mill pretty fast. But I'm surprised you only got three."

"Well, technically we got four, but one's some geezer from Wisconsin," said Pat. "He seems to be down here just to stir up some shit. He's been spouting off on how bidding on the car is the same as being a Jew-hating closet Nazi."

Pat shook his head and continued, "You should have been here earlier today. There was like a hundred people on Henderson and Race with signs and such. I heard the old guy was doing some preaching to them, so he might be some kinda religious nut up there in cheese-head country."

Pat smiled and continued, "Anyway, because he ponied up the bidder bond, he's got VIB parking. That stands for Very Important Bidder, like VIP but for auctions."

"I get it," replied Jack. "Cute."

"Anyway, VIB's get to park on the property and he had some of those signs in his car. Earlier today he was actually trying to hand them out to people in the featured car section, where the Hitler car is. We put an immediate stop to that. He paid to be here, but not to advertise his viewpoints. Do you want to go see the car? There's plenty of light left."

"Sure," said Jack. "Absolutely, but in a bit. So, this guy with the signs, it sounds like good TV. Was Andy on it?"

"I think so, but it's hard to tell. He's doing this Candid Camera production stuff, so it's not real apparent exactly what, or who he's filming."

Jack just nodded his head and said, "That's a new hook we're working on. Just trying to make the shows more interesting. You said you didn't know where Andy was?"

"No, not exactly," replied Pat. "But it's not that big a place. The auction is about over for today, maybe he's at the bar. As a seller, he gets free drinks."

"Yeah, he told me he was here to sell a car," said Jack, remembering that Andy was pretty vague about that aspect of the deal. He had implied, but not specifically stated, that it had been part of his *plan*.

"That he is. Lucky for him because it got him into the auction… legally," replied Pat with a smile that suggested he would never do it any other way. "In fact, if he's not on the auction floor, or at the bar, then he's probably out at the cars. I've seen him by his 911 a couple of times today. He doesn't look very happy about selling it."

"He's selling his 911?" exclaimed Jack. "He loves that car. I remember when he first bought it. He's always said he was going to be buried in it."

"Yeah, well, whatever," said Pat. "He signed the consignment papers a week or so ago and delivered the car on Wednesday. It's a nice car, it will likely do…" he paused, thought a bit, and continued, "at least sixty-five or seventy, maybe more. Vintage 911s are red-hot right now and that one is in great condition."

"Yeah," agreed Jack, "air-cooled 911s are definitely in demand. But Andy's not a collector. He's not in the *buy and flip* business. For him to part with his baby, well that's pretty…" Jack paused and thought for a moment remembering that first phone call with Andy just a week or so ago, "I'd say that's pretty drastic."

"None of my business," said Pat, "Some people sell, some people buy. I'm just the middleman bringing them together. Let's go check out the Tourenwagen before they cover it up for the night. You'll be able to see if Andy is out there by the 911."

"Ok, but I really need to talk to him," replied Jack. "If he's not out by the cars, I need to go find him. I doubt he's left before the auction is completely over."

"As always; whatever I can do to help," replied Pat with a practiced, used car salesman smile.

Jack replied, with as much sincerity as he could muster, "Thanks, Pat. I appreciate it; as always."

Andy, Bobby, Dean, and the Twins had all seen Calman as he blustered his way into the auction arena. If he had bothered with more than a curtsy glance around the room as he hustled over to the auction office, he would certainly have seen them as well.

Andy gave Bobby a look that asked, "*Why the hell is Jack here?*" It was just as clear a question as if he had used a megaphone to voice it.

Bobby gave a shrug that just as clearly stated, "*How the hell should I know?*"

"Why don't you guys go visit with Dean's buddies back stage and I'll go see why Jack's here," said Andy.

"Good idea," replied Bobby, who then turned to Dean and the Twins. "We'll talk with Jack, see what's what, and catch up with you in a bit." He turned to Andy and more stated than asked, "Isn't that right, partner?"

Andy paused, thinking that this partner thing was going to take some getting used too. He replied, "Huh, yeah. Sure."

Andy then turned to Dean and the Twins. "This shouldn't take too long."

"And after the room clears, I'm going to want to set up a few transmitters with omnis to capture ambient. We'll need it for the surround sound mix," said Bobby. "Make sure you let the AV guys know that. See if you can get me the freqs they are using for their wireless and also see if you can get the keys to the scissor lift. I've also got a couple of new devices I want to try out and I need to mount them in the grid."

"Roger that," replied Dean. "I told them we'd wait until after the last car, but I have a feeling they won't mind if we're a bit early." He turned to the Twins and, in a courtly manner, bowed and gestured to the stage with a flourish. "Ladies, your future admirers await."

The Twins looked at each other, rolled their eyes, and shook their heads.

"Ok," said Mandy.

"Lead the way," said Brandy.

Andy turned to Bobby, who was staring at the Twins as they walked away. "Again, I remember when cameras were huge and camera guys were… guys. And normally big guys at that."

"I remember, " replied Bobby, never taking his eyes off the Twins. "And I've decided I'm not missing those big guys one bit."

"Now that I think about it," said Andy. "Neither am I. But they certainly do stand out in the crowd."

"Yes, they do," replied Bobby. "I'm surprised we didn't get outed more often today," he continued. "That Peerman guy was OK, but the two in the morning weren't so understanding."

"Yeah, I was thinking we need to tone down their whole *production crew* vibe, but I'm not quite sure how," replied Andy as they started walking to the auction office.

"I've got some thoughts on that," replied Bobby with a smile. "I think we'll do a little shopping tonight."

Andy looked over at him, about to ask what kind of shopping, when McMillian and Calman walked out of the office.

"Hey, Jack! What the hell are you doing here?" Andy called out, immediately forgetting about the shopping discussion and thinking, with some trepidation, that things were about to get very interesting.

When he saw the expression on Calman's face, Guidry's smile slipped just a bit. He thought that *very interesting* might not be a strong enough description.

## CHAPTER 32
# Finalize The Deal

*Friday – August 25 – 6:24 PM CDT*

> "There'll be lighting, period graphics, and flanking sixty-five inch, 4k monitors showing actual footage of Hitler in a Tourenwagen."
> — Pat McMillian

"Hello, Andy," Jack Calman said with a smile that didn't quite reach his eyes. "You're looking well."

Guidry paused for a minute, realizing that it had actually been quite some time since he and Calman had met face-to-face.

"You, too," replied Andy, with an expression that was a cross between suspicion and relief. "And what a surprise. What could have pried you away from that desk you love with such short notice?"

Guidry knew exactly why Calman was in New Orleans and was instantly juggling all the ramifications that his appearance might have on his deal, both with Neiderland and A-Bear, and not to mention with Raston.

"I couldn't get you on the phone and we really need to finalize this deal," replied Jack, suddenly realizing how desperate he must have sounded. His negotiator instincts kicked in and he continued in a more off-hand manner, "I really just need to get this off my plate. I've got bigger deals that need my full attention."

"Jack," said Andy in his best *I'm so sorry* tone of voice. "I would have gotten back to you sooner but..."

"But," interjected Bobby, "we really should be talking about this," Bobby stopped and looked at Pat. He flashed him a brief smile and turned back to Andy and continued with, "in private."

Jack looked at Bobby and simply said, "Hello, Bobby."

"Hello, Jack," replied Bobby.

Then all three of them turned to look at Pat, who immediately replied, "Of course, I was just waiting for a lull so I could excuse myself." His voice shifted to a mildly exaggerated southern drawl, "Down here in the South, we're pretty big on manners," Pat then gestured to the glass double doors leading out to the car pavilion and continued in his normal voice, "Oh, and might I suggest you take Jack out to see the car?"

"They'll be covering it up for the night soon, and we'll be moving it inside first thing in the morning," Pat explained. "Once we close the doors tonight, we're building a presentation stage for it right over there, house left of the stage. There'll be lighting, period graphics, and flanking sixty-five inch, 4k monitors showing actual footage of Hitler in a Tourenwagen.

Maybe even *our* Tourenwagen." Pat stopped, glanced at Jack, then sighed and continued, "It'll be in the auction hall all day tomorrow to entice the crowd. It will look stunning, but without a badge I'm afraid you won't be able to…"

Jack interrupted with a big sigh, "Yeah Pat. I know. You've explained it." Jack stopped and plastered as fake a smile as he could manage, with just the right amount of eye squint. "I appreciate you letting me in today, what with me being a media asshole and all."

"Jack," implored McMillian. "Sometimes you have to talk to people on their own level. It was just a way of letting the guards know that, under the terms of the A-Bear agreement with the seller, there are certain rules we have to follow. If we don't, there is a substantial financial penalty. And I mean *very* substantial. It's just business."

McMillian stopped, leaning in a bit for emphasis, lowered his voice and continued, "I tell them *no media assholes* simply so I don't have to go into details. They understand that kind of language." He straightened up and continued in a more jovial tone of voice. "And besides, you know I LOVE the media! Andy and I found a way to work together on this and I suppose, by extension," McMillian paused, smiled and looked at Jack as he continued, "with Neiderland… again… assuming you can *finalize the deal?*"

Jack's producer radar tingled a bit, and he quickly smiled and replied, "I don't consider it much of an issue, just a matter of some terminology; mainly paperwork details." Jack paused and shot a questioning look at Andy, who returned it with a shrug and a quick nod of the head. Jack continued with, "We like to have all the details buttoned up before the production goes too far."

Jack then paused, lowered his voice and continued in a conspiratorial tone, "But in all honesty, it's really more an excuse to get out of the house, get a nice dinner, maybe hear some live music on the company dime."

"Excellent," replied Pat. "Andy, I'm sure I'll see you later. If not, then tomorrow." He held out his hand to Bobby, "And I'm Pat. Did I hear that your name is… Bobby?"

"Yes it is," replied Bobby, shaking Pat's hand. "Pleased to meet you."

"And you do?" asked Pat.

"As far as the production, I'm the sound engineer. But I'm also a partner in this venture."

"Really?" replied McMillian, with genuine surprise in his voice. "I wasn't aware Andy had a partner."

"Neither was I," said Jack, now with a real squint in his eye as he looked at Andy and Bobby.

"It's a rather recent development," said Andy, who quickly continued with, "And Pat's right, we better go look at that car. We can talk business anytime."

"Excellent," replied Pat. "Jack, I've got more to do in the office. It was a pleasure seeing you again. If you need anything, let me know. Anything that I *can do*, I'll be happy to."

McMillian turned and walked back towards the office area. Andy turned and started off to the right, towards the double doors leading to the outside. He walked in a purposeful manner, like someone used to being followed. Jack and Bobby just stood there looking at each other for a full three seconds before Jack spoke.

"Partners?" asked Jack.

"For this venture, yes," replied Bobby. "Problem?"

"You tell me," said Jack.

"Not for me," smiled Bobby. "But, I'll bet you're thinking, 'How am I going to tell this to that, huh, what was that term? Oh yes, how fitting. To that *media asshole,* J. Roger Winters."

"Tell him what?" replied Jack. "What do we care if Andy has a partner? It doesn't change the deal as far as we're concerned."

"Hey," yelled Andy from the doorway. He was holding the door open and gesturing to them. "They're going to start covering up the car."

Jack looked at Bobby and said, "I really do want to see this car." He then walked off towards the doors.

Raston shook his head and followed Calman. He was thinking that a deal is not a deal until it's a *done* deal, and that this one wasn't quite ready for the fork.

Raston walked through the doors and into the low, long light of a late Louisiana afternoon, right at that transitional period when the humidity level and temperature were reaching parity.

As Calman immediately walked over to where Guidry was standing, Raston took a detour to the high tensile wire fence that separated the concrete platform from the Mississippi River. With his hands on the thick metal cable, he took a deep breath, savored the smell, and looked over the river to the other bank. Unlike the side he was on, which was a solid mass of buildings and docks as far as the eye could see, the other bank was only sparsely developed. Dense, dark green vegetation filled in the gaps between the small piers and docks that dotted that side of the vast expanse of slow moving water.

He stood for a moment, enjoying the view, and then glanced at the Tourenwagen, almost hidden in the shadows.

He noticed that Guidry and Calman were standing by the car, but not paying it much attention. They seemed to have already launched into the *finalization*.

Raston then sauntered over to join the conversation He was thinking it was a bit like playing poker when you absolutely, positively, without a doubt, knew you had the winning hand. It hardly seemed fair, but Raston didn't mind. He never had before and he certainly didn't now.

## CHAPTER 33
# Funky Chicken

*Friday – August 25 – 6:25 PM CDT*

> "It's a blues bar and the Funky Chicken
> isn't exactly a blues dance style."
> — DEAN PRESTON

"Well, well, well…" said Malcolm Walker, as Dean and the Twins walked into the back stage area designated as the *Video Village*. Even though it had no walls, the arrangement of the rack mounted banks of equipment, with integrated desktops, certainly presented itself as an exclusive area.

"Look what the cat done drug in," said Brian Simmons as he smiled at Dean and the Twins. His smile dropped as he turned to Malcolm and said, "We've still got two cars to go. Let's keep on top of it."

"I am always on top of it, Cool-B," replied Malcolm with a huge smile. "And to heck with what the cat drug in… look at the angels that done flown down from heaven!"

*"Ready camera 3,"* said Brian, *"Take 3. Camera 3, let the car leave the frame. Ready camera 1."* He paused, staring intently at the screen.

The Twins looked at each other. The older guy's total concentration was something they could relate to. They didn't often see an intensity that matched their own and they found it fascinating.

*"Take 1,"* said Brian as he lightly tapped the appropriate button with the deft, sure hands of a concert pianist. On smaller shows like this, Brian preferred to work the video switcher himself. *"Ready Audio 1, they're going to start."*

Malcolm rolled his eyes at Dean and the twins, but replied almost instantly, *"Audio 1 ready."*

He gestured for Dean to come over and lowered his voice to a whisper as Brian called the shots between the cameras. "We'll be done in a few minutes. You know your way around. Explain it to your lady friends."

*"I said, pan 4 to position 2,"* came a controlled, but agitated command from Brian.

Malcolm reached over to the robotic camera control panel and pressed the button that made the camera pan and zoom into one of the angles they had pre-programmed during setup.

*"Cam 4 in position 2,"* replied Malcolm.

*"Ready-4-take-4,"* replied Brian, so fast that the four words sounded like one. He looked over at Malcolm who looked up at Dean and gestured with his head to the back of the village.

"Let's stand over here," said Dean, gesturing for the Twins to join him as he moved over to stand behind a large, folding producer's table whose four chairs were all facing the control area. "Things can get pretty hectic when Cool-B is calling the show. Besides, he's fun to watch."

Fifteen minutes later the auctioneer's image filled the program monitor screen as he announced, "And that, ladies and gentlemen, concludes day one of the *Muscles on the Mississippi* automobile auction. Please join us again tomorrow when we will proudly offer another fine selection of investment grade automobiles, including the…"

*"Ready roll in #4, take it,"* said Brian as he tapped the switcher and the big screens flanking the stage displayed footage from earlier in the day, shot on a small HD cam attached to a Steadicam Jr.

"1940 Mercedes 770k W150 Grosser Tourenwagen," finished the auctioneer. He then paused for a few seconds to let the crowd appreciate the footage, although the vast majority seemed to be spending more effort in getting a bartender's attention before the open bar shut down for the day.

"Please remember that you must have your credentials to be admitted into the auction tomorrow and that there will be no general admission tickets available," the auctioneer continued. "And due to the heightened interest in this auction, please bring a photo ID as well. You will not be allowed access without it. All credentials will be individually checked, so plan to arrive early. Bidding on the morning lots will begin precisely at ten am."

*"Ready camera 4, position 1,"* called Brian.

Malcolm was so used to the closing flow, his finger was poised above the button assigned to that position and he pushed it a millisecond after it was called.

*"Camera 4 in position 1"* replied Malcolm, *"ready for pull."*

*"Take 4,"* said Brian as he tapped the button that fed the robotic camera's image to the program monitors, as well as the big screens flanking the stages and the smaller, fifty five inch monitors mounted on stands strategically located about the room and above the bar. *"Sneak in house music."*

It was a relatively tight shot of the auctioneer and his onstage staff. They were obviously congratulating each other on a successful day as they began to gather up their stuff.

*"Start the move, ready for logo,"* instructed Brian as his finger lightly caressed the button that would switch the video screen to the Doremi video server that was already playing the logo animation of *A-Bear Presents - Muscles On The Mississippi*.

As the robotic camera began to pan left and tilt down, it also began an incredibly smooth pull to an artfully distorted wide-angle view of the nearly empty auction floor. As the isolated pockets of remaining bidders stood up and began to make their way to the aisles, Brian called out, *"90 frame dissolve to logo with music swell. Slow drop to walk out level. Perfect, hold, and..."* Brian paused, *"that's a wrap for the production crew."*

Brian then took a deep breath and continued speaking into the Telex he was wearing. *"Good job today guys... and gal."* He remembered that one of the camera ops was female, a bit burly, but female nonetheless. *"Call time is eight, but you heard the man. It's likely going to be a bit slow getting in tomorrow. Plan accordingly."*

The camera ops were from the local office, and Brian had only worked with one of them previously. But if they were good enough to be hired by United A/V, then they were going to be, at the very least, a few steps above merely professional.

With the production buttoned down for the day, Brian's demeanor turned from clinical to carnival. "Dean!" he barked out, as if he was just now noticing who he was.

"How the hell are you and who are these beautiful ladies who have the distinct misfortune to be hanging around with you?" Brian asked with a huge smile on his face. He walked over, his wide-open arms virtually demanding a hug.

After the hugging and requisite back slapping, Dean turned to the Twins and said, "Mandy, Brandy... I'd like to introduce Malcolm Walker and Brian *Cool-B* Simmons. Boys, I'd like you to meet the best camera ops you have met, and most likely ever WILL meet; Mandy and Brandy Fukui."

"A true pleasure," said Malcolm. "Now I know why Dean was so eager to leave us and jump into the high profile world of broadcast TV."

"Yeah," replied Dean with a smile. "It might be higher profile, but it is certainly lower paying! Although, as you can see, it does have its advantages," he replied smiling at the Twins, who just rolled their eyes and shook their heads in unison.

"Although, the advantages are not what you two hacks have in mind," said Dean. "Watching Mandy and Brandy shoot video is like watching poetry in motion. It is as far removed from regular video production as ball room dancing is from," Dean paused and smiled, "is from Malcolm doing his *Funky Chicken*. Like that time in Indy."

"Whoa, whoa, whoa... there is no call to bring that up. I was very drunk that night, and that band was laying down some seriously funky tunes. Besides, I was good." Malcolm turned and smiled at the Twins, "I was real good!"

Dean smiled and said, "Really, that's your story? First of all it was blues night. It's always blues night at the Slippery Noodle. It's a blues bar and the Funky Chicken isn't exactly a blues dance style. Now, as to being good, or rather, *real good*," Dean paused and held up his phone and innocently asked, "Shall I show the video?"

Malcolm eyes got big and he blurted out, "What! You still have that?" He made a half-hearted lunge at the phone, but Dean pulled it away, laughing.

"Yes, I do. One false move and it's on Facebook!" threatened Dean.

"Ok," laughed Malcolm, "I'll behave."

Brian looked at the Twins and asked, "So, how long have you young ladies been in the business? You hardly look old enough to be as good as Dean says you are, but Dean knows his stuff and doesn't praise lightly."

"I had a good teacher," said Dean, acknowledging the compliment and then turning to the Twins. "When you work with Cool-B, you rise to the occasion or you get left behind." Dean paused, and realized just how little he knew about the Twins, other than their incredible *camera dance* production style and their rapidly rising reputations within the industry. "So, how long HAVE you gals been shooting professionally?"

The Twins looked at each other and gave a *might as well* shrug.

"We began shooting, *professionally*, almost four years ago," started Mandy.

"Three years, nine months, and fourteen days," said Brandy, more to Mandy than the group. "The first job we got paid for was a music video for DanYells, when he was promoting his debut album. Although we didn't shoot it multi-cam. We just alternated between working the b-camera and being one of *da bitches*." Brandy paused, stared straight ahead while she thought for a second or so and then continued, "Yes, I believe that was the name of the background players, *da bitches*. We didn't even work camera in the last scene."

"That's when we both appeared in the last scene," continued Mandy. "That revealed the surprise ending of there being... *twin bitches*."

Brian and Malcolm gave each other a puzzled look. Malcolm spoke up, "I can certainly see that. You gals got that music video look, especially a DanYells video. But how did that turn into top drawer, camera op gigs?"

"Nine days after the shoot, we got a call from Josh Borman, the director, who had finally gotten around to logging the B-camera footage," answered Brandy. "He said he wanted to hire us as camera ops for his next production."

"That was the infomercial for the Hair-B-Gone ultraviolet hair removal system," said Mandy.

"Josh introduced us to multi-cam production," said Brandy.

"And we've been doing it ever since," said Mandy, "People seem to like how the angles cut together."

"*Like* isn't the right word for it. It's more like *astounded* at how well they cut together," said Dean. "You've never seen camera ops more in sync with each other. The first time I saw them work was on a *Power Tour* segment. It was one of those Edelbrock sponsored carb-rebuilding competitions during a stop in Ohio. The director was very adamant about having monitor feeds from the cameras and comms to the ops. He insisted that he had to able to call the shots."

Dean stopped and smiled at the memory. "I think it was more that he didn't believe gals that looked like this, could actually shoot." Dean's smile got even bigger as he continued, "Actually, none of us did. Jack Calman hired them as camera ops during the middle of the gig when two other ops got food poisoning."

"Food poisoning," Malcolm interrupted with a smile. "Wasn't that your term for the massive hangover you had on that Intel job in Miami?"

"It was food poisoning and you know it," replied an indignant Dean. "And I still did my job."

"Yeah, in-between a couple of dozen bathroom breaks," teased Malcolm.

"Yeah, whatever. Anyway, back to the Twins and *Power Tour*," said Dean, obviously enjoying his recounting of the event. "I was just a PA then, so I was shadowing the director in case anything came up. He called the cameras for the first minute or so, but then every time he opened his mouth, one of the Twins had already moved onto the next shot. It was incredible coverage, just the right amount of overlap; always in the right position for the close-ups. Like I said, it was poetry in motion. The last twenty minutes we all just stood there, looking at the monitors. The director was just nodding his head without saying a word. He didn't ask for monitors, or comms, for the rest of the tour."

"Well," said Brian with a slight air of disapproval, "I suppose that's possible, but it would seem that something like that would take years of practice, and would not be something that you want on a directed shoot. I've called the shots for a number of great camera ops, guys that seem to know ahead of time what shots you want, but I'm not fond of ops changing shots before they're told."

"I understand totally," replied Dean, "and pretty much agree with you with normal camera ops. But as you can see," Dean smiled and gestured to the Twins, "these are not *normal* camera ops. I've had the pleasure to watch them work on four different productions as a PA. And I've gotten to work with them as field producer for the last week or so, first at Amelia Island and now here, on this production."

"Speaking of which," said Brian, "what exactly are you doing here? Although it's hard to miss seeing these delightful young ladies shooting with their DSLR's, it doesn't come across as a real production. There's no lighting, no interview setups, no audio guys."

"Funny you should mention that," said Dean. "What we're doing is a…"

"What we're doing is talking about these young ladies and how they obtained these mad camera skills," said Malcolm, "So where did you go to school? And who taught you this director-less shooting system?"

"The first university, which I assume you mean by school, was UCLA," answered Mandy, "Before that we attended the Buckley School, until the third grade."

"That's when we were diagnosed," finished Brandy. "Between third grade and UCLA, we were homeschooled by our Mother."

"Diagnosed?" blurted Dean. "Diagnosed with what, if you don't mind me asking."

"We have Asperger Syndrome," said Mandy.

"Which is a lot like High-Functioning Autism," said Brandy.

"At least that's what we're told," said Mandy.

"We don't really worry about it," said Brandy.

"We just see things a little..." said Mandy.

"Differently," finished Brandy.

The Twins stopped and looked at the men, who were just staring at them. Dean's lips were moving just a bit, as if he were trying hard start a sentence but just couldn't think of something to say.

# CHAPTER 34
# Either Way, I'm Buying

*Friday – August 25 – 6:31 PM CDT*

> "You're funding it because you knew
> Andy had a deal; a deal with us."
> — JACK CALMAN

Bobby Raston was watching the workers as they carefully covered up the Tourenwagen. They lifted the cover up and over before laying it gently on top of the car. They were trying hard not to disturb any more of the dust than was absolutely necessary. He was, however, also listening intently to Guidry and Calman having a rather heated discussion.

"Look, our deal was contingent upon the first payment being in my bank account before EOB... two DAYS ago," Andy was saying to Jack. "It didn't happen. I made other arrangements."

"Technically it was yesterday that the money was supposed to be paid. That's only one day," replied Jack.

"Yesterday AND today," replied Andy, "that's two days. No money, no deal. But I don't want to quibble. It's like you said to McMillian, it's only *details*. I'm sure we can work this out."

"Good," said Jack, "I hope so, too. That's why I'm here. Obviously we're still interested and here's what we're willing to do." Jack took a deep breath and started, "First of all, and this is probably the most important, the money is still the same. It's only paid out a little differently. We agree to the full pilot fee and the per episode amount."

"What about the cancellation fee if you don't pick it up as a series?" asked Andy. "I had waived that in lieu of getting the deposit… which didn't happen."

Jack sighed, "Look, I got royally reamed by upper management on this whole deal. So let me just put all my cards on the table instead of all this screwing around."

"Sounds like a Winters reaming to me," said Bobby who, while listening, was still watching the workmen.

Jack shot Raston a look, rolled his eyes with a sigh and continued, "We'll pay the hundred grand for the pilot. And we want the first right of refusal for the next thirteen shows, at the sixty per."

"Plus travel?" interjected Andy.

"Yes, plus travel," confirmed Jack and continued. "We'll agree to an additional twenty-five g's as a cancellation fee, if we don't pick up the series. But, and this isn't so bad if you think of the entire deal and our commitment to it, we get a total buyout on all shows we purchase, as well as the concept and name."

Andy looked at Jack for a full five seconds and then started shaking his head and smiling, "You know… that would of worked.

I would have gone for that." He then glanced over at Bobby, who looked back, rolled his eyes and gave him a *told you so* shrug.

Jack looked at Andy, waited an identical full five seconds before asking, "Would have?"

Andy smiled and said, "Jack, it's obviously all part of a game. You knew I needed the money, probably not exactly how bad I needed it, but you knew. You dangled the carrot out there, made me feel I had it; that all I had to do was reach out and grab it, knowing I would start planning as if it were already in the bank. And then you snatched it away to put yourself in the driver's seat; to get a better deal. A different deal than the one you had already *agreed* too. That's just not the Jack I know, or used to know."

Bobby couldn't help but smile. He was thinking that Jack was looking more than a bit uncomfortable during that description. He only wished that Winters had also been there. He'd love seeing that SOB squirm.

"Anyway," continued Andy, finishing the thought with an exaggerated shrug, "so things have changed. Still, I really do want to make a deal on this. How about fifty grand for the cancellation clause and I give you twenty percent... no, that's way too much, let's say twelve percent of the US rights. Then if someone outbids you for US syndication, at least you'll be recouping some of your investment."

"Seventy-five percent," countered Jack quickly, "It's our money funding the series."

"Last I checked," said Bobby finally turning to face the other two men, "the only one who's shelled out any money for this production is me."

"So what," replied Jack, having already figured out why Andy hadn't been returning his calls. "You're funding it because you knew Andy had a deal; a deal with us. You'll get paid and then some. It's just easy money for you. And I doubt you'd be so free with the cash if this deal hadn't already been in the works. And, at this point, I'm not so sure it is."

Jack turned to Andy, looked him in the eyes and said, "How about this. We fund it... fully. We do a hundred for the pilot. We do sixty, plus travel, per show for another twelve shows... IF we pick it up. And we get first right of refusal for another thirteen at the same sixty per. By then, economies of scale and overall experience will have substantially cut your internal cost per show. It'll be like getting a huge fee bump. But we really do need to own seventy-five percent of the show as well as the concept and name."

Andy looked down for a minute. Deep in thought, he nodded his head up and down like he was flipping the beads on an abacus. He then shook his head from side-to-side, looked up and said, "Jack, I want to make a deal, but we may be too far apart. I have partners now, who all own pieces of this show. Not the company, I still control that so the decision is mine, but they do get a chunk of the revenue from this show, as well as any others we produce under the same arrangement."

Andy's voice wavered just a bit as he continued, "If we even went fifty-fifty, I'd end up with nothing and that's just not going to work. I'll give up twenty percent of the Pilot, and fifteen of all succeeding shows in the first series, contingent on your purchase. If you pick up another set of shows, past the first thirteen, I'll give up twenty percent of those shows and continue with that for as long as Neiderland is the first-run buyer, at the agreed upon price. But I own the name and the concept. No negotiations on that. I think that under the present conditions, that's really as good as I can do. I'm already giving up far more than our original agreement but…" he turned, gestured to the massive river and continued with, "that's just water under the bridge."

Jack smiled at the reference, and then put on a contemplative expression. He looked out at the river and began slowly stroking his chin in a seemingly unhurried manner. Internally, however, he was seething at having his hands tied, remembering Winters' *fifty percent and no less* bullshit.

"Well, I wish I could say we have a deal," Jack finally replied while still looking at the river. He then turned back to Andy and Bobby and continued with, "And we might. But that's quite a bit more than the bottom line I was authorized to offer. I'll present your terms to…" he stopped and looked directly at Bobby, who returned the look with a big knowing smile. Jack sighed and returned an acknowledging nod, continuing with, "I'll present them to my management team. I'll certainly know by tomorrow, at the latest, and maybe even later this evening."

"I believe the west coast is two hours behind us," said Bobby, making a show of looking at the Breitling before continuing. "Seems to be there should be plenty of time to know tonight." Bobby looked at Andy, who nodded at him. "And I think we really *do* need to know tonight. If not, we'll just move on with the understanding that this," Bobby paused, and made a big gesture of looking at the workers tying down the cover on the Tourenwagen. He then looked back at Jack and continued, "that this *exclusive* is up for grabs. And you know I know a few people with more than willing hands."

"OK," answered Jack with a sigh. "If I can get this approved, I'll just need to change the figures in the contract. I've got the file with me and can print it at my hotel. I've already checked and they have a notary on staff. Can we meet at the Royal Sonesta this evening?"

Andy was about to speak when Bobby beat him to it, "Yeah, we can meet you there." Bobby then continued in a more friendly voice, "And since you're modifying the contract, go ahead and add that fifty thousand dollar deposit back into it and schedule it for immediate payment. Like you said, it's the same amount of money, just paid a little *differently*. And also add a clause that the contract isn't valid until that fifty is paid." Bobby stopped and smiled, "That should help speed things up with your *upper management*."

Andy looked at Bobby. He seemed about to say something to him but then just smiled. He really couldn't think of anything more to add. Andy turned to Jack and simply said, "Seems fair enough to me. Do you want to set a time or just play it by ear? I don't want to be out too late; it's gonna be a big day tomorrow." He paused, briefly smiled at Bobby and turned back to Jack and continued, "For some of us anyway."

Jack shifted his eyes from Andy to Bobby and back to Andy. He just nodded his head, smiled and said, "Why don't we meet for dinner at eight in the lobby. I'll either be there with a notary and a contract, or by myself with an appetite. Either way, I'm buying."

"I've got a crew that needs to be fed," said Andy.

"Of course," replied Jack. "I assumed it would be a crew dinner." Having reached the pause point in this negotiation, he was already mentally moving on to the next task at hand. He was thinking about what he was going to say to Stan Niemec, from the SN auction in Florida.

Even though Niemec's personnel approval clause didn't extend to camera ops, per se, it would be hard not to notice that the Twins were no longer around. Jack was pretty sure the six voicemails he had received from Niemec, none of which he had yet been able to listen too, were concerning that very subject.

"Ok," said Andy.

"Eight o'clock at the Royal Sonesta," said Bobby.

"Excellent! Now, if you will excuse me," said Jack, "I have a few phone calls to make." He paused and looked over at the Tourenwagen. It was all covered up and barely visible in the rapidly deepening shadows. "I sure wish I'd gotten a better look at that before they covered it up," he said to Jack and Bobby.

"Guess you'll just have to wait and see it on TV... somewhere," Andy replied.

"Yup," replied Jack with a rueful grin, "I guess so." He then turned and walked down the side of the building towards the Race Street gate.

# CHAPTER 35
# It's Convenient

*Friday – August 25 – 6:33 PM CDT*

> "I know exactly what is allowed
> during the auction."
> — DEAN PRESTON

"Once we were diagnosed, our mother decided we would be better off being homeschooled," said Mandy.

"The other kids had been…" said Brandy.

"*Cruel* would be a good word, although we didn't always realize it," said Mandy. "Our Mom did though."

"She was very protective," said Brandy.

"We didn't associate with other kids very much," said Mandy.

"Not until we went to university," said Brandy.

"That's when we discovered photography," said Mandy.

"Which lead to cinematography," said Brandy.

"That's what we got our degree in," said Mandy.

There was a pause, and when it became apparent that the Twins were finished speaking, Malcolm cleared his throat and spoke, in a somewhat forced yet genuinely jovial manner, "Well, isn't that interesting? So you two graduated from UCLA Film School?"

The Twins looked at each other and then turned to Malcolm. Mandy said, "No. We started off at UCLA."

"But it was very... big," said Brandy.

"After six semesters we transferred to the Brooks Institute and started over again," said Mandy.

"As freshman," said Brandy.

"As freshman?" asked Dean. "Why did you have to start over again? Didn't your UCLA credits transfer?"

"Maybe," said Brandy.

"We never asked," said Mandy.

"We wanted to see how Brooks taught the classes," said Brandy.

"And I'd imagine your grades improved on the second shot at college. Especially since it was, huh, 'smaller,'" said Dean in a sympathetic voice.

The Twins looked at each other, then back at Dean, then shrugged simultaneously.

"Not really," said Mandy.

"We made the best grades available at both schools," said Brandy.

"Heck, if you can afford it, why not go to school for seven or eight years," said Malcolm. "I wish I could have gone for seven or eight months!"

"We could afford it," said Brandy.

"Or, to be more accurate..." said Mandy.

"Our father can afford it," continued Brandy in a matter-of-fact tone, devoid of any self-consciousness. "He is extremely wealthy."

Mandy, nodding her head in agreement, simply said, "Extremely."

"It's convenient," said Brandy to the three men, who were all staring at her with their mouths slightly agape. Brandy continued as if the three men's looks somehow conveyed a non-understanding of the word. "For example, if we had not been able to secure rooms at the Best Western, we could have had the French Quarter house opened up and stayed there."

Mandy nodded her head in agreement, "Our family has lots of houses, all over the world. It can be very convenient."

"Very," agreed Brandy.

Dean turned from Mandy to Malcolm and Brian. They were still transfixed by the Twins. When they both turned to him with an incredulous look on their faces, as if sensing some sort of practical joke, Dean just spread his palms out and shook his head from side-to-side.

Malcolm cocked his head and, in more a statement than a question, asked, "So let me get this straight. You're incredible, almost psychic camera ops. You're drop-dead gorgeous. And you come from some sort of *Lifestyles of the Rich and Famous* family?"

"No," replied Brandy. "Never on that show. But our New York, London, and Vail homes have all been on *Million Dollar Rooms*."

"And the one here, too," reminded Mandy, "The bar, remember?"

"Oh, yeah," replied Brandy, turning to the guys she said, almost apologetically, "Sorry, it's sometimes hard to remember. Plus, we haven't been here in years."

"Well, that certainly is… interesting," said Dean. After a big sigh and a shake of the head to clear it, he continued. "But, before we got distracted and ended up going WAY too deep into the personal lives of Mandy and Brandy, I was explaining what we were doing here, and how you might be of help."

Brian quickly cut in with, "Before we do any *helping*, we'll have to clear it with Pat McMillian; he's the client lead on this."

"Why, yes," came a voice that seemingly appeared out of nowhere. "Yes, I am," said Pat as he walked into the Video Village, as if on cue.

Dean was wondering how long he had been there, and what he might have heard, as the dapper man brushed past him and walked directly to the Twins.

Shaking each Twin's hand in turn, he continued, "Hello, I'm Pat McMillian and this is my little event. I've heard a lot about you two, and frankly," Pat paused, dropped his right eyebrow and plastered a smile on his face that was just short of leering, "who could help but notice you around the auction today."

The Twins just stared at him, as if wondering which of the usual compliments or come-ons would be next. Not receiving the desired response to his statement, Pat continued in a more jovial manner, "Andy told me you two were the best in the business, and that no one would ever know you were doing anything more than just shooting the cars… like any other attendee. Naturally, I could see what you were doing, but I don't think any of the bidders you interviewed today could tell," Pat paused and then smiled as if about to share a funny story.

"I thought one of the off-duty cops guarding the car had it figured out. He asked to speak with me, but all he wanted to know was if it were OK if he, huh…" Pat paused, looked at the Twins and continued, "if he fraternized with an attendee."

Pat stopped and plastered another more conspiratorial smile, lowered his voice just a bit and continued, "He basically wanted to know if he'd get fired from the gig if made advances to the lady in question. You see, I pay my people pretty well and easy money isn't all that easy to find; at least not here in the…" Pat paused for effect before finishing the sentence, "the 'Big Easy.'"

"Hello Mr. McMillian," said Dean, a bit louder than he had too. "I'm Dean Preston. I'm the field producer for *CarAlity*. I was just about to brief Brian and Malcolm on what we're going to be wanting them to cover during the Tourenwagen auction."

Pat looked over at Dean as if he had just noticed him. "Well son, that's going to be a bit tricky. I've already talked with Andy about this. There's a lot of money at stake and this is all got to be done *within the loopholes*, so to speak."

"Yes, sir," said Dean, "I know exactly what is allowed during the auction. Both in how it applies to the general public, as well as the more *inclusive* individual deals you have with both Mr. Guidry and the owner of the vehicle."

Seeing the frown rapidly developing on McMillian's face, Dean quickly added, "Or at least as much I need to know.

Which is basically just enough to do my job. No more and hopefully," Dean paused for effect and then smiled and continued, "no less. Because I'm here to tell you, knowing less than enough to do your job REALLY sucks!"

As Brian and Malcolm nodded their heads, muttering agreement sounds almost too low to hear, McMillian looked at Dean for a very long three seconds.

He then broke out into a big smile and said, "I'm sure it would. Now lets talk about what my guys can, and cannot do for you during the, uh, the *big show.*"

# CHAPTER 36
# This is HUGE

*Friday – August 25 – 6:41 PM CDT*

> "We're still working on that aspect of
> the story and we'll have an exclusive
> interview with this mystery collector
> on the FOX 15 News at 10."
> — Sandra Melancon

"*Back in five, four, three...*" the floor director finished the countdown with two fingers, then one, then pointed at the news desk. Frank LaVere and Clarice Courville finished their pseudo conversation with a nod and a smile.

*"Ready 1, take 1,"* the camera op heard in his Telex as LaVere turned to his close-up camera with a practiced smile. It was the one he reserved for stories that had a lot of human interest, but no overt tragedy.

"The sixth annual *Muscles on the Mississippi* classic car auction started today, but a very controversial, last minute addition to the auction roster was causing a bit of uproar." LaVere paused for effect and continued with a concerned, yet friendly demeanor, "And not necessarily in a good way."

*"Ready 3, take 3, with graphic"* said the director as the screen switched to Courville's close-up camera with the *Muscles on the Mississippi* logo above her right shoulder.

Clarice picked up the narrative, reading from the teleprompter in a practiced, conversational manner, "The car is a 1940 Mercedes 770k Tourenwagen…"

*"Ready car pic one. Take it,"* said the director as the PIP insert changed from the auction logo to a still frame of the Tourenwagen.

"And its claim to fame is that it might just have had a very famous prior owner. Or, perhaps, infamous is a better word. FOX 15's automotive reporter, Sandra Melancon, is live… just outside the River City Complex, where this car will be the final offering in tomorrow's auction."

*"Ready split screen with live feed,"* said the director as the technical director tapped a button on the video console and the program screen switched to Clarice at her desk paired with a live shot of Sandra standing outside of the Race Street entrance to the River City Complex. Behind her, in the distance, were rows of classic cars, with a dozen or so people still wandering about.

"Sandra," said Clarice, "it seems pretty peaceful out there now, but I understand that wasn't exactly the case this morning?"

"That's correct, Clarice," replied Sandra. The flat, even light of the battery powered Astra 1x1 Bi-Color LED

Litepanel made Sandra pop off the screen, in contrast to the long, low shadows behind her.

Joey had adjusted the light level to more closely match the background and set the neutral density filter to four. The large lens aperture the camera now required turned the rows of cars behind her into a soft focused, multi-hued work of impressionist art.

"It is pretty calm now, but earlier today…" Sandra said talking directly into the camera. She turned and gestured behind her.

*"Ready roll in with audio,"* said the director from the FOX 15 Newsroom, just over five miles away.

"…it was a very different scene," finished Sandra and stared into the camera until she heard *"Clear"* in her ear-prompter.

*"Take roll-in,"* said the director. All across New Orleans, TV screens changed to a low angle, rolling shot of protesters waving signs and chanting, "No Bids for Hitler hate."

The director turned to the TD, sitting next to him in the FOX 15 control room, and said, "Great shot. That's got to be Joey. He always goes the extra mile."

The scene changed to Sandra doing a stand-up with the chanting crowd in the background. As she spoke, the scene cut to various shots of the Tourenwagen under its display awning, and the people gathered to look at it.

"Earlier this week, a surprising email went out to thousands of classic car enthusiasts across the country. It explained that a recently discovered 1940 Mercedes 770k Tourenwagen was going to be a last minute addition to this year's *Muscles on the Mississippi* classic car auction. And the fact that the car might actually have been used by Adolph Hitler has created quite a bit of controversy."

The scene changed to a series of short sound bites, with lower third IDs.

"It should be destroyed," said Melvin Akins, of Slidell, LA. "Anything to do with that SOB should be crushed up, melted down, and buried."

"Can you imagine that car all in the dirt, with some dub-dubs, band-aid rubber, and an LS1 under the hood?" said Horace Brooks, a young man from Houston, TX. He was in his mid-twenties, six foot four, and weighed at least three hundred and fifty pounds. He had a round face, three chins, and an infectious grin.

"It is a magnificent automobile," said Bruce Ferryman, of Tuscaloosa, AL. "The sign says it's a survivor, and it looks it. But looks can be deceiving. I'm looking forward to the auction tomorrow and to seeing the provenance."

Sandra's voice-over continued the narrative with a series of close-ups of the magnificent automobile and a brief PIP of Pat McMillian.

"And whether it's the real deal is indeed the million-dollar question, or in this case the six million dollar plus question, which is the pre-auction estimate according to Pat McMillian, A-Bear's director of auto auctions."

The scene cut to a series of slow pushes into photos of Hitler in various, yet almost identical Tourenwagens, saluting vast crowds. Sandra's VO continued with, "There were only 7 known Tourenwagens used by the Nazi leader, and all were thought to been documented and accounted for. The consigner of this car, who declined to be interviewed, states that he will present proof of its claim to fame just before bidding starts on this, the last car that will be offered in this year's event."

*"Ready live two-shot aaannnddd take it,"* said the director.

"Sandra," asked Frank LaVere from the studio news set, "why would the seller wait until just before the auction to offer proof of the Hitler connection. I would think that the sooner the car is proven to be authentic, the more money the car would bring?"

"That's what I would think as well," replied Sandra, still standing in front of the River City Complex. "But the seller claims that the provenance is also quite valuable and the rights to it will be included with the car. When, how, and even if it is shared with the world, will be decided by the winning bidder."

*"Ready camera 3, take 3, on a split with live,"* said the director as Clarice Courville popped into view on the left side of the split screen with Sandra on the right.

"All the protests seem to be outside the River City Complex. What was it like inside the actual auction site?" asked Clarice.

"Well, while the Tourenwagen certainly attracted a lot of attention, A-Bear management did not allow the same sort of protesting on the property. There are quite a number of very valuable cars on-site. We also found out they suspended sales of spectator tickets very early today, shortly after the demonstrations started."

*"Ready camera 1, take 1 in the split,"* said the director as LaVere replaced Courville in the left side of the screen. The teleprompter feed, with the pre-arranged Q&A between the anchors and Sandra, made calling the newscast relatively easy.

"Will they be selling tickets tomorrow?" asked LaVere. "I think I'd like to see this!"

"Sorry, Frank," replied Sandra. "Under a rather unusual agreement with the seller, only buyers and sellers who were pre-registered, before the Hitler car's last minute addition, will be granted access to tomorrow's event. And there are no media passes available. If you, or anyone who isn't already registered, wants to attend tomorrow's auction they will have to post a bidder bond to get in."

"And I would think that the bidder bond would be… substantial?" asked Frank in a polished, conversational tone which belied the fact he was reading the question from the teleprompter.

"Substantial is a good description," replied Sandra with a smile, "for five million dollars."

"WOW," replied Frank, "Five million! That's a little too rich for my blood."

*"Ready 3, take 3,"* said the director as Clarice Courville replaced Frank LaVere on the left side of the screen.

"Sandra," asked Clarice, "has anyone actually posted a five million dollar bidder bond?"

"Our sources tells us that, as of this evening, there have been four people that have posted the bond and are expected to bid on the Tourenwagen during tomorrow's auction," replied Sandra. "Three are well known classic car enthusiasts, but one is a newcomer to the world of multi-million dollar car collecting. We're still working on that aspect of the story and we'll have an exclusive interview with this mystery collector on the FOX 15 News at 10."

*"Ready camera 2, two-shot in the split,"* said the director.

"Oh, and Frank…" said Sandra, with a smile on her face.

*"Take 2,"* said the director.

"Yes, Sandra?" replied Frank.

"The deadline to post that five million is noon tomorrow," said Sandra. "There's still time if you change your mind."

*"Ready to go to 2, full screen,"* said the director.

"I'll keep that in mind," said Frank with a practiced smile as he gathered up a few papers on his desk, as if organizing them for the next story. The same papers had been on that desk for the last three years.

*"Take 2 full,"* said the director.

"Can you believe you have to post a five million dollar bond to bid on the car, before you even see any proof that it was used by Hitler?" Frank asked Clarice.

"And, can you believe what old cars go for these days?" replied Clarice. "I understand that in a 1973 auction, another Hitler car set a world's record for a car sold at auction."

"I didn't know that," replied Frank. "And how many millions of dollars did it go for?"

"One hundred and fifty three… thousand dollars" replied Clarice, with a smile. "Times change."

"That's still too rich for my blood," said Frank. "And besides…" he grimaced convincingly, "Hitler?"

"Yeah," agreed Clarice, "I know."

*"Ready on 3, take 3,"* said the director.

"Let's find out what the weather's going to be like for that big auction," said Clarice. "What's it going to be like Ernest?"

*"Ready 5, take 5,"* said the director.

"It's going to be a hot auction, in more ways than one," replied a dapper Ernest Morgan. "Here in the Crescent City we're expecting the morning highs to be…"

*"You're clear,"* said a voice in Sandra's ear prompter.

Joey left the tripod-mounted camera, walked to the Litepanel and turned it off.

"That was a nice piece," Joey said to Sandra. "But why didn't you use the interview with the old guy in it? Why carry it over to the ten o'clock and, more importantly, do we have to come back here to do a live toss to it?"

"There is something more to that Saul Wittmann than meets the eye, so I decided to save it until Blake Fontenot could poke around a bit."

"Blake, the intern from last year?" asked Joey.

"Yeah, he got a job with WCEZ, the FOX affiliate in La Crosse, Wisconsin," said Sandra. "I had to sweet talk their news director into letting him drive down to where Wittmann lives. It's a little town called Richland Center. They sure do talk funny up there."

"I'll bet they do," replied Joey. He was an Illinois native but had called New Orleans home for over fifteen years. "And I'll bet they think you do, too."

With a very pronounced, way over-the-top New Orleans drawl, Sandra replied, "Why, I do believe they thought my accent was quite charming." Reverting back to her normal speech pattern she continued, "Anyway, they let Blake take a news van and a camera guy to try and dig up some background info. Basically, I wanted to save the Wittmann interview until I heard from him."

She felt a slight buzzing in her pocket and said, "And, that might be him now."

As she pulled the phone from her jacket pocket, something in the auction area caught her eye. She looked down at the phone, answered it and said quickly, "Hold on Blake, I'll be right with you." She looked over at Joey and said, "See that guy walking around the cars, with that big cloud of smoke? Get some B-roll on him."

Joey looked over at the guy and then up at the still relatively bright blue sky. He spun the neutral density filter to one, flipped a lever on the lens that doubled the focal length, put his eye on the viewfinder and hit the record button.

Sandra lifted the phone to her ear and said, "Hey, Blake. Thanks for calling. What do you have for me?"

As she listened, her eyes grew larger and she started to smile. "Really! No! REALLY! And you have that on video?"

Joey called out to her, "That guy's gone. He went into the building. Wrap it up?"

"Hold on Blake," she said into the phone and held it to her chest. Turning to Joey she replied in a rapid, demanding, and very excited voice, "Don't bother packing! Just toss it in the van. We've got to get back to the station NOW. This is HUGE!"

As she rapidly walked to the van she said, "I'm back, Blake. Now, tell me that again but with more detail. Do not leave out a SINGLE thing!"

## CHAPTER 37
# Bad Moon Arising

*Friday – August 25 – 6:52 PM CDT*

> "There's a little thing called the *truth*
> that you may have forgotten."
> — HERMAN ADLER

"All your worrying and I wasn't even in the story," snorted Saul Wittmann as he pointed the remote at the flat panel LG television and turned it off. "And just whom do you think she was talking about in that *newcomer to the car collecting world, more at ten* line?" replied Herman Adler as he got up from the king bed in Saul's River View room. They were on the thirty-fourth floor of the New Orleans Marriott. Herman walked to the window and gazed out at the magnificent view. The festive, multi-hued lights of the French Quarter were just starting to compete with the long, slow-moving shadows of a late Louisiana day.

Although you could easily see the faint white disk of the moon against the deepening indigo blue of the sky, it would be at least another hour before the sun finally relinquished its fiery grasp on the city, and the raw, humid heat turned into a sultry New Orleans evening.

"They're just saving the *crazy guy* video for later so they'll have something new to add to the story," replied Saul. "Besides, like I said, I hope to hell they play it up so that there's even more people out there tomorrow." Saul looked a bit rueful as he continued in an accusatory tone, "I told you we should have waited for the news people to set up before we went into the auction. I could have given another pep talk to my followers for the cameras."

Herman turned from the window with an astonished look on his face. "Your followers? Have you gotten even more insane?" he demanded of Saul. "There's a little thing called the *truth* that you may have forgotten. You came here to buy that car for YOUR museum. A museum that not only features Hitler, but glorifies him! Have you even considered what might happen if the truth about *Brother Saul* gets out before the auction tomorrow?"

Saul walked over to window and nodded slowly as he gazed at the wide brown ribbon of river. The city was clustered up close to it, seeming to feed off its power as it had for centuries. From this height, the old parts of the city blended in with the mid-century and ultra-modern in a mashup that illustrated the very march of time itself.

"We all do what we can, what we have to do, to make a difference in the world we leave behind," Saul replied, never taking his eyes off the city. "Sometimes things are just meant to be, just like that river. It was meant to flow there, in that very place, so this city could spring up around it."

Herman looked at Saul with his mouth slightly agape. "Have you had a stroke you aren't telling me about?" he asked. "If word gets out about your real reason for being here, there's no way you're going to be able to buy that car."

Herman suddenly stopped and looked up at the ceiling, hands raised with palms up, as if he just had an epiphany. He almost shouted, "Which is probably a good thing!"

He then lowered his eyes to Saul and asked in a agitated tone, "Why am I even worrying about this? I should be praying that the truth comes out; praying that reporter figures out who you are and why you're here!"

Throughout this mini-tirade, Saul just kept looking at the river. After a long pause, he just nodded his head, then slightly shook it back and forth, and then nodded it again. It was as if he was having an internal argument and neither side could claim a decisive victory. Finally, he looked at his watch and turned to Herman, who seemed to be waiting, with some trepidation, for a response to his outburst.

"Okay, boy," said Saul, "we've got to get moving if we're going to get something to eat before we go to the meeting."

"Meeting?" asked Herman. "What meeting?"

"Mason invited me to speak at his church tonight; the First Free Mission Baptist Church. We've got to be there at eight o'clock." He pulled a piece of paper from his pocket, handed it to Herman and said, "Here's the address."

Herman just shook his head. He realized he had as much chance in stopping Saul from continuing down this path as he did in making that big river stop flowing. He just took the paper from Saul, sighed and said, "I'll grab my stuff." He then walked though the door to his own, adjoining room.

As he was gathering his things, that song started playing in his mind again. He couldn't remember when he had last heard it, but the lyrics and melody were as clear as if it were playing on the clock radio beside the bed.

Saul called out from his room, "Get a movin' boy, we don't want to be late and I'm hungry. I wanna get some of that gumbo stuff the gate guard told us about."

Herman didn't say anything, but just walked back into Saul's room. Saul opened the door to the hall and sort of shooed Herman through it. Herman started humming in time to the lyrics that were positively ringing in his head.

*Don't go around tonight,*
*Well, it's bound to take your life,*
*There's a bad moon on the rise.*

# CHAPTER 38
# Personal Arrangement

*Friday – August 25 – 6:53 PM CDT*

> "I won't let you have more than one, no matter how much you want another."
> — Pat McMillian

Bobby Raston pulled the RigMaster from his pocket. He tapped a few buttons and then smiled as video appeared on the screen, complete with cross hairs for proper aiming.

The long black tube of a Sennheiser 816 and a small, lipstick camera with a mild telephoto lens were attached to a remote controlled pan/tilt head. Although quite a bit smaller, they closely resembled the robotic cams that were also in the rigging and controlled by Malcolm Walker in the Video Village. Bobby had two of these custom modified mic mounts with him. He had designed and built these nearly a month ago, but this was the first time he'd gotten to use them in an actual shoot.

He was working twenty feet up on a scissor lift. It was parked just a bit front of the spot where the Tourenwagen Display stage was ready to be built. It would be against the wall to the left of the stage, directly opposite the doorway leading to the courtyard. The room was now empty of bidders and sellers. It had been taken over by the various cleaning and maintenance crews prepping the hall for tomorrow's big event.

The riggers and grips had brought in the last of the materials for the stage and were standing around waiting for Bobby to drive the lift out of the way so they could get started. As union workers, they were used to the *hurry up and wait* nature of their occupation. On the clock was on the clock, whether you were busting your hump or sipping on coffee while waiting to get started.

Bobby plugged in his earbuds and used the RigMaster control screen to point the Sennheiser towards a group of three riggers sitting on a stack of staging. From his perch above the staging area, he could barely hear the low murmurs of their conversation. But when the crosshairs on the aiming camera settled on the group he could clearly hear every word. It was far from cinema quality, but it was legible, distinct and well isolated from the rest of the noise on the auction floor.

"I told her we was working late on the set up for that cigar convention. If it comes to it, you guys gotta back me up," said one of the workers to the group.

"And, like she didn't smell all that whiskey on your breath," said another in the group. "That woman of yours ain't stupid."

"She ain't no night owl neither," replied the first worker. "She was sleeping when I got home, so I just brushed my teeth, slipped under the covers and it was done."

"If she finds out you was at the club again, she's gonna cut your…" said another rigger in the group. His words faded away as Bobby redirected the mic at a man straightening out the chairs in the middle of the room.

Bobby could hear the chair legs scrapping the floor as the worker aligned them with each other. When the walkie talkie the man had on his belt squawked to life, he clearly heard "Al, can you bring the air tank back to the warehouse?" Ignoring the message, the floor worker continued at his task as the voice on the walkie talkie gave instructions on exactly where in the warehouse the air tank was needed. Bobby pulled out the earbuds and nodded with a smile. From his position on the lift he could barely hear that the walkie talkie conversation was even happening, and he most certainly couldn't make out any words.

"Okay, guys," Bobby said in a loud voice, "I'm done here. Thanks for waiting."

Bobby grabbed the small joystick that operated the scissor lift and started its slow journey to mount the next mic to the rigging directly in front of the main stage.

"No worries," shouted the nightclubbing man as he waved at Bobby and continued his conversation with the other two riggers.

As Bobby was maneuvering the scissor lift to the gap between the chairs and the front of the main stage, he saw McMillian come into the room from backstage. Pat stopped, looked at him for a very long moment, shrugged his shoulders and walked over to the staging area. He walked up to the riggers with an authoritative air, and they rose to their feet when they saw him coming.

Pat started talking to the nightclub guy, who was obviously explaining something and pointing at Bobby. Bobby turned his back to them, retrieved the RigMaster and earbuds, and tapped the icon that returned the mic to its last position. Watching the video on his screen, the conversation became clear as soon as the camera found the group. Two more taps on the screen started the unit recording the audio and the 720p video signal. Bobby slipped the RigMaster back into his shirt pocket. He began to mount the second mic head as he listened to the conversation.

"That guy had the scissor lift right where the stage is going," said the nightclub man, obviously the lead rigger on the crew. "We brought in all the staging and were just waiting on him to finish mounting his uhh… well, whatever it was he was mounting."

"Looks to me like it's all clear now," replied McMillian in an accusatory voice. "Looks to me like you guys were just sitting around bullshitting on my dime."

"You're right, Mr. McMillian," replied the rigger who had long ago realized the best way to diffuse this sort of situation was to admit it and move on. After all, it's not like this was a rare conversation, and it's not like it was really all that important. The man needed his stage built, they were here to build it, and they were, after all, *Union*.

"We'll get right on it. Shouldn't take more than four hours," he said with a smile as he gestured for the rest of the men to get up and start working. "Exactly what the book says."

"Yeah, well it won't get built with you guys sitting around on your ass," replied Pat. "And I won't pay for a penny over the four hours."

Raston just shook his head as he snuck a look at McMillian.

Raston had been dealing with *McMillians* for a long time and they neither impressed nor scared him. After all, he also was a Union man. As McMillian continued to berate the workers for not having started on the stage, and making useless threats about withholding overtime, Bobby noticed a tall, slender man enter the building from the courtyard doors.

The man stopped at the doorway and looked around the room. He held a device to his lips for a moment and then exhaled a huge plume of white smoke.

Raston's eyes widened at the impressive cloud and thought that guy certainly wasn't using the same king of vape juice Guidry did, or he wouldn't be able to walk.

Raston had finished mounting the mic but continued to pretend to adjust it as the vape man strode across the floor towards McMillian. His clipped, purposeful stride accented the vaguely militaristic outfit he was wearing.

Pulling out the RigMaster, and glancing at the screen, Raston was able to both see and hear McMillian say, in a voice just a little too loud, "Ok guys, that's going to work. Glad I could clear that up."

As McMillian walked out of frame, Raston put his finger on the screen, controlling the mic/camera mount to follow him as he walked up to the vape man. Once they started talking, he slipped the RigMaster back into his pocket and continued to pretend to fiddle with the second remote controlled mic mount.

"Guten Abend, Herr Heinzburg. I see you have fixed your, uh, your device," said Pat in a somewhat forced, yet friendly tone.

"Ya," replied Heinrich Heinzburg in a clipped professional tone. "There is a shop in your French Quarter that had the necessary parts." Heinrich stopped and became almost friendly as he continued the conversation on a subject he obviously enjoyed. "Indeed, it was quite well stocked, although a bit crowded and somewhat understaffed. Unfortunately, I did not get to fully discuss the various eLiquids they offer. There were some regional flavors which I intend to try at my first opportunity." Heinrich paused, thought for a second and asked, "What is a praline?"

"It's a local candy, normally made with pecans," Pat replied. "It's quite good, and when it's fresh it just melts in your mouth. Perhaps you should try the actual candy first, so you know what it tastes like?"

"Yes," replied Heinrich, reverting to his more formal manner. "Perhaps, so."

Heinrich stopped and looked at the workers who were beginning to set up the frame that would hold the backdrop graphics. They wouldn't start on the actual stage until Raston gave up the scissor lift and they could hang the stage lighting in the grid.

"This does not look like it will take very long," said Heinrich. "Why will we not move the Tourenwagen into the building tonight?"

"A number of reasons," replied Pat. "But mainly because the car movers are gone for the day. Bringing them back this evening and having them work all day tomorrow would incur some hefty overtime charges, and we wouldn't be able to keep the same crew until the auction. It would go past the union workday rules."

"And is that important, having the same car movers?" asked Heinrich. "It is merely a laborer position and the car would be safer inside."

"It's *skilled labor* and they are the best in the New Orleans," replied Pat. "That's a big car. Without being able to actually roll it on its tires, much less drive it, it needs to be handled gently. Besides, I have my best security men watching the car. They are armed, and very dangerous. The car will be fine."

"And what time will be the car be moved into the hall and onto its stage?" asked Heinrich.

"As we discussed, the workers will arrive at eight a.m. and attach the dollies," said Pat. "It will take approximately one hour from the time they start until the car is safely secured onto this stage."

"And the security measures to allow only *authorized* participants into the hall?" asked Heinrich.

"All in place," replied Pat. "We've tripled our normal security to handle the extra requirements of matching photo ID with their badges. We'll also have uniformed NOPD officers at each entrance, and at each edge of the stage," Pat pointed to the right and left of where the stage would be, "there and there."

Pat stopped and shook his head with a smile, "Everything will be exactly as we discussed. I am very detail oriented."

"So it would seem," replied Heinrich, idly watching the workmen constructing the back truss, where the photo graphics and back lighting would be attached.

Heinrich then turned, looked directly into Pat eyes and said "Our mutual banker from the Caymans told me you have checked to ensure our *personal arrangement* was still in place. Actually checked twice, according to him."

Bobby was still pretending to be adjusting items in the grid while he listened. The phrase *personal arrangement* stopped him in his tracks. He pulled out the RigMaster and looked at the video feed in time to see Pat straighten up and look quickly around.

Bobby tapped on the screen to bring up the audio controls, made sure he was still recording and had sufficient audio levels. He saw the green digital meters drop to a fraction of their previous levels as Pat lowered his voice in reply.

"Yes," said Pat barely above a whisper.

As he continued to speak, Bobby tried boosting the audio gain to full, but that just amplified the ambient audio. He could make out that Pat was talking, but not the actual words. Sennheiser 816s were great, but they weren't magic. He'd try filtering the ambient out later, but high up in the grid he couldn't hear the rest of the conversation.

"Of course, I checked with our banker," replied Pat. "And I'll be checking again tomorrow, and likely more than twice. Do you have a problem with that?"

Heinrich looked at Pat for a moment and then finally broke into a smile. "Not at all," he replied. "I want you to be secure that our personal arrangement will also be followed, to the letter."

McMillian returned the smile. He briefly thought about bringing up the fact he knew Herr Heinzburg had also made a confirmation call to the escrow account manager, to ensure everything was still in place according to their agreement. He decided that nothing would be gained from that disclosure.

Then, in a more jovial mood and a much louder level, Pat bellowed out, "So, how about a Hurricane at Pat O'Briens?"

The sudden increase in volume blasted into Raston's earbuds and made him jump a bit, banging against the rigging as his right hand reflexively started for the RigMaster screen to lower the level. On the screen he saw the back of McMillian's head as he quickly looked up and away, in his direction. Raston saw the other man follow McMillian's gaze and look towards him as well.

Bobby, thinking fast, put a finger in his mouth, pulled it out and start shaking his hand. "Damn it, damn it, damn it" he said just loud enough to be heard on the floor. He then stuck his finger back into his mouth, pulled it out again and pretended to be observing it while actually looking past it and at the RigMaster screen.

He saw Heinrich turn back to Pat. Through the earbuds, heard him ask in a low voice, "Problem?"

Pat was still looking at Bobby, but at Heinrich's question he quickly replied, "No. No problem whatsoever."

"Hey you! On the lift," shouted Pat. The shout literally blasted into Bobby ears but this time he was ready for it and barely flinched. He slipped the RigMaster into his pocket as he turned around and replied, "Yes, Mr. McMillian?"

"Did you hurt yourself?" asked Pat, finally allowing himself to wonder why Raston was on the lift.

Then he saw the long, black-on-black tube on the pan tilt head. Mounted in the rigging with all the lighting gear and other cameras, it pretty much looked like it belonged. His eyebrows lifted involuntarily. It was all he could do not to immediately turn and scan the grid above and behind him.

"It's nothing," replied Bobby. "Just pinched it on a hanger."

McMillian looked back at Heinzburg, who was watching the workmen installing another section to the background truss. He then snuck a glance at the grid directly above where the stage would go. Looking closely, he identified an identical black tube on the same sort of mounting device. He could also see a light reflecting off the front of a smaller tube mounted directly underneath the longer one.

He immediately knew he was looking at a mic with a camera attached and that it was pointing directly at him. H struggled to keep the smile on his face, trying hard not to let the expression on his face reveal his sudden change in mood.

He turned back to Bobby and called out in slow measured tone between semi-clenched teeth, "Then, be careful. I don't need any Workers Comp claims."

He then asked Heinrich, "So, how about that Hurricane?"

"What is this… Hurricane?" Heinrich asked. "There was also an eLiquid of that name."

"It's a New Orleans tradition. Goes down easy and kicks like a mule. I won't let you have more than one, no matter how much you want another," said Pat, just a little bit too jovial. "And you most certainly will want another. But we've got a big day tomorrow and we've both got to be on top of our game."

Pat's phone buzzed in his pocket. He pulled it out and saw it was from Sandra Melancon. He held it up to Heinrich and said "Reporters. We're going to get a lot of that tomorrow, but don't worry. I'll handle it." He tapped the button that sent the call to voice mail and said, "Let's go. We'll park at your hotel and walk to Pat O'Brian's."

As they passed the scissor lift, on their way to the exit, Pat stopped and called up to Bobby, "Andy's your supervisor, right?"

Bobby didn't know what to say so he just replied in a slow voice, stretching out the word, "Yeeaaaah."

"Tell him we'll need to talk tomorrow morning. First thing. And hurry up with that lift, the riggers need to use it before they can build the stage."

"No worries, Mr. McMillian," Bobby replied. "Almost done."

As they walked out the door, Bobby manipulated the controls and the scissor lift started lowering to the floor.

"Damn," he thought as the lift settled onto the base and he started to climb down the short ladder to the floor. "This spy stuff seems so easy on a movie set."

# CHAPTER 39
# Just SOP

*Friday – August 25 – 7:05 PM CDT*

> "Of course we'd LOVE to be able to show you the provenance video, but it's really intense and, well…"
> — MALCOLM WALKER

"I see you are still one client schmoozing S.O.B.," said Brian Simmons after McMillian had left the Video Village to check on the staging for the Tourenwagen.

"Hey," replied Dean. "You gotta do what it takes to get the job done. And I get the job done."

"Well, now that we've got the *can and cannot* instructions, I think it's high time to start thinking about where we're all going for drinks," said Malcolm with a big smile.

"I'm pretty sure the boss will have other plans," replied Dean. "But I'll check."

"Bring the boss along," said Malcolm. He was talking to Dean, but smiling at the Twins.

"I said I'll check," replied Dean. "So let's go over this once more. There are actually two videos that will be shown during the Tourenwagen auction. The first is *Discovery,* and it's mainly a fluff piece about the area, and then about the finding of the car. The other is what they are calling the *Provenance* video."

"Yup, that's right," confirmed Brian. "During the first video, it's business as usual. We can shoot whatever we'd like, although both IMAG screens will be showing the video, so whatever we're on is just feeding the ISO recorders."

"Yeah," said Malcolm, "It's the provenance video that they're really concerned about, and I don't blame them. That's pretty rough stuff. It should have a disclaimer on it."

"Wait a minute. You've seen it?" asked Dean. "I thought McMillian just said it was embargoed and that they were bringing you a Blu-ray just before the auction?"

"Mr. McMillian did seem to think it was AWFULLY impressive that he'd been the ONLY one to see it in the United States," said Mandy.

"Actually, he seemed to think HE was awfully impressive in general," said Brandy.

Dean nodded his head in agreement, and then asked Malcolm, "So, that being the case, how do you know how *rough* it is?"

Malcolm looked over at Brian, who just rolled his eyes and shook his head. Malcolm raised his hands, palm up, and shrugged his shoulders.

"Well, they brought the disk in during set-up to…" Malcolm broke into a passable German accent, "to ve shur zee disk is compatible vit ur equipment."

Dean smiled and said, "And so while it was playing, you thought you might as well dump it into the Doremi because Cool-B doesn't like playing a disk live."

Brian Simmons just shrugged and said, "The man said follow SOP, and my SOP includes not relying on a disk to load up and be ready to play on cue."

Just then Dean's phone buzzed in his pocket. He held up a finger to Brian to wait while he fished it out of his pocket. He looked at the caller ID and saw it was Andy and said, "Excuse me. It's the boss. I've got to take it."

As he walked out of earshot, he heard Malcolm say, "So ladies, what kind of music do you like and have you ever sipped on a Green Fairy?"

"Hello, Andy," said Dean into his phone.

"Where are you?" asked Andy. He didn't believe in wasting time with formalities, especially not when he was on the job, and even more especially not with the crew.

"We're still backstage in the Video Village. We also met Pat McMillian who was very adamant that we follow the procedures that he and you worked out," said Dean. "Where are you?"

"I'm out by the cars," Andy said into cell phone as he stared at his beautiful 911T. It was parked in the rapidly darkening parking lot with all the other cars that would also soon have a new garage to call home. "I needed to think a bit after my talk with Jack Calman. Have you seen Bobby?"

"Well," replied Dean, "as of about twenty minutes ago, he was on a scissor lift doing something up in the grid. He'd gone back to the Escalade and gotten a couple of cases."

"Yeah, he said he had yet another audio gizmo he wanted to set up," said Andy as he continued looking at the classic lines on his beloved Porsche. He started to speak, but his voice croaked a bit, so he cleared it, took a breath and tried again. This time he succeeded.

"We're all going to dinner with Jack," said Andy. "We're going to meet him at the Royal Sonesta on Bourbon Street. We're supposed to be there at eight, so we should probably leave by seven thirty. Check with Bobby to see if he's done and if not, how long it will take."

"Roger that," replied Dean, thinking that officially pulled the plug on having drinks with Malcolm and Cool-B. "I'll call you if Bobby needs more time."

"Ok," said Andy. "I'll meet you and the rest of the crew in the hall in twenty minutes." Andy hit the "end" button on his iPhone and almost in the same motion, put it in his pocket and pulled out his vaping device. He took a deep drag. As he held the vapor in his lungs, he looked at the Porsche, shook his head and thought, "Max, I'm going to miss you."

As the cannabis infused vapor tickled the back of his brain, he imagined the car was also looking a bit sad, almost as if it was going to miss him as well.

Andy checked his watch, noted the time, took another, smaller drag and slipped the slender device back into his pocket. He just stood there and continued staring at the car.

Dean walked out from behind the stage and saw Bobby pulling a couple of obviously empty cases from the scissor lift platform. He walked over and said, "Andy says we need to leave by seven thirty to make a dinner with Jack Calman. He wanted to know if you were done."

"I'm done in the grid. I just want to hide a few small omnis around the room for surround and ambient. It'll only take another fifteen minutes or so," said Bobby. "Did you see those two guys that were in here?"

"What two guys?" asked Dean, looking around. "There's fifteen people in here now."

"One was Pat McMillian, the auction manager," said Bobby.

"Yeah," interrupted Dean. "I met him in the Video Village."

"The other was the guy who owns the Tourenwagen. He came in and talked with McMillian a bit and then they left to go have drinks," said Bobby.

"Did he see you?" asked Dean. "We can't have a worker show up as a bidder."

"No," replied Bobby, "I don't think Herr Heinzburg was very interested in a rig worker. At least I think that's the name McMillian called him."

"OK, good," replied Dean. "I'll go rescue the Twins and be back before you finish." Dean looked at his watch and said, "We've got about twenty minutes."

As Dean was walking into the Video Village he heard Malcolm, who was very obviously trying hard to impress the Twins, "Of course we'd LOVE to be able to show you the provenance video, but it's really intense and, well…"

"And well that's the sort of thing that loses gigs and gets you blacklisted," Brian finished with an authoritative air.

The Twins didn't look like they cared one way or the other, but Dean was very interested.

"How long is it?" Dean asked Brian.

"Eight minutes, twenty-seven seconds, and fourteen frames," replied Brian. It was his job to be precise.

"Well… the way I see it," said Dean, "if it's so intense, so rough, then we really NEED to know what's on it to properly do our job. It's like when you're running audience cams on a

Keynote gig. You need to know where the jokes are so you're set to capture the laughs."

Brian's demeanor softened somewhat. He personally made it a habit to preview any available video from any speaker he didn't know for just that reason. If you knew when to expect an audience reaction, then you weren't caught flatfooted; like in the middle of panning the audience camera or adjusting angles when the money shot happened. That was *Live Event 101*, and he believed he might well have taught that to Dean, back in the day.

"We're going to see it anyway," said Dean. "And in less than twenty-four hours. Again, it's just part of being prepared to do our job. And you heard McMillian. Anything you can do to help us…"

Dean could see that Brian was just about ready to tip. "Besides," he continued, "SOP is SOP, and this is certainly SOP."

"SOP would be to watch both videos, just like the audience will see them. *Discovery* is only five minutes long," said Brian. He then shook his head, sighed and turned to Malcolm, "Cut the feed to the IMAG, position the PTZ cameras on stage right and left so we can keep an eye on them."

"Roger that, Cool-B," replied Malcolm. With the speed and grace of a concert pianist, he hit a few buttons on the camera control panel, tapped a couple of more on the video switcher, and finally called up the video rundown on the Doremi control panel. "And how about I just go stand over there to make sure we don't get any *visitors* from the backstage entrance. I've seen these videos and I don't need to see 'em again… ever."

As Malcolm stood up, he paused and looked at Dean with a smile, "Want me to show you how to press play? This can be a bit complicated for a *field hand*."

Dean smiled at the jab. "That's *field producer*, and I'll manage," he replied as he sat down in Malcolm's chair. He looked at the screen and saw two videos in a sub-menu under the heading Tourenwagen. One was titled "Discovery" and the other titled "Provenance."

"*Playing Discovery in 3, 2, 1,*" Dean said in a practiced cadence as he tapped the screen and started the playback.

"Then we'll see what so damn intense about the provenance," he muttered under his breath as *Discovery* started to play on the large program monitor. Five minutes later it was finished.

"Nice work," said Mandy.

"Very nice," said Brandy. "We don't get to see that very often."

"You don't get to see what very often?" asked Dean.

"Finished video," replied Mandy.

Dean looked puzzled and was about to speak when his phone buzzed, signifying a text message. It was from Andy. "In the hall in ten. Be ready."

"Crap," he muttered and announced, "*Playing Provenance in 3, 2, 1,*" and tapped the button.

Eight minutes, twenty seven seconds, and fourteen frames later the video stopped, frozen on the last frame. Dean reached out and tapped a button that switched the video on the screens to black.

"Holy shit," he whispered, still trying to absorb what he had just seen. He shook his head, as if he just remembered where he was, and looked at the Twins. They were looking at the screen with the same look of mild boredom they usually had when they weren't in shooting mode.

Dean stared at them, wondering if that was what this Asperger thing was all about. Does it so deaden you to normal human emotions that you watch something like they had just seen and not blink an eye.

Malcolm walked back into the center of Video Village and said, "Those Nazi bastards were some true sons of bitches. Almost makes you want to skip going out and head straight to the hotel room." He stopped, smiled, and finished with, "Almost."

"It's hard to believe that this would make you want to buy that car at all," said Brian. "Let alone pay two or three times the market value just because it was part of... part of that," he said as the pointed to the now black screen. They knew what he meant.

"I don't know that it will," replied Dean, staring at the screen as if he could still see the images. The clanging of metal on metal and the muted voices of the workmen working on the stage only accented the quiet of the group standing mutely in the Video Village.

Suddenly the phone in Dean's pocket buzzed and shook him from his thoughts. He pulled it from his pocket, looked at the caller ID and answered, "This is Dean."

"I hope so. That's who I called," replied Andy. "I'm in front of the stage with Bobby. Are you ready to go?"

"Uh, yeah. Sure," replied Dean. "Wait until I tell you about the..."

"You can tell me later," interrupted Andy. "Come out and let Bobby show you this audio rig of his. You're going to need to see, and hear, what it can do so you'll be ready for tomorrow. Then we've got to hightail it over to hotel to meet Jack."

"Ok," replied Dean. He tapped his phone to end the conversation and said to Brian, "Thanks for showing us the videos. I think."

"Well, at least you know what to expect from the crowd when it plays tomorrow," replied Brian. "But you DID NOT see it here first, correct?"

"Correct," replied Dean. "I won't burn you. You know that."

"And I certainly hope I get to see you lovely ladies again," Malcolm said to the Twins. "Perhaps after your business dinner, we could meet up for a nightcap?" He pulled out his phone and innocently asked, "What's your number?"

"It's five, five, five, none ya," interjected Dean with a smile. "I'll call you if we're out after dinner and the boss doesn't mind. But I wouldn't hold my breath. It's a big day tomorrow and I'm pretty sure we'll be sleeping when you're ordering your third round. And certainly by the fourth."

Dean turned to the Twins and said, "Let's go. Andy's out front and we need to be leaving soon." As the Twins walked out and towards the front of the stage, Dean turned to Brian and Malcolm. "See you tomorrow guys. And thanks again. I think," he laughed. "But it's better to get over the shock now than during the shoot."

"No worries," replied Brian with a shrug. "Just SOP."

Brian and Malcolm both watched them leave in silence. Once they rounded the back of the stage and entered the hall, Brian looked down at the camera monitors and saw them walk up to Andy and Bobby.

Brian, still looking at the cameras, said to Malcolm. "I was really surprised at those gals' reaction. Or, rather, their *lack* of reaction. It's like it didn't faze them a bit. I guess that's what that As-Burg-Whatever does to a person."

"Maybe," replied Malcolm. Brian looked up to him as he continued. "I don't know. I was watching them while it played and you're right. They were watching it closely, but almost in a clinical way. They didn't flinch. Not once. And there are plenty of places to be flinching in that video."

Malcolm just shook his head and continued, "It's hard to believe there's all that *heat* on the outside and all that *chill* on the inside. Still, all cashed up and fine as wine. That's quite a package."

"I wouldn't mind seeing some of their camera work," said Brian. "Ask them for a link to something they've done. That's if you just happen to run into them before this gig's over."

Malcolm smiled and said, "Well, you do never know, now do you."

"Sometimes you do," replied Brian with a smile. "Let's wrap it up and get out of here. I'm thinking a drink or two before dinner."

"That's just one of the things I like about you, Cool-B," said Malcolm with a smile; a smile which only slightly dimmed when he glanced back at the monitor where the video had been playing. He turned back to Brian and said, "Let's go for the two drink option."

# CHAPTER 40
# No Spielberg

*Friday – August 25 – 7:15 PM CDT*

> "Perhaps you thought I was too stupid to
> understand your half-witted explanation
> of this so-called deal you came up with?"
> — J. ROGER WINTERS

"WHY CAN'T YOU DO ANYTHING RIGHT?" screamed J. Roger Winters.

Jack was lying on the hotel room bed, eyes closed with the phone on speaker. He held it high above his prone body. The angry voice filled his room and spilled out onto the balcony. It actually drowned out the sounds of early evening revelry that floated up from Bourbon Street. Jack had just filled him in on the deal he and Andy had negotiated. Not surprisingly, Winters wasn't happy.

"I specifically told you that our minimum was a fifty-fifty deal on ownership! You should have started out at seventy-five or eighty and then let him Jew you down to fifty."

Jack idly wondered why ethnic slurs didn't count as cursing.

"I started out at a full buyout and dropped to seventy-five percent," said Jack.

"FULL BUYOUT!" screamed Winters. "No wonder you pissed him off. You came across too greedy, like you were taking advantage of the situation. And yet ANOTHER stupid move on your part!"

Jack wanted to point out it was exactly what Winters had told him to do, but knew it would only add fuel to this fire.

"He said he would have taken the deal, if we had sent him the money." he told Winters. "As we had promised."

"As YOU promised," shouted Winters. "You've been mucking this up from the beginning. I don't know how, but I'm sure it had something to do with that nimrod Raston being in on this. Obviously, I'll have to start keeping a closer watch on you."

Other than a big sigh, Jack made no reply.

"So IF you've got the details right, the money is all right. It's the ownership percentage that's in question?" asked Winters. When there was no reply he yelled out, "CORRECT?"

"Yes, sir," said Jack, trying hard to unclench his teeth. "That is correct. That and they want the original fifty grand deposit, that we, huh, that I promised them. The contract isn't valid until the deposit is in Andy's account."

"Big deal," replied Winters. " I knew this would happen. That's why I told you to have everything ready for the deposit. I assume you DID manage to accomplish that little task?"

"Yes, sir," Jack replied.

"OK," said Winters. "Let me think about this for a moment."

There was a long pause in the conversation. Jack could hear laughter on the street and a surprisingly melodious blend of music coming from the variety of bands playing in the open-air clubs. He was more than ready for a drink, and he licked his lips remembering a shop he had seen earlier, not two blocks away. Its walls were lined with large commercial-sized frozen drink machines. They were all churning away, their glass fronts showing all the hues of the rainbow. The huge menu above each bank of machines boasted names like *MoJo Juju Juice*, *Blueberry Blood*, and the ever-present *Hurricane*.

"Ok," said Winters. "Here's what you do. Make up two contracts, one with us getting the twenty percent on the pilot, fifteen on first season and twenty on any successive seasons. That is what he wants, right? You didn't screw that up, did you?"

"That's what he said was his bottom line," replied Jack.

"OK, but also make up a contract with us getting twenty percent on the pilot but thirty on a subsequent twelve show order respectively," instructed Winters in a commanding tone. "That way he'll get what he wants on the first show. That's what's *real* to him because he's working on it right now. The remaining twelve shows of the first season might be on his radar, but he doesn't know how the pilot will turn out. AND, by the way, NEITHER DO WE. Anyway, he'll be willing to negotiate more on the remaining twelve. Negotiating a second season before the pilot is even done is ludicrous. He's no Spielberg. Are you writing this down?"

Jack rolled his eyes and made writing gestures with his free hand, "Yes, sir, twenty on the pilot and thirty on the first twelve shows. But no deal on the second season," Jack paused a bit, sighed knowing that he could not help but continue, "But the percentage on season two was contingent on us picking up the show. And it's just locking a percentage in place, without a commitment to purchase. It really is to our benefit."

"I'm sorry," replied Winters in a sarcastic, solicitous tone; easily one of his favorites. "Perhaps you thought I was too stupid to understand your half-witted explanation of this so-called deal you came up with?"

"If you're already talking about second season," continued Winters in his *teaching the kids from the short bus* tone, "then you've showed your cards on the first season deal." Winters took a deep sigh and continued, "You start off by telling him you're not interested in a second season until you at least see the pilot. Use that Spielberg line. It'll show him you're not just bending over and giving up the glory hole."

"And so I take it that you want me to present the twenty-thirty contract first," said Jack. "Press him that this is as good as we can do. But if he won't get on board, go with the twenty-fifteen-twenty. Or did you want me to remove the twenty percent for a second season clause?"

"No, if it gets to that, you've been rolled in flour and the wet spot is showing," said Winters. "That's a bone he's throwing us, so we might as well pick it up and gnaw on it. If you'd just think about it for a second, you'd see it's to our benefit."

"What about the deposit?" asked Jack, ignoring the regurgitated benefit comment. "He was adamant that the contract wouldn't be valid unless the deposit was paid."

"Well, you can't give him the money until the contract is signed now can you?" demanded Winters. "Tell him you'll have the money transferred as soon as accounting opens up in the morning. I'll call 'em and tell 'em to have their hineys in the office by six. You call them at eight, your time, and get this deal done. Do you have all that? Have you been writing this down? It would be most UNFORTUNATE if you continue to drop the ball on this simple deal."

Jack again made a writing gesture with his hand raised high. "Yes sir, I've got it all down; every detail. Twenty-thirty first. No Spielberg. Twenty-fifteen-twenty if he plays hardball. Call to approve the wire transfer at eight, New Orleans time, assuming the contract is signed. Don't drop any more balls."

"Ok, good," replied Winters. "And there's one more little thing."

"Yes, sir?" said Jack.

"We're going to have a fair amount of money, and a lot of reputation riding on this," said Winters in a slow deliberate tone. "I've already sold this as a ByDemand exclusive to our new network level sponsors. I've already collected their money to lock them in at that level. These are some very big boys; high roller, personal friends of mine that I wouldn't want to embarrass. Having their brands associated with a program about some schmoe getting duped into paying millions for a fake car *would not be good*. I'm holding you personally responsible that this whole thing is on the up and up. If it's not, we might… no, we *most definitely would* have to find someone more adept at this sort of work."

"I… well, I don't know how I can do that," stammered Jack. "I'm not even allowed into the actual auction. I haven't even gotten to take a good look at the car."

"DO I HAVE TO DO EVERYTHING FOR YOU?" Winters immediately replied, at a volume just under screaming.

"CAN'T YOU FIGURE OUT THE SIMPLEST DETAILS? I AM DONE WITH THIS CONVERSATION."

"Mr. Winters, I don't think you..." Jack said quickly, but not quite quick enough. Winters had ended the call.

"Fuck, fuck, fuck," said Jack. He then sighed a bit. He got off the bed, tapped a few notes into the open MacBook on the desk, and then launched the Contacts app on his phone. He typed in Stan, and then tapped on Stan Niemec name from the long list his phone produced.

As the phone started ringing, he let out a big sigh and then put a smile on his face. "Smile on your face, smile in your voice," he mumbled. It was a mnemonic device he often used, and liked to pass on to friends and associates. He had been telling it to himself a lot more often since Winters came into his life. The call finally connected and yet another angry voice came pouring out of it.

"Jack, what's this crap about pulling those girls from my production?" demanded Stan. "Blackman says they are the best he's ever seen and somehow they just disappeared from my shoot... along with that Prescott kid. Now I've got two local geezers who look like they'd be more at home shooting a mud race than a Maserati."

"Preston," replied Jack absentmindedly, wondering if the guys from *In The Dirt TV* had been bragging about their normal gig. He had told them to keep that on the down-low. He then realized that Blackman had likely worked with them before.

"What?" asked Stan.

"Preston," replied Jack, who quickly continued. "The kid's name is Preston. But never mind, it's not important.

What's important is that Burt Blackman's on the job. And that was our deal. Now let me tell you about those two *very experienced* shooters I sent to you, and for a *very* good reason."

Jack glanced at the clock radio by the bed, calculated the time he had to placate Niemec, prep the two versions of contracts, get them printed, arrange for the notary, and meet Andy and crew in the lobby by eight o'clock. The warm breeze, wafting in from the open balcony, blew away any chances of one of those frozen, fruity concoctions before then.

He sighed and continued, "Basically, it was really just a mistake. My mistake. Just a huge mistake on my part for using those gals in the first place. I'm sorry and I'll tell you how it happened. I think you're going to appreciate this. You see…"

## CHAPTER 41
# Live Shot At 10:10

*Friday – August 25 – 7:37 PM CDT*

> "Blake tells me there's a couple of establishing shots, three interviews with sound bites, and an *undercover* scene that's going to be nothing but money."
> — SANDRA MELANCON

"Whatever you're doing, stop it," said Sandra Melancon as she bustled into the edit bay holding a small notepad filled with scribbles.

Alton Briggs didn't even look up from the computer screen as he replied, "Give me a few minutes. I've got one last tweak before I hit export." Looking up at the corner of the screen he continued, "And I'm off the clock in one hour and twenty-three minutes."

Sandra didn't say a word, but plopped down in the producer chair and started writing on the pad. She paused every few lines to shift through the pages and check on a previously written note.

After seven minutes, Ton tapped a button on the keyboard with a flourish and announced, to no one in particular, "Another masterpiece of the editing arts, ready for consumer consumption." Turning to Sandra he asked, "And what may I do for you?" And that's when he noticed the gleam in her eye. He'd seen that gleam before and he knew this was going to be good.

"We need to recut the *Muscles on the Mississippi* recap for the ten o'clock," she said quickly, as if there was no time to waste.

"Oh, yeah, the Hitler Car," replied Ton. "I wanted to show you something about that car. I noticed it in the footage after you left."

"Tell me in a minute, after I explain the recut, and if we have time," said Sandra. "That guy Wittmann isn't what he seems. And he just out-and-out lied about why he's here. At least I think he's lying. Blair Fontenot did some digging for me this afternoon and came up with some incredible stuff. And he has video to back it up!"

Ton immediately asked, "Where are the clips?"

"We're downloading the raw now," replied Sandra. "They'll be on Server Five in about," she paused and checked her watch, looked at the note pad and continued, "twenty minutes."

"How big is the recut?" asked Ton. "If I can't get started for another twenty minutes, that won't leave me a lot of time."

"I've got your overtime authorized," said Sandra. "This is going to be big. EMMY® big. Maybe NATIONAL EMMY® BIG."

"Cool," replied Ton with a smile. Overtime at his rate didn't get approved very often and he could always use the money. "So what's the deal with the guy? He's not really some preacher stirring up a big ole bucket of Hitler hate? Is he really a car collector hoping to keep the price down? That's kinda what I was thinking."

"Oh, he's a collector all right," replied Sandra, "But not a car collector. And forget Hitler hate, it's more like a Hitler hard-on!"

She went to the last page of the notepad that she had been writing on, tore it out, and handed it to Ton. "Here's the script. Sorry I don't have time code on the clip descriptions, but I haven't actually seen them yet." Ton took the sheet of paper, knowing that the handwriting would be rushed, but legible and organized. It always was when Sandra was on a breaking story.

Sandra continued, "I'll be doing a live standup for the ten o'clock, ten minutes in."

"Prime spot," replied Ton. "Nice." He was starting to think this really must be big if the News Director gave that slot to a car story.

Sandra continued, "I'll tease the interview as not being exactly what it seems and then we'll run the Wittmann piece."

"Do we have to recut it or use it as is?" asked Ton. "It's a minute ten."

"It's good the way it is," said Sandra, "I want him to come across all pious and sanctimonious. It's when we go back to the live shot that I drop the bomb with the Fontenot footage."

Sandra looked at her notes and continued, "Blake tells me there's a couple of establishing shots, three interviews with sound bites, and an *undercover* scene that's going to be nothing but money."

"How long do you want this second roll in?" asked Ton, who glanced at his watch to see how long it would be before he could check out the video clips.

"I've got a thirteen second VO to go over the intro and a ten second VO to go over the money shot. We'll fill the middle with sound bites," said Sandra looking at her notes. She looked up at Ton with pursed lips, nodding her head for a bit as she calculated the time, then said, "I'm thinking a minute to a minute ten for this piece should be plenty. I've got four minutes for the whole story and I'm going to try and get one more interview to wrap it up. If I can, I'll do that interview live, during the standup, to cap the story."

Ton nodded his head, laying it out in his mind and replied, "How long are the interviews?"

"Pretty short from what Blake told me," Sandra replied. "But like I said, I haven't seen 'em."

"And what's the money shot?" asked Ton.

Sandra looked at Ton and a huge smile slowly wiped the all-business demeanor from her face. "Again, I haven't seen it. I could tell you what Blake told me, but I think I'd rather surprise you and get your first impression later."

Sandra stood up, "I'm going to go cut the VO's. I'll put them in the same folder with the Blake clips on Server Five." Sandra looked at her watch and continued her rapid fire instructions, "It shouldn't take more that about ten minutes. Then I'll come back and we can edit the new roll-in."

As she turned to walk out the door, Ton stopped her with a "Wait just a second. I want to show you something before you set the story in stone."

Sandra stopped, looked at her watch again, and sighed. "Ok, but I don't have a lot of time."

"I don't know what you can do with it," replied Ton. "But I think you'll find it interesting."

He manipulated the mouse and clicked it a few times. He then tapped on the keyboard and the timeline for the Wittmann roll-in filled the screen. He moved the cursor to a shot of the Tourenwagen, found his *Phillip* flag on the timeline and pressed a hot key to call up the original clip. He then held down a key while scrolling on the mouse and the shot zoomed into a spot to the inside of the driver's side front fender.

"See that little flag pole," he asked Sandra.

"Yes," replied Sandra, looking up from her notes. She had begun writing again while Ton had called up the clip. "What about it?"

Ton zoomed in even further into the shot.

"See those little screws?" he asked with a smile on his face.

"Yes," said Sandra, trying to keep the impatience out of her voice, but not really succeeding.

"Those are Phillips screws," said Ton.

"AND???" asked Sandra.

"Phillips screws first appeared on Cadillacs in 1936," said Ton. "I know because my brother-in-law was dinged for having them on his '32 V-12 at a Concours last year."

"I didn't know you were an old car guy," said Sandra.

"I'm not," replied Ton, "But my brother-in-law is and he's been bitching about it ever since."

"Ok," said Sandra, "So what do these screws have to do with anything? This is a 1940 car and you said the screws were available since '36."

"Yeah," said Ton. "Here in the U. S. of A. But technology didn't move that quickly back then, especially not at the beginning of the war. I'll bet if you take a good look at that car, you won't find any other Phillips head screws on it. And take away those flags and it doesn't scream *Hitler Car* quite so loud."

"Humm," said Sandra, "that is interesting, but I don't know what to do with it, or how to use it. I'll see what I can dig up tomorrow, but for now I've got to go do these voice overs and then find Joey and tell him we'll doing a live shot tonight."

"That'll be the third time today you're at Mardi Gras World," said Ton. "They'll be loving the air time."

"We're not going to Mardi Gras World," replied Sandra with a smile.

"Really?" asked Ton. "Then where's the live shot?"

As Sandra stood up she looked at her notes and read out loud, "The First Free Mission Baptist Church." She looked at Ton and continued, "That's where most of this morning's protesters were from."

Ton just nodded his head and smiled. This gal was good, damn good.

"I'll be back A.S.A.P.," said Sandra as she walked out the door. As she left she told Ton, "Don't let anyone else snatch you up for some bullshit promo work." She was gone before she heard the answer.

"Not a chance," said Ton as he turned to the editing console. He called up Server Five and saw that a few of the clips had finished downloading. He dropped them into a bin, double clicked on the first clip to load it into the preview monitor. "Not a chance in hell," he muttered again as he pushed the play key and the video began.

## CHAPTER 42
# Exactly Like The Storm

*Friday – August 25 – 7:59 PM CDT*

> "Kind of an acquired taste,
> but very New Orleans."
> — Antoine Guidry

"There they are!" exclaimed a jovial Jack Calman. He had a folder in his hand and a smile on his lips. "And right on time!"

"Of course. It's a big day tomorrow," replied Andy Guidry. "We're here to take care of business, then eat and sleep."

"This is a nice place, and right on Bourbon," said Dean looking around the opulent lobby with its marble floors and crystal chandeliers. There was an impressive blend of artwork on the walls and precisely placed antique tables were topped with massive vases of fresh flowers. Bobby and the Twins didn't look as impressed. It took a lot to impress Bobby, and the Twins simply didn't notice.

"Yeah," replied Jack with a shrug and a smile, "I like to stay here when I'm in town and I *always* get a room overlooking Bourbon. It can get noisy, but it's New Orleans. It's supposed to be noisy!"

Jack then held up a folder and said, "Let's get our business out of the way, and then we can decide where to eat. Andy, we can talk a bit over there," said Jack pointing to a sitting area with elegant, high back chairs and a small sofa flanking an ornate, early French coffee table. He then pointed across the lobby and continued, "If the rest of you want to go to the bar and get a drink and a dozen or two on the half shell, just charge it to me. My room number is two thirty one."

"We can do that," said Dean with a huge smile. He always liked it when Mr. Calman was onsite. It didn't happen often, but when it did, he really knew how to treat the crew.

"Bobby will stay with us," Andy said to Jack. "We'll meet the rest of you in…" he stopped to look at the name of the bar, "huh, we'll meet you in *Desire* in a few minutes."

As Dean and the Twins went off to the bar, Jack motioned toward the sitting area with a courtly gesture and said, "Gentlemen."

Andy and Bobby remained standing. Jack's smile faltered just a bit and asked, "Would you prefer not to sit?"

"Do we need to?" asked Andy. "You either have, or don't have the contract. If you do, let's get it signed and get some food. If you don't, then… well, then let's just get some food cause I'm starving." Andy looked at Bobby with his palms up and shrugged his shoulders as if to ask "Am I right?"

Bobby just nodded in agreement and looked at Jack. With a smile and a shrug, he said, "Seems pretty clear."

Jack's smile faded just a bit as he studied the two men's faces. Despite Winters' disparaging remarks, Jack was a master at negotiations. He could read people's subtle *tells* as if they had their intentions tattooed across their forehead. These two weren't going to budge. And considering the circumstances, the deal they offered wasn't a bad one, no matter what that nickel-squeezing asshole thought.

Jack let his smile turn a bit rueful, inhaled deeply and said, with firm conviction, "J. Roger Winters is a dick."

"Understatement of the year," Bobby quickly replied. "So, I'm guessing that means that folder does not contain a contract with our terms in it." Bobby gestured to the bar and said, "Good, let's go get them before they order and we can go eat. Or are we eating here?"

Jack just stood there and said, "The money's not an issue, it's the ownership percentage. You guys know that giving up ANY ownership to a production company is rare these days. We think you giving us twenty percent of the pilot, and thirty percent of the remaining twelve shows in the first season is more than fair. We'll negotiate for season two, if there is one... once we see how this one goes."

"Ok, then," said Bobby. "That's clear enough. Basically, you can't meet our terms. Again, are we eating here?"

Andy stared at Jack for a long three seconds, studying his face. Finally he asked, "Really?"

Jack looked back, staring into Andy's eyes and said, "Just following instructions. So that's a 'No?'"

Andy just continued to look at Jack, waiting for him to continue.

"Andy," said Jack, "I'm an ethical man in a difficult situation. I need to hear it from you. Are you declining this offer?"

"Yes," said Andy, pausing a bit before he continued, "I am declining your offer."

"Good," said Bobby with a huge smile. "Now that's settled, let's go."

Andy kept looking at Jack, who kept looking back at him.

While by no means the best of friends, or even friends for that matter, they were associates. And they had been for a long time. Jack had literally given him his start in the business, at least the business of producing. If it weren't for Jack believing in him, he wouldn't be where he was today. And although the current circumstances weren't exactly great, it was better than being an aging camera guy listening to young pups like Dean telling him how to frame a shot.

Jack stared at Andy and then calmly said, "OK, then I've got another contract, with your exact terms. I'll sign it right now, but I'll catch hell for it. Like I said, and I truly can't say it often enough, Winters is a dick."

"Even better," Bobby chimed in. "Let's sign it and be done."

Jack and Andy ignored him and continued looking at each other.

"Andy, I could use a bone here and a fixed percentage on our first right of refusal for season two isn't it," said Jack, all traces of a smile gone. "If I give you exactly what you want, I'll never hear the end of it."

"Damn. It sucks to be you," said Bobby. "So, are we going to get this signed and get going? I'm getting hungry."

Andy continued looking at Jack for another three seconds. Jack returned the stare with unwavering eyes.

"How about we just do a straight twenty percent across the board? I give you twenty percent ownership on the pilot, on season one shows, and a twenty percent lock on season two with the first right of refusal," said Andy.

"WHAT?" cried Bobby.

"Deal," said Jack.

"Hold the fuck up for a moment," said Bobby, dismay with a touch of anger creeping into his voice. "What happened to the deal we just had? Why the fuck are we giving up more?"

Andy looked at Bobby, his eyes beginning to spark as his own temper started to flair. "I don't believe this concerns you Bobby. There is no *we* in this. Our deal is our deal, and it's only for the revenue split. The company is mine and this is a company level negotiation." Andy paused and cocked his head a bit, emphasizing his height over the much shorter man. "Do you have a problem with that?"

"What I have a problem with is the producer giving up so much he's no longer interested in the property," replied Bobby. "If my share is going to be worth anything close to the money I'm putting in, that I've *already* put in, you need to be *enthused* about this project, now and going forward."

"I appreciate your concerns," said Andy in a tone bordering on sarcasm. "But, I don't have any problems remaining *enthused*." He then turned to Jack and asked, "Speaking of money, I believe there was a deposit clause in the negotiation?"

"If we sign the contract tonight," said Jack, "There will be fifty thousand dollars in your account before... well, certainly before noon tomorrow. The west coast is two hours behind us."

"Can you get it done by nine am New Orleans time? Before we start rolling tomorrow? It's not like you have to go stand in line at the teller."

Jack smiled and said, "Deal, deal, and done." He held up a small thumb drive and said, "I've got the contract file on this. I'll go over to the business center and make the changes you suggested," he paused and sent an unspoken *thank you* with a nod and a smile to Andy. "It'll be ready to sign in ten minutes or less."

He then turned and waved at a smartly dressed woman that was standing next to the concierge desk. He turned back to Andy and Bobby and said, "That young lady is a notary and will witness the signatures. We'll get this done and then go do a little celebrating."

As Jack walked off, Andy and Bobby finally sat down in the seating area to wait for the new contract.

"Why did you give up anything to that asshole Winters?" asked Bobby in disgust.

"I didn't," replied Andy. "My deal is with Jack and I told you, this is company business. MY company business."

Bobby just shrugged and they both sat in silence for a full minute.

"I appreciate what you've done for me," said Andy. "More than you know. But Jack's been good to me over the years and I'm a loyal guy. I'll refund all your money after the auction tomorrow, with your percentage. It doesn't change our deal at all."

"I never thought it would," replied Bobby. "It's all just business. I just don't believe in getting anything less than the best deal possible."

Bobby then stood up and stretched a bit, "It was a long day today. I think I'll go wait in the bar and let Jack buy me a drink... or two."

Twenty minutes later Bobby was slurping down the last of a dozen oysters, with an accompanying stereo soundtrack of "EEWWWW" from the Twins. Jack and Andy joined them, after having first stopped at the bar for a quick discussion with the bartender.

"Let's finish up," announced Jack. "We now have a signed airtime deal for... *CarAlity*."

Jack looked at Andy who just shrugged, smiled, and said, "It was just a working title, but it's starting to grow on me."

A waiter showed up with a tray of six small glasses with about an inch of amber liquid in them. He handed one to each of them and then went back to the bar.

"A toast to Season One of *CarAlity*, a joint venture of Pure Entertainment and NGTV," said Jack raising his glass.

Dean and the Twins gave their glasses a sniff. The Twins wrinkled their noses at each other, then to Dean. He returned the look, shrugged his shoulders and said, "Salute!"

They all drained their glasses and, almost in unison, the Twins, Bobby and Dean all cried out, "Yuck!"

Andy smiled and said, "It's a Sazerac. Kind of an acquired taste, but very New Orleans."

Dean was making smacking noises as if trying to clear the taste from his mouth, "I don't think I'm going to spend the time it would take to *acquire* it. If we're eating here, I'm going to order another beer." Dean looked at his empty glass with a cocked eye and stated, "That was just nasty."

"I managed to get reservations at Brennan's, but not until nine-fifteen. We've got a little time to kill," said Jack.

"So we're going to go for another New Orleans classic drink, and this one that I guarantee you'll like," said Andy.

"I hope so," replied Bobby, pointing at his empty glass. "Because that was indeed *nasty*."

As they all stood up, the waiter brought the bill to Jack. He added a very generous tip and signed it with a flourish.

As the group made their way out the door and onto Bourbon Street, Andy held back, thinking briefly about the vape pen in his pocket. He then just shook his head and smiled. He just couldn't believe how much things had turned around in the last forty-eight hours. It sucked that he was losing Max, but if he hadn't bit the bullet and put him in the auction, none of this would have happened."

As he caught up with the group, Dean asked, "So where are we going and what are we drinking?"

"It's four blocks up and a right turn on St. Peters," said Andy. "It's called Pat O'Brian's and they are famous for their Hurricanes."

"Like the storm?" asked Dean.

"Yep," replied a jovial Andy, patting Dean on the back. "*Exactly* like the storm."

## CHAPTER 43
# Let It Shine

### Friday – August 25 – 8:04 PM CDT

"He looks strong, but he's an old man."
— HERMAN ADLER

"And the Lord Jesus spoke unto me and said 'Saul, there's a reason I've blessed you with the time and the money to tackle this task.'" Saul paused and looked at the sea of faces, almost entirely black, that packed the First Free Mission Baptist Church. A sprinkling of "Amen" and "Praise the Lord" floated above the crowd.

"He said to me, 'It is to do my will! To shine the bright white light of the Lord and expose this evil for what it is!'" Saul Wittmann cried out, his right arm was raised high with fingers splayed. He then visibly sagged at the lectern and slowly lowered his arm. The congregation was completely silent as they waited.

Saul lowered his head and took a deep breath. He looked every bit the tired old man, burdened by his mission, that he hoped to portray. With another deep breath, still staring at the podium, he seemed to gather his strength. He slowly stood up, straight and tall, and scanned the room with a steely stare. His voice then exploded with, "And with your help, and the blessings of our Lord Jesus Christ, that is EXACTLY what I'm going to do. It's taken every penny I have, and every ounce of energy this old body has in it, but I AM going to shine a light on this evil!"

The entire congregation leapt to their feet amid fervent shouts of "Praise Jesus," "Hallelujah," and "Mercy, Mercy, Mercy!"

The choir, dressed in voluminous royal blue and white robes broke out into a riotous rendition of "This Little Light Of Mine." By the fourth verse, the entire church was clapping, singing, and dancing in place as best they could, considering the packed conditions.

Pastor Jay Rollins Broussard strutted up to the podium. He was smiling, clapping, and almost dancing to the music. When he reached Saul he reached out to him, shaking his hand with his right and grasping Saul's forearm with his left. He then released the forearm and pulled Saul close, grasping Saul's shoulder and leaning in to be heard over the singing.

"Brother Saul, Brother Saul," shouted Pastor Broussard. "That was uplifting and a righteous salute to the Lord! Are you sure you've never done any preaching?"

"Never in my life, Brother Jay," Saul shouted back. "Before this evil transpired, I suppose I never had to."

"Then Jesus is working through you," replied Broussard. "All praise to his holy name."

The pastor then signaled for Saul to sit in the chair next to the ornate lectern, turned to the choir and, continuing to clap along, he gave them the smile and nod of the head that signaled them to wrap it up after the next chorus.

"Let it shine, let it shine, Leeetttt iiiitttt ssshhhhiiiinnn-neeee!" As the last note still reverberated, Pastor Broussard turned to his congregation and scanned the room. The crowd was silent as they waited for him to speak.

"I... believe!" he shouted.

"Amen" and "Praise Jesus" squeaked out from a few of the congregation, as if they had no more control over it than they would a sudden hiccup.

Jay Rollins Broussard had been the pastor of the First Free Mission Baptist Church for well over thirty years. He knew his congregation. He knew how to bring them up and how to make them dig deep to do the Lord's work.

"I believe that the Lord works not in mysterious ways, but in ways that righteous people can see just as plain as the nose on their face," said Broussard, scanning the congregation with a knowing smile.

"I believe it is plain to see that our Lord Jesus Christ has brought Brother Saul to us," said Broussard in a commanding tone. "Brought him to us because he needs our help... our presence... our holy intervention to bring the attention of the world to this unholy exchange of filthy lucre; an exchange for an object that does nothing but glorify EEEE-vil."

The mass of people had long ago overwhelmed the air conditioning. The crowd stood sweating in their church clothes, the air made even more humid by the residual heavy breathing as they recovered from the song. They hung on Broussard's every word, waiting for their cue to respond.

"Will Brother Saul fight the good fight alone; a stranger in a strange land?"

"NO!" came the thunderous reply.

"Will we help Brother Saul, just as the Good Samaritan helped his fellow man?"

"YES!" came the reply, even louder.

Pastor Broussard nodded to Mason LaCroix who was at the back of the church with the other members of the church's *Young Adults For Jesus* group. The forty-three members were split up between those holding a stack of printouts and those holding collection baskets.

"Young Brother Mason, a willing instrument of the Lord who brought Brother Saul to us, will be coming among you with the members of our youth group. Can I get an AMEN?"

"AMEN!" shouted the crowd.

"Praise Jesus," Broussard replied and continued, "Brother Mason will be passing out information on this evil automobile, so you will know about this travesty and be able to spread the word yourselves. It will also tell you when the buses will be leaving tomorrow morning and what you need to bring to participate in this righteous battle against Satan himself. Can I get a Hallelujah?"

"HALLELUJAH," came the almost immediate reply.

"Amen," Broussard replied and continued, "They will also be passing the collection baskets so you can help with this holy endeavor. We need materials for signs, gas for the busses, food for the masses. As you know, being righteous isn't cheap, but the rewards are great. Can I get a Praise Jesus?"

"PRAISE JESUS," came the ear splitting reply.

"So true, so true," replied Broussard dropping his tone to imply the impartation of a serious communication. "We do need to praise Jesus, every day and in every way. We have been called upon. We have been chosen." Broussard looked around the room, head held high. He raised his right hand, fist clenched, to just over shoulder height and gave it a slight pump to add inflection to his words, "We are NEEDED to shine a LIGHT on this dark EVIL and... we... WILL!" On his last word, he slammed his fist onto the lectern.

The opening chord from the Hammond B-3 poured from the dual Leslie 122 speakers. With all the drawbars out, the single chord reverberated throughout the room for exactly three seconds. Then the choir, with perfect timing, began to sing again.

The sound of "This Little Light Of Mine" again filled the Church, and spilled out into the hot humid night. Each member of the congregation paused their clapping and singing only long enough to drop some change, or a few wadded up dollar bills, into the collection baskets. The members of the First Free Mission Baptist Church were far from wealthy, but they were always willing to share what little they had.

Herman Adler stood at the edge of the choir platform, which was directly behind the lectern. Herman looked up at the massive crucifix. The Christ figure had a decidedly darker complexion than the one in the Wisconsin church; the church he had attended Sunday services in with his mother and father.

"Jesus," Herman whispered, "I know I don't talk to you very much anymore. And I know this is the first time I've been in a church since..." Herman stopped a bit as his breath caught in his chest. He closed his eyes, forced his chest to expand, blew out a little puff of air and continued, "Since the funeral."

Herman turned and looked at the crowd, joyously clapping and singing along with the choir. He then looked over at Saul, who was positively beaming, nodding his head in time with the music and looking around the room with wide-eyed amazement. Saul looked happier and more alive than anytime Herman could remember. He then turned back to the crucifix and continued his prayer, "But if you could, please watch over us tomorrow. And especially watch over Saul."

Herman looked at Saul again and saw he had gotten up from his seat and was vigorously clapping, actually almost dancing, and singing at the top of his lungs with Pastor Broussard. Herman continued praying, "He looks strong, but he's an old man. Help him get his way, if that's your will. And help him accept it, if it's not."

Herman crossed himself, said, "Thy will be done," and then smiled. He was thinking that praying was a lot like riding a bike. Once you figure out how to do it, you never really forget.

He then realized that the choir had come around to the first set of lyrics for the third time. He looked out at the crowd, still singing with wild abandon and digging even deeper into their pockets and handbags.

He saw Mason, about halfway down the aisle, laughing with an elderly black man. The man had a slight stoop and a natty black straw hat with a thin brim and a multi-hued band. Mason held out the basket and the man dropped a well-worn dollar bill into it. He could read the words on Mason's lips, "Bless you, brother!"

As Mason turned to scan the room for another donor, his eyes locked on to Herman's. Mason gave Herman a big smile, a thumbs-up, and was then sidetracked by a large woman with a bright yellow dress and a huge hat that almost matched the color. She was waving a five-dollar bill in the air, as if conducting the choir, and Mason hurried over to collect it.

Herman shook his head in both wonder and resignation. With a smile he thought to himself, literally for the very first time, "This might actually work."

He then joined in, his slightly flat voice being swallowed up in the choir's mighty wall of sound. The fact he could barely hear himself just made his smile bigger and his singing louder.

*Ev'ry where I go,*
*I'm going to let it shine.*
*Ev'ry where I go,*
*I'm going to let it shine.*
*Hallelujah*
*Ev'ry where I go,*
*I'm going to let it shine.*
*Let it shine, let it shine, LET IT SHINE!*

# CHAPTER 44
# Big Money, Beautiful Women

*Friday – August 25 – 8:23 PM CDT*

> "One guy has a car to sell tomorrow, a sweet little 911."
> — Pat McMillian

"You were correct," said Heinrich Heinzburg as he stood by their small, square, wrought iron table topped with a thick pane of glass. It was one of dozens of similar tables in the crowded Pat O'Brien's courtyard. It was butted up next to the bar's famous fountain, shaped like a martini glass. The fountain was bathed in blue, pink and yellow lights with huge, foot-high flames dancing in the bowl. The brick walls of the courtyard were also splashed in the vibrant hues contrasting with the huge, seemingly random placed planters of dark green ferns.

As he swayed back and forth, he continued speaking, "Das Hurricane does indeed *kick like a mule* and I should not have had more than one." He looked down at the tall, curvy glass in front of his seat, made to resemble the glass chimneys on an old-fashioned kerosene hurricane lamp. There was less than a quarter of the dark red liquid missing, but this was the third one the waiter had brought him. Heinzburg hadn't realized just how strong the drinks were until he stood up to go to the bathroom.

Shrugging his shoulders, he reached down and picked up the glass. After a big draw on the straw, he put it back down and said, "I vill be back shortly."

"Take your time," replied Pat with a big smile. He was still nursing his first Hurricane, and there was still an inch or two left at the bottom, diluted to a pale pink by the melting ice. "But we really should go get some food. You're looking like you could use it."

Heinrich straightened up, ramrod straight but still swaying a bit, and announced, "I am fine. But perhaps some dinner would be a good idea. It vill be, as you say, a big day tomorrow."

"You're right about that. I'll call and see if NOLA can get us in for dinner," relied Pat as he pulled his phone from a pocket.

"NOLA?" asked Heinrich.

"It's an Emeril Lagasse restaurant," replied Pat. "It's pretty close and the food is outstanding."

"Excellent," replied Heinrich, "I shall be back momentarily and then we can leave, unless you want another?"

"Noooo," Pat replied with a smile, "I'm good."

He watched Heinzburg work his way towards the restrooms and thought that by this time tomorrow he would be even better. A quarter of a million dollars better.

McMillian spent the next few minutes running numbers in his head, his smile getting larger as he did. He glanced at his watch and then to the courtyard entrance to see if Heinzburg was coming back. His smile instantly vanished as his eyebrows went up in alarm.

Calman, Guidry, Raston, Preston, and the Twins had just walked into the courtyard and were looking around for a table. He was trying to decide whether to try and hide his face while they looked for a table or to just get up and meet Heinzburg at the bathrooms. That's when Preston saw him, raised a hand in greeting and pointed him out to Guidry and Calman.

McMillian plastered a smile on his face, still wondering what to do. He certainly didn't want to be making any introductions between Heinzburg and the TV crew. He quickly glanced around and, as always, the courtyard was packed. He then decided what to do and waived them over.

As they arrived, Jack took the lead in the conversation, "Hello Pat."

"Hello Jack, Andy," he paused to look at Bobby and continued, "and it's the *grid man*. I believe it's Bobby?"

"Yes, it is," replied Bobby in a flat tone.

"And, of course, Dean and these most delightful ladies, Mandy and Brandy," said Pat. The Twins had already started taking photos of the picturesque courtyard, albeit in a casual manner.

Pat managed to tear his eyes from Mandy as she leaned over the squat potted ferns that surrounded the fountain. She reached out with the camera pointing up to get a low angle shot of the flames. There were numerous people staring at the

Twins. Whether those looks were subtle or overt seemed to depend on the number of Hurricanes having been consumed.

Andy looked around and said, "Looks pretty crowded."

Pat immediately replied, "Take my table, I was just leaving. It's small table, but it's better than no table. And it's right by the fountain."

Jack looked down at the two glasses, one over half full, and asked Pat, "Someone not like the drink?"

Pat smiled and replied, "Liked it too much. That's the third and he doesn't need to finish it."

Pat then leaned in and said, "I'm with the owner of the Tourenwagen and it wouldn't be good for him to meet you, for a lot of reasons. He just went to the bathroom. I'll go meet him there. See you tomorrow."

Heinzburg was currently standing in the main bar, a dark brick-walled room with an enormous bar; massive wooden beams and pillars; huge prints of old New Orleans; and hundreds of German beer steins hanging from the ceiling. It was very crowded and loud, with the piano stage in the adjoining room in full swing. Dotted around the walls were collections of framed black-and-white photos of past patrons, both famous and infamous.

Heinzburg needed to think and the Hurricanes weren't making that process very easy. Just a couple of minutes ago, as Heinrich was waiting in line for the restroom, he had heard, "Holy shit, look at that!"

He turned his attention to where two young men, even more inebriated than he was, were staring. He had only caught their profiles and backs as they walked through the large hallway, past the bar and into the courtyard. But that brief glimpse was enough. It was those twin girls, the *Asperger*

*Socialites.* An uneasy feeling of alarm was fighting with the alcohol-induced calm.

He decided that peeing could wait and walked out to the edge of the courtyard entrance. He was even more confused when the men that had accompanied the Twins immediately went over and started talking to McMillian. He briefly thought of joining the conversation, but immediately changed his mind.

He looked more closely at the men. The older one he had seen at the auction just a few hours before, when he had gone to check on the indoor stage for the Tourenwagen. He had been out by the auction cars, staring at an early 911. He had noticed him mainly because he was vaping, but it was more like an e-cig than a vaping mod. He didn't think he'd seen the other men, although the short, fat one looked somehow familiar.

Heinzburg was most concerned about the Twins and why they were here. He shook his head a bit in a vain effort to clear it. He backed up and stood in the hallway to think. As he stared up at the antique rifles that formed an arch over the hallway, he decided it was more dangerous to let the Twins see him than it was not to know why they were here. Then it came to him.

He thought that since the group was talking to McMillian, that he would know why they were here. He then tried to think of a way to get McMillian to leave the table, so he wouldn't have to go back into the courtyard.

Just then, McMillian walked into the hallway, saw him standing there, and smiled. McMillian mistook the confusion on Heinzburg face as being alcohol induced, which wasn't entirely wrong.

"There you are," said Pat, "I got us reservations at NOLA, but we've got to be going. They had a hard time squeezing us in, but the name A-Bear Auctions does carry a fair amount of weight in this city."

"Very good," replied Heinrich with a very theatrical rub of his temples with his fingertips. "I believe you are correct in that I could very much use some food."

As they walked out of Pat O'Brien's and onto St. Peter's Street, Heinrich turned to Pat and asked in a drawl that was plainly someone drunk, pretending to be drunker, "Who ver those people you were talking to at our table?"

"Huh," replied Pat, trying to buy time so he could think of an answer. He also wondered why Heinrich was trying to appear more tipsy than he actually was. "Which people?"

"The four men and the beautiful girls," replied Heinrich with a big smile plastered on his face, "The very, very, wunderschön frauleins!"

'Oh, those people," replied Pat, "One guy has a car to sell tomorrow, a sweet little 911. The others are actually buyers, perhaps even for your car. I don't know about the gals." Pat stopped, shrugged and with a sly smile continued, "Big money, beautiful women… they kinda go together."

"Ah, yes," replied Heinrich, "I hope to find this out very soon. So how far to this, this NOLA?"

"Not far," replied Pat, "Just a few blocks."

As they walked, Heinrich actually broke out into some sort of German song. Pat looked at him more closely and wondered if maybe he really was that drunk?

A disturbing thought suddenly occurred to him. He realized he should have told Guidry they were going to NOLA for dinner because he certainly didn't want to meet up with them again.

As they walked down the street, Heinzburg sang his German ditty while McMillian texted furiously on his phone.

# CHAPTER 45
# Minibar Whiskey

*Friday – August 25 – 8:47 PM CDT*

> "In The HO-LY Name Of JEEE-SASSSS!"
> — Herman Adler

"That went very well," said Saul Wittmann, smiling broadly as he and Herman Adler drove away from the First Free Mission Baptist Church.

"You think?" Herman replied, genuinely happy for the first time since they landed in New Orleans. "You had them in the palm of your hand. You had me, too. I was beginning to think you were being tru... well, being serious about this."

"What do you mean?" blustered Saul. "Of course, I was being serious."

"Has something changed that I don't know about?" asked Herman. "Aren't we drumming up bad PR to try and keep the price down on that car? Keep it low enough so we can swoop in and buy it; so you can put it in the HEIL?"

When Saul didn't immediately answer, Herman glanced over at him. The old man was staring straight ahead. A pensive look had replaced the beaming smile that had been there just moments before.

"Well, has something changed?" Herman demanded.

"No," replied Saul. "No, that is still the plan. The ends justify the means, but that doesn't mean I can't be a bit…" Saul's voice trailed off as he continued to stare out the car window.

"A bit what?" asked Herman.

"Nothing, it's nothing," replied Saul as he straightened up and assumed the ramrod posture that Herman knew so well.

"You were enjoying yourself, out there preaching to the crowd," teased Herman, "firing them up," Herman switched to a passable imitation of Pastor Jay Rollins Broussard, "In The HO-LY Name Of JEEE-SASSSS!"

"I'm just doing what has to be done," replied Saul. But as he sat there thinking, a small smile developed on his lips and he continued with, "but I was pretty good up there."

"Yup," replied Herman, "you surely were."

"Alright then," said Wittmann, "Let's go back to the hotel. It's been a long day for an old man, and I'm ready to have a minibar whiskey and hit the hay."

"Good idea," replied Herman. "I'm with you, except for the whiskey part. It has been a long day, and it's going to be an even longer one tomorrow."

As they rode in silence, Saul started to hum a bit. After a couple of bars, Herman joined in. After two more bars they both began singing, low at first, but then at the top of their lungs.

Two elderly black men were standing on the corner, sipping on pint bottles of Kamchatka vodka nestled inside small brown paper bags. As the Impala turned the corner, a full block away, they heard the singing. As it rolled by them, they saw the two men inside, swaying in their seats and singing to each other in joyous abandon, and almost in harmony, "I'm going to let it shine! Let it shine, let it shine, let it shine."

They looked at each other and started laughing. The laughing soon turned into coughing so they stopped, took another sip from their respective bottles and looked back at the car.

Even though the Impala was now two blocks away, they could still hear the singing. They then looked at each other. In unison, they shrugged, nodded, and said, "White people." They then started laughing again. To them, that said it all.

## CHAPTER 46
# Make It Two Orders

*Friday – August 25 – 8:49 PM CDT*

> "Seems to me, I was the one humping that big ass Sony HDCAM all over the frigging desert while you pretended to study the shot list."
> — ANTOINE GUIDRY

"Hurricanes all around," Jack Calman said to the waiter who was bending over to hear his order. The waiter was a thin young man with a scraggly beard that looked as though it would always stay that way. He was dressed in a stark white shirt, thin bow tie, and an emerald green coat with white piping.

Jack pointed to the Twins, who were huddled together on the other side of the fountain, comparing the screens on their Canon 5D cameras, and said "Including the ladies." The waiter glanced over at the Twins, smiled, and made a notation on his order pad.

Jack paused a bit, perused the menu, and continued, "And bring us two orders each of the Pecan Crusted Duck and the Alligator Bites." Jack paused and looked at the men getting situated around the tables. It had only taken ten minutes or so for the waiter to find a couple more of the small, square tables and position them next to the one they had inherited from McMillian.

"Should we get some Popcorn Crusted Oysters?" Jack asked. "They are really tasty, but kinda rich. I'd hate to spoil our dinner."

Andy just shrugged and made a gesture that conveyed, "Why do I care? You're buying."

Dean jumped in with, "Well the Twins won't eat 'em, but I will. Who knew oysters were so good? Can we get at least one order?"

Jack looked at the waiter and said, "And an order of Popcorn Crusted Oysters... oh, what the hell. Make it two orders."

"Good choice, sir," said the waiter, who straightened up and said, "I'll be right back with your drinks."

Andy added, "And can I get a glass of water?"

Bobby and Dean immediately echoed with a "Me, too."

The waiter made a courtly bow, glanced at the Twins with an involuntary eyebrow raise, and confirmed, "And six waters." He then left the table.

Andy leaned over to Jack and said with a smile, "Big day tomorrow. We don't want to get all Moab'd."

He was referring to a shoot for the old *Four Wheels TV* program many years prior, when he was a camera op and Jack was filling in for a suddenly ill field producer. Between setups they had rushed into one of the state run liquor stores and snatched up some peppermint schnapps to fortify the three point two beer that was the Utah standard.

Relaxing after the day's shoot, they were tipping a few. Unfortunately, they hadn't realized it was one hundred and one proof schnapps, verses the more normal forty proof, until it was too late; MUCH too late. What they remembered of the night was fun, but the next day... not so much.

"We managed to pull that one off," Jack said with a sly smile.

"We?" replied Andy. "Seems to me, I was the one humping that big ass Sony HDCAM all over the frigging desert while you pretended to study the shot list. Like your eyes were open behind those Ray-Bans! Anyway, I'm a bit too old, and way too smart, for that kinda nonsense."

"I agree... one hundred and ten percent," replied Jack. "One drink, a few bites to soak up the alcohol, a nice dinner and I'm off to bed. I plan on being fast asleep long before midnight. Well, one a.m. at the latest. I've got a plane to catch first thing in the morning. Right after I make the call about your deposit."

"Excellent," replied Andy as the waiter showed up. He carried a large tray filled with the tall, curvy glasses. Each was filled to the brim with ruby red liquid and topped with an orange slice.

As the waiter placed one in front of Andy he immediately lifted it and said, "And I'll drink to that!" And so he did. Actually, they all did.

## CHAPTER 47
# FOX 15 News At 10

*Friday – August 25 – 10:00 PM CDT*

> "It was a stretch to come up with the bidder bond, but since I don't plan on actually buying anything, it will be returned to me."
> — SAUL WITTMANN

"*W*ere *in the open, in five, four, three,*" the floor director stopped at three and continued the count down with his fingers.

At the same moment the director in the control room said, *"Roll open and swell music. Ready 2 with two-shot."* As if he was conducting an orchestra, he raised his left arm, with the palm up, while intently watching the screen as the animated graphic reminded the audience they were watching "FOX 15 at 10!"

407

"*Fade music on my cue,*" called out the director. An overweight young lady, way too fond of red beans, rice and her Momma's smothered pork chops, lightly laid her finger on the audio fader. She was ready to slowly pull it down in relation to the director's outstretched arm.

"*Take 2, start audio fade,*" the director called out as he started to slowly lower his arm. He looked at the bank of monitors to make sure that camera three was on a medium close up of Frank LaVere. Currently on screen, camera two was showing the two anchors pretending to be engaged in a casual conversation.

"*Ready 3 and lose music in three, two, one, take 3,*" said the director as his hand dropped to the desk, the last of the music trailed away and the program monitor changed to the MCU of Frank LaVere. The audience heard his last word of the pseudo conversation, "Absolutely," and then LaVere turned to the camera. The director called out, "*Ready 1 on MCU.*"

"Welcome to FOX 15 News at 10, I'm Frank LeVere."

"*Take 1,*" said the director as the screen changed to a matching MCU of Corville. "*Ready to go back to 3.*"

"And I'm Clarice Corville," said the woman on camera.

"*Take 3,*" said the director as the program switched back to the man.

"In our six p.m. newscast, Sandra Melancon, FOX 15's Automotive Reporter, told us about a last minute addition to the *Muscles on the Mississippi* classic car auction," said LaVere in the deep tone he reserved for serious news delivery.

"*Ready camera 1, frame for insert, ready roll in,*" called out the director.

LaVere continued speaking directly into camera three, using his peripheral vision to note the floor director walking over to the middle camera, "The car, purported to having been owned by Adolph Hitler, was creating quite a stir."

*"Take 1 with roll in,"* instructed the director.

The program switched to Clarice Courville, who seamlessly picked up the story line off the teleprompter. Above her left shoulder was a picture-in-picture insert of the protesters.

"Dozens of people, most, if not all, from a local church, were protesting the auction," said Courville.

*"Ready to insert remote in the PIP, then a split with the remote,"* said the director. *"Insert remote."*

As Courville continued, a live shot of Sandra in front of the First Mission Baptist Church replaced the recorded video of the protesters in the box above her shoulder. "Sandra Melancon is now live in front of that church..."

*"Ready for split,"* called the director hurriedly, *"take split."*

"Sandra, I understand you have some interesting updates to your earlier story?" asked Courville.

"Yes I do, Clarice," replied Sandra.

*"Ready to go to roll-in,"* called the director, looking at his show rundown for the first time since the broadcast started.

On screen, the two women stared directly into their respective cameras as they performed the short, preplanned conversation that led into the video roll-in.

"In the earlier broadcast, I told you that in order to gain entrance into the auction you had to post a five million dollar bidder bond," said Sandra.

"I remember," replied Clarice with a smile.

*"Ready to put camera 2 in split with remote, on the movement,"* said the director.

"I believe Frank is still thinking about it," continued Clarice taking her gaze from the camera and looking towards LaVere.

*"Take 2 in split,"* called out the director. Exactly in the middle of Clarice's head turn the studio feed in the split screen turned into a two-shot.

Frank LaVere was shaking his head and said, "And it's still too rich for me; way too rich and not just a little bit too creepy."

*"Ready camera 3 in split, on the move,"* called the director. As LaVere shifted his gaze to his close-up camera the director said, *"Take 3 in split."*

"Sandra, I understand you have an interview, from earlier today, with one of the men who actually did post a bidder bond?" asked LaVere.

"Yes, during today's auction I managed to talk with Saul Wittmann, from Richland Center, Wisconsin, about why he posted the multi-million dollar bidder bond."

*"Ready roll-in full,"* called the director.

"And how he managed to gather this much support for his SUPPOSED position," finished Sandra.

The technical director, anticipating the cue started the Wittmann interview. The director eyebrows flew up in alarm. *"Not yet,"* he cried out. *"Don't take it, re-cue! Wait for me to call it!"*

On screen, Frank LaVere slowly nodded his head for emphasis, "And that is the operative word…" he said, now shaking his head from side to side to show a combination of dismay missed with disgust, "supposed."

*"Take roll-in full,"* said the director. As the video clip started to play, the director looked at the TD with a slightly askew grin. The technical director raised his hands and shrugged his shoulders. The director rolled his eyes, and then looked at a smaller monitor that was showing the same interview that was going to air, but with a time code window.

*"We're back in a minute ten,"* he called out. The floor director, whose precise mental clock was a prerequisite for the position, adjusted the time and called out *"Back live in a minute eight."*

"When I realized that selling this car was tantamount to glorifying the most evil person ever born…" Saul Wittmann was saying, looking off screen to his right. He was identified with a lower third ID that had his name, his town, and identified this as a FOX 15 exclusive.

As he continued talking, the cameraman zoomed out to a two-shot to reveal he was talking to Sandra with the Tourenwagen directly behind them, "I just couldn't stay home and see this happen. I had to come to New Orleans and do whatever I could to stop this unholy, glorification of Satan incarnate."

"But five million dollars is a lot of money," replied Sandra.

"It's a bond, not a fee," replied Saul with a smile. "The good Lord has blessed me with a comfortable cushion in the sunset of my life. It was a stretch to come up with the bidder bond, but since I don't plan on actually buying anything, it will be returned to me."

"And how did you manage to rally the kind of support that is literally lining the roads as we speak; protesting against this car behind us?" Sandra asked, gesturing to the Tourenwagen. There was a smattering of people by the car that were staring directly into the camera, some were waving. There were always a few *video bombers*.

As she continued, the scene cut to a low angle close up of the front of the massive automobile, "It is, after all, just a car."

"Sandra," said Saul in a pastoral tone. "The Lord works in mysterious ways. Within hours of arriving in New Orleans, he led me to a young man whom he immediately touched with his mighty hand; a young man who had the veil of indifference lifted from his eyes; a young man that was transformed into an instrument of his will." He stopped, lowered his voice and continued, "Obviously the Lord does not think of this as *just a car*."

Saul paused for a second and then continued, "If not for the timely intervention of Jesus Christ, all praise his holy name, the only demonstration against this monstrosity would have been a tired old man, holding but a single sign of protest." He paused again and a sly smile broke out on his craggy, weather-lined face as he continued, "And I doubt that would have been enough to call out the news and publicize this travesty."

*"Ready to cut to live,"* announced the director.

"The Lord does truly work in mysterious ways," continued Saul with a huge smile. "And I am but one of his humble servants."

*"Cut to live,"* said the director as the program monitor again showed Sandra against the backdrop of the squat brick building that was the First Mission Baptist Church.

"Unfortunately," said Sandra, "in the high stakes world of top tier collector automobiles, all is not always what it seems. Earlier this morning we asked our affiliate sister station, FOX's WCEZ in La Crosse, Wisconsin, if they could get us a little background on Saul Wittmann."

*"Ready roll-in,"* said the director looking at one of the smaller monitors to make sure it was the correct one.

"What they found shocked us," said Sandra. "And it should shock you as well."

*"Roll it and take,"* said the director as the video was broadcast to thousands of New Orleanians looking to catch up on the day's news before they went to sleep.

Sandra's VO described the scene as the video cut to various clips in sync with her words, "Richland Center, Wisconsin is a typical little town. They have a main street, a city square, a community college, and a town library."

The scene cut to a middle-aged woman who looked rather surprised to be on camera. "Mr. Wittmann used to come in a lot. He was a big reader," she said. The woman was standing inside the library entryway, with rows of bookshelves behind her. The lower third ID'd her as Sheryl Binderhoff, Richland Center Librarian.

"For a time, he was very interested in World War Two, basically anything to do with it. Then he stopped checking out books." Her face took on a puzzled expression as she continued, "The last time he returned one, he said we needed to upgrade to books with a more accurate viewpoint."

The scene cut to the exterior of a building with a sign that proclaimed it as the First Harvest Methodist Church of Richland Center. A distinguished looking man with a full head of impeccable salt and pepper hair, combed straight back, was standing by the low sign. He was ID'd as Pastor Frank McWarren.

"I know Saul Wittmann well," the man said. "He is… well, he's an asset to the community. He's not a regular parishioner, not here or at any other church that I'm aware of. I actually don't recall the last time he attended a service, but there's a lot of people that have yet to receive the word of the Lord."

The scene cut to panning shot of a small gas station, unique in that it was still a service station, not just a convenience store with gas pumps. There were three pump islands and a small office next to two service bays. There was a 1986 Crown Vic up on a lift in one of the bays and a '79 Silverado parked in the other. Signs above the office and bays read Oil Change, Tune-up, and Service.

The scene then cut to an older, somewhat craggy guy in overalls, standing by the pumps with the service bays behind him. He was wiping his hands on a rag and was ID'd on-screen with Frank Castleman and Castleman Shell.

"Yeah, I know Wittmann. Known him for years. He's a big man in these parts, really big. He used to own a lot of property, still has a bit. Most of it farmland, some of it… well, some of it isn't." He started to say something and then very obviously thought better of it. "That's all I got to say. You need some gas?"

Sandra's VO started up again as the scene cut to a shot of low rolling hills, obviously captured out of a moving car, "The majority of the people we talked to declined to be on-camera, but some of those that were unwilling to speak *strongly* suggested we drive out to a building they said Mr. Wittmann owns." As the rolling camera shot slowed down, it turned into a gravel driveway and into the parking lot of a large red steel building. "And so we did."

There were a variety of camera shots from different angles, obviously edited together mainly to cover the time while the Sandra's VO set-up the money shot.

"We were told by many people that this building is where Saul Wittmann spends the majority of his time; that his truck is seen going back and forth to this building on an almost daily basis. And what is this building? Some called it his workshop. Some said it was his storeroom. But others, multiple others, called it his..."

The scene then changed to show a tight close-up of the canvas-wrapped sign. The angle of the sun made the name pop. There was no mistaking what it spelled. Especially since Ton Briggs had added a bit of contrast to the shot to make it all the more apparent. As the screen filled with the word HEIL, Sandra's VO finished the sentence, "museum."

The director just stared at the image for nearly a split second, an eternity for someone in his position. He quickly snapped out of it and called "*Cut to live.*" When nothing happened, he repeated the command, *"Cut to live, cut to live, cut to live!"* until the also dumbfounded TD pushed the proper button and Sandra once again filled the screen, now with Pastor Broussard, looking somewhat stunned, standing next to her.

At Sandra's request, Joey had set up a portable digital TV receiver so that the Pastor could watch the video segment as it played. He barely got the volume turned off, before the control room switched to his camera. As he walked up to the camera he looked at the Pastor's face and tried to decide if his expression was shock, anger, or disappointment. Deciding it was a bit of all three, he gently laid his hand on the camera controls to avoid disturbing the live shot.

"With me is Pastor Jay Rollins Broussard," said Sandra, staring directly into the camera, "from the First Free Mission Baptist Church, in which the majority of today's demonstrators are members. Pastor Broussard, thank you for joining me."

"Thank you for having me, Sandra," replied the Pastor. A southern church leader has to be equal parts politician and pontificator if he's going to succeed in this line of work. He flashed a carefully chosen rueful grin and continued, "And for discovering the wicked truth behind this Godless charlatan."

"Before we went live," continued Sandra, "You told me that Mr. Wittmann actually visited this church and spoke to your congregation earlier this evening."

"Sandra, I am ashamed to say he did," replied Broussard. "I am mortified that we welcomed this evil man into the house of the Lord and let him spin his wicked web of lies to the entire congregation. But as a pastor, and a man of God, I have to pray that the Lord will have mercy on his soul for this heinous transgression."

"You also told me that the First Free Mission Baptist Church was planning on demonstrating again tomorrow, with even more people," said Sandra. "May I assume that might change?"

*"Tell her to wrap it,"* the director said into the telex system, which was being transmitted to Joey. *"She's ten seconds over."*

The pastor was silent as he thought about the question; only the slight narrowing of his eyes betrayed his boiling anger. Finally he said, "Sandra, as that… that transgressor pointed out, the Lord works in mysterious ways. What is meant to be, will be. In the end, we are all but servants of his divine will."

Sandra was about to press for clarification, but when she looked over at Joey, he was twirling his upheld finger; the universal gesture for *wrap it up*.

Instead of a follow-up question, Sandra simply said, "Thank you for being with us, Pastor Broussard."

*"Ready 2 for a split with live. Have them toss immediately after the comment,"* said the director. On the preview monitor the anchors received the instructions and then each assumed a surprised persona. Unlike the director, who had only had a rundown with times, they had already seen the roll-in.

Joey started a slow zoom into a Sandra MCU as she continued, "What an amazing turn of events on the eve of the final day of the *Muscles on the Mississippi* classic car auction. And the story is not over yet. We are also investigating an allegation that the *supposed* Hitler Car may not be quite as it's portrayed. More on that as we uncover the truth."

*"Take the split with a two-shot on camera 2,"* said the director.

"That truly is an amazing turn of events, simply incredible," said Frank LaVere. "Sandra… great job!"

*"Ready to lose the live split,"* called the director.

"Thanks Frank," replied Sandra, "I am personally appalled, and can only imagine what the parishioners of this church are feeling right now."

"Sandra," said Clarice Courville, "what's going to happen now?"

Sandra paused, as if she had to think of the answer to the pre-scripted question, and then replied with a shrug and a smile, "An auction, I suppose. This is Sandra Melancon, reporting live for FOX 15 news."

"*Lose the split,*" called out the director. "*Wrap 'em up... now! Ready camera 3.*"

The floor directors frantic wrap up gesture involved his entire arm, while LaVere slowly shook his head and said to Courville, in a tone of wonderment, "That Sandra is incredible. FOX 15 is lucky to have her."

As he turned to his camera the director called out, "*Cut to 3... ready 2 on full wide with music. We're killing the promo.*"

"We'll be right back with a story on a Rolex watch scam in the French Quarter, a Kajun Kitchen review you won't want to miss, and of course, breaking news as it happens. Don't go away," said LaVere, picking up the short stack of papers he kept on the desk as a prop.

As he turned to Courville for a little bogus conversation, the director called out, "*Cut to 2, no promo, roll in music full.*" He watched the screen until the master control operator took over the feed and ran the first spot. He looked at his rundown sheet, marked an X over the segment they had just completed and called out, "*We're clear, back in four.*"

Almost immediately the glass door to the control room slid open as Preston Moralas stepped in and demanded, "Who the hell said you could cut the promo to my Kajun Kitchen segment?"

The director looked over at the TD who just shrugged his shoulders.

Three miles from the station, Joey was packing up the camera and lighting gear while Sandra was thanking Pastor Broussard.

The pastor smiled and graciously excused himself. He walked into the church, closed the door, and immediately dug the vibrating phone from his pocket. "Yes, Mason," he managed to get in before the young man started talking. "Mason," said the Pastor, but the voice on the other end continued without pause.

"MASON!" Pastor Broussard almost shouted into the phone, "Hold on now. I understand your concern, and your feelings, but you are looking at this in an unchristian-like manner. Yes, we do have to do something, so be quiet and listen. This is how we're going to handle this."

Seven miles away, Herman Adler was lying on his hotel room bed, staring at the TV with his mouth slightly agape. He blinked his eyes three times in rapid succession. He closed his month, swallowed, and then muttered "Holy shit."

He walked into the adjoining room with the full intention of waking Wittmann up, telling him what he just saw, and demanding they start packing. Then he saw the old man sleeping, looking every bit of the eighty plus years he'd been on this earth. Whatever he decided to do, he would need his sleep.

Adler slowly walked back into his room and opened the minibar. Since he didn't have a lot of drinking experience, he just selected a bottle at random, twisted off the cap, and drained it.

"Holy shit," he muttered to himself. "HO-LEE-SHIT!" he repeated almost shouting. He then reached for another of the miniature bottles. He was thinking it would be a long night as there was no way he was going to be able to fall asleep.

He looked over at the TV. The male anchor was talking to a reporter about some restaurant. When the video switched to a couple of guys holding hands at one of the tables, Adler picked up the remote, muted the audio, and plopped onto the bed. He tipped the new bottle up to his lips and drained it.

It actually wasn't as long a night as he thought it would be.

# CHAPTER 48
# Kids

*Friday – August 25 – 10:03 PM CDT*

> "I have a feeling that this will either be really, really good or really, really bad."
> — Jack Calman

"And just then a black guy ran by with two purses in his hands," said Andy, taking a mighty pull at the straw as the last of the red liquid drained from the bottom of his third Hurricane.

"So, I told the cops, 'I think I'd be checking that out instead of worrying about him peeing on a wall!'" said Jack. "So they handed Andy his license and took off after the guy. We ran the other way and made it to the hotel with time to spare."

"Yeah," howled Andy, "If you consider two hours 'till the six a.m. call, *time to spare!*"

"We were still drunk as hell when the cars started leaving, but at least the hangover didn't start until noon!" laughed Jack. "And boy, did that one suck!"

"Not as much as missing that turn and driving eighty miles in the wrong direction!" said Andy, bringing on another set of howls.

Andy and Jack were laughing so hard they didn't really notice the rest of the group wasn't exactly sharing in their enjoyment.

"Speaking of hangovers and call times," interrupted Bobby. He was overtly tapping on his Breitling Chrono-Matic to emphasize the point.

Andy looked at Bobby with a somewhat quizzical yet amused look, his lips pursed and his eyebrows lowered. He then looked at Dean and the Twins. The Twins were huddled with their heads almost touching, looking at the backs of their cameras. The bright LCD screens lit their faces as they scanned through the photos and video clips they had taken that evening.

Dean had actually been listening with rapt attention as Andy and Jack talked about the *old days*, but at Bobby's interruption he suddenly leaned back and yawned.

The waiter had long ago cleared their table of the remains of their dinner. Midway through the second round of Hurricanes, they had abandoned the idea of going to Brennan's and instead choose to dine on the Pat O'Brien's versions of Jambalaya, Etouffée, Shrimp Creole, and Red Beans and Rice.

He now approached them, pointed to the empty glasses in front of Andy and Jack and asked, "Another round?"

Bobby's glass, his second, was half full, and had been for a while. Dean was actually on his third, but just barely. The Twins had switched to Diet Coke halfway through their first one.

"It's getting late and I've got an hour of gear prep before I'll be ready to start. The Twins and I have still got to go clothes shopping, and even the Bourbon Street stores likely close at midnight." said Bobby. "I'm done and heading out."

Andy and Jack looked at each other and smiled.

"Just like that time in Oaxaca," said Andy, and he and Jack broke into another round of laughter.

Jack looked up at the waiter, who was waiting somewhat less than patiently for an answer, and said, "No, I think we're done." Jack handed the waiter his company credit card and said, "Just the check."

Jack turned to the group, looked at the final inch or so in his glass and raised it, "Good luck tomorrow. I have a feeling that this will either be really, really good or really, really bad. And I can't wait to find out which."

Andy bristled a bit and replied, "There is no way in hell it will be anything but great! We've got a great concept, a good plan of attack, incredible shooters, the world's best audio guy and," he stopped, smiled, shot a quick glance at Dean and continued, "and… we've got Dean."

Dean made a wry face and said, "Thanks."

"Just kidding," said Andy. "Jack insisted that you, Mandy, and Brandy were a team and if I wanted them, I had to take you." He stopped at looked at Jack and then continued, "And as always, Jack was right."

Dean shot a glance at Jack and mentally thanked him, thinking how much the executive had done for him in just the last year.

"No, it's not the team, or the concept, that might make this really, really bad. Although the name might need a little work," said Jack, looking at Andy.

"What's wrong with *CarAlity*?" replied Andy, "It is really starting to grow on me!"

"Yeah, maybe. We can cross that bridge later," replied Jack, with a touch of slur in his voice. "What's wrong is this whole Hitler thing," he continued. "The setup is really wonky. Bidder bonds, secret provenance, mysterious seller… it just doesn't feel right. And it really needs to be…" Jack paused, sighed and shook his head.

"Be what?" asked Andy.

"Be right," replied Jack.

"Looked *right* to me," interjected Dean. "When I, huh, when we saw the provenance video, it looked very right. Too right!"

"Like I said when you told us earlier, I don't want to know anything about that video. I want to see it when the audience does," said Andy quickly.

"Yeah, I know," replied Dean, "That was no spoiler alert, I was just saying that it was pretty compelling. At least it was to me."

"What did you gals think?" asked Jack. The guys at the table all turned to look at the Twins, still huddled together and looking at their camera display screens. "Mandy, Brandy?" asked Jack at about twice the volume.

They looked up in stereographic loveliness, eyes blinking to refocus on the table, both physically and mentally.

"I'm sorry," said Mandy.

"Did you ask us a question?" asked Brandy.

"Yes," said Jack, "What did you think of the Hitler Car videos?"

"We thought it was a good job," said Brandy.

"Well edited," said Mandy.

Jack looked puzzled and then shot Dean a look and a questioning shrug.

"He means the provenance video," said Dean. "Not the introduction video."

Mandy and Brandy looked at each other and then back at Dean.

"That one, too," said Brandy and they both went back to looking at the camera screens.

Dean looked at Jack, shrugged his shoulders and spread his arms palms up in gesture that clearly meant he didn't understand it either.

"I just hope the auction doesn't bomb, that it brings big money, and that it makes good TV," said Jack as the waiter brought the credit card and the check. As Jack signed the slip, he continued, "And I hope to hell that car is real."

"Why would you care if the car is real?" asked Andy as they all stood up to leave.

"I personally don't care. It's Winters. For some reason, he cares," replied Jack as he stood up and swayed a bit. "Whew, those Hurricanes certainly live up to their name. It's making my head spin a bit."

"To hell with Winters," Bobby said, "the only thing that guy knows about good TV is how to screw people out of it."

"Yeah," replied Jack, "and if anyone knows that, it's certainly you."

Andy looked at Jack, and then at Bobby. The look on Andy's face negated the need to ask Bobby the question.

"It's a long story," said Bobby. "I'll tell you later. After tomorrow.'

"Anyway," continued Jack, "For some reason Winters thinks it would be a catastrophe of biblical proportions if that frigging car isn't what they claim it is. And I didn't even get a good look at it."

"My vote would be that it's exactly what they claim it is," said Dean. "Sure the setup is a bit, huh, theatrical. But since when is that a crime, or even a bad thing?"

Dean held up his iPhone and said, "And it's been blowing up on the *Interweb*. If this was all a plan to build social chatter on this car, it's working."

"Well, I hope so," replied Jack with a smile, "Or I might be asking Andy for your job on the next installment of," Jack lifted his hands like a conductor and he, Andy, and Dean all chimed in together and said "CARALITY!"

Bobby just rolled his eyes and the Twins didn't seem to notice.

"All right then," said Jack with a big smile on his face. "Let's recap. First thing in the morning, I'll get the deposit wired into your account. It should show up by nine or so; certainly no later than ten. If it doesn't, or anything happens that needs some attention, call me. I have a direct flight to LA in," he looked at his watch and continued, "in about eight hours. I should be at my desk by, hum, let's see," Jack did some mental calculating and then continued, "by one in the afternoon your time."

Jack stopped and smiled at Andy, "It's good to be working together again."

Andy smiled back and replied, "Yeah, real good."

"Why don't you guys just kiss and be done with it?" asked Bobby. "I'm leaving. Girls, are you ready to go do some shopping?" The Twins just looked up, looked at each other, then looked back at Bobby and nodded.

"Yeah," said Dean who then gave a mighty yawn. "I'm done, too. I'm heading back to the hotel."

Andy looked at Jack and shrugged. Jack smiled back, shook his head and just said, "Kids."

They then smiled and said, in long ago practiced unison, "One more round… to sleep on?" and they started laughing again.

# CHAPTER 49
# Coin Flip

*Friday – August 25 – 11:59 PM CDT*

> "You can't possibly be more
> beautiful than you are right now,
> Mandy... or, huh, Brandy?"
> — DEAN PRESTON

"**W**hat the hell?" Dean thought as he opened his eyes and tilted his head to look at the clock radio. The red numbers showed eleven fifty-nine, which meant he had been in bed barely twenty minutes. He was wondering if he had imagined it when it happened again. Three soft knocks on his door, a pause, then three more.

Dean threw back the covers. He was wearing his Ferrari boxers, the red prancing horse logo printed all over the smooth white fabric. He briefly thought about slipping on his pants, but instead just walked over to the door and opened it a crack.

As he peeked through, his first thought was to shake his head to make sure he was awake. Then he thought better of it. If this was a dream, he didn't want to wake up. It was one of the Twins.

"Hello," she said.

Dean opened the door a little wider to reveal his face but still hiding his body behind it.

"Huh. Hello Mandy... or, huh, Brandy," Dean paused waiting for an identification confirmation that didn't come. "Do you need something?"

"Maybe," the Twin replied and shrugged. "I wasn't really tired and thought you might like some... company."

"Well, huh, sure," replied Dean, his mind racing with the possible meanings of the word, but also aware that this was the first time he had seen a Twin alone, without her sibling.

"Company? Sure. Just let me put on some clothes," Dean said. He was about to close the door, and then thought that would be rude. He left it open a crack and walked back into the room to where his clothes were draped on a chair in front of a small desk.

As he reached for his pants he heard the door close behind him with a soft click. He turned to see the Twin standing in front of it.

"I don't think that will be necessary," she said with a smile. "I'll just join you."

She then peeled off her t-shirt and tossed it onto the extra bed in the room. The pink Fruit of the Loom sports bra that covered her perfectly round, grapefruit-sized breasts couldn't have been sexier if they had been a featured item from *Fredrick's of Hollywood*.

She then reached down and undid the button on the top of her jeans, unzipped them, and let them fall into a heap about her feet. She stepped out of the heap and stood there. Her short-legged panties, also in pink, were far sexier than any thong would have been.

"There," she said with a mischievous smile. "Much better, don't you think?"

Dean opened his mouth to say something, but then realized he really didn't know what to say. So he just closed it and nodded. His Ferrari boxers were pup-tented in front of him, the fly button was straining to remain closed.

With a playful smirk, the Twin looked down at the boxers, then up at his face and said, "We're going to have to make this rather quick. It's going to be a big day tomorrow and I need my beauty sleep."

Dean smiled back at her. He finally regained his voice, although it was a bit thick in his increasing excitement. Hoping to sound at least a little debonair, he said, "I completely agree. Except for the part about you needing beauty sleep. You can't possibly be more beautiful than you are right now, Mandy… or, huh, Brandy?"

"So sweet," she replied. She then giggled, pushed him onto the bed, pulled off his boxers, and fell onto him. The giggles quickly subsided.

Just ten minutes earlier, the Twins had been in their room. They had flipped a coin and it came up *heads*. The Twin that called *tails* had softly knocked on a different hotel room door. Within seconds, that door had flown open, accompanied with an exasperated, "What the…"

The words had died on Bobby's lips as he saw the other Twin standing there. A grin, so big it actually hurt, plastered itself on Bobby's face as he regained his composure. He then just stepped to the side of the doorway and simply said, "Come on in!"

Before the coin flip, the Twins had briefly thought of Andy Guidry as the booby prize in their little wager. But after a very brief moment of contemplation, they had looked at each other, scrunched up their noses, and said "Ewweeuu."

It wouldn't have mattered. Guidry wasn't in his room.

## CHAPTER 50
# I'm No Reporter

*Saturday – August 26 – 1:07 AM CDT*

> "It doesn't matter what it is, racing,
> building, talking… it's gotta be fast!"
> — BRADLEY MENDENHALL

"Hey, buddy! We got yer beau-ti-ful girls right chere. Got big-butt women and the coldest beer in de Quarter," said the young hustler; his thick black hair was slicked back and his shirt was unbuttoned to the middle of his chest. There was a heavy gold chain intertwined with the thick pelt of chest hair.

Andy just smiled and shook his head and kept walking. His practiced hand snaked into his pocket and brought out the thin purple battery topped with the vaping cartridge. As he walked, he took a light drag on it, more out of habit than need. He had more than sufficiently medicated himself, as the San Diego dispensaries had once referred to it.

When he hit this level of *medication*, when the cannabis-saturated bloodstream bathed his brain, seemingly random ideas would race around his head. Obtuse connections formed, merging random thoughts, as a thousand *what if's* dashed about, most hitting roadblocks and falling away. Those ideas with the best chance of success would somehow emerge from the wreckage, like the proverbial phoenix arising from the ashes. At least they always had before.

So much had happened, and happened so fast, that he hadn't really had much time to think about it. Only two days ago he had arrived, more or less destitute, on his last legs financially as well as emotionally.

It all started when his show had been cancelled by Redline as being *too stale*. At least that's what that young twerp, Bradley Mendenhall, Junior VP of Programming, had told him when he had finally accepted the call. They had actually cancelled his show with a letter. And not even a registered one.

"Listen, dude," Mendenhall had told him, his peculiar accent a combination of upper crust, East Coast snobbery and West Coast surfer wanna-be. "No offense, but the name of the network is Redline, and there's nothing remotely rapid about your show. It's just a bunch of geezers talking about old cars, and how many years it took to *bring'em back*."

Andy recognized the tone all too well. It was the same one he used when telling a PA why he was firing him because he showed up thirty minutes past the call time. It was the *you just don't get it* tone.

"People don't want to hear about restorations that take years. Six month paint jobs; scouring junkyards for the correct, date-coded carburetor intake; debating over polyurethane bushings or factory rubber. Dude, nobody cares!" exclaimed Mendenhall. "On Redline, things have to move fast. It doesn't matter what it is, racing, building, talking… it's gotta be fast!"

"Ok," Andy had replied, hating himself for even trying, knowing that any effort was futile. "I can revamp, speed it up, push it to the Redline."

"Really?" asked Mendenhall, "How? By speeding up the zooms on those crappy old photographs? Especially the ones of how they found the car and what condition it was in? Listen Mr., huh," there was a slight pause and a few taps on the keyboard and then he continued, "Mr. Guydry. It's not just the show that's stale, it's the whole concept."

"Guidry," said Andy.

"What?" asked Mendenhall.

"The name is Guidry. The first syllable is pronounced *Gid,* as in Gidget, not *guy.*"

"Yeah, well, OK, Mr. Gidget," said Mendenhall. "Have I answered your questions? Are we done here?"

"On that subject, yes, I suppose so," said Andy, ignoring the Gidget as a sidetrack he didn't want to take. "But I've got lots of concepts. When can we have a meeting so we can talk about my next show for Redline? You're going to need something to fill my slot."

"Your, huh, previous slot," replied Mendenhall, the tapping on the keyboard and detached tone of his voice signifying that he had, mentally at least, moved on from this conversation. "We've already got a replacement for that slot, it's a new show called "Loud & Proud" out of Oklahoma. They build show cars in a week, and they use new parts. You know, parts from companies that actually advertise."

"Sounds great," replied Andy. "I can't, huh, can't wait to see it. So, anyway, how about a meeting so I can pitch a couple of ideas. I think you're going to love them."

"Yeah, OK, huh, WOW, oh, huh, yeah" came the obviously distracted voice. "Listen, brofus, my schedule is really jammed, but I'll have my admin slot you in ASAP. She'll be in touch." And then the little cockalorum actually hung up on him.

Needless to say, the call hadn't come. And when he called the next week, and the week after that, he got the same answer, "Mr. Mendenhall's calendar is still completely full. We'll call you when there's an opening."

That was three months ago. It doesn't take long to run out of money when you have to keep spending and there's nothing coming in.

Andy suddenly noticed he had stopped in front of a shop named Vapor Eyes, on St. Louis between Bourbon and Royal. He stood there thinking about whether he needed another battery. His current one didn't seem to be lasting as long between charges.

He then thought, with a rueful half grin, that it was probably just that it was getting a lot more use lately. During the last couple of years, his occasional cannabis vaping had slowly but surely turned into a daily habit. Once he let the office go, and gave the video editors their notice, it had gotten harder and harder to leave that particular *pen* in his pocket.

He was simultaneously having this mental debate about the battery, reliving the humiliation of his Redline dismissal, and devising an editing workflow for *CarAlity*, when he realized that someone had spoken to him.

"Guten Abend," said the voice again. Andy shook his head a bit to clear it, put on a smile and turned to the voice. It was Heinrich Heinzburg and he looked pleasantly curious. "I have seen you at the auction. And, I believe, earlier this evening at the Pat O'Brien's."

"Huh," said Andy, his brain now entirely devoted to deciphering the situation at hand. Questions bounced around his brain while he continued to smile. "Had this guy followed him? Was he suspicious? What was his agreement with McMillian? Who the hell was he supposed to be?"

"Yes, at the auction, certainly," replied a cordial Andy, "But I don't recall seeing you at Pat O'Brien's."

"I was leaving when you came in," said Heinrich. "Who could have missed you with those, and forgive me if I am being too bold, those stunning young ladies in your company."

"No forgiveness needed," replied Andy with a smile. "It is kinda hard to overlook them."

"And why, may I ask, are you at the auction?" Heinrich asked with a friendly, yet somewhat guarded smile.

Andy thought as fast as the cannabis would allow. He was about to introduce himself when he realized that if Heinrich saw him tomorrow, he would be wearing Dean's *A-Bear AV Crew* badge. He decided to use the KISS principle and the simpler the better, although that might be hard.

"I'm sort of working the show," he replied, hoping the huge smile might offset the vagueness of the answer. "My name is Dean," Andy continued, holding out his hand.

"And I am Heinrich," the man replied as he shook *Dean's* hand. He dropped it and looked at *Dean* with a quizzical expression.

"Working ze show?" replied Heinrich, letting a little more accent slip into his speech. "This is a bit confusing to me. At ze Pat O'Brien's, Mr. McMillian told me you were selling a car?"

"Oh," replied Andy, letting some Cajun slip into his speech along with a more sheepish grin. "Oh yeah, dat too. Actually, I'm doin' boat."

"Boat?" asked Heinrich with a genuine look of puzzlement.

"Boat o' dem," said Andy. He didn't know why he brought up the thick Cajun accent of his youth, but it was too late to change. "Boat sellin' da car and workin' de show." He leaned in to Heinrich and continued, "Me, I gets a deal dat way cause I don't have to pay de house dey full cut. Dey's gimme a discount."

"I see," replied Heinrich. The Hurricanes from earlier still had a hold on him, although the very excellent meal at NOLA's had helped more than a little bit. During dinner he had wisely abstained from any more alcohol, opting for the local sweet tea and two cups of the Community Coffee. Still, it had been a long day, and an even longer week, and with three of those very strong drinks in him, things were still a bit fuzzy.

"Vell," said Heinrich, gesturing to Vapor Eyes, "I see ve share the habit."

"Yeah, dat's true," Andy replied, pulling his vape pen from his pocket. "But not like you, no. When you vape, dat's a whole 'nutter ballgame."

Heinrich smiled as his fingers first danced over his vape mod holder, and then smoothly removed it. "Yes," he replied to Andy, "This is a step or two above your, huh, your device."

"Poo Yai," joked Andy, "If that's only a step or two, dem's some big-ass steps!"

Heinrich smiled with a hint of appreciation, and tried to match the accent in the phrase, "Ya, certainly some *beeg ahss steeps!*"

They both politely chuckled a bit, which Heinrich ended with a gesture towards Vapor Eyes and saying, "Zee night is fading fast and it will be a big day tomorrow. I'm going to get Mark, I believe that's his name, to custom mix some of their Hurricane e-Juice with a bit more nicotine than usual."

"You a bigga man dan me," laughed Andy, "I don't want to hear the word Hurricane, but less be vaping something that tastes like it!"

"It is a strong drink," said Heinrich, "I too, know this!"

They both politely chuckled again as Heinrich continued, "But it was a unique and pleasant taste. Plus, I'm told I can *try it before I buy it*, so I shall see."

Heinrich looked down at the slender eCig device in Andy's hands, looking up at Andy he said, "I also started out with that. Then it was, as your Guns and Roses says," Heinrich paused, stood up a little straighter and recited in a cadence closer to rap than rock. To emphasize the rap delivery, he held his arms in front of him, palms down, fingers together and extended. As he delivered the lines, his hands crossed over each other in time with the rhythm.

> *"I used ta do a little,*
> *but a little wouldn't do,*
> *so the little got more and more."*

It was surprisingly good, and Andy's genuine smile showed his appreciation. "Mais, thas 'xactly how it is! And wit mo things den just a little vapin'!"

Heinrich gave a little twisting nod of the head to show his appreciation and gestured to the front door of Vapor Eyes.

"I'm good," said Andy, shaking his head. "Me, I was jest walking 'round, letting the food and alcohol go down a bit." Andy tapped on his sternum with the thumb side edge of his closed fist. "Dat Acid Reflux can shore be hell when you old. But I won't hold ya here. It was nice talking to you. Good luck with your car."

Heinrich turned to go to the store and then stopped. Andy was already ten steps away when Heinrich called out, "How did you know I was selling a car? This is the first we've talked and I haven't told you that."

Andy stopped and turned around, "Mistar, jest cause you ain't talked wit dem, don't mean people don't know who you is… and what car you're selling. Jest like dat vaping rig o' yers, you big time."

Heinrich looked at him for a second and asked in a low serious tone, "You're not a reporter are you?"

Andy smiled, chuckled a bit more than was polite, and replied, "Me, a reporter. No sir. Thanks for the compliment, but I'm no reporter. You have a good evening."

As he turned around he brought the pen to his lips, slowly sucked on it and blew out a thin plume of vapor as he walked away. He was actually successful in blocking an almost overpowering urge to turnaround and see if Heinrich was still looking at him.

"Shit, shit, shit," Andy muttered as he walked. He said it again, through clenched teeth, when he realized he had turned and walked the wrong way.

Heinrich watched for the first ten steps or so as Andy walked away. He looked very thoughtful, with just a hint of confusion. He then shrugged and walked into Vapor Eyes, a smile on his face and an anticipatory gleam in his eye.

## CHAPTER 51
# Discretion

*Saturday – August 26 – 5:26 AM CDT*

> "You work for me and it's not a problem unless I say it's a problem."
> — Antoine Guidry

"Wow," said Dean as he was staring at the ceiling. He was wide-awake and it wasn't even five thirty.

They had been naked within minutes of the Twin's arrival, and she had made fast and furious love to him. He had been both highly aroused and a bit dismayed, but certainly not unwilling.

Afterwards they had squeezed into the bathtub shower together. Dean was amazed that he had been ready to go again so soon, and with just a little soapy provocation. They coupled again after the shower, slower and more tender this time. It was more what Dean would have classified as making love versus the previous passionate rutting, although he wasn't opposed to either process. They had finally fallen asleep around one.

"Wow, what?" murmured the Twin. Her head was on his arm as she nestled next to him.

"Wow, everything," answered Dean. "I mean *Wow* that you knocked on my door. *Wow* that someone like you would want to… to…"

"To have sex?" she asked.

"Ok, yes," he replied, "To have sex with someone like me. And the sex, oh-my-god, the sex was the biggest *WOW* of all."

"Well, thank you," she replied with a smile. "But it was nothing, and don't think of it as anything more than that."

"Nothing?" replied Dean, smiling but sounding a bit wounded. "I thought I was doing a little better than *nothing*."

"Oh, you were great!" she said. "That's not what I meant. I meant that it was nothing, that it was my pleasure as well. I'm afraid that my sister and I have a more… well, a more *continental* view of sex than most people. To us it can be more like being playful with a good friend."

"Speaking of your sister," said Dean with a smile, "You never did tell me which, huh, which sister…"

"Hush," said the beautiful women, placing a finger to his lips. "That's part of being playful. Isn't it more fun that you don't know?" Her teasing smile made it clear that it certainly was for her.

"Huh," he started, paused and then continued. "Huh, well I guess." Dean paused until the *wow* overwhelmed him again. "But that was something, I mean REALLY something!"

The beautiful woman lying next to him just smiled.

Dean then blurted out, "I mean, both of you are so... so reserved. I thought it was your... huh, your condition that made you, huh..."

"You thought the Asperger precluded passion?" asked the woman, propping herself up on one elbow to look at Dean's face. The thin sheet slipped away, exposing the perfect breasts.

Dean's eyes couldn't help but dart down, back up to her face, and then down again.

"Huh," he said, forcing himself to look into her eyes. "It's just that, well, that you and your sister are always so... so... serious. Yes, I guess that's the word. It's all work, you're always shooting. Even when you're being, huh, being conversational, it's for a reason. To get something you want." Dean paused and continued. "I've noticed how you and your sister can turn on the charm. It's overpowering, but it's also a bit... maybe *calculating* is the right word?"

The beautiful young woman was no longer smiling, but she didn't look angry either. She had a somewhat detached look of mild interest.

"Go on," she said to Dean.

"No," he replied, "I'm not doing a good job at this, and I don't, huh, I don't want to... to spoil anything." He looked into her face, ignoring the look. "Last night was, literally, the most incredible night of my life."

The Twin just smiled at the comment and said, "I'm glad. But it wasn't meant to be *incredible*. It's just a little fun between friends." She reached out, touched his bare chest with a single finger, and continued, "We are still friends, aren't we?"

Dean could barely manage a low moan as she traced that lone finger slowly down his chest and drew a little circle around his belly button.

As she continued the slow circle with just the tip of her finger, she said, "But I am interested in your perception of my sister and I. It is a symptom of our condition that it is sometimes hard for us to judge these things. Especially when we are together. Tell me more about how you perceive us."

"Huh, OK," said Dean. The finger was deliciously distracting. So much so that he entirely missed the smoldering fire that had lit up behind her smile.

"It's like when we saw those videos yesterday," Dean started. He was now staring at the ceiling so he could think, basking in the afterglow of the experience; her proximity getting him aroused. "The first one was beautifully done, the shots were amazing and all you commented on was the *editing*? And then the provenance video! That was easily the most brutal thing I've ever seen and it didn't seem to faze you two at all. I... I didn't know what to think. I don't know what to think now. And then, then there was last night!"

He smiled, and continued while he turned to look at her face, "And last night was..." Dean stopped in midsentence as he saw the look on her face.

"You think we are devoid of feelings?" she asked. "That our Asperger condition makes us incapable of human emotion?" she asked. The Twin then threw back their covers, exposing the naked and now erect Dean. She looked down, and then up into Dean's face. She then shrugged and simply said "Pity."

She then rolled out of the bed, looked about the room, and began gathering her clothes.

"What?" said Dean, alarmed at the sudden change in both temperature and temperament. He propped himself up and stammered "Wha, wha, what did I do. I'm sorry! I shouldn't have said anything!"

As she dressed, she simply said, "You actually should have said something earlier. We were impressed with the editing because we shot that video, everything but the drone work. Our father had taken us to Cologne, to look at the new cameras. We were offered the gig when the director saw us shooting with some demo units at an open-air market. We had to travel, of course, and the location was very remote… but we're used to that."

Dean, mentally scrambling for something to say, blurted out, "Huh, the huh, the *breaking the wall* sequence was incredible."

She stood there looking at him and then rolled her eyes. She was now dressed from the waist down, holding the sports bra and t-shirt in her hands. She tossed the t-shirt onto the bed, spun the bra around so that it was in the proper orientation, and then continued as she put it on, "As to the provenance video," she said pausing a bit. "It was gory, yes, and brutal. And, it too, was very well done. It was all practicals by the way; no CG. As to why we weren't as *moved* by it as you were? Well, we were. The first time we saw it."

"Wait a second," said Dean, shaking his head as if to shake out the disbelief. "You've seen the provenance video before?"

"Yes," replied the woman. She then reached down to pickup the t-shirt. "It had the same director as the video that…" she paused as she had almost called out her sister by name. She then put the t-shirt on and continued, "The same director as the video my sister and I shot. It was a complicated production, what with the time difference the two videos represented and how they needed them to blend together. Not to mention all the set and prop work to represent the different eras."

She turned to look in the mirror that was on the wall next to the TV. She fluffed her hair a bit, practiced a smile, nodded her approval, and turned back to Dean.

"Anyway, about a month after we shot the video parts of the script, we ran into the director at an industry party in Frankford. They had finished the film portion of the shoot and he had done the transfer at CineNova that morning. He had the footage on a hard drive and insisted we come to his room for a viewing. He said that only we could truly appreciate it, as the beauty was in the camera work."

The Twin paused and stared up at the wall for a couple of seconds. It was as if she were replaying the video in her mind. She then continued with, "Actually, the camera work isn't that complicated, but the framing is very precise, especially for a film camera. And I did think the effects were quite convincing, even in black and white. He was extremely proud they had done most of it in one take, although I seem to remember it was not the first take. He also said it was top secret; that sadly, no one could ever know it was his work."

"Then why did he show it to you?" asked Dean.

She tucked in her chin and dropped one eyebrow. It was a look that clearly asked if he could really be that stupid?

"To get us to come to his room. And he was quite persuasive. "

Not wanting to ask, but not being able to help himself, Dean stammered, "So you, huh, both of you…"

The fire in her eyes, which had tamped down a bit in the story telling, immediately flared up. "I said we have a *continental* view of sex, not a concubine's. We flipped a coin. We often do. That time my sister won."

"Wait a second!" exclaimed a somewhat dazed Dean, finally understanding exactly what she was telling him signified. "That means the car isn't real!"

"Real?" she replied, looking around the room to be sure she hadn't forgotten anything. "Of course, it's real. You've seen it."

"I mean *isn't real* in that it's not *really* a car that belonged to Hitler; that the provenance video isn't real," Dean explained.

She looked at him with a sympathetic, somewhat puzzled expression like she was talking to a child, and one that was somewhat slow.

"It is what it is. It's an old car. Who it belonged to, or who rode in it..." she stopped and shrugged, "who can say? The provenance video? Of course it's real. I told you. I know the man who made it. Besides, how do you know the video isn't just a recreation of an actual event? Or that it won't be presented as such during the auction?"

She turned to the door, stopped, and turned back to look at Dean. Her gaze softened a bit at the sad confusion on his face. "Look, I had a nice time. You're a nice guy, and a very sweet lover. But, like I said, in the end it really is nothing."

Dean was still trying to absorb what she was telling him about the car. He replied in a distracted tone, "Ok, I understand." Then realizing what he was replying to, he suddenly sat up a little straighter and asked, "But, will we do this," he shook his head a bit and continued, hoping he was phrasing it correctly, "will we do this *nothing* again?"

She smiled, turned and walked to the door, and then turned back to Dean. "Perhaps," she said. "It would depend on your discretion. To be discreet is also *very continental.*" As she finished the sentence, she peeked out the door, turned and smiled at Dean and then slipped into the hallway, the door closing with a soft click.

Preston sat on the bed trying to think. It was more than just a little overwhelming to a rather naive Midwestern boy, barely three years out of Iowa State's film school.

With a rueful smile, he thought that he must have skipped the class that dealt with situations like this. He then reached over and picked up his cell phone. He tapped on the previous call list, and then tapped on Guidry's name. It rang six times and went to voice mail. Preston hung up and just sat there for a moment.

He breathed deep and caught a fleeting wisp of the Twins' scent. He leaned over with his nose hovering over the rapidly fading depression where she had been lying only minutes before.

He then sat more upright and shook his head. "Think, Preston, think!" he commanded himself. Then his eyes got big as he remembered Jack Calman's last comments from the night before.

Fifteen minutes later he was walking out of the shower, smiling at the soapy memory of just a few hours earlier. Then his phone started buzzing on the nightstand.

He quickly walked over to it, saw it was Andy, tapped answer and said, "Hello."

"What do you need," came the brusque voice.

"Andy, I just found out the Hitler Car isn't real. At least I don't think so. Actually, I think it's a total fraud… probably," he blurted out.

"How the hell did you *just find out*?" Andy asked, "It's not even six. Is this some Twittergram crap?"

"No, no it's nothing like that," Dean paused, the word discretion, and the consequences of its lack, weighed heavily on his mind, "It's nothing I can get into right now, but I'm pretty certain the car is a fake. And last night Jack made it pretty clear that if it turned out to be a fake, it was a going to be a huge issue."

"Listen to me," Andy replied sternly. "Regardless of why you believe this, do not fuck this up. You work for me and it's not a problem unless I say it's a problem. And whatever you do, don't say anything to anybody unless I say it's OK. *Especially* not to Jack Calman. We do not want our sponsor to pull the rug out from under us because of some bullshit rumor. Breakfast in the lobby at seven. Don't be late," finished Andy, who immediately hung up.

"I guess I fucked it up," Dean said softly, shaking his head as he put down the phone and slowly started to get dressed.

# CHAPTER 52
# Caveat Emptor

*Saturday – August 26 – 7:15 AM CDT*

> "I fully understand that this car is the top security priority and that it is imperative that nothing happen to prevent it from being sold."
> — MAURICE SCHAFER

"So where are the cops?" asked Pat McMillian as he walked up to the Tourenwagen. It was a quarter past seven and the thick heavy air, although still relatively cool, promised the inevitable arrival of a classic New Orleans summer day.

The tarp protecting the car from the early morning mist had been removed and was lying behind and next to the short platform. The all-important patina looked none the worse from the tarp's careful installation the night before. A huge dragonfly had settled on the top of one of the flagpoles, its iridescent wings spread wide and ready for immediate flight.

"On their way, Mr. McMillian," replied Maurice Schafer. He looked very imposing in his black tacti-cool garments. "I just talked with them and they're running just a bit late."

"Late?" asked Pat, as if he couldn't believe what he was hearing. "I told you this car was the absolute top priority. I told you that nothing, and I mean NOTHING, gets between this car and the auction block and you're telling me that YOUR cops, whom I am paying VERY well, are *running a bit late*! How long has this car been unprotected due to your incompetence?"

"No time at all," replied Maurice in a dull, flat voice. It was a voice that, if you knew him, meant you were treading on dangerous ground. Pat McMillian paid well, very well, and Maurice appreciated the work. But he didn't like being talked to this way, and it didn't happen often. He had a well-deserved reputation as someone you didn't want to anger.

"I've been here since four thirty, when I relieved the night crew," said Maurice. "I fully understand that this car is the top security priority and that it is imperative that nothing happen to prevent it from being sold." He stopped and put on a practiced smile. Back in the day, that smile had often been the precursor to a very sudden headache for whatever *perp* was on the receiving end of that grin.

"Do you not think that I can provide adequate protection?" Maurice asked, with a slow, deliberate pronunciation on every word.

"Yeah, yeah, yeah," replied Pat in a condescending tone while he visually inspected the Tourenwagen.

It wasn't that McMillian did not find Schafer to be intimidating, because he most certainly did. That's why he hired him. More than once, a client with a side deal had decided that they no longer wanted to participate at the agreed upon financial contribution. Schafer had a way of ensuring that once a deal was agreed upon, it was fully consummated.

His interventions had never actually come to violence, at least nothing that left a mark. But it was always clear, and with absolute certainty, that it could easily escalate to that level. This had always ensured that participants upheld their end of the bargain, despite the absence of a written agreement.

"Where are the car movers?" asked Pat.

"The lazy fucks went to check on the indoor stage; or so they said," replied Maurice, still smoldering a bit. He was thinking that they were more likely checking on the coffee and pastry vendors who were starting their set up routine inside the auction venue.

McMillian paused to survey his little temporary car kingdom. The bridges over the Mississippi had a smattering of cars crossing them, barely audible in the soft early morning quiet.

He then looked out at the wide brown highway of water, slowly moving as it had for centuries, and likely would for centuries to come. He looked over to the lines of cars waiting their turn on the auction block. The ranks had been somewhat decimated by the previous day's auctions, but many of the sold cars were still there, waiting for their new owners to arrange for transportation to their new homes.

McMillian truly lived for the excitement of the auction; people yelling, bids climbing higher, and the moneymaking shout of *Sold!* But this was also nice.

It took months of effort to put on an auction. The planning, organization, and thousands of details that made for a polished buyer/seller experience all came together in a two-day whirlwind of serious money changing hands. This calm before the final day tempest, when the last-minute wrinkles had been ironed away, was a time to reflect on the simple satisfaction of another enormous job well done.

That he would soon be another quarter of a million dollars closer to opening his own auction house made his self-satisfied smirk just a little bit wider.

Suddenly, the tone of the occasional soft chatter changed on McMillian's walkie talkie. Someone was urgently calling his name. He turned up the volume and spoke into it, "Go for McMillian."

"I's tried to stop him Mr. Mac, but he jest pushed right passed me!" said Clovis, the gate guard.

"Who pushed right past you?" asked Pat. Pat noticed Maurice had turned up the volume on his walkie talkie. There was a small speaker, with integral mic, clipped to a loop on his shirt, at the juncture of the collar bone and shoulder. A curly cord connected it to the walkie talkie clipped to his thick leather belt.

"Dat mister… huh… mister… huh… dat mister Calzone from yesterday. He just pushed right past me and I didn't know whats to do," came the obviously rattled voice. "You let him in yesterday, and you seemed to know him so I didn't wants to be too… huh… you knows…"

McMillian rolled his eyes and looked at Schafer, who simply shrugged back and gave a shake of his head. The gesture clearly conveyed the message the guard wasn't one of *his* guys.

"He jes now walking 'round the building, heading toward the riverfront entrance," came the reply. "What's you want me to do, Mr. Mac?"

"I want you to try and do your job," said Pat, more than a hint of anger in voice. "McMillian out."

"Yes sir, I will but I..." came the reply. McMillian muted the walkie-talkie as he saw Jack Calman come storming around the edge of the building. McMillian's opinion of the incompetence level of the gate guard actually softened somewhat. Calman was clearly a man on mission. When Calman saw him standing by the Tourenwagen, he sped up even more.

"Pat!" Jack yelled out. "Stay right there! I need to talk to you!"

McMillian looked around and held up his hands in a gesture that conveyed he wasn't going anywhere.

Calman walked swiftly up to McMillian, his face red and sweaty with the combination of anger, the humid air, and more than a few years of desk jockey duties.

"You've got to..." Jack panted a bit and then continued, "You've got to... pull this car... from the auction." Jack's eyes were wide and wild, the antithesis of his normal demeanor.

"I'm not sure I'm following you, Jack," replied Pat. The slightly quizzical look on his face gave no hit of the alarm bells going off in his head.

"What's... not... to... follow?" asked Jack, gaining his breath back a bit, which only fanned the fire in his eyes. "You need to pull this car from the auction. It's a fucking fake and you know it!"

It wasn't hard for McMillian to look surprised, although shocked was a more apt description of what was coursing through his brain.

"First!" Pat replied, holding up one finger and mustering up some indignation, "I have no idea of what you're talking about and I resent the accusation that I do!"

"Second!" continued Pat, adding another finger to join the first. "As the producers of this event, we have examined all relevant documentation and provenance related to this vehicle. In our opinion, this car is *exactly* as portrayed."

"Third!" he added, adding his ring finger to the other two, and subtly changing the tone of his voice to that of someone explaining a concept to someone he was already sure wasn't going to get it. "This is a classic car auto auction, basically a big, temporary used car lot. We don't guarantee any of these cars as to anything. Not structural, not mechanical, and certainly not historical."

Pat paused and smiled, "And if even discounting one and two," he said, dropping his fore and ring finger, leaving the middle standing alone in the classic gesture, "the third item rules. Caveat emptor, Jack. Let the buyer beware."

"Listen here, asshole," replied Jack, pointing his finger at Pat, "And fuck you very much, too."

As Calman began speaking, he almost unconsciously started to invade McMillian's personal space. With an odd, anticipatory grin on his face, Schafer started to glide towards the two, reaching his hand into a back pocket.

McMillian looked past Calman to Schafer, caught his eye, and ever so slightly shook his head from side-to-side. Schafer stopped walking towards them, but didn't return to his former position.

"It's all about the money with you! Nothing else," said Jack, who also stopped his forward progression, and also did not return to his former position. "And don't say it's not!

But for the sake of argument, let's just say you and the entire A-Bear Auction staff were duped into believing this car was indeed a barn find. And one that just happened to have chauffeured around that Nazi asshole."

Jack stopped, took a breath to try and calm himself, and continued. "Well, then I am here to tell you that we have uncovered incontrovertible evidence that this car is, at best, a tribute. And that I, as the supervising producer of the network that is funding the production about the auction of this car, *demand* that it be immediately identified as such."

"And, if I refuse to accept your… unsubstantiated claim, whatever it may be?" asked Pat. His eyes narrowed as they flitted over to Schafer to see if he was paying attention. He was.

"Then I will blow this fuckin' auction right out of the water," replied Jack, his eyes starting to flare again. "Our discovery of this fraud, and your part in it, will be blasted across our social media networks within the hour. I will personally call every single media contact I have and they'll be talking about this on FOX and MSNBC before noon. A nice, non-partisan story about greed and corruption in *The Big Easy* will be a nice change of pace for both of those networks. And I guarantee that you will be the pivot man in that media circle jerk!"

"Let's calm down," said Pat, shaking his head a smiling a bit. "It's way too early for all this drama. I haven't said I wasn't going to pull the car. I've only said that we don't have any reason to do so… yet." Pat put what he hoped was a genuine look of concern on his face. "So, exactly why do you believe that this magnificent car," Pat gestured to the Tourenwagen not five feet behind them and continued, "is not exactly what it is portrayed to be? As I told you, I have seen the provenance and it is very compelling. It isn't a stack of old paperwork in fading fountain pen, it is — and this is entirely off the record — a video from when this car was... was put away for safekeeping. It is compelling... brutal... and..." Pat paused, searching for the next word.

"And faked," interjected Jack. "It was made less than a year ago. And all that blood and gore is just old-school movie magic."

McMillian was stunned. He wondered how Calman even knew about the video, much less that it had blood and gore. He tried to come up with possible scenarios as Calman continued his rant.

"So you either pull the car from auction or, at the very least, announce that you have reservations about the provenance," said Jack, holding up his huge iPhone, "or in ten minutes you'll be the talk of the entire industry, if not the country."

"Jack," replied McMillian, with what he hoped was a sincere look on his face, "I'm stunned. I don't know what to say." McMillian shook his head as if bewildered and continued, "I've personally seen the video, and it was very convincing. But nobody else is supposed to have seen it, other than the seller and myself. How did you see the video and why do you think it's faked?"

Jack thought briefly about the phone call he had received less than an hour ago. He hadn't taken the time to think this part out. He didn't know how much, if any, he wanted to divulge about his sources.

"I haven't actually seen the video," replied Jack. "I know people who have, and people who say they know the man who made it."

"So this accusation, something that could potentially derail an auction involving millions of dollars, all boils down to a guy, who knows a guy, who knows a guy?" Pat said, shaking his head at the statement. "Can't you hear how ludicrous this sounds? I have a responsibility to my customers, both sellers and buyers, to protect their interests. What if it's your accusations that were fabricated? Then you've deprived the seller of his money, and the buyer of a once-in-a-lifetime opportunity to own a piece of history."

Pat smiled and shook his head, "Jack, as much as I respect you, I can't just pull the car on your word alone. Nor can I make any unfounded statements as to its veracity. I have a reputation to maintain."

"I should have known I'd be wasting my breath!" said Jack. He stepped up to within a foot of Pat and said, "I don't have time for this shit. I've got a plane to catch and a lot of calls to make, including one to Prescott Hébert. I guarantee this car isn't going to be auctioned today. As to your reputation," Jack held up a finger pointing directly into Pat's face, and then lowered it so he could emphasize each word with a poke on Pat's chest. "Kiss… it… goodbye!"

McMillian's eyes narrowed to slits as he looked past Calman and nodded his head at Schafer.

Jack saw the look, remembered the hulk of a guard he had blown past, thought "What the…" and started to spin around.

Schafer prided himself on his skill with the well worn, Boston Leather 5417 Denver Sap. He always joked it was like the old AmEx commercial, saying, "Ya don't leave home without it." Many a New Orleans lowlife had taken a sudden nap at its less-than-gentle persuasion. For the most part, they awoke with nothing more than a raging headache and a tender lump to remind them of the error of their ways.

Schafer's carefully aimed swing was intended to be a glancing blow just above and behind Calman's right ear. It would have caused his brain to slam against the skull, squishing past it's bath of protective blood and inducing immediate unconsciousness. It killed a few million brain cells in the process, but was otherwise relatively harmless.

Once the blow connected, Calman's knees would buckle, he would fall backward, and Schafer would catch and lower him to the ground to prevent any further, and more visible, damage. In his long career with the NOPD, he had literally lost count of the number of times he had delivered this particular coup de grâce as his own personal brand of street justice.

But brute force, no matter how skillfully applied, always has to potential to go wrong. And this time it went horribly wrong.

Calman swung around to his right as Schafer was in midswing. Ten point five ounces of lead shot, backed by a spring steel shank and covered in smooth, heavy gauge leather, slammed into Calman's nose. It instantly shoved the cartilage into the septum, splintering the delicate bones and shattering the skull socket surrounding it. It then continued it's destructive arc, crushing the right eye socket, and causing extensive, concussive damage to the eyeball. The skin above the socket split open, and the blood that immediately poured out only added to the copious amount flooding into and from the ruined nasal structure.

What the blow had not done was cause immediate unconsciousness. It would come soon enough, but there were still a few moments of lucidity in which to feel the pain, and to see his attacker.

"Damn it," hissed Maurice through clenched teeth, momentarily stunned by the misplaced blow and its bloody aftermath.

It only took that split second, and the fact that Calman was now stumbling away from him, to make him miss his catch. Calman's heels got entangled in the edge of the discarded tarp and he fell straight back. The thin, nylon fabric offered no cushion as the back of his head hit the underlying concrete. It sounded like a baseball bat splitting a melon.

McMillian and Schafer stood completely still, staring at Calman as the blood poured down his face, mingling with the pool already spreading from the back of his head. The deep red was in stark contrast to the light blue of the tarp.

"Oh, fuck," murmured Pat. "I think you killed him."

Schafer surveyed Calman with eyes long immune to bloody handiwork, including his own.

"Might have," Maurice agreed with a slow nod of his head.

"Why the hell did you do that?" Pat asked, still staring at Jack's completely inert body.

"I believe your exact words were, *nothing gets between this car and the auction block. Nothing.*" answered Maurice, whose eyes had quit looking at Jack and were now quickly scanning around them, looking for any potential witnesses. He sighed a bit when he saw that there had been no one around to see the blow... other than Pat McMillian.

"Mr. McMillian, you hire me to provide security," said Maurice, closely watching Pat to gauge his reaction. He knew the man was in shock right now, but that it wouldn't last long. He continued, "A higher level of security than you get from people like that gate guard. Who, by the way, let this man onto the grounds in the first place."

"But you didn't have to... have to," stammered Pat, who then pointed at Jack. "You didn't have to do that!"

"Accidents happen," replied Maurice, his voice eerily calm. "If he hadn't turned around, it'd be all good right now. He'd just be taking a nap. It's really his own fault. Besides, we don't know if he's dead."

"Then check him," said Pat between clenched teeth. He then also looked around and was relieved that there was no one within eyeshot. He could, however, hear plenty of activity within the auction hall. They wouldn't be alone for very long.

Maurice knelt down and put two fingers against Jack's neck, the side that wasn't covered with blood. He then stood up and looked at Pat with a shrug. "I'm no doctor, but there doesn't seem to be much of a pulse. He *might* be breathing, but it's hard to tell. I'm thinking he's pretty much dead, or he will be pretty quick."

"Fuck, fuck, fuck," said Pat, to himself and under his breath. "This is not fucking good. Not fucking good at all. Think, think, think!"

As Schafer looked at him, McMillian stood there, nodding his head rapidly as one plan after another ran through his head and was quickly dismissed. He looked at the bridge, and then down at the massive river.

Unlike the other side of the river, with its tall, tree-lined banks, this side was heavily developed. The large expanse of concrete that faced the river was built on huge pylons that rose up from the river itself. These were once docks that huge riverboats tied up too and unloaded their cargo, both human and otherwise.

Bordering the huge concrete pavilion on the riverside was a nautical style three-wire fence. Directly past that was a steep drop into nothing but deep, fast moving water. McMillian looked down at Calman, and then again at the river, then downstream, and then finally at Schafer. Schafer was staring at him. His eyes were slitted; his expression one of sinister anticipation.

McMillian thought that under any other circumstances he'd just call the cops. He'd then throw Schafer so far under the bus, he could do a lube and oil change before anyone could pull him out. But he knew if this was declared a crime scene, they'd close down the auction and he could kiss that quarter million goodbye.

McMillian looked down at the now motionless body and thought that at least he was bleeding on the tarp. He thanked God for small favors. He then thought, with a bit of a smile, that if they tossed Calman in the river, what happens to him next would be out of his control. His smile lessened a bit as he thought that was maybe *too much* out of his control. Various options ping-ponged about his head, until he finally decided on one, more out of desperation than conviction.

"Okay," he said, shaking his head a bit, hoping he was making the right decision. He looked at Maurice and asked, "First of all, do you have any problems, any problems what-so-ever, with getting rid of this little *issue*, without alerting the… proper authorities?"

"Nope," replied Maurice, looking Pat straight in the eye with a slight smile on his lips. "None what-so-ever. I've gotten rid of more than a few *issues* in my day."

"Good," said Pat, "Then here's what we're going to do."

Ten minutes later, Schafer was once again standing guard. He had put on his sunglasses and was watching as the car movers flitted around the massive automobile.

Dennis Blanchard was attaching ramps to the back of the Tourenwagen's platform. He paused for a second, looked around, and called out "Hey, Landry!"

Landry Babineaux was attaching GoJak dollies under the front tires of the massive automobile. He had already attached the steel cable from an electric winch mounted on the front of the platform to the front axle. Once the ramps were in place, and the wheel dollies attached, they would remove the jacks holding up the frame and then back the car off the ramp, letting the winch do the heavy work.

Once on level ground, the GoJaks would let the men push the car into the auction hall. They could have easily done it by themselves, as they were pretty big guys. But with a car this big, and this valuable, once they got the car onto the ground, they would call for more help.

Once inside the auction hall, they would reverse the process until the car was positioned onto its own little side stage. It would sit there, dramatically lit against a backdrop of massive photos of Adolph Hitler, riding in what seemed to be that very car.

"Landry!!" exclaimed Dennis, almost shouting despite the short distance between them.

"What you want?" Landry loudly asked. "I'm busy here and me, I need to concentrate. This ain't no Chevy on the levee."

"What happened to da car tarp?" asked Dennis. "It was right here when we left."

"How the hell would I know?" replied Landry, studying the ancient tire as the wheel dolly started to come together underneath it.

"Huh, sir…" Dennis asked loudly, directing his attention to Maurice Schafer, who hadn't moved an inch since they had returned and started working on the car. "Do you know what happened to that tarp?"

"Yes, I do," came the monotone reply.

"Oh," replied Dennis, "Okay, huh, well, where is it?"

"Nunya," replied Maurice. "Any more questions? Or do you think it might be a good idea to shut the fuck up and get back to doing your fuckin' jobs?"

"Dat's a great idea sir!" Landry called out.

As far as he was concerned, the sooner he was done with this job, the better. That big guy scared him. Once he was satisfied that this wheel dolly was on correctly, he moved over and began mounting the next one. This one was on the opposite side of the car, putting the Tourenwagen between him and Schafer.

Dennis called out, "Ramps done. What's next?"

"Come over here and work on da bottle jacks," said Landry.

Once Dennis got close enough, he lowered his voice and whispered, "Quit fuckin' around. Your flirtin' with Lucille and that second cup of coffee is why we're late. It's bad enough with *him* watching us like a hawk," he said, pointing his head in Schafer direction. "I don't feel like dealing with that McMillian asshole today."

"You can say that again," replied Dennis, also in a whisper. "That little Yankee's a killer."

Maurice Schafer had excellent hearing, but only the slightest hint of a smile indicated that he had heard the men. As he walked around the car to watch the men working he decided that since the scope had changed, he wasn't getting paid nearly enough for this job. He also decided he'd have to figure out a way to change that.

## CHAPTER 53
# Who Dat

*Saturday – August 26 – 8:25 AM CDT*

> "When they went back to the
> live shot, he looked like he'd been
> poleaxed right between the eyes."
> — HERMAN ADLER

"Oh crap, I can hear them from here," said Herman Adler. He was driving on Tchoupitoulas Street and was still at least two blocks away from Henderson, where the majority of the protesters had been the day before.

"Yeah, what did you expect?" muttered a somewhat distracted Saul Wittmann. He was sitting in the back of the rented Impala with a hotel bedspread splayed out across his lap, still trying to come to grips with that morning's turn of events.

Saul had walked into Herman's room at just after seven a.m. and found the young man lying on his bed fully clothed, with an even half-dozen minibar bottles strewn across it. The

TV was on, but muted. *FOX 15 News at 7* was well underway, as the morning anchors smiled cheerily and sipped on coffee cups with huge FOX 15 logos on them.

"What the hell is going on in here?" shouted Wittmann.

Herman had jolted awake and sat straight up in the bed. He then moaned a bit, rubbed his temples and plopped back onto his back.

"Boy, I don't know what your problem is, or why you think you can solve it with high-priced minibar booze," said Wittmann, "but we can deal with that later… and we most certainly will. But for now, git yer ass up and off'n that bed. I plan for us to be at that auction when the doors open."

"Yeah, I'm sure you do… or did," said Herman, still lying on the bed with his eyes closed. "After last night, I think your plans may have changed."

"What the hell are you talking about?" asked Saul, a smile creeping onto his face as he thought about the incredible reception he had received at the First Free Mission Baptist Church. "Last night couldn't have been better. There's likely to be twice as many people protesting against the Hit… Der Führer's car today. I intend to get there early enough to do a little more preach… huh, I mean *persuading* before we go into the auction. Now get your ass up!"

Herman swung his legs over the bed, letting their momentum pull his upper body into a sitting position on the bed. He moaned at the sudden movement.

'I can't believe you were getting drunk the night before the biggest day of our lives," said Saul in an accusatory tone. "Do you have a problem that I don't know about?"

"Yeah," replied Herman. "We both do."

"Both!" exclaimed Saul, "I'm not the one drinking alone 'till I pass out on top the covers!"

"No," replied Herman looking up at Saul with bloodshot eyes and a rueful expression, "you're the one whose cover is blown."

Saul's eyes narrowed as he looked at Herman. "What's wrong boy? Stop dancing around and spill it."

Herman slowly stood up and walked over to the minibar. Saul was wondering if he was going back for more booze and was about to say something, when Herman pulled out a little bottle of orange juice. He popped the cap, drained it, and let out a big sigh as the cold, sweet liquid seemed to revitalize him.

"After you went to bed, I was watching TV," Herman started. "I was watching the news to see your interview with that reporter lady. And just like I thought would happen, she has blown this whole thing out of the water."

"What are you talking about?" asked Herman. "How is this *whole thing* blown out of the water?"

"Somehow she got a camera crew up to Richland Center. They were interviewing people about you. Nobody said anything too bad, but nobody said anything too good either."

"So," replied Saul, "What difference does that make?"

"Somebody told them where the museum is, and that you owned it. They showed the sign."

"They showed the sign?" shouted Saul. "They uncovered my sign, on my property, and took pictures of it?"

"No," replied Herman, "They didn't uncover it. They didn't have to. At the angle of the shot, and with the sun going down, you could read the name clear as day. They ended the story with that big ass HEIL filling the screen."

"Oh, shit," replied Wittmann, trying desperately to think, hoping like hell those fine people at the church hadn't seen the story.

"They must have sprung it on that Pastor Broussard when they showed it on TV," continued Herman. "When they went back to the live shot, he looked like he'd been poleaxed right between the eyes."

"Pastor Broussard was on the TV?" Saul croaked, his voice filled with pain.

"They did the story in front of the church and had him there for commentary," said Herman. "And boy oh boy, did he comment."

Saul was silent. He stood there swaying slightly from side to side until his silence started to alarm Herman. Herman walked over and took the old man by the arm, led him to a chair, and sat him down.

"The first flight out of here is at ten forty-two," said Herman softly. "The tickets were on your credit card, so you'll have to change them." Herman looked over at the clock on the nightstand and continued. "We've got plenty of time to pack and get out to the airport."

Saul just sat there, staring at the TV. Suddenly his eyes got big as he realized he was watching what had to have been the previous night's story playing on the screen.

"The sound, boy," Saul nearly shouted, "turn on the sound."

Herman turned and saw what was on the TV and walked over to the bed and picked up the remote. He hit the mute button just as the huge HEIL was on the screen.

"Sandra, that is quite a story," said the pretty blond morning show anchor, "And I understand that you are working on further developments concerning the car itself?"

"Yes, we are," replied Sandra, looking very smart and put together for a woman who had gotten less than three hours sleep. "The story about this car is that it's in *as found* condition, but an anomaly has been detected by the FOX 15 news team that may refute that particular claim. And, perhaps, even the authenticity of the car itself, at least as it concerns its ties to Adolph Hitler."

"This just keeps getting better and better," replied the anchor, "I can't wait to hear what's next!"

The shot changed to the co-anchor, a late-fifties white guy with capped teeth and a bronzed complexion. "In other news, the Riverbank Revitalization project may be stalled once again due to the discovery of…" Herman again hit the mute button.

"And now the car might not even really be a Hitler car?" said Herman. "Even more reason to get on a plane and get the hell out of here."

Herman stood there watching the old man in the chair. Saul's eyes were straight ahead and completely still. They were pointed at the TV but obviously not watching.

"Saul…" said Herman, starting to get concerned. This was a lot to spring on an old man. He thought that plenty of old people probably had strokes from less pressure than this.

"Saul, are you OK?" he asked again, his voice low and full of concern.

"Here's what we're going to do…" started Saul as he slowly started speaking. That had taken place less than two hours ago, and they were currently in the first phase of the somewhat modified bidding plan.

"I still can't make out what they're saying," said Herman, as they crawled along with the other cars heading to the auction. "But we're coming up on some of the demonstrators,"

"Okay then," said Saul as he gathered up the bedspread. "Put on that hat and keep it low." Saul then laid across the seat and covered himself with the bedspread.

Herman picked up the cap they had bought from a tourist shop on Canal Street before leaving for the auction. It was a cheaply made cap with a black mesh back and a plastic sizing band too short for any normal head. The foam fabric front was printed with *Who Dat?* above a Fleur de Lis. He tugged it down so that the brim was barely above his eyebrows. He then turned onto Henderson Street and into abject chaos.

## CHAPTER 54
# Not Too Interesting

*Saturday – August 26 – 8:27 AM CDT*

> "I was taking care of some banking
> business and was informed of the
> rather unusual arrangement you have
> with the seller of this automobile."
> — Prescott Hébert

"It's your job to stand there and try to look at least mildly intimidating," said Pat McMillian to the rent-a-cops, who had finally showed up. He looked at them and just shook his head, as if he had a hard time believing that was a possibility.

"Nobody, and I mean NOBODY gets on this platform without my personal approval. In fact, if they aren't accompanied by me, or Schafer, they don't get within 5 feet of this car. And I don't care who they are," continued Pat. "Basically, nobody gets anywhere close enough to even spit on this car. Am I completely clear on this?"

The off-duty policemen just nodded their heads in a somewhat lackadaisical manner.

Maurice Schafer, who had been standing behind and to the left of McMillian, stood up a little straighter and gave them a stern look.

The cop on the left, Joe Fontenot, was trying unsuccessfully to suppress a yawn. The cop on the right, Charlie Bonet, just stood there, impassive and immobile. He actually did look a lot more than just *mildly intimidating* behind his vintage Ray-Ban Wayfarers.

The two police officers were partners and had just gotten off an eight hour shift which had run into an extra three hours of OT, which was why they were late. They had busted some petty hucksters running a fake Rolex scam in the Quarter at the very end of their shift. It had gotten a bit bloody, and two of the perps were in the hospital, with one not expected to leave any time soon; at least not under his own power. The paperwork had taken a bit of collaboration so as to fully explain the altercation from an acceptable point of view.

They weren't really looking forward to a full day of standing around, backed up by another shift on the street. But the money was great; almost a week's pay to work a single day, so Joe Fontenot spoke up.

"Yes, sir. We understand," said Joe. "Nobody spits on the car."

McMillian had just turned to ask Schafer what he was thinking when he hired these idiots, when he saw the man strolling across the room.

"Oh, crap," he muttered under his breath. "What the hell is he doing here?"

Prescott Hébert was, as always, impeccably dressed... albeit in a style just this side of a well-to-do pimp.

He was on a first name basis with old Sam Meyer, the third generation hat man at Meyer the Hatter. The store on St. Charles Street was an institution and had been providing the well-dressed men of New Orleans with the finest quality hats for over one hundred and twenty years.

Hébert always wore a hat, as his baldhead was somewhat lumpy, dotted with patchy wisps of hair, blotchy skin and an even half-dozen actinic keratosis'. Today he was topped with a dark purple Stetson Tailgate Straw Porkpie wrapped in a wide, bright gold silk band.

His lightweight, bespoke linen suit was in the same bright shade of gold, worn over a lilac polo shirt. His belt and shoes were made from alligator, and dyed in the same dark purple as the hat. He delighted in wearing garish hosiery, most often in violent contrast with his otherwise carefully coordinated ensembles.

Today, under the perfectly hung pants, the cuffs breaking precisely at the arch of the shoe, you would likely have chuckled at the clashing bright green silk socks with red crawfish prints. But only if you knew him very well, and weren't dependent upon him for your income.

Hébert had grown up as poor white trash in Ville Platte, Louisiana. Deep in Cajun country, Ville Platte is widely considered to be one of, if not the, worst places to live in the entire state.

By the time he was thirteen, he had wheeled and dealed his way into driving a fairly late model pickup, with a wink and a nod from the local police. "After all," they thought, "he might be poor, but at least he was working hard... and he was white." He quit school on his sixteenth birthday so he could concentrate full time on his *bidness*.

He had started off just buying and selling. He'd search out the old things from Cajun families that lived way back in the country, in communities so small they weren't on any map. So small that a trip to Ville Platte was considered *going to the city*.

Hébert spoke their language, a French dialect that was linguistically closer to the 1700's than modern-day Parisian. They were amazed when he would offer what they considered vast sums for their *old stuff*, furniture items that were often handed down through multiple generations. The antique beds, chests, chifforobes, and tables were well loved and well worn, producing a patina that made antique collectors drool, as well as ignore just how deep they had to dig into their pockets to possess it.

Hébert would, however, buy almost anything if it were old enough, especially once he discovered the thrill of the auction barn. He had an eye for what would sell, and an innate sense for what the market would pay.

By the time he was twenty, he had started his own auction company and never looked back. Now in his early seventies, the tall, dapper man was very wealthy indeed.

While he had, of course, a residence in the French Quarter, he spent the majority of his time in Natchitoches... a small town sixty miles south of Shreveport. Natchitoches had begun as a small French fort in 1714 and was the first permanent settlement in the entire Louisiana Purchase.

Hébert had a sprawling, fully renovated 1800's plantation home on almost two acres that fronted Cane River. Cane River was once part of the Red River, and a major trade route, but was now a long oxbow lake and the major recreational outlet of the small town.

The main street of Natchitoches was still paved with the bricks on which countless horse carts had once maneuvered, laden with goods from huge white steamboats that constantly plied the river. All that bustle had turned to bust when, as an unintended result of river-clearing efforts by the nineteenth century Army Corps of Engineers, the Red River changed its course. This transformed Cane River into a long meandering, high-banked lake that was so glassy you could see the ripples from bugs landing on it in the early morning hours. At least you could until the ski boats and party barges made their inevitable appearance.

A-Bear Auctions, a tongue-in-cheek correctional jab at the way the way non-Louisianans always mispronounced his name, was now a multi-billion dollar corporation. There were divisions that specialized in everything from maritime vessels, to fine art, to big-city media properties. If it could be sold at auction, there was an A-Bear division that did so. There were rumors of a merger with Sotheby's, although which business was acquiring which was still in speculation.

Consequently, the classic car side of his business was actually a very small part of the overall operation, which explained why Pat McMillian had so much autonomy in running it. As long as the numbers showed a profit — and they had always showed a profit — McMillian was left to his own devices.

In fact, counting the day he was hired, he had laid eyes on the old man no more than a few dozen times. Other than the distasteful incident after NGTV had dropped them from the

*Bid Battle* roster, most of those meetings comprised of just a nod and a wave. But since Mr. Hébert's taste in automobiles tended to be in the very new, very expensive, very luxurious side of the industry, McMillian correctly surmised he wasn't here to browse.

"Take care of this," Pat hissed at Maurice and then plastered a huge smile on his face as he hurried off to greet his employer.

"Mr. Hébert," he exclaimed as he walked up to his employer, "What a great surprise! What can I do for you?" Just in time he stopped himself from extending his hand. Prescott Hébert didn't like shaking hands, at least not with employees.

"Hello Pat," replied Prescott, stopping his forward momentum as Pat rushed up to him. Prescott looked at Pat, and then looked over at the Tourenwagen about thirty feet away. Maurice was in deep discussion with the two uniformed police officers in front of the car.

Prescott looked back at Pat and said, "That is quite a presentation." It was in a flat, noncommittal tone that showed neither approval nor disapproval.

Pat responded like he had just been highly complemented, "Quite a presentation for quite a car!" he said beaming. "I assume you just had to come and take a look at it for yourself, before it goes home with some very lucky bidder…" he paused, lowered his voice, and leaned in as if sharing a secret with an old friend, "for some obscene amount of money."

"Not exactly," replied Prescott. "I was taking care of some banking business and was informed of the rather unusual arrangement you have with the seller of this automobile. I'm not sure I understand it, or approve of it. With something so far out of the normal way that we do business, I also don't understand why you set this up without my knowledge, or my approval."

Pat's expression turned to one of surprise, while his mind raced around trying to come up with a plausible explanation. "I, huh, I thought you knew about it. I emailed you what the seller wanted to do, and was, quite frankly, surprised that you didn't respond. But because it's such an advantageous deal for us, I just assumed you were pleased and had moved onto other more important matters. You are a very busy man."

"I never got any email from you about this financial arrangement," said Prescott.

"I don't know how that could have happened," replied Pat. "I... I..." he stammered and then slapped his forehead with the palm of his hand. "I must have sent it to you from one of my personal email addresses. I get confused when I'm on my iPad. It must be in your spam folder."

Prescott Hébert just continued looking at him, not saying a word.

McMillian returned the look; his smile not entirely making its way to his eyes. He was thinking that if he could just pull this off, he wouldn't have to take any more crap from this old geezer; or anyone else for that matter.

"I'm sorry if you didn't get the information," replied Pat. "But if the banker explained it to you properly, then you see this is a great deal for the company. Instead of our usual commission we get anything over the... well, I guess you might call it a *soft* reserve. With us receiving anything over three point seven five million, we stand, huh, I mean the company stands to make millions on a single car. This car, a verified Hitler-used 770 Tourenwagen should easily bring five, six, or even seven million dollars."

"What the bank told me is that we are *guaranteeing* the money," replied Hébert. "That I have three million, seven hundred and fifty thousand dollars in escrow; along with an contractual agreement to transfer up to that amount into a Cayman Island account, immediately after the sale. Immediately! Before we collect a single dime from the buyer."

"Yes, that's true," replied Pat, carefully choosing his words. "But we're completely covered there. Everyone who's anyone, that even remotely has the ability to purchase a car like this, has already put up a cash bond of five million. Even if they overbid, beyond their ability or desire to pay, we will immediately make at least one point two five million on this transaction because we already have the money."

"Son," said Prescott, looking Pat dead in the eye. "What if someone else, someone you don't have a bond on, bids on the car? There are lots of bidders that signed up well before your bidder bond nonsense. How do you know that one of them won't get caught in the frenzy, get in way over their heads, and then default on their bid. What if one of those bidders is in cahoots with the seller, and then just disappears? Disappears like my money will after the guy with the gavel yells, *Sold!*"

Hébert could tell by the rapid blinking in McMillian eyes that he hadn't thought of that. He sighed, wondering what ever possessed him to hire this fast-talking Yankee huckster.

"Doesn't this seem like a far more likely situation than some mysterious seller falling into our laps with a multi-million dollar payday just to auction the car?" Prescott asked. "One that only wants half of what the car is worth, but wants it right away?"

Pat gulped. He actually hadn't considered that possibility, and it made sense. It could well be. But he'd be damned if he'd give up his *stipend* when he was so close he could smell it.

"Okay, sir," said Pat, trying to sound both humble and very sure of himself. "I'll admit that could be a... a possibility. But most of the pre-registered people — the ones that registered before we announced the car and required the bidder bond — well, they are also known entities. We did our due diligence on the sellers. As to the buyers... even more so. Sure the scale is vastly different, but we never want shysters at our auctions, whether it's five million or fifty thousand. The controls we have in place are designed to prevent any *issues*, regardless of the dollars in question."

Prescott looked him in the eye for what seemed an eternity, but was in reality only a few very long seconds. Finally, while still staring him down, Prescott asked, "Boy, are you trying to fuck me out of my money?"

Pat's eyes grew wide with shock, and this time it wasn't an act. "WHAT?" he cried out, so loud that the people beginning to file into the auction hall turned to look at them. Immediately he lowered his voice and continued, "Sir, I resent that statement. Maybe I'm being duped, but I don't think so. Maybe this is a bad deal, but I also don't think so. But one thing I do know, with rock solid certainty, is that I have never once taken a single dime out of this company that wasn't on my paycheck!" Pat stood tall, with true indignation on his face. "I think this is a great deal, and one that's going to make the company, going to make *you*, a lot of money. And after this car is sold, you're going to thank me and be sorry you ever accused me of... of..."

"Settle down, son," Prescott said, "I didn't accuse you of anything. I just asked you a question. Now here's what I want you to do. When that car is being auctioned, I want you up there with the auctioneer. If anyone bids that you don't personally know to be on the up and up, you disregard that bid. You tell the auctioneer it doesn't count. You make an immediate announcement to that effect so the entire audience knows why you're not taking the bid."

Prescott paused and let the instructions sink in before he continued, "Am I completely clear?"

"Yes, sir," replied Pat. He was actually thinking that wasn't going to be an issue. Mainly because there was no way he was going to be more than fifty feet away from that car for even a second. Not until it was sold, the auction was over, and he had a chance to *prepare it* for delivery.

Pat then put on his big, confident grin and replied, "Completely clear, Mr. Hébert. And I will be the first person to call you after the auction. I am looking forward to telling you exactly how much money we will have made on the deal."

"You won't have to call me," said Prescott with a smile. "I'll be right here, watching every move." He then looked around the room and said, "It's been a while since I've been this deep into the weeds. It'll be fun."

"Excellent," replied Pat, thinking the exact opposite. "I'm sure it will. Now if you'll excuse me, the auction begins in under two hours and there is always lots to do."

"Oh, and when the seller shows up," instructed Prescott, "I'd like to meet with him… alone."

"Absolutely," said Pat, nodding his head in agreement and looking thoughtful. "Sounds like a great idea. You'll find him very interesting."

"I hope not too interesting," replied Prescott.

McMillian, for once, didn't know what to say. So he just smiled weakly and walked away.

## CHAPTER 55
# Heinous Hate Incarnate

*Saturday – August 26 – 8:29 AM CDT*

> "I don't want anything, 'ceptin' to serve the Lord."
> — Mason LaCroix

"What's going on?" asked Saul Wittmann. His voice was muffled from underneath the bedspread.

It was extremely slow going on the road to the auction entrance. Mainly because the gate guards were turning away more cars than they were letting in. The auction was now big news and a lot of people had figured it would be a good way to spend a Saturday. The explanations as to why they couldn't attend, and occasional arguments over the denial, had slowed the progress to a fraction of what it been the day before.

Lining the road of mostly stopped cars was easily twice the number of demonstrators as from the day before.

"Nothing different from yesterday. Just a lot more of it," replied Herman Adler.

"All I hear is the same chants from yesterday," said Saul. "What do the signs say? Anything about me? And turn up the A/C, I'm dying under this blanket!"

Herman lifted the brim on his *Who Dat* cap and peered out the driver's side window. "The signs are about the same, just more of them. I don't see anything about…"

The sharp rap on the passenger window made Adler jump. His head spun around to find Mason LaCroix standing there. There was a big stack of flyers in his hands, identical to the ones from yesterday. Adler pulled down his cap and waved his hand in a *go away* gesture.

"Not interested," he called out, trying to lower his voice an octave or two.

Mason just smiled and continued tapping on the window with the first knuckle of his right hand index finger. Herman lowered the window a couple of inches and repeated in his lowered voice, "Not interested."

"Hello Brother Herman," said Mason with a smile. He looked into the backseat, smiled at the bedspread covering the man sized lump and said, "And a great, good morning to you, Brother Saul!"

"What's going on?" Saul hissed in a loud whisper, still under the blanket. "Who're you talking to?"

"Brother Saul, it's me, Mason," said the young man, his smile getting broader. "Why are you all covered up?"

Saul lowered the bedspread just enough to peek out and see Mason smiling at him. He then sat up in the seat and tore the cover completely off. He eyed Mason suspiciously and asked, "What do you want?"

"Want? Me? I don't want anything, 'ceptin' to serve the Lord," Mason replied with a big smile.

Wittmann stared at LaCroix, blinked a couple of times, and then looked around. Adler was right. It was the same as yesterday, with demonstrators holding signs, shouting out slogans interspersed with *Praise Jesus* and *Hallelujah*. Wittmann had truly expected to see signs of a more *personal* nature. In fact, he half expected to see a few dangling Saul doll effigies.

"Did you, huh, happen to see the, huh…" asked Saul.

Mason pulled back a bit, first pointing to the small opening in the window and then to his ear. He leaned back in and spoke into the crack, "I'm sorry Brother Saul, but I can't hear you. It's kinda loud out here!"

"Roll down the window," Saul said to Herman. When he complied, Saul started again.

"Mason, didn't you see the news last night? Or talk to Pastor Broussard?" Saul asked.

"I did most certainly see the news. And yes, I did talk to Pastor Broussard," said a smiling Mason. "And to be honest, I was very angry with you. But Pastor Broussard explained to me that this was just another example of how the Lord works in mysterious ways. And that whatever your reasons for being lying and deceitful really have no bearing on the matter at hand. Praise Jesus!"

Mason then stood up and yelled out, *PRAISE JESUS!* The crowd returned the call in a mighty roar, *PAAARAAAIIISSSEE JESUS!"*

Mason leaned back into the car and continued, "Pastor Broussard explained that the Lord needed this particular travesty, the marketing of this heinous hate incarnate, to be uncovered. And to do so, he was using you as his unwitting vessel."

"So, you're not, huh, you're not mad?" asked Saul.

"Mad? No. Not now, anyways. I was, but it's just not the Christian way," said Mason with a huge smile on his face. "I've made my peace with the Lord, and I guess you'll have to do the same."

"But I lied to you," said Saul. "And all these people. And you're not angry?"

"Like I said Brother Saul, the Lord works in mysterious ways," replied Mason. "Whether you knew it or not, you were doing his work. And we are, too… by shining a light on this evil transaction. Go in peace, Brother Saul. And you as well, Brother Herman. You don't need to hide and, in reality, you can't. No one can hide from the eyes of the Lord."

Mason smiled at both of them, then stood up and sung out to the crowd, "This little light of mine, I'm going to let it shine!"

The crowd immediately picked up the song, belting it out as the cars in front of Mason started moving.

> *"This little light of mine,*
> *I'm gonna let it shine.*
> *And no Hitler car,*
> *will ever be mine… mine… mine."*

As Adler slowly drove forward, Wittmann stared out the window at the joyous crowd, his mouth slightly agape. As some of the crowd recognized him, they poked and nudged each other and pointed him out. A few gave him a stern look, a few more made the sign of the cross, a few even made the sign of the horns, but they all kept singing.

By the third verse, Wittmann was softly singing under his breath as well, including the new Hitler verse. Adler heard him, but just shook his head and continued the slow drive to the gate guard.

## CHAPTER 56
# Twice In Two Days

*Saturday – August 26 – 10:33 AM CDT*

> "We do not interfere with it,
> alter it, or contribute to it."
> — ANTOINE GUIDRY

"The kid's doing great," Bobby Raston told Andy Guidry. His face was still plastered with that same goofy smile that had been there since he'd showed up for breakfast. "Everybody's doing great! You've got an audio monitor. Isn't everything going great?"

Guidry just nodded his head. He'd been splitting his time between sitting in the Escalade and monitoring the audio feeds, standing in the holding area and staring at Max, and checking to see if the deposit had made it into his bank account. It hadn't.

He tried calling Jack Calman once, but remembered he was on a plane and so didn't try again. He'd be landing at about noon our time, so he'd just call then. He thought briefly of calling Nina Perez, Jack's admin, but decided against it. He figured it would either go through or it wouldn't and nothing he could say to Nina would change it.

"This is gonna be one hell of a great show!" said Bobby with virtually unbridled enthusiasm.

Andy's eyes grew a bit wide as he looked around to see who might be within earshot. Seeing no one paying them any attention, he looked down at the clipboard he was carrying as a prop and replied through clenched teeth, "Pipe down. We're supposed to be incognito, remember?"

"Oh yeah," replied Bobby, still smiling, "I forgot. Incognito. Got it." Although *incognito* might be the last word one would use to describe Bobby and the Twins today.

Since there was no getting around that the Twins created a stir, it had been decided it would be best to use a bit of reverse psychology on the crowd. They would call as much attention to themselves as possible, right off the bat, so that interest might die down more quickly.

Raston and Guidry had reasoned it would be like how your nose will eventually ignore a constant, pungent odor, yet continually wrinkle at the occasional whiff. They hoped it would work.

After leaving Pat O'Brian's the night before, Raston and the Twins had located a clothing store, just off Bourbon Street, that specialized in high-priced clothing that made a statement. It was, coincidently, a store that Prescott Hébert was also intimately familiar with.

Raston sported a garish, yellow silk shirt, patterned with various Lamborghini models. It had a high collar and French cuffs, studded with heavy gold cuff links shaped like Marti Gras masks. A thick gold herringbone necklace was easily visible against his pudgy, hairless chest as the shirt was unbuttoned to just above his sternum. His hair was slicked back and shiny and he had a diamond stud in his left ear, albeit attached via a magnet. He also wore a pair of RayBan Aviator Gradient sunglasses with the Silver/Pink mirror lens treatment. To finish the effect, he had white linen slacks with rolled cuffs that showed his sockless feet shod in brand new, white Sperry Top-Siders.

With that outfit, the ever-present RigMaster seemed a more-than-appropriate accessory.

The Twins were simply stunning, albeit in a slutty, well-kept woman sorta way. They wore matching purple silk Capri pants, also paired with brand new, white Top-Siders. Their shirts were expensive men's white broadcloth dress shirts with the sleeves rolled up and the tails tied in a knot just above their belly buttons, exposing smooth flat tummies with just the hint of highly toned abs. Their shirts were also unbuttoned to mid sternum, exposing thin purple sports bras that tried, with noticeably less that complete success, to keep their breasts from jiggling as they moved.

They also wore huge sunglasses with gradient tints, albeit propped up on top of their heads. The only jewelry on them was large gold hoop earrings, and man sized Diesel DZ7258 watches that looked far more expensive than they were.

Of course, they had their Canon EOS-1D X Mk II cameras on the trick monopods. Coupled with their flamboyant outfits, they now seemed more like expensive accessories than high technology tools.

Dean Preston was far more conservative, in both his dress and manner. When they had all met for breakfast in the Best

Western French Quarter's dining area, Guidry also noticed that he was markedly more subdued than normal.

During breakfast, while Guidry was going over the production workflow for what seemed like the tenth time, he noticed that Raston had a huge, decidedly out-of-character grin on his face. And while Raston was being almost abnormally attentive to the Twins — which was saying a lot — Preston was also very much out of character. He was almost moody, slowly picking at the complimentary waffle and eggs while stealing long glances at the Twins. The glances, however, seemed more like a clinical examination than the usual unabashed admiration.

But just because Guidry noticed, didn't mean he paid it much attention. There was always drama in a field production and, with a crew like this, on a job like this; well, a few mood swings were to be expected. As long as people did their jobs, he really didn't care to get into their personal lives.

Dean had tried to bring up the validity of the Hitler car, but Andy immediately shut him down with a "This is a reality shoot. We shoot the reality of the situation. We do not interfere with it, alter it, or contribute to it. Is that understood?"

Preston acknowledged that it was understood, then studied the gals to see if his question might make his mystery Twin give her identity away. It did not. They barely glanced at each other and seemingly hadn't even heard Guidry's pronouncement.

The insane traffic, with all the demonstrators, lookie-loos, and media trucks, had made them arrive at the auction more fashionably late than they had planned, but they still went ahead with their pre-arranged crowd-desensitizing plan.

When they first arrived, Bobby and the Twins made a big production of strolling about the cars displayed outside, with the Twins *oooing* and *ahhhing* over various cars that Raston pointed out. They took a copious amount of photos, with the intent of getting the other attendees used to this behavior. After about thirty minutes of the charade, they entered the auction hall.

Looking like a man with the world on a string, Raston had strutted into the hall with a Twin on each arm. After his surprise visitation of the night before, the *world on a string* attitude wasn't far off the mark. As far as Raston was concerned, this was a top drawer, top of the bucket list experience, and the smirk on his face showed it.

Like Preston, he also didn't know which Twin had been the *lucky lady*. But unlike Preston, he didn't really care. He was more than willing to be discreet if it enhanced the chances of another nocturnal encounter.

Once they had made their entrance, Raston had then made a point to shoo the Twins off as demonstratively as possible. He then settled into the sparsely populated rear section of chairs, inserted a pair of Bose QuietComfort noise-cancelling earbuds, and started studying the RigMaster with the intensity of a teenager with a burgeoning social cyber-life.

Dean Preston was wearing brown leather Adidas sneakers, tan chinos, a blue polo shirt, and the microphone enhanced glasses. Just like Raston, the Twins, and everyone else in the room, his entry credentials were in a clear pouch, attached to a lanyard about his neck.

Since they had VIB parking, they were able to drive into the reserved parking next to the auction car holding area.

They had just handed their badges and photo ID's to the gate guard in a single handful. If he had thought it strange that a member of the A-Bear A/V crew was in with a group of VIB attendees, he didn't show it.

Preston had taken only a short trip through the cars outside before entering the auction hall. He had then bought a coffee and stood drinking it at one of the tall concessionaire tables while waiting for Guidry, who was dressed in camera black from head to toe. While they talked, Guidry made a show of checking a clipboard he was carrying and talking in an expressive manner, as if Preston were asking questions about the order of the cars.

Actually, Guidry had been pointing out two of the *whales*, the high-dollar car collectors who were expected to be the big bidders on the Hitler car. He also reminded Preston they needed to get some footage with the old guy from yesterday. The one he had seen talking with that reporter gal, Sandra Melancon. He wished he'd have had time to check out the local news. Partially to see what the locals were saying about the car and all the commotion, but mainly because he wouldn't mind seeing Melancon again, even it was on the *small screen*.

He then reminded himself to ask McMillian about that old guy and why he had a VIB badge. He didn't look like the kind of guy that would, or could, plop down five mill to bid on a car, yet he was definitely on the list that McMillian had emailed him last night.

He had also told Preston that he'd keep an eye out for Dave Givens, who had yet to make an appearance. He told him he'd point him out as soon as he arrived.

Givens' main business was supplying authentic movie cars to A-list Hollywood production companies. He had an impressive automotive stable that were either actually used in the films, or were used as *blueprints* to build replicas when the cars were scheduled to be somewhat abused during the production.

Whether you needed six identical '76 Mustang IIs in Cobra livery, four identical '49 Cadillac Series 62 Club Coupes, or even a single, pristine '63 Ferrari 250 GT Spyder California… Dave Givens was the guy you called.

Jay Bozeman, a whale from Dallas, was a different kind of collector. He could have been a poster boy for third generation big oil money. He had not only been there when they had arrived, he had actually been among the first of the attendees to walk in the door. He was also the very first to hit the bar. Whether he was hung over or still drunk was hard to tell, by himself or anyone around him. By mid-morning he was on his third Bloody Mary and had already purchased two cars.

He had, of course, tried hitting on the Twins, but they had shot him down with a combination of haughty looks and speaking entirely in Chinese. Their Mandarin was actually pretty poor, no more than a third grade level, but his was non-existent.

Mark Hanson, the whale from St. Paul, Minnesota, was also there. He was incredibly wealthy, having been one of the early backers of the Mall of America and having owned a large percentage of the land it was built upon. Despite the vast wealth, he tended to be decidedly low-key in both dress and manner.

His collection centered on pre-war classics in general and Mercedes 500ks in particular. His collection of these rare and beautiful cars included three Roadsters, two Cabriolets, and a single, unrestored Coupé. If it were his choice, there would be no Hitler provenance attached to the Tourenwagen. He was far more interested in the actual vehicle than its evil association.

Since arriving, Hanson had been sitting quietly in an aisle seat, sipping coffee and watching the cars cross the block. He hadn't bid on a single one, but seemed to be very interested in the proceedings. Although if you were paying attention to him, you might have noticed that he seemed to be more interested in the auctioneer, and the cadence of the sell, than he was in any one particular car.

During the morning, both Hanson and Bozeman had repeatedly wandered over to the Tourenwagen display to study the car. Dean had been able to *interview* each of them multiple times. But whereas Bozeman was positively effusive about the car, Hanson was much more reclusive than overtly enthused.

Dean was able to switch his tone to match each man's demeanor and get some decent sound bites from both. He still marveled at the Twins, who had nonchalantly video recorded each encounter. If you hadn't known what they were doing, you wouldn't have guessed they were doing it.

"Hell fucking yes, I'm going to buy this car," Bozeman had said to Dean as they were standing in from of the Tourenwagen. "I've got the most bitchin' car collection in the entire metroplex… if not the fucking state. And there's a lot of Texans with bitchin' car collections!"

"Cool," Dean had replied. "Do you have a lot of these old, pre-war cars in it?"

"Nah," said Bozeman, "Mainly 60's and 70's. Mostly Muscle but I've got me some Exotics. I have four Lambo Countachs, three matching '76s in red, white, and blue and a twenty-fifth anniversary model in silver. Son, I tell you what, those cars are fuckin' chick magnets."

"I'll bet," replied Dean, thinking how all the *beeping* would get a laugh with the audience. It always does.

"If I had one of my Countachs here, those hot Chink twins would be pulling each other's hair out to see who be climbing in with me. Guaren-fuckin-teed!"

"So if your collection doesn't have pre-war cars, why are you interested in this one?" Dean had asked.

"Because it's a Hitler car, of course!" laughed Bozeman. He then leaned in to Dean, lowering his voice, but with the effect of making the recorded audio even clearer. "I mean, don't get me wrong, this will be a good investment. Cars like this don't go down in value. But I've got this totally smoking-hot Jew girlfriend and we will be banging six ways from Sunday in the back of this car. Have you seen the seats? Flip up them jump seats and the back is a fuckin' playpen!"

With that, Bozeman slapped Dean on the back, spilling a bit of his Bloody Mary on the polished concrete floor. He then lifted his half-empty glass, carefully eyed the ice to liquid ratio and announced, "Time for another. You should try one! I've been tipping ten bucks a drink to that totally hot *high yella* babe working the bar. And she is really doin' 'em right. And she could really do me right, if you catch my drift."

Dean just smiled and wondered if the man would be this stupid and obnoxious if he didn't have all that money. He decided he likely would, it just wouldn't be as entertaining.

Dean had talked to him twice since, once again at the Tourenwagen display and the other time after he had just bought a Royal Blue '66 Chevelle. The auctioneer had described it as having "a blown and stroked Edelbrock prepped LS3 with a 5 speed - 5 lever Lenco Street tranny twisting on a 12 bolt rear with 4.10 gears."

"I like my cars like I like my women," he had told Dean. "Super sexy, super fast... and a little bit weird!"

Hanson, on the other hand, had been more subdued. Actually, way more subdued.

"Nice car," Dean had commented to Hanson. The man was standing at the very edge of the Tourenwagen's platform.

Hanson had looked at him, sized him up, and turned back to the car. Still staring at the car he had responded with, "Yes it is. It's a very nice car. Looks to be very original."

"So, are you going to bid on it?" Dean had asked in what he hoped was a casual manner.

Hanson looked back at Dean, with his left eyebrow raised a bit, and responded with, "Perhaps. Why do you want to know?"

"Just wondering," replied Dean. "You look like a man who knows what he's looking at, and has more than just a casual interest."

Hanson pursed his lips, cocked his head, gave Dean the once-over and decided he didn't seem to be any competition. "Yes, I might bid on this car. I do have more than a casual interest. And you?"

"I think it's cool, what with the Hitler connection and all, but it's way out of my price range. Besides," Dean said, lifting his badge, "I'm here as a seller, not a buyer."

Hanson's eyebrows lowered a bit as he replied in a serious tone, "Are you the seller of this car?"

"Oh, no," replied Dean. "I'm selling my, huh… my Dad's '68 Porsche."

"It's pronounced Por-sha," replied Hanson, almost absent-mindedly. He squatted down onto his haunches to look at the undercarriage, or as least as much of it as he could see.

"Why don't you just go up and get a closer look?" asked Dean, making a show of looking at Hanson's badge. "You're one of those VIBs, I'm sure they'll let you onto the platform."

Still peering up at the car from his squatting position, Hanson replied, "Yes, you would think so. But the guards said it had to be cleared by Pat McMillian. I asked them to call him, but he hasn't gotten back to them yet."

"So what makes this car so interesting to you," asked Dean. He pretended to "remember" what he had seen on the badge. "Mr., huh, I believe I read Hanson on your badge?"

"Yes, it's Hanson, but I don't talk about cars, or my interest in them — if there is one — before an auction. It's not good business," said Hanson as he stood up, and then leaned down and wiped the dust off of one knee. "Now if you'll excuse me, I'm going to try to find this Mr. McMillian."

Hanson then walked off towards the auction office entrance to the right of the main stage.

A soft voice came though the small Bluetooth device that was in Preston's ear.

"Now that guy is nothing but good TV," Dean heard Bobby whisper, the sarcasm coming through loud and clear.

"Well, you never know. I'll try to talk to him again when he's not by the car," said Dean, also in a whisper and moving his lips as little as possible. "It's pretty weird that they won't let a VIB up on the platform to check out the car. I would think that people spending millions would want to get up close and personal with what they're buying."

"He just said it had to be cleared by McMillian," replied Bobby. "I can understand they don't want a bunch of muscle heads kicking the tires on a car like that."

Bobby then said, "How about you gals? Everything good on your end? The audio feed is good? Either of you need some coffee? I mean, just in case you didn't get enough, huh, enough sleep."

Preston's ears perked up. Was he imagining the veiled innuendo? Could Raston actually know about him and her? Whichever *her* it might me.

"We're all good," replied Mandy from the far edge of the main stage where she was feigning interest in the pristine 1978 Lincoln Mark V Givenchy Edition in Midnight Jade with a matching Majestic Velour interior. Actually she was more than just pretending. This would make a great gag gift for her father. She smiled when she thought of the look on his face when he went into the garage of the New Orleans house. She made a mental note to see who won the auction so she might offer them some instant profit on the luxury automobile.

"We don't drink coffee. We're tea gals, but we're fine," added Brandy from just to the left of the Tourenwagen platform. "I had to move my camera during that last interview so we lost the second angle. Some people came to talk to the guard and blocked my view." She looked over at her sister, who was gesturing at the big Lincoln with a simple tilt of her head that spoke volumes to her sister. Brandy just smiled and nodded.

"No worries," replied Bobby. "I'm also recording the aiming camera feed from my shotgun setup in the grid. I think we're covered."

The strangest interview of the morning was when Preston had walked over and plopped down next to the old guy from Wisconsin. As he tried to strike up a conversation, the young guy sitting one chair over was unsuccessfully trying to appear as if he wasn't eavesdropping.

"Didn't I see you here yesterday?" Dean asked.

After an few uncomfortable seconds, Saul finally replied, "I was here. So I suppose that's possible."

"I noticed you were hanging around the Hitler car when it was outside," said Dean. "Are you going to be a bidder?"

Saul continued to sit there without speaking.

"So, what did that reporter gal ask you yesterday?" asked Dean. "I was going to see if I could catch it on the news but never got a chance to watch it."

Saul took a deep breath and slowly let it out. He then turned to Dean and said, "She asked a lot of questions. Questions I shouldn't have answered."

Staring into Dean's eyes for an uncomfortable three seconds, he continued with, "So I'm not really in the mood for any more questions. Do you understand me?"

"Oh, absolutely," Dean said apologetically. "I'm sorry if I've upset you. I was just wondering about all those protesters outside and whether that would have any effect on a potential bidder. You know, just curious."

Wittmann's eyes narrowed as he looked at Preston and then slowly stood up and walked away.

Preston watched him leave and then looked over at Adler who was sitting there watching him with a quizzical look in his eye.

"Wow, what's up with him?" asked Dean.

"Off hand," replied Herman as he also stood up, "I'd say it was none of your fucking business." Herman then walked after the old man, but looked none too eager to catch up.

As the morning slid past noon, and cars continued to cross the auction block, it was, as Bobby was saying to Andy, going "Really, really great!"

Guidry slowly nodded his head as a smile started blooming on his face. He looked out at the auction floor for his crew.

The Twins were, of course, easy to find, but Preston seemed to be lost. Then Guidry had the idea to imagine an intersecting line between the Twins camera lenses and, sure enough, there was Preston. He was casually talking to an older couple, dressed in matching GTO shirts. He then started pointing to the Tourenwagen and Guidry briefly thought of turning on his audio monitor to hear the conversation, but then decided that he really didn't need to. He had already heard enough that morning and anything else was icing on the cake.

Guidry was lost in thought, thinking that it really was going to be one hell of a great show. He also threw out a mental, *screw you very much Bradley Mendenhall*. He was hoping like hell he wouldn't have to suck up to the preppy little twerp to pitch this show to Redline. He really wanted Calman and, by extension, NGTV, to pick this up.

He tapped a few buttons on his phone and saw his account still had the rather dismal negative balance it had this morning at nine a.m., and every other time he'd checked it since then.

Guidry just sighed and shook his head. He wondered why Calman hadn't held up his end of the bargain. That was twice in two days and it just wasn't like him. Or at least it wasn't like the old Jack Calman.

## CHAPTER 57
# Period Correct

*Saturday – August 26 – 12:25 AM CDT*

> "Yeah, baby, that's how WE roll."
> — Sandra Melancon

"You can let me out here," said Dave Givens, handing the taxi driver a fifty and telling him to keep the change. It was a long ride from the airport, and the traffic was still pretty heavy on Tchoupitoulas. The actual auction had started a couple of hours ago, and the doors had opened hours before that. Dave was thinking that most of the attendees should have been inside by now, but they literally hadn't moved more than a few car lengths in the last twenty minutes.

Dave's plan was to fly in, buy the car, and be out the same day. They were in the middle of producing the cars for *Mobile & Mad 13* and he didn't want to be away from the shop any longer than he had to. He grabbed the vintage, thick brown leather satchel he'd had for over twenty years, exited the cab, and started walking.

He was both amused and amazed at the scores of people that were lining the road leading to the parking area. The sheer number of black people with a sprinkling of white faces here and there reminded him of *Selma*, for which he had also supplied both background and hero period cars.

He walked by the crowd, nodding and smiling at the various derogatory chants about Hitler in general and the Tourenwagen in particular. He was thinking that if there was ever a movie about this auction, this crowd scene would not be cheap to recreate.

He passed three local news trucks, their microwave booms extended and cables snaking out to the camera crews. Mostly the camera ops were standing around, trying to hide from the sun, which had just crossed the line from merely blazing to intensely brutal. Huge white, puffy clouds occasionally offered a fleeting bit of relief as they blocked the direct sun on their slow journey to the west. Another source of shade came from the 10x10 silks each of the TV crews had set up to diffuse the light at the reporter's position. Each was supported by massive chrome stands, their wheeled tripod bases weighed down by heavy sandbags.

Dave was thinking that perhaps a sport coat hadn't been his best wardrobe decision that morning, although it had been quite comfortable in LA's cool, early morning climate. He could feel the sweat breaking through his antiperspirant. It dampened his shirt around his armpits as he trudged towards the entry gate. He just shrugged and continued walking. He was, after all, here to buy a car, not to try out for *The Face*.

Even from a couple of hundred feet away, he could see the gate guard was checking ID's against the credentials that hung around the attendee's necks. There was also a pre-check guard station that made sure you were wearing your credentials before you could even get into the line.

A bit surprised by the intensity of the security, he dug into his bag and retrieved his credentials with the little VIB sticker on them. He slung it around his neck as he continued walking, slowing down a bit as he passed the Ford Transit with the call signs WFNO FOX 15.

"Now there's someone who could be on *The Face*," thought Dave as he paused to watch the beautiful woman talking earnestly into the camera. She was pausing occasionally to hear and respond to questions. He walked up close enough to hear what she was saying, but not so close as to make the crew nervous.

"Well, Eric," she said directly into the camera, "I guess that would depend on how the car is presented to the attendees, but this certainly raises questions as to its authenticity."

She paused a bit to listen, laughed, and responded with, "Yes, I supposed someone could get *screwed* on this deal, but I suppose that only time will tell, and in this case..." she paused and looked at her watch, "it will be in just under six hours."

After another short pause, she smiled, nodded and then held her gaze until the camera op called out, "We're clear."

The relief on the woman's face was mixed with equal parts elation as she smiled at the camera op and said, "FOX – News – National! Yeah, baby, that's how WE roll."

Station management had been very pleased with the attention that Sandra's story was getting. For this live feed, they sent out their best and biggest truck and had actually supplied a sound guy and a microwave technician. It's not every day that one of their reporters had a breaking story that was picked up by the network for a live feed.

As the small, three-man crew started to break down the equipment, Sandra wandered over and sat in the open doorway in the side of the truck. The air-conditioned breeze from the trucks control room washed over her back as she looked at her notes.

"Hello," said Dave as he walked up to her, but still keeping a respectful distance. "Did I hear you say you were reporting for FOX News National?"

Sandra looked up and saw a trim, well-dressed man, roughly five foot ten or so, in his late forties or maybe early fifties. The close-cropped fringe of hair that surrounded his bald pate was more silver than black, but his face was relatively unlined and his smile was engaging. She then looked down at his credentials. Immediately noticing the VIB badge, she stood up and went over to shake his hand.

"Yes, indeed, Mr. Givens," we were just on "The Cost of Freedom" talking about our recent discoveries in the Tourenwagen auction, and its supposed connection to Adolph Hitler."

She made a show of looking at his badge, although both of them knew she didn't really need to, "And I see by your VIB sticker that you might also be interested in that particular automobile?"

"Well," replied David, "it was interesting enough to at least come and take a look."

Sandra paused long enough to put on her investigative reporter face and said, "L.A.'s a long way to just come for a look. And I'm told that VIB sticker on your badge means you're very interested. And since you're coming into the auction rather late…" Sandra paused to turn and look at the still massive line to get into the auction complex. She then looked back at David, now with a playful smile on her face that carried into her voice, "I would assume that the car in question is likely the only vehicle you are interested in?"

David paused, cocked his head a bit and then returned the smile. "Yes, at least it was until I heard you mention something about an issue that raises questions about its *authenticity*. At least I think that's how you phrased it. Why do you think there is some doubt?"

"I'd be happy to explain it to you… on camera," said Sandra.

David looked over at the slowly diminishing line of people, then at the Omega Speedmaster strapped to his wrist. He then looked up and smiled at Sandra. "Okay," he said with a shrug. "Why not? It looks as though I have plenty of time."

"Joey," Sandra called out as the camera op walked past her, camera in one hand, tripod in the other. "We need to do an interview with Mr. Givens. Could you reset the camera," she paused and looked at the other two crewmembers who were taking down the huge sun diffuser. "And the silk?"

Joey stood there, sighed and replied, "Sure, no problem. It'll be ten minutes," he then paused and looked at progress being made by the two members lowering the Century stands and continued with, "maybe fifteen." He then turned around, walked back to the camera position and called out, "Hey, guys. There's a change in plans."

Sandra turned to him and said, "While we're waiting, let me get a little background info. So you're from Los Angeles and, I would assume, a car collector. Anything else I can mention in your intro?"

It was actually more like twenty-five minutes when Joey finally called out, "Roll tape. And four, three, two..." he paused for the silent *one* and then pointed at Sandra and Dave standing in front of the camera. The two younger members of the crew, seated at the audio board and transmitter console, looked at each other, mouthed, "Roll Tape," then snickered. They weren't old enough to have ever *rolled tape* on anything.

"This is Sandra Melancon with a WFNO FOX News exclusive." Sandra then paused and thought for a second, held up two fingers and said, "Take two."

Sandra then smiled at the camera, mentally counted herself down and continued, "This is Sandra Melancon with a FOX News exclusive, outside the River City Complex of Mardi Gras World. With me is Dave Givens, owner of Cue The Cars, one of the largest suppliers of specialty and period correct cars to the movie industry. Dave, thank you for being with me today."

"It's my pleasure Sandra," replied Dave with a practiced smile. "But, just to be clear, we are *the* largest supplier of cars to the motion picture industry."

"I stand corrected," said Sandra with a practiced smile that didn't give away the pre-arranged gaffe. "You are also one of the VIB's, or Very Important Bidders, which means you are interested in the 1940 Mercedes 770k W150 Grosser Tourenwagen, also known as the *Hitler Car*."

"Yes, Sandra, I am interested in the *Hitler Car*, although not for any business purposes other than perhaps as a model. Although it might certainly be used as a reference vehicle, sort of a time capsule. It's not every day, or even every decade, that an unmolested barn find of this magnitude becomes available."

"As I understand it," Sandra continued, "You haven't gotten to actually look at the automobile yet, at least not in person. Nor have you been able to view the, well *mysterious* is the only word for it, the mysterious provenance that is supposed to tie this car to the Nazi leader."

"That is correct, Sandra," replied Dave. "Once our bidder bond was submitted we received a link to a set of high resolution photographs of all four sides of the car, as well as close-ups of the dashboard and interior upholstery. We were invited to examine the car in person, with or without expert advice, anytime up until today. I understand that it is now on the auction floor, and no longer available for a complete inspection."

"What do you mean by a *complete* inspection?" asked Sandra.

"A complete inspection would be to go over the entire car, top to bottom, inch by inch. But in a car like this, it's really not that big a deal."

"With a car that's estimated to sell in the millions of dollars, why wouldn't the lack of a complete inspection be a *big deal?*"

"That's a good question," Dave replied. "You'd be insistent on performing a complete inspection on a car that would be more prone to forgery. For example, if you were planning to bid on that long-lost '65 Z16 Malibu convertible, specially built for Bunkie Knudsen, you'd better do a complete inspection. You need to be absolutely sure that the car hadn't actually left the factory as a basic '65 Malibu convertible before you raise your paddle."

"And why wouldn't you have the same concerns with the Tourenwagen?" asked Sandra.

"It comes down to the availability of the source material," replied Dave. "There are thousands of '65 Malibu convertibles to use as a *starting point* towards your Z16 tribute build. That's just not the case with the Tourenwagen. It's not the authenticity of the car that's in question. The Mercedes-Benz Classic Center has already verified that it is a correct car. I also received a copy of their report in my VIB package. What is in question is the Hitler connection and that seems to depend on the... well, the *veracity* of its provenance. Basically, I'm not concerned if the car is *real*. There is no doubt that the car is a 1940 Mercedes 770k W150 Grosser Tourenwagen. But it was worth it to me to come and see for myself why they think it was a Hitler staff car, and to bid accordingly."

"And if the provenance is less than convincing," said Sandra, "will you still be a bidder?"

"The 1940 Tourenwagen is a rare and wonderful car. It is worth quite a bit of money, to me at least, without any tie whatsoever to that evil SOB. Being half Jewish, on my mother's side, and working in an industry that is famous for its Jewish heritage... personally I would prefer that it had no connection to Hitler. It would certainly be cheaper. Although, perhaps less expensive is a better term."

"As an expert in period-correct automobiles," said Sandra, laying the groundwork. "We'd like to get your opinion on a discrepancy that our news team has discovered in the presentation of this automobile."

"Happy to do it," said Dave. "Discrepancies at this level of the game can be an expensive issue." He paused and smiled before continuing, "Now whether it's an issue for the buyer or the seller, depends on the timing."

"In our coverage of this car," Sandra began, "we noticed the Nazi flags are attached to the car's flag poles utilizing Phillips-head hardware. As Phillips-head screws weren't introduced to the automotive market place until 1936, we found it odd to find that technology on this car. We independently contacted the Mercedes-Benz Classic Center, to ask when Phillips-head screws were first used in Mercedes-Benz cars. They told us, and I'm paraphrasing from an email written by the Supervisor of Parts Operations at the Mercedes-Benz Classic Center, that they did not believe that Phillips head screws were used on any Mercedes automobile until the mid-fifties."

Sandra paused for effect and then asked Dave, "Don't you think this is odd? That the Phillips head screws on this car would, at the very least, casts doubt on its... I believe you used the word *veracity*?"

Dave looked both surprised and thoughtful for a bit, and then carefully replied, "It certainly is unusual, but not definitive. The description of the car doesn't necessarily preclude any *additions* to the vehicle. As I remember it, the official report from the M-B Center merely states that the accessories are period correct. This doesn't necessarily mean they are original to the car, although one would certainly hope, or even assume them to be."

Dave stopped and thought for a moment and then continued, "So, in my opinion, is it odd? Certainly. But everything about this is odd. Selling a car like this, in a venue like this... that's odd. Selling a car like this, with this kind of lead time... that's odd. Not revealing the provenance on a car until during the actual auction... that's odd. But will Phillips-head fasteners being used to attach period correct flags to the car going to be a definitive factor, either in the selling or in my willingness to bid? Well… it's certainly something to keep in mind."

"Thank you for your time, Mr. Givens," replied Sandra, "And good luck in there. Perhaps you'll join us again after the auction to give us your expert opinion on the car, the process, and the provenance?"

"Perhaps," replied Dave with a big smile. "Perhaps, I will."

# CHAPTER 58
# Mildly Intimidating

*Saturday – August 26 – 1:07 PM CDT*

> "Especially since, he remembered with a smile, that it was his job to look mildly intimidating and make sure nobody spits on the car."
> — Joe Fontenot

Joe Fontenot was not looking forward to his evening shift. He was standing at his post, guarding the stairs at the rear of the Tourenwagen platform. For the last two hours, he'd had to try extremely hard to stifle his yawning, while comforting himself with the thoughts of the big payday ahead. And, he thought, regardless of the money, you just couldn't beat the view.

He was referring to the Twins, who certainly gave off a different vibe today than yesterday, at least as far as their outfits were concerned.

Yesterday they were very much in a *working casual* mode. Their high-end cameras were obviously tools of the trade; at least they were to someone used to sizing up people at a glance. Even so, it had taken him a while before he realized what they were doing. The casual observer might not have noticed they had been shooting an old guy while he talked to various people about the car. But Joe Fontenot wasn't a casual observer.

When he had first noticed it, he had quietly informed Schafer of the undercover camera work. Schafer had then checked with the powers that be and told him to disregard it; that it was an authorized activity.

Today, however, the Twins were dressed in far different outfits, bordering on the slutty side of stylish. It was a look that was even more alluring to the young beat cop. They were still doing their surreptitious shooting of unwitting subjects, although this time it was a much younger guy doing the interviewing.

He had found it hard not to laugh out loud when that rich asshole tried to pick up on one of the Twins and she would only speak to him in what he assumed was Chinese. Obviously he was either not her type or that she was working and didn't want to be bothered. Or both.

The short, fat guy who came in with them was paying a lot of attention to his oversized mobile, just as he had been yesterday. Joe figured it was some sort of monitoring device. Today he noticed that when the young guy was talking to people in front of the Tourenwagen stage, the fat guy's fingers were tapping and dragging on the device. Finally, out of the corner of his eye, he noticed the long tube of the microphone moving in the rigging and realized the guy was controlling it with the device. It was impressive.

He'd been security on enough TV production gigs to see that these people were pros, and high-level pros at that.

Plus, watching the undercover TV crew work was at least mildly interesting and gave him something to think about as he tried keeping the yawnies at bay. This was in direct opposition to how his partner Charlie Bonet handled the boredom.

Charlie had ten years' seniority on him, and three ex-wives to show for it. Charlie always wore sunglasses on these gigs, even indoors. If they bothered to ask, he'd tell his temporary employers it was so people couldn't see where he was looking, or at whom. The truth was that Charlie had developed an enviable ability to actually nap while standing. He would stand there in a modified parade rest, occasionally turning his head from side to side, but with his eyes very much closed. For all intents and purposes, he was sleeping on his feet. This was a very useful ability for someone with a lot of alimony to pay and no other ways to supplement his income. Or none he wanted to pursue.

Suddenly Joe's ears perked up as the heard the music again. It was the old BTO song, "Taking Care Of Business." Earlier in the day, when he had first heard the music, the auction hall hadn't been as crowded or as noisy. It had been pretty easy to ascertain it was coming from the massive trunk of the old Nazi car. He was pretty sure it was some kind of ringtone, although it wasn't always the same tune. Now that the hall was both much more crowded, and the decibel level much higher, there had to be a lull at just the right time for him to be able to just barely hear it.

When Fontenot had first heard the music, shortly after he and Bonet had taken their positions, he'd thought about telling Schafer. He almost immediately decided against it. He'd likely just be told to *shut up and guard*. Of course, it might have something to do with the mysterious presentation that would take place during the selling of the automobile. Even the more likely scenario, that it was some worker's phone that had been inadvertently left in the trunk, had a downside to letting Schafer know about it. It might end up saving McMillian some embarrassment during the sale, which was pretty much the last thing that Fontenot would want. Especially since, he remembered with a smile, that it was his job to look mildly intimidating and make sure nobody spits on the car.

Fontenot then looked over at one of the Twins, who was pretending to be studying her nail polish on her right hand while the left hand slowly twisted the DSLR on the monopod. He glanced over to where the camera was pointing and saw the young guy was talking to someone who was stooped down and trying to look under the car. It was the same guy who had asked him to contact McMillian about getting up on the platform. As the guy moved from the back to the front of the car in a sort of duck walk, the interview guy casually followed him, asking questions.

Joe looked back at the Twin and realized she was keeping the two in frame as they moved. He then looked around and saw the other twin, talking with one of the A/V guys, but also keeping her camera pointed at the two people in front of the Nazi car.

He then looked up and saw the long black tube of the Sennheiser was also tracking the two as they moved across the front of the stage.

Fontenot just nodded his head. He appreciated professionalism and these guys, and gals, were certainly that.

He paused for a second, listened intently, and then looked over at the Tourenwagen. He realized it was playing another song. This time it was "Whipping Post" by the Allman Brothers. Fontenot gently nodded his head in time with the music, his memory of the song filling in the sections that the auction noise drowned out.

He thought, with a smile, that the person who left the phone in the trunk was either an old guy or a true lover of classic rock. His smile faded a bit as he realized he hadn't noticed anyone on the A-Bear crew that would fit either of those descriptions.

## CHAPTER 59
# Very Weird Indeed

*Saturday – August 26 – 12:12 PM PDT*

> "Although I will be happy to confer with Human Resources to see if my title was somehow changed to *girl* without my knowledge."
> — NINA

"Hello Mr. Winters," Nina Perez had answered for the fourth time in less than two hours.

"Have you heard from him?" demanded J. Roger Winters.

"No, sir," replied Nina. "As you have requested, I will inform you the moment I do." Nina was polite, as always. Actually, the only way you ever knew if Nina was upset with you was when she became extremely, over-the-top, über polite. Which pretty much described her current tone.

"You're his girl! You're supposed to know where he is!" yelled Winters.

"Mr. Winters, I believe the proper term is administrative assistant," replied Nina. "Although I will be happy to confer with Human Resources to see if my title was somehow changed to *girl* without my knowledge."

She paused to let that statement sink in before she continued, "As to Mr. Calman's whereabouts, I have only been able to confirm that he did not show up for his flight out of New Orleans. Nor did he cancel it." The last part Nina had found more than a bit disturbing. Jack often had to rearrange his plans when he was in the field, but he always cancelled his flights, or at least he always called her to do it.

Nina continued, "I have tried calling his cell phone numerous times this morning. As he has not answered, or otherwise communicated with me, I have no way of knowing where he is. As you have requested, multiple times, I will let you know as soon as I have any information concerning Mr. Calman's whereabouts."

"Did you check with accounting again?" Winters demanded. He noticed, but choose to ignore Nina's tone. He had no doubt she was serious about the HR comment. "They still haven't heard from him about transferring the money to that Guidry guy?"

"Again, as you requested, I have checked with accounting. As of," Nina paused to look at the time on her computer screen, "thirty two minutes ago, they also have not had any communication with Mr. Calman. I have left word for them to immediately contact me if they do, as well as to inform Mr. Calman that you are anxious to speak with him. Would you like to authorize the transfer of the funds?"

"NO!" Winters screamed. "We can't transfer the money until we know we have a deal, a *signed contract* deal. That's what Calman is supposed to be taking care of! Something has gone wrong and I don't like it," replied Winters, now in a lower tone but just as angry. "I just tried calling him myself, for the third time this morning! I know gosh darned well he wouldn't be ignoring my calls. You did call the hotel?"

"Yes, sir," said Nina, not mentioning this was the second time he had asked that question. "They said his room was unoccupied, but that he had not checked out. They said his personal effects had been partially packed, whatever that means."

"Well shuckems and dag nab it!" muttered Winters. "Give me the number for that Guidry fellow."

With a mouse stroke and a few key taps, Nina had the number and gave it to him.

"And, just in case," added Winters with an audible sigh. "Do you happen to have a number for Bobby Raston, the audio guy? It somehow seems to have been deleted from my contacts file."

"Perhaps," she replied. "Let me check." Nina's contacts file was legendary. She had no doubt as to whether she had Raston's number. She paused for a three count. Then, sensing the impatience on the other side of the phone, she smiled and paused for another three count. She then gave him the number.

"Okay," said Winters, "I want you to call Jack every five minutes until he answers the phone or turns up dead. Do you understand me?"

"Perfectly," said Nina, "And would you like…" Nina quit talking when she realized the SOB had hung up on her. As she slowly replaced the handset back onto the phone base. With a wry smile she wondered if he had said every five minutes or every fifty. She just shook her head and thought about how hard it was for a *girl* to remember all those pesky little details.

Nina then sighed as the smile left her face. She knew Jack. She knew his likes, dislikes, and his ways of doing business. It wasn't like him to just go off the grid, especially not in the middle of a deal. First it was turning off his phone when he knew Andy Guidry would be calling about the deposit. Now it's him missing a plane and not even calling in, and not even checking out of the hotel.

She knew something was wrong, but she didn't know what it was or what to do about it. It wasn't like her not to know exactly what to do in any situation, and she didn't like it. She finally decided to call Calman's ex-wife to see if she had heard anything. She knew that with Calman and his ex's current relationship, she was truly just clutching at straws. Unfortunately, she couldn't think of anything else to do.

She shook her head a bit, wondering why Winters' statement about Jack turning up dead kept echoing in her mind. She decided to try calling his cell just one more time.

After five rings Jack's voice mail message came on and said, "What? I'm not answering my phone? Weird! Oh well, I guess you'd better just leave a message."

Nina just hung up and thought the message was very accurate; that his not answering was very weird indeed. She then took a deep breath and dialed the number for his ex-wife.

## CHAPTER 60
# Long Story

*Saturday – August 26 – 5:12 PM CDT*

> "Make it quick, cause I'm a busy man
> and we're making TV history here."
> — BOBBY RASTON

"I haven't said thank you. You know, for buying my car," said Andy. He was standing by Raston's chair, looking down at his clipboard like he was answering a question about an upcoming auction item.

Raston looked up at him with a quizzical look on his face. He had expected a reaction from Guidry, and certainly much earlier, but this wasn't it.

"Huh, no problem," Bobby replied. "It's a nice car and it was going way below market. Couldn't let someone steal it."

Andy cocked his head a bit in surprise and asked, "How do you know what *market* is?"

"You'd have to live under a rock not to know that vintage 911s have tripled in value in just the last couple of years… again," replied Bobby.

Actually, for three weeks last August, Raston had run the sound crew on the real estate reality show, "Beverly Hills Hi/Low." One of the agents, a stunning black woman as hot as she was ruthless, had driven an immaculate '67 911S. Raston had done a little research on Porsches in general, and early 911s in particular.

While he personally mic'd her up, he tried to engage her with surefire conversation starters like, "That sure is a SAA-weet 911 you're driving!" and "Wasn't that was the first year of the S model?" Since these attempts had been acknowledged with little more than a nod and a grunt, the next time he mic'd her up he went for the *urban* approach and asked, "Vintage nine-one-one's are totally price. Am I right or am I right, girlfriend?"

Once she found out that, due to contractual issues, they couldn't fire him, she required that Raston would not only never speak to her again, but that he would also not be allowed within twenty feet of her. Raston had just shrugged when told about it. It wasn't the first time.

A big smile came on Bobby's face as he thought about it. Compared to the Twins, the agent was a dried-up old hag. His smile got even larger as his thoughts wandered back, yet again, to his very unexpected, yet oh so welcome nocturnal visitation.

"I know my way around a 911, or at least what they are going for these days," Bobby said to Andy. "How I know it is a long story, but I figured there was at least fifteen grand being left on the table."

"I thought so, too," said Andy, "but I guess the final price didn't really matter. All we're on the hook for is the buyer premium."

Bobby thought about setting the record straight on this, but then decided it could, and should, wait. Instead he said, "Obviously, *Muscles on the Mississippi* isn't the right venue for vintage European. Why'd you pick this auction to sell your car?"

"Long story," said Andy. "Well, probably not so long. Pat McMillian told me that this wasn't the right auction for my car, but I already knew that. As you are already well aware of, I just needed cash and needed it quick."

Bobby looked over at the side stage with the Tourenwagen on it. There were a few people milling around it, but it was nothing like earlier in the day. There was a really big guy in his early twenties taking a selfie in front of it. There were two cops guarding the platform stairs at the front and rear of the vehicle. They looked bored, but alert. At least the cop without the sunglasses did. The one with sunglasses barely moved.

"The real question," said Bobby, "actually, the *multi-million dollar question*, is why did our German friend choose this venue for his *very vintage* European?"

Andy paused to look over at the car currently being auctioned, a 1965 Corvair Sprint. The auctioneer was pumping up the crowd with descriptions of the John Fitch modifications and reading excerpts from the September '65 issue of *Car & Driver* that featured it.

He then looked down at the clipboard. Earlier he had clipped the rundown page from the auction catalog. He'd been asked, more than once, when a particular car would be on the block.

He looked up at Bobby and replied, "Three more cars and we'll find out."

Andy pushed the transmit button on his earpiece and said, "Heads up, team. Only three more cars after this Corvair."

The auctioneer then banged the gavel, pointed to a man in the crowd, and called out "*SOLD!*"

"Correction, one more car after this '61 Bubbletop Chevy and it's showtime," said Andy to the crew. "The last car before the Hitler car is a chopped and channeled, '59 Chrysler Imperial. That's when Mandy and Brandy need to get to their positions. Remember, we are not shooting the auctioneer or the car owner or anything else the house cameras will cover. We want audience reaction, especially during the provenance video. We'll be the only live cameras in the room and we've got to be on top of it."

Andy stopped and scanned the huge room, noting the locations of Mandy, Brandy, and Dean. They were all looking back at him, although doing a good job of not being overt while doing it.

"Mandy, Brandy," Andy continued, "Be ready to switch the ISO on your cameras after the Imperial. They are going to cut the lights for the first video so it's going to get dark."

Despite being nearly thirty yards apart, the Twins simultaneously rolled their eyes.

"Don't worry, boss. We've got this," Andy heard Dean reply. Andy smiled, looked down at Bobby, pointed to the earpiece and did an OK gesture with his thumb and forefinger. The fake Bluetooth comms did a really great job.

He pressed the transmit button and continued, "During the presentation, I'll be in the Video Village with your buddies. I want to have a good idea of what we'll have to work with in post. After the Hitler Car auction, we'll pick up again and get as many interviews as possible, hopefully with the winner. You got that Dean?"

"Roger that, Andy," Dean replied. "Just let him try to get away without talking to me!"

"Alright then," said Andy. "Let's make a show."

Bobby made a big show of standing up and stretching while he murmured, "I guess I don't need to ask if the money was transferred?"

"Not as of twenty minutes ago," replied Andy. "And I've given up on calling Jack. He should have been at his desk hours ago."

"Have you called Nina, his admin?" asked Bobby.

"Yes, but I didn't get anything out of her. Just that he's currently *unavailable* and she's not *at liberty* to say when he might be." Andy paused in contemplation and continued, "Something's not right."

"Yeah," replied Bobby. "What's *not right* is that we don't have a deposit yet, which means we don't have a valid contract. Maybe we were playing a little more hardball than we should have?"

"I don't think so," replied Andy. "But that's not what I'm talking about. It was almost like Nina was pumping me for information, but in a very skillful way."

Guidry felt his phone vibrate, but when he looked at the caller ID, he didn't recognize it. It was the fourth time he gotten a call from that number in the last fifteen minutes. He just sighed and tapped the icon that sent it to voice mail. Mentally cursing the entire bill collection industry as a whole, and whichever asshole it was calling him in particular, he put the phone back into his shirt pocket. He thought briefly about just turning it off, but decided against it. Calman still might call.

A moment later, Bobby felt the iPhone in his front pants pocket vibrate. He immediately checked the room, hoping to see one of the Twins with their phone out. But they were both looking at the display screens on their monopod mounted DSLRs.

He sighed, pulled out his phone and looked at the caller ID. His smile immediately turned into a scowl. He swiped the phone, pressed the answer button and barked out, "What the hell do you want, Winters? Make it quick, cause I'm a busy man and we're making TV history here."

"That's exactly what I'm calling about," came the smarmy voice of a man who brokered multi-million dollar deals with people he detested, or detested him, on a more or less regular basis. "Our deal seems to have gotten a bit off track, and I'm hoping I can put it back on the rails."

"Well that train has left the station and you missed it," replied Raston. "I should have known if you were involved, this would be a *fuck you* deal from the get go. I might still be willing to talk to Calman, but I told you a long time ago, I'm not interested in anything you have to say. Not then, not now, not ever. And, as you well know, the deposit on the Carality series *somehow* didn't happen, which is not exactly *shocking* when you're involved. And since we don't have a deal, we're already talking to… well, who else we're talking to is proprietary information."

He then lowered his phone and tapped the screen with a lot more force than was needed. He then took a deep breath, as if to calm himself. He turned his head and saw Andy watching him with a look of disturbed interest. Bobby just smiled, shrugged his shoulders and said, "Now that... *that* is a long story."

"Shouldn't you have at least heard what he had to say?" replied Andy. "Or at least conferred with me before you hung up on our *network*? This is still my company."

"And it seems it's still my money that's funding this project. Believe me, if they don't pick up this show, someone else will," replied Bobby. "Besides, they're obviously worried... very worried. If they weren't, he would *never* have called me."

"And why is that?" asked Andy. "What's the deal between you two?"

"I told you," replied Bobby. "I'll tell you later. It's a long story." He paused and looked at the '59 Imperial, with vintage slot mags and thin chrome side pipes, waiting to drive onto the auction block. "And it's just about *showtime*."

Andy looked at him for a long three seconds. He then heard the auctioneer call out "SOLD" on the Chevy, and the color man begin introducing the Imperial. Andy pushed the transmitter button and said, "It's on like Donkey Kong. Let's do this."

## CHAPTER 61
# None Of My Business

*Saturday – August 26 – 5:29 PM CDT*

> "If I look as *Jew-boy* as you tell
> me I do, it just might work."
> — HERMAN ADLER

"It's almost time," Herman Adler said to Saul Wittmann, as they sat in the back of the auction hall. When there was no response, he reached out and shook the old man's shoulder a bit. Wittmann seemed to suddenly come too, like he had been in a trance.

"What?" Saul replied, more statement than question. His paper thin, old man eyelids were lined with red, as if he had been crying or maybe just forgetting to blink. Saul then looked around the room, as if he had forgotten where he was and then continued, "OK… yes… it's time.

"So," replied Herman in a resigned tone. "Let's go over this one more time. Our cap is four million, firm. Before the bidding starts, we split up to opposite sides of the room. I'll take the bid up to three point five, and then you'll jump in and start bidding against me. We'll go back and forth, but in small increments... no more than fifty grand. Having you jump in at that point, as if we're bidding against each other, should confuse the other bidders and get them rooting for me. Especially those that watched the news last night."

"Or this morning," muttered Saul, looking down at the ground and slowly shaking his head.

Judging from the looks, points, and whispers they'd received since arriving that morning, that was the majority of the attendees.

"When you hit three point eight million," Herman continued, "I'll jump up, pretend to be angry, and call you a Nazi-loving asshole. I'll yell something about how it's my people, *God's chosen people,* that deserve this car and I'll be damned if I let you have it. I'll yell that I'm all in and take the bid to four million, a two hundred grand bump, and then start staring you down. If I look as *Jew-boy* as you tell me I do, it just might work. The other bidders, if there are any left, might let me have it, just so you don't get it."

Saul just sat there, as if he hadn't heard a word. Just as Herman was about to repeat the plan, Saul replied, "Yes." He then heaved a big sigh, which seemed to strengthen his resolve, and continued, "Yes, that's the plan. That is why we're here." He then continued, more to himself than to Herman, "Stay the course. Stay the course. That is why we're here."

At the bar, Jay Bozeman was ordering a margarita on the rocks, having switched over from the Bloody Marys precisely at noon. He was very disciplined that way. "Shake a leg, sweetheart!" he called out and then whistled. He was holding up a ten-dollar bill and once he was sure she'd seen it, he stuffed it with a flourish into the large brandy sniffer that was collecting tips. He figured she must be up to sixty or seventy bucks in tips from him. He had actually lost count, and really didn't care. He never did when it came to tipping the bar staff.

Mark Hanson was seated at the far left of the audience section, on the side with the Tourenwagen display. He had positioned himself so he could easily turn to see the auctioneer, the Tourenwagen, as well as any other bidders. He sat calmly, with his legs crossed and the auction program on his lap. Only the incessant, rhythmic tapping on the program with his right hand index finger betrayed any excitement.

Dave Givens was standing at the rear of the audience section. He had recognized Guidry almost immediately, despite being dressed in camera black and wearing his cap pulled down low. It was no surprise when the young man he had seen Guidry talking with casually came over and tried to spark a conversation.

They'd talked about the car, what he thought about it, why he wanted to bid on it, and what he thought it would go for.

After Preston had left, Givens nodded his head in appreciation. The kid was good, as were the beautiful twin girls who had been nonchalantly pointing their Canon DSLRs at him during the *conversation*. He realized that if he wasn't in the biz, he likely wouldn't have realized he was being interviewed.

He didn't know exactly what was going on, but he didn't really care. He always felt that any publicity was good publicity. He smiled, thinking how he had managed to slip in both his name and his company within the first three sentences, and then wandered over to the Tourenwagen for the fourth or fifth time that day. He once again stared at the screws holding the Nazi flags to the poles. They were, of course, Phillips head. He'd expected that. It was the fact they were really old Phillips head fasteners that were a concern. If they had been new, it would have seemed more forthright.

Joe Fontenot smiled as he heard "Whipping Post" again. Someone was very anxious to talk to whoever owns that phone. It then occurred to him that it might be the owner of the phone, calling over and over to try and find it. He imagined some poor goober on the car detailing crew walking around the sold cars right now, listening for a little Dicky and Duane. For the twentieth time that day, he thought about just opening the trunk and getting the phone out, but for the twentieth time decided against it. Then the bidding on the Imperial began to heat up and he couldn't tell if he just couldn't hear it anymore, or it had stopped playing.

Fontenot tried, rather unsuccessfully, to cover up yet another yawn. He was past ready to get this Hitler Car auction over with. The sooner it was sold, the sooner he got off, and the longer his nap would be before he went back on duty.

Suddenly, he thought he heard something a bit different, something that seemed out of context in the noisy environment. He looked about the hall, trying to identify the source and couldn't find one. He then looked at the car, took a couple of steps closer to it, leaned over to listen more closely, and decided he was hearing things.

Fontenot then went back to his post by the rear platform stairs. He checked his watch, shook his head to clear it and wondered if the lack of sleep was finally catching up to him. He tried willing himself not to yawn again, but almost immediately lost the battle.

## CHAPTER 62
# It's Showtime

*Saturday – August 26 – 5:36 PM CDT*

> "As I have promised, here is the disk."
> — Heinrich Heinzburg

"Ah, it is my vaping companion from last night," said Heinrich Heinzburg as he walked into the Video Village with Pat McMillian.

Immediately recognizing the voice, Guidry froze for a moment. He wondered how much of his conversation with Simmons and Walker had been overheard. He then thought that since they had just been talking tech, it likely didn't matter.

Turning towards Heinzburg, and seeing the confident smile on the young man's face, he returned it. McMillian however, didn't look nearly as composed. His eyes were darting back and forth and there was a heavy sheen of sweat on his forehead. It was as if he had been standing outside all day instead of in the cool dry air of the River City Complex.

"Hello," said Andy. "It's nice to see you again. And hello to you, Mr. McMillian."

McMillian looked at Heinzburg to judge his expression and then at Guidry. What did the *vaping companion* and *see you again* mean? When and where had they met?

"Hello, Andy," replied a somewhat wary Pat. "I saw your car cross the block. Pity. I would have thought it would bring more."

"That's why they call it an auction," replied Andy.

"Andy?" asked Heinrich in a puzzled tone. "I thought your name was Dean?"

"Uhh, yeah," said Andy shooting a quick glance over to Pat and then back to Heinrich, "Andy's my middle name. We go by middle names a lot here in the south."

"I see," said Heinrich looking at Andy and then Pat. The look on his face showed he actually didn't. He was also thinking that the man's accent seems to come and go at will. He decided that something wasn't quite kosher, smiled at his mental use of the word, and decided it didn't really matter.

He had figured that McMillian would be running some sort of side deal. After all, it was his own side deal with the man that was the true guarantee their financial arrangement would be consummated. At this point, whatever other deals McMillian may have concocted were of no concern. All was in place for his plan and whatever happened after its conclusion was nothing he need worry about. That would be between McMillian and the new owner of the Tourenwagen.

Heinzburg walked over to Brian Simmons and handed him the Blu-ray disk he was carrying. "As I have promised, here is the disk," he said.

Brian took the disk and immediately handed it over to the Malcolm. Malcolm removed it from the case and inserted it into one of his machines.

"Now, we should go over the playback schedule," said Heinzburg.

"Absolutely," replied Brian. He looked at the bank of monitors as a wave of applause signified the end of the Imperial auction. He said to Malcolm, "Go to the Hitler Car countdown graphic and start it at…" he looked up at Heinrich and asked, "ten minutes?"

"Yes, precisely," replied Heinrich. "Now, the presentation begins with a dark room. You play the first video, Chapter One, the Introduction. As that video ends, the lights on the Tourenwagen pop on. Not slowly, but immediate. Pop them on so as to startle the audience. Do you understand?"

Brian just nodded his head and repeated, "Lights pop on. Got it. How about a sound effect to emphasize the pop on?"

"That would be excellent," replied Heinrich.

Malcolm piped up with, "I've got just the one."

"Wunderbar," replied Heinrich. "At that point, when everyone is looking at the Tourenwagen, I will position myself on stage, in front of the auctioneer platform, where the other cars have been. As I begin speaking, you slowly bring up the lights on the stage. I will speak for approximately three minutes and start the bidding. Once the bidding plateaus I will introduce the Chapter Two of the disk, the Provenance. Then you will…" Heinrich stopped and looked at Brian, who was alternating between eyeing the monitors, now displaying a graphic showing the Tourenwagen with a countdown clock, and his ever-present *bible*.

"You do not seem to be taking any notes?" Heinrich asked Brian. "It is imperative that this be conducted in this precise manner."

Brian looked up at Heinzburg and replied, "I took plenty of notes the last time you were here. So far," he tilted the large, three ring binder towards Heinrich to display the copious amount of handwritten notes, "nothing has changed in the rundown, except for the sound effect." He then pointed to a handwritten note that read *w/SFX* next to the lighting note.

Heinrich smiled and continued with, "Very good. Thank you for your attention to detail."

Heinrich looked over to Pat to compliment him on his crew, but saw he wasn't paying any attention to the exchange. Instead he was staring at the various camera monitors. In the auction lull, people were starting to wander over to the Tourenwagen stage.

Pat then put a walkie-talkie to his lips and hissed out, "McMillian here. Nobody gets onto that platform. Acknowledge!"

On the screen, Joe Fontenot raised his radio. His voice came out of Pat's walkie talkie, "Acknowledged." Joe looked over at his partner and pretended to have seen a confirming sign from Charlie, and continued. "Both guards understand, no one on the platform."

"Schafer copies," came another voice out of Pat's walkie-talkie.

Heinrich wondered about the virulence in Pat's command, but again thought that at this point it didn't really matter. He continued with his rundown to the A/V crew chief.

"When I introduce the Provenance, I will explain that this is, in and of itself, of great value. I will point out that your camera people will remove the cameras from their shoulders and point them away from the stage. The crane operator will also secure his camera and point it away from the stage."

"Jib," corrected Malcolm. When Brian, Heinrich, and Pat all turned to look at him, he continued with, "It's a jib, not a crane." He then smiled sheepishly and turned back to his console.

"As will the *jib* operator. I will then point out the robotic cameras in the…" Heinrich stopped at looked at Malcolm. Malcolm, without turning around piped up with, "The rigging."

"I will also point out the robotic cameras in the rigging. At that point, when they are all looking at them, you will point the cameras towards the back of the room. You will then cut the lights. No dimming, just a cut to darkness," said Heinrich.

Brian looked up from his binder and stated, "OK, that's different." This time he made a big show of scribbling the note into the binder.

"Once the provenance video has played, you will once again, *pop* the lights onto the Tourenwagen. After an appropriate time, I will begin speaking and you will slowly increase the light level on the stage." Heinrich paused and, reassured by Brian's nodding head, continued his instructions. "That is when the bidding will resume, with what I anticipate will be increased vigor, although it may take a while for the *provenance viewing experience* to subside. From that point on, it is simply an auction."

Brian looked up from his binder and simply said, "OK, got it."

"Then it is, as you say, *showtime*," said Heinrich. He clicked his heels, gave a short nod and walked out of video village. As he left, Pat looked up from the monitors as if he just realized the conversation was over and started to follow Heinrich.

Andy spoke up in somewhat of a whisper, "Pat, a moment?"

Pat sighed, turned and hissed, "What?"

"Tell these guys it's alright to hook up my recorder to their program feed," Andy said, holding up a small Black Magic Video Assist portable monitor and HD recorder.

"I told you I'd get you all the footage after the show," whispered Pat. "Why do you need to hook that up?"

"Lots of reasons," replied Andy. "But mainly because it reassures me to be able to walk away with something tangible at the end of the auction. Humor me on this. What can it hurt?"

Suddenly Joe Fontenot's voice crackled over the walkie-talkie, "Mr. McMillian, Mr. Hanson is asking why he can't get on the platform to examine the car before the bidding. You never got back to me about his earlier request."

"I'll be right out," Pat said into the walkie-talkie and then turned to Brian and pointed at Andy. "If it doesn't screw anything up, do what he wants."

Pat then stormed out of Video Village and towards the entrance between the auction stage and the Tourenwagen platform.

"Are you embedding audio into the signal?" Andy asked, as he handed the portable recorder to Brian along with a blue HD-SDI cable.

"Of course," Brian replied in a tone that asked why wouldn't they.

He then handed the device and cable to Malcolm, who looked at it, attached it onto a spare BNC feed on the patch panel, and then powered it on. Once he saw the Tourenwagen countdown animation on the monitor, overlaid with audio meters that displayed the music he was sending to the house PA, he looked up and asked, "When do you want to start recording?"

Andy looked at the countdown graphic that had just clicked past the six-minute mark. "I've got plenty of battery and a clean sixty-four gig card," he replied thoughtfully, mentally calculating the available recording capacity. "Might as well start now. As the man said, it's *showtime*."

# CHAPTER 63
# Es Ist Hier

*Saturday – August 26 – 5:42 PM CDT*

> "What's the record for a
> Hitler car at auction?"
> — FRANK HILLMAN

"It is what it is," Pat McMillian said to Mark Hanson as they stood in front of the Tourenwagen platform. They were standing among a dozen or so people who had wandered over to take a look at the featured car and take a few selfies in front of it. "It was available for inspection all day yesterday. That window has closed."

"It was never communicated to me, or my people, that we would not be able to do a close-up inspection of the car," Hanson replied. "You're expecting people to pay seven figures for a car they aren't able to personally inspect for authenticity? I have tied up a lot of money to attend this auction, solely for the purpose of bidding on this car. And now you're telling me I can't get within ten feet of it?"

"A copy of the M-B Classic Center report was sent to you with your VIB packet. They have verified the car," replied Pat, glancing up at the count down animation just as it clicked past three minutes. Prescott Hébert was standing just off the left side entrance of the main stage, where the stairs to the auctioneer balcony were located. He pointed at Pat, then up to the auctioneer balcony, and then pointed two fingers to his eyes.

"Mr. Hanson," said Pat, "I appreciate you coming, but as you might expect, today has been a very busy day. We have telephone bidders who will be bidding based solely on the Classic Center report. They have also submitted a bidder bond and they haven't seen the car as closely as you have. I'm sorry if we can't accommodate your request, but again… it *is* what it *is*."

He turned, looked at Hébert, held up his forefinger as if to say *one moment*, and then said to Hanson. "I'm afraid I'm needed elsewhere. Good luck in your bidding, should you decide to do so." McMillian then turned and walked towards the back stage entrance. He smiled as he walked past Prescott Hébert, pointed to the auctioneer balcony and then at his own eyes with two fingers.

McMillian's gesture clearly communicated that he would be watching.

Hébert's steely nod conveyed the message that he'd better be.

McMillian's smile immediately left his face as he walked back stage and climbed the stairs to the auctioneer's balcony. For the thousandth time since the incident he asked himself how the hell he was going to get out of this mess.

He'd left strict instructions that no one was to be allowed near the car, even after it was sold. Somehow he needed to keep the new owner, whoever it might be, away from the car, and the trunk, until Schafer could take care of the *issue*. It suddenly dawned on him that the whole process would be far easier if a telephone bidder won the auction.

He took a seat next to the auctioneer, on the small platform that loomed above the main stage, just as the pre-recorded announcement boomed out over the PA system.

"Ladies and gentlemen. Please take your seats. The presentation of the 1940 Mercedes 770k W150 Grosser Tourenwagen will begin in two minutes," it concluded and the milling crowd began to make their way towards their seats.

Frank Hillman had been the auctioneer of choice for A-Bear auctions for the last thirteen years. He was a master at cajoling the last dollar, or thousand dollars, from a bidder. He was also adept at convincing car consigners to lift the reserve if it were anywhere close to the current bid. There was rarely any money *left on the table* at an auction that Frank Hillman was calling.

"So, what's the record?" Frank asked Pat as he sat down next to him and put on the Clear-Com headset. The headset provided communications with the staging crew, the car wranglers, and the A/V guys in Video Village.

When McMillian didn't answer, Frank asked again.

"What?" Pat replied. He had been looking at the cop who was guarding the rear platform entrance. The cop was turned and looking at the car with his head cocked over towards it a strange way.

"What's the record for a Hitler car at auction?" Frank asked for the third time.

"Huh, the last one that went to auction was in the early 70s and it barely broke one-fifty, but that was a lot back then. The record for any car actually," replied Pat as he scanned the crowd who were settling into their seats. From his vantage point he saw that Prescott had gone back stage and was talking to Heinrich, who was waiting in the wings. He continued with "One changed hands privately in 2009. Some Russian billionaire supposedly paid a few million Euros for it."

"Well then," said Frank with a smile. "Let's make a little history."

"We better," muttered Pat, looking down at the flat screen monitors embedded into the table. They mirrored whatever was on the big screens flanking the stages. Currently the animation was counting down from thirty seconds. "I want you to pay particular attention to the phone bidders," Pat instructed Frank. "There might be some distance delays as some are calling in from Europe. Give them as much leeway as possible, more than we normally do."

Frank shot him a glance, thinking that was the direct opposite of his normal instructions. But this wasn't a normal auction, so he just shrugged and replied, "Roger that, Mr. Mac."

"You've got the rundown on this?" asked McMillian. "We start with a video, run it up a bit, play the second video, and then sell the car."

"Yup," replied Frank. "I've got it. Basically, if it's dark or a video's playing, I keep quiet."

The lights then started to dim and as the countdown hit zero they went completely out. Music slowly swelled up. On the screens, a slow fade up revealed the opening shot.

It was winter in the Austrian Alps, and the scene was every bit as beautiful as that phrase implies. The air was achingly clear and the snow that blanketed the scene glistened and sparkled as if inset with diamond flakes. The camera was flying. It seemed to be going a hundred miles per hour just inches from the treetops. It darted back and forth, almost playfully, barely missing the taller branches.

Suddenly, the trees stopped at the edge of a huge gorge, flanked by craggy mountaintops. The white dusting of snow across the tips stood out in high contrast against the deep blue sky, devoid of a single cloud.

There was a subtle gasp from the audience as the camera launched itself over the cliff, seeming to fall and climb simultaneously. As the camera banked into a long sweeping right hand turn, the mildly accented voice of Heinrich Heinzburg began streaming out of the speakers..

"Austria… perhaps the most beautiful place in the world. Home to majestic mountains, gorgeous glens, raging rivers, lipid lakes and… foreboding forests, Austria is the Aryan paradise."

McMillian looked down at Heinzburg, still in the wings and talking to Prescott, thinking that the man had obviously decided that *more was more* since he recorded this voice over, at least as far as accents were concerned.

"Austria is also the home of two rather notable residences of Herr Adolph Hitler."

The drone camera was now flying straight up the side of a steep cliff. Tall scraggly pine trees were interspersed along the sharp, craggy face of the mountain, tucked into the crevices, and seemingly anchored to bare rock.

Suddenly, a multi-story brick house appeared at the pinnacle. The rather plain architecture only highlighted the incredible view the house enjoyed at virtually any angle.

"Perhaps the most famous is this, the Kehisteinhaus, also known as The Eagles Nest. Many are under the impression that this was der Führer's primary residence. It certainly seemed to have been thought so by the various Allied armies who rushed to lay claim to it at the conclusion of the war."

The drone camera was now circling the building, keeping the house precisely centered so that the stunning background seemed to whirl behind it.

"This magnificent building was a gift from a grateful German people to Adolph Hitler in celebration of his fiftieth birthday. It was completed in only thirteen months and at the time cost thirty million Reichsmarks... about one hundred and fifty million Euros in today's economy. It was presented to Herr Hitler on the twentieth of April, 1939."

As the gorgeous scene slowly faded to black, the music faded completely away and the voice over continued in a dry, emotionless tone, "Der Führer only visited Kehlsteinhaus a handful of times. By some estimates, as few as ten. He stayed an average of thirty minutes per visit."

The screens slowly came back to life. The flying camera was now navigating a more heavily wooded cliff, not nearly as steep. It broke through the trees and turned onto an obviously very little used, very old roadway. The camera hopped above the barely recognizable remains of a wall and gate and followed the gently banking roadway. It stopped before a huge field of rubble so overgrown and dilapidated, that were it not for the decaying bits of concrete construction, you might have thought it had been this way since time began.

"This is what remains of the Berghof, Hitler's *true* alpine home."

The scene was then overlaid with a semi-transparent black and white photo of the house, perfectly aligned with the rubble-strewn ruins.

The video then dissolved into Eva Braun's famous home movies, some in black and white, but most in color. They were infused with soft pastel hues that only added to the jovial atmosphere and on-camera camaraderie of Adolph Hitler, Hermann Göring, Martin Bormann, and various other Nazi leaders. Their clothing alternated between nappy civilian attire and ornate Nazi uniforms.

Heinrich's voice continued over the vintage films as they changed to clearer, black and white films and photos; these having being taken by official German military photographers. "The Berghof was where Hitler relaxed, recuperated, and reflected with friends and family. It was also where he received many visitors of state, impressing notables such as Benito Mussolini, the Aga Kahn, and Neville Chamberlain. The British Prime Minister is seen in this photo arriving to the Berghof in a Mercedes Benz 770 W150 cabriolet, as did virtually everyone who came to the Berghof… including der Führer himself."

The scene then dissolved into an extremely high, overhead shot of the entire valley. It was live video, but remarkably steady; a testament to the quality of the equipment and the expertise of the operator. As the voice-over continued, photorealistic structures began to overlay the valley, each with a graphic identifying the structure. The structures seemed planted in place, moving with every motion, no matter how slight, of the background video. The post-production artist was obviously also quite talented.

"It is not known how many 770s were required to support the Berghof compound, and the other official buildings and residences that occupied it…"

On the screen, the buildings were identified as the SS barracks, hotels, guesthouses, garages, hay barns and pigsties. Buildings higher up on the hill and mountainsides were labeled as Bormann's house, Göring's house, and the Berghof. Little squiggly lines started snaking throughout the valley as the voice over continued.

"The entire valley, known as the Obersalzberg, was riddled with tunnels connecting the various buildings to each other, as well as to air raid shelters and storage facilities. Most of these shelters and storage facilities were destroyed. Some during the war… some immediately after… some as late as the early 2000's. Some of these storage facilities were never destroyed because… they were never found."

Suddenly, the camera dropped out of the sky into a free fall flight towards the valley floor. Just as it seemed it would surely crash, it did a mid-air pirouette and, with a flash of blue sky, the camera started blasting down an overgrown road that was little more than a trail. There were fresh tracks in the snow. They were obviously made by a heavy vehicle as they were deep and had churned up frozen ground to mix with the otherwise pristine snow.

The drone made a wide sweeping arc around a left hand turn and then slowed to a hover. Blocking the snow-covered road was a Mercedes-Benz G63 AMG 6x6. Attached to the rear was a large enclosed 4-axle trailer with massive, oversized tires.

The bed of the G63 was covered in canvas, with the back of it pulled open and snapped to the sides. The tailgate of the four-door, go-anywhere vehicle was lowered and various picks and shovels were leaning against it. A diesel-powered air compressor was chugging on the road alongside an electrical generator. Hoses and cables snaked into the hillside, through a moss-covered stone archway. Next to the archway was a pile of rubble; the fresh breaks from its recent demolition contrasting against the mossy exterior that matched the archway.

The drone slowly made its way to the tunnel. As it approached, it rose in the air to show the number "32" pressed into the concrete, weather worn and barely visible in the top of the arch.

It then dove into the tunnel, following the cables and hoses, as the sounds of construction slowly became louder. It rounded a corner and stopped. Before it was a line of three archways. The left and center archways led to large rooms whose walls were lined with huge, yet empty wooden racks. Despite their obvious age, they still looked very sturdy. The archway to the right was bricked in, almost flush to the stone of the archway. It was not a perfect example of the bricklayer's art, but its age gave it dignity.

Three people were in front of the wall, their backs to the drone, their breath visible in the cold air. One of them held a small air powered chisel and was carefully chipping away at the mortar of a brick. The scene was lit with four banks of Kino Flo LED video lights. A Panasonic HC-X1000 4K video camera was mounted on a small Sachtler carbon fiber tripod with an FSB 4 video head.

As the crew worked on the wall, the drone camera flew behind the video camera. On the small, flip out monitor, the onscreen display revealed the moderately wide angle shot it was recording. As the drone drew closer to the monitor, the monitor seemed to fill the screen. The onscreen indicators seemed to fade away as the picture from the ultra high definition camera now filled the screen.

The young man working on the wall then stopped the air chisel. He tugged at the brick, felt it loosen and then tugged on it some more. Finally, it came out of the wall. He handed the brick to one of other workers and pulled a SureFire LED flashlight from a small holster on his belt.

The man, whose back was still turned to the camera, took a very obvious deep breath. He then put his face to the opening in the wall, poked the small flashlight into the opening and hit the end cap switch with his thumb. He then stood completely still for a full five seconds and then switched the light off. The man then turned around. It was Heinrich Heinzburg. Rapidly blinking, as if to keep the tears at bay, but with a huge smile on his face he simply said, "Es ist hier. Es ist eigentlich hier."

The smile then slowly faded, as the energy seemed to drain from his body. With his back against the wall, he slowly slid down it until he was sitting on the ground. He then clutched his knees and began to cry.

The screens began to slowly darken to black, as the sound of his soft sobbing continued to fill the room. The lights on the Tourenwagen platform suddenly blazed to life, painfully bright and perfectly synced with the sound of a heavy steel door slamming shut, albeit with a bit too much reverb. Dozens of faces jerked away from the brilliant platform, their eyes dilated by the darkness, and then slowly turned back as they adjusted to the light.

"I apologize for my lack of control," said Heinrich Heinzburg, standing in the center of the still darkened main stage. "It was an emotional moment."

The backlights slowly came alive, silhouetting Heinzburg who was centered on the stage, from right to left, but about four feet beyond the middle. He was fully enveloped in a massive cloud of white vapor. The backlighting made the cloud seem almost alive as it swirled in eddies, pushed about by the now visible currents of the air-conditioning system.

Heinrich took one more deep drag on his vaping mod and blew it out in front of him. The massive, glowing cloud of billowing white almost totally obscured his body. He then stepped through the cloud to the center of the stage as the front lights slowly rose to full power. "That was a very emotional time for me. It was more than just the culmination of years of effort. It was the realization of generations of family lore, finally vindicated; proven to be true."

Heinrich paused and looked over at the massive automobile and smiled. He then turned back to the crowd and continued, "Many of you have heard about the provenance video, and that once played, will secure this car's place in history. The video you just saw was NOT the provenance video. That video will be revealed to you momentarily and you will decide for yourself as to its…" Heinrich paused, as if searching for the right word. He then finished the sentence, "as to its veracity."

Heinrich took another massive drag on his vaping mod, closed his eyes, tilted his head back, and released the plume of vapor towards the ceiling. He then lowered his head back to the audience and smiled. "But let us take a few minutes to look at that resplendent automobile, that wonderful, glorious, *survivor*. Even without any provenance, without any proof of its rightful place in history, it is... magnificent."

A murmur of agreement swept through the audience as dozens of faces, illuminated by the stage lights, turned to look at the Tourenwagen.

"On its own merit... as it sits... what would it be worth?" asked Heinrich. He glanced up at the auctioneers' platform, nodded to Pat and Frank and continued with, "Shall we find out?"

The room lights suddenly turned on and, as they did, the bidding began.

"We have a very nice, 1940 Mercedes 770k W150 Grosser Tourenwagen; unrestored and completely original," announced Frank Hillman. "Shall we start the bidding at one hundred thousand dollars?"

A sea of hands shot up. It seemed as though the entire audience were waving their hands, clutching their bidder credentials with the numbers facing the stage.

"Two hundred thousand dollars?" he asked.

Not a single hand went down.

"Three hundred... four hundred... five hundred?"

Finally, reality started creeping into the frenzy and people began lowering their hands, leaving about fifty or so still waving in the air. Frank picked one at random, because at this point it didn't really matter. He pointed to the bidder and said, "I have your five hundred thousand, sir."

For a brief moment, a muscle car flipper from Yazoo City, Mississippi was the lead bidder. It was a very brief moment indeed as Frank paused and then continued with, "Now looking for one million. Do I hear one million dollars?"

## CHAPTER 64
# PROV-E-NANCE

*Saturday – August 26 – 6:13 PM CDT*

"As I was saying, this is what you came for."
— Heinrich Heinzburg

"Travesty!" exclaimed Saul Wittmann to no one in particular, and at a level just this side of shouting. He was pacing the floor between the seating area and the bars in the back of the auction hall.

During the last few hours he had developed an epiphany of sorts. An epiphany that seemed to mesh with his most recent, yet mostly forgotten plan to purchase the Tourenwagen. This new *understanding* was amplified by a lack of food, a low-grade fever from some bug he'd picked up, and just generally being old. As the bidding climbed higher and higher, before the Hitler connection had even been offered, he had been getting more and more agitated.

A few of the A-Bear regulars had stayed with the bidding until it jumped over the two million mark. The bidding then slowed down dramatically at that monetary juncture, until only the whales and Herman Adler were left, as well as two very motivated telephone bidders.

For a while, the bids had been going up a hundred grand at a time. And, for a very short interval, Adler's three point five million was the high bid. But, almost immediately, it was raised by a five hundred grand bid to an even four million. Saul Wittmann never even had a chance to begin bidding, if indeed he realized it was his cue to do so. It then jumped another two hundred and fifty grand and stalled at four and a quarter million.

Herman Adler breathed a sigh of relief. He was happy all this craziness was finally over, but was a bit disappointed he didn't get to call Wittmann a Nazi-loving asshole. Adler looked over at the old man to see his reaction to the loss. He didn't like what he saw. Now that this insane quest for the Hitler Car was over, it was time to get the old man home.

Heinrich Heinzburg, however, was very impressed. Even though his take was capped, the more was indeed the better, at least it was in the overall scheme of things. Still, he thought, it was a pity to leave so much money on the table.

"Trés bien," muttered a still wary Prescott Hébert. He was thinking that perhaps this screwball McMillian deal might actually be a beaucoup moneymaker.

Mark Hanson, although certainly in the thick of it, had decided he wouldn't bid another penny until he saw the provenance. Like it or not, at this point the car's value was going to be intrinsically tied to its Hitler connection.

Pat McMillian was actually praying, desperately petitioning God that the winner would be one of the phone-in bidders.

It didn't even cross his mind that the reason behind his request might preclude any sort of divine intervention.

Bobby Raston was staring at the RigMaster with a huge smirk on his face. He had the display set to show the recording levels from all the mics he had placed throughout the room and was mentally congratulating himself on how great the 7.1 mix would sound.

Jay Bozeman had been the big bidder that pushed it to four million. He had been hoping that a huge jump in the bid increment would shut down the rest of the bidders and get this over with. It had worked before and, basically, he was ready to be done with this auction. He was thinking he'd rather be on Bourbon Street, drinking some… bourbon, that is. He smiled at his internal witticism.

Dean Preston, now that there was a lull in his interviewing duties, was getting more angry by the second. He just couldn't believe the auction had gone this far, and the bidding had gotten this high. He wondered for the thousandth time if he had done the right thing; if maybe he should have done more to expose the car. Overpaying for the car probably wasn't going to hurt these rich guys. But if Mr. Calman was right, when the truth came out, it was going to kill the man.

Herman Adler began to think that Saul Wittmann might have finally gone off the deep end. He watched the old man pacing back and forth at the back of the hall, obviously talking to himself. From his agitated gestures, and the sideways glances from the bar patrons, it was quite a conversation.

"Mandy, Brandy. Someone get the old guy," said Andy, standing in the wings of the stage and pressing the transmit button on his earpiece. "He's acting crazy, but he could be faking. We need at least…" his voice trailed off as he saw one of the Twins seemed to be looking at the auction, but her mono-pod mounted camera was pointing at Wittmann. "OK, you've got it. Never mind." As he took his finger off the transmit button, the little itch in the back of his brain was trying to guide his hand to the vape pen in his pocket.

Joe Fontenot was thinking that was a new one, as he slowly maneuvered himself closer to the Tourenwagen to better hear the latest ringtone. He nodded his head in time to the beat as he asked himself whatever happened to that Hammer guy? He was also thinking that whatever kind of phone was in the trunk, it had some serious *thump* to it. He looked at the Tourenwagen, then the crowd, and then whispered the title to himself, "Can't Touch This!"

Frank Hillman pointed to Dave Givens, the current high bidder, and announced in a rapid, urgent cadence, "I have four point two five, looking for four point five. I have four point two five …" he then swung his arm around to Mark Hanson and asked, "Do I have four point five? Do I have four point five? Do I have four point five?" and then abruptly stopped to wait for the answer.

The hall was actually almost quiet as Mark Hanson stood up and asked in a loud, but calm voice, "Do you have the provenance?"

Pat McMillian reached to the Clear-Com clipped to his belt and pushed the transmit button. "Get ready to roll the provenance video!"

From the other side of the auction hall, a beefy southern drawl yelled out, "Yeah! What about dat video? Where's the provenance?"

A chant began in the hall, slowly at first but rapidly rising, "Provenance. Provenance. Prov-E-nance! Prov-E-nance!! PROV-E-NANCE!!! PROV-E-NANCE!!!"

Andy Guidry was standing in the stage wings and looking at the crowd coming to their feet. Visions of an EMMY˚ award danced through his head as he surreptitiously took a hit on the vape pen. He slowly blew out the vapor, realized what he was doing, and then stared at the pen. It seemed to have appeared into his hand of its own volition. He jumped a bit when he suddenly felt a tap on his shoulder.

Andy whirled around and saw Heinrich standing behind him with a huge, almost manic smile on his face. "It is time for me to go on," he said. "Please forgive me, but I cannot stand the taste of the Hurricane vaping fluid any longer. Do you have an extra cartridge that I may purchase from you?"

Andy jaw dropped open a bit in surprise, but he quickly closed it. "Huh, I'm sorry. I don't have any extra cartridges. All I have is this one," he said as he held up the vape pen. The cannabis infused liquid in the cartridge was down to about one third of the clear, plastic vial.

"Then I suppose it will have to do," said Heinrich as he plucked the pen from Andy's hand.

"But, huh, you see," Andy stammered as he watched Heinrich unscrew the cartridge from the slim battery.

"But I'm afraid your battery is not up to this task," Heinrich said with a smile as he handed the battery back to Andy. "Let's see if this will work," he said as he screwed the cartridge into the inner threads of his ornate vape mod. He looked at the mouthpiece, shrugged, and wiped it off with his thumb and forefinger. He then pushed a button on the side of his device, sucked mightily on the cartridge, and then exhaled a massive plume of vapor.

He smacked his lips and tongue, and then shrugged again. "Unusual. Perhaps a bit grassy tasting," he said to Andy, "but *anything* is better than the Hurricane fluid!" He then said, "I'm a bit busy at the moment, but I shall pay you for this cartridge immediately after the auction."

"Huh, I don't think you should…" said Andy slowly, wondering when that massive drag was going to hit Heinrich. While Heinrich had been testing the vape cartridge, Andy thought he could actually see the liquid in the cartridge getting lower.

"Nonsense, I insist on paying you," interjected Heinrich. "After all, I am certainly able to afford it!" He smiled at Andy, took another deep pull on the vaping mod and walked out onto the stage, a huge cloud of vapor trailing behind him.

Guidry stood there watching him walk to center stage. He reached up and pushed the transmitter button. He opened his mouth to speak, realized he didn't know what to say, so he released the button and just stood transfixed as the scene unfolded.

As soon as Heinzburg appeared on stage the chanting immediately stopped. Heinzburg took another massive hit on the vaping device and blew it out. He then looked down at the device and squinted at the cartridge. His felt his head was wobbling a bit, although only on the inside, and he seemed to have trouble focusing. He then closed his eyes, shook his head, and then opened them. As he did, he seemed to finally notice the sea of faces looking at him.

Heinzburg stopped and smiled. He imaged the faces as big daisies turning to the sun. His smile grew even bigger when he realized that he was the sun. Suddenly, with a start, he remembered why he was on stage. He was thinking that something was very, very wrong as his hand lifted the vaping device to his lips.

Heinzburg felt he was moving in slow motion as he turned and looked over to Guidry. The wide-eyed look of concern on Guidry's face was both horrifying and comical. Guidry was making a *cut* gesture, four fingers together, palm facing down, wrist pivoting as the fingers waved across his throat. He was also shaking his head in an emphatic *NO!*

Heinzburg then pulled the vaping device away from his lips, looked at it, and asked himself if he might be in trouble. He immediately answered himself with the confirmation he most definitely was. He then smiled and giggled a bit at his internal conversation. He then looked up at the sea of faces, still intently watching him, and slowly returned his vape mod to its custom holster.

He looked over at Guidry, who was now just standing there watching him; eyes wide open in a combination of shock and fascination. Heinzburg shook a finger at him, smiled, and then turned to the audience.

"Ah yes, the provenance," he started. His previous sharp, controlled gestures were now past the point of being sloppy. He smiled and continued, taking great care to enunciate each word in the car's name, "The proof that this car, this 1940… 770k… W150… Grosser… Tourenwagen, was once," he stopped, smiled, and continued, "Well, more than once, but was used, huh, was ridden in, by…" the smile remained on his lips, but drained away from his eyes and voice, "Herr Adolph Hitler… also known as, der Führer."

He paused and looked at the crowd. They were still looking at him, but with a different kind of look; a look that plainly wondered what the hell had happened to him.

Jay Bozeman was just shaking his head, thinking that Heinzburg guy obviously couldn't hold his liquor. He drained the plastic glass of his third margarita and raised his arm to signal the bartender gal. Almost immediately the auctioneer's voice boomed out with, "Sir, we are not taking bids at this moment."

The entire audience turned to look at Bozeman, who just smiled and slowly lowered his arm. Noticing the bartender was now looking at him, he called her over with a crook of his finger.

The audience turned back just in time to see Heinrich exhaling a much smaller cloud of vapor with a somewhat goofy smile on his face. "As I was saying, this is what you came for. The proof that you are in the presence of a car that was touched, ridden in, and appreciated by Herr Hitler himself. Well then, let us proceed."

Heinrich paused, brought his vape mod up to his lips and then stopped. He looked at it, smiled, then lowered it and continued. "But first, a little assurance that this proof, this provenance, remains in the sole possession of the new owner. I have had to shoulder this… this revelation for far too long. It is time to pass it on."

Heinrich then walked to the front of the stage, looked up at each of the camera turrets in the rigging and then slowly looked out to the crowd. "There will be no cell phone videos allowed during this presentation," he said. He paused for a second and then shouted, "NONE!"

He then gestured to the rigging and said, "If you look up, you will see the cameras turn away from the stage." The crowd looked up and, as if their movement was a cue, the cameras simultaneously spun around and faced the back of the hall.

Heinrich then pointed to the jib camera. "And this one as well," he said as the jib arm swooped over the heads of the audience and rested on its stand, camera pointed away from the stage.

"And the cameramen." Heinrich said as each of the camera operators removed the huge cameras from their shoulders and placed them on the floor in front of them.

Heinrich then smiled. Shading his eyes, he scanned the room and, once he found them, wagged his finger at each Twin individually. "And that means you as well, Mandy and Brandy. And may I say how nice it is to see you two again."

The Twins were on opposite ends of the room, just outside the audience area. Until Heinzburg had taken the stage they had been pretending to photograph the Mardi Gras props that lined the perimeter. They shrugged and turned their cameras away from the stage as well.

Bobby Raston just smiled and looked down at the RigMaster. The screen was showing the 720p feed that was being recorded from one of his mic rigs. His fingers danced over the controls to point the other one towards Heinrich as well.

Heinrich then walked over to the massive IMAG screen on stage left, the side that Andy was on. He turned to the audience, gestured to the screen and began speaking, "And now…" he started, pausing for effect.

Suddenly Saul Wittmann yelled out from the back of the room, "NO BIDS FOR HITLER HATE!"

The room was dead silent for three seconds until Heinrich smiled and broke the silence. With his German accent more pronounced than ever, he wagged his finger at the back of the room and said, "Vee shall see."

The room suddenly went dark as the provenance video began to play.

## CHAPTER 65

# If There Are No Questions

*Saturday – August 26 – 6:31 PM CDT*

> "Start... the... bidding!"
> — Pat McMillian

"Speicher Dokumentation, Lager 32, Filmteam 5, 12. Juli 1944" was written on a small chalkboard in front of the camera. The black and white film looked remarkably good, with just enough film artifacts to suggest its age.

There was no audio on the film and the room was silent as all eyes were on the two massive screens.

As the chalkboard was removed, the entrance to the hillside cavern was revealed, looking far less overgrown. The camera tilted up to see the number 32, plainly visible over the entrance. As the camera tilted down, a young man in a

German officer's uniform stepped in front of the camera. His insignia identified him as a Sonderführer, a propaganda specialist. He looked up at the number, asked a question of the camera operator, and then gave the universal signal to "cut the camera."

The scene then changed to the interior of the cavern. The camera now shot through a very wide-angle lens and was panning the three rooms. The two on the left had the strong wooden shelves from the earlier video, although now they looked newly built. The top shelves were filled with large paintings stacked vertically on end, their ornate frames touching each other. The bottom shelves held wooden crates, interspersed with small statues.

As the camera panned to the third room, the auction audience gasped. In it was the Tourenwagen, albeit a lot more shiny. Two skinny, ragged-looking civilian men are working on the car, obviously prepping it for storage, while a third is mixing something in a wheelbarrow by the entrance. A German soldier is guarding them, holding a Maschinenpistole 40 submachine gun. The guard is obviously cognizant of the camera, as he stands a bit stiffer and more attentive than seems appropriate for the duty at hand.

The massive automobile is on jack stands, the tires a couple of inches off the ground. Large metal pans are under the car. Radiator fluid is draining into one of the front ones, with another is positioned under the engine to catch the oil. One of the workers is holding a siphon hose at the rear of the car, draining the gas tank into a large metal container. Behind the car there were more of the wooden shelving racks. These, however, are stacked with metal containers, presumably filled with fresh fluids for the car. On the side of the room are pallets of bricks, next to the man working at wheelbarrow.

The young Sonderführer steps into the scene and begins to indicate what he would like for the next shot. He uses his hands as a framing device; index fingers pointing up with thumbs out to the sides and touching each other.

Suddenly, the director snaps to attention. The camera then shakes a bit, as if the operator has quickly removed his hands. The guard also comes to full attention, making his previous *on-camera* stance seem almost leisurely in comparison.

A man then strides briskly into the frame, his back to the camera. He is wearing an impressive light-colored uniform with a peaked cap and a swastika armband. He is followed by two men, each wearing identical, long black leather overcoats. One is about the leader's height and the other a head taller. They all walk directly to the car, without even acknowledging the others in the room. The shorter officer opens a rear door for the man with the armband. With his back to the camera, the man takes off his gloves and lays them on the seat. He then reaches in, opens a small compartment, peers inside, and then shakes his head.

He stands up, obviously agitated. He then leans speaks rapidly to the taller of the men in the leather coats. The man immediately begins shouting at the guard and a flurry of activity ensues. Just as the man in the lighter colored uniform is turning around, the director steps in front of the camera for a moment and its view is blocked.

Only seconds later, the director steps away and the civilians are now being lined up against the left wall of the

Tourenwagen room. The shorter officer has a Walther PP pointing at them. As the guard searches them, his MP 40 is slung around on its shoulder strap and resting against his back. The man with the armband is now standing in the foreground of the shot, at the edge of the frame; his back is to the camera with his hands clasped behind him.

The guard then pulls a small, shiny revolver from the pocket of one of the workers. The man immediately drops to his knees, puts his face in his hands, and quite obviously starts to sob. The guard, paying no attention to the crying man, walks over and presents the revolver to the taller of the leather-clad men. That man cradles it in his hands, as if it were an object of extreme value. He then walks over to the short man with the armband, whose back is still to the camera.

The man unclasps his hands from behind his back and takes the revolver from the officer. He looks down at it for a moment, and then slips it into his pocket. He then speaks to the officer, who immediately raises his arm and mouths, "Heil, Hitler!"

The tall man then turns and says something to his companion. The shorter man takes two steps forward and shoots the kneeling man through the top of his head and into his body The man topples over onto his face, and black blood begins to seep out from the hole in his skull.

The taller man then asks the guard, who is now standing at attention, a short question. The guard points to one of the two remaining workers. The tall man speaks to the shorter one again. The short man uses the pistol to motion the indicated worker to step away from the other one. He then calmly shoots the remaining worker. While a relatively small hole appears on the man's forehead, just above the left eye, the wall behind him is splattered with blood, brains, and skull fragments.

The director, barely visible at the extreme right edge of the frame, leans over and vomits onto the ground. His stomach is visually convulsing as the thick, chunky fluid is ejected from his mouth. No one pays attention to him.

The man with the armband gestures to the Tourenwagen and, with a circular motion, references the large opening to the room.

The guard then shouts at the remaining civilian who is staring down at his dead companions. The guard shouts again and the civilian seems to shake uncontrollably for a couple of seconds. He then slowly walks back to the wheelbarrow, where he had been working just moments before.

The guard, the men in the black coats, and the somewhat shaky director all turn and salute the man with his back still to the camera, but whose swastika armband is clearly visible. The man returns the stiff armed salute and turns to leave. He is so close to the camera, that only the bottom half of his face is visible. But while it is somewhat out of focus, the black toothbrush mustache is unmistakable.

As the two SS officers follow the man out of frame, the guard begins yelling at the remaining worker. The man picks up a trowel from the ground, dips it into the wheelbarrow and slathers a bit of mortar onto the concrete floor. He then places one of the bricks onto it and repeats the process.

As the man is laying the bricks, the picture seamlessly dissolves into the last scene of the previous video. The registration of the two scenes is so perfect, the finished brick wall seems to magically appear into the opening. The video changes to color as film grain gives way to high definition crispness. On the screen, Heinzburg is once again sitting with his back against the bricks, the sound of his sobbing filling the room.

Suddenly, the on-screen Heinzburg looks up, takes a deep breath, and gracefully rises to his feet. He then walks over and looks directly into to the camera. With his breath just barely visible in the cold, and his cheeks plainly showing tear tracks against dusty skin, he says, "Lass uns das machen." A subtitle appears that reads, "Let's do this," and he turns and starts shouting to the crew.

One of the crew rushes in with a small air chisel and hands it to Heinzburg. He looks at it briefly, as if savoring a monumental moment. He then turns and attacks the wall.

The hard metallic sound of the compressed air slamming the chisel back and forth blends with the gritty, cracking sounds of the wall being hammered open and chunks of brick falling to the concrete floor. The noise, reverberating in the stone chamber, pours out of the speakers and fills the auction hall.

The scene then cuts from the stationary, tripod-mounted camera to a series of beautiful images, seamlessly edited together. From close-ups of the chisel tip as it effortlessly batters its way through timeworn brick and mortar, to low, wide-angle shots of the wall with Heinzburg attacking it, to ground-level macro shots as large clumps of brick fall and bounce into the frame before being snatched up and tossed to the side by other members of the crew. The variety of the shots, combined with the intricate editing, compress the actual demolition time to well under ten seconds. But those ten seconds are incredibly compelling; it leaves the viewer wanting more.

The cacophony abruptly ends as the scene cuts to an extreme close up of Heinzburg. Sweat has beaded up and rolled down his face, leaving wet tracks from their passage. His heavy breath is now clearly visible in the air. The camera cuts to an over the shoulder shot, revealing the destroyed wall with the Tourenwagen beautifully framed in the now open alcove.

Just as the air chisel slips from his grasp, the camera cuts to a ground-level shot. In slow motion, the tool slams onto the concrete floor. The audio, also slowed down, sounds like a gunshot as it reverberates against the cavern walls, and then echoes through the large auction hall. As Heinzburg walks towards the car, the compressed air hissing from the now still hammer mixes with the sound of his boots as they crunch across the debris-laden floor.

The shot changes to a POV as he steps over the archway and into the alcove. The car fills the frame. It is covered in dust and cobwebs but otherwise looks exactly as it had in the Speicher Dokumentation film.

The scene then does a slow dissolve from the POV shot of the car to a flurry of quick cuts, all in close-up. The sequence details the process of taking the car off the jacks, moving it out of the cavern and into the large trailer attached to the M-B G63. What certainly took hours is seamlessly compressed into less than a minute of screen time. The final shot is a road-level view of massive tires rolling across the screen. As the trailer passes it, the camera pans over to watch the truck and trailer, with the Tourenwagen strapped onto it, slowing driving away.

As the video faded to black, the Tourenwagen graphic appeared and the lights slowly came back on. Heinzburg was standing by one of the screens, still staring at it, seemingly lost in the moment.

Suddenly, he turned and smiled at the audience, most of which looked as though they had just awakened from a trance. Murmurs of sound began to float above them, as they started to jabber about the video among themselves.

In Heinzburg's highly altered state of mind, he thought he could actually hear snippets of the various conversations. And, as he heard them, he felt he could almost see the sound bites as written words floating above the audience; *Incredible, Mind Blowing, Stunning, Tour de Force.*

Heinzburg smiled at that last one, his eyes a bit hooded as he slightly swayed from side to side. He then realized someone was calling his name. He shook his head and managed to push his attention through the cannabis haze just as the sentence ended with, "More to add, Herr Heinzburg?"

He looked up at the auction platform and saw that both the auctioneer and Pat McMillian were looking at him. They both looked a bit alarmed, but Heinzburg thought that McMillian looked especially agitated. For a moment he was lost in thought as he wondered why. He started to open his mouth to ask him, actually forgetting he was on a stage in front of hundreds of people.

A sudden burst of applause, as people rose to their feet, made him remember where he was, and what he was supposed to be doing. Heinzburg smiled at the applause, walked to the front of the stage and bowed. Then, as if pointing out a co-star, he gestured to the Tourenwagen, bathed in lights on its own stage. The applause doubled. Heinzburg's smile grew even larger.

"Danke," he said to the audience. "Danke sehr... Thank you very much. And now, if there are no questions, let us continue with the auction."

Pat McMillian's attention was cemented on the whale bidders. From the looks on their faces, it wasn't going to be that simple. Not by a long shot.

"Start the bidding," Pat hissed to Frank, who himself seemed to be mentally digesting what he just experienced on the screen. "Start it!"

Frank turned to him and asked, "What?"

Pat's eyes blazed as he said in a low, slow, forceful tone, "Start... the... bidding!"

Frank snapped too and immediately called out, while pointing to Dave Givens to indicate he was the last bidder, "The bid is four point two five million dollars. I have four point two five million dollars." He then swung his arm over to Mark Hanson and asked, "Do I have four point FIVE million, four point FIVE million, do I have four point FIVE million dollars?"

The crowd was silent while Mark Hanson was very obviously thinking about it. He was about to raise his arm, when Dave Givens called out, "Herr Heinzburg! I do have a question about the provenance."

Heinrich smiled. He held out his arms, palms up. As he rapidly curled his fingers into his palms he replied, "Bring it on!" His accent was far more Brooklyn than Bavaria. Then, as if realizing a gaffe, his eyes got a bit bigger as he shrugged and sheepishly continued, in his previous accent, "As you Americans are so fond of saying."

McMillian just shook his head and decided that he had to get Heinzburg off the stage. He stood up and started to leave the platform when he glanced over to where Prescott Hébert was standing. Hébert's gaze was focused directly on Pat and he was slowly shaking his head. Prescott pointed at him, and then a bit lower, signifying he should sit down. McMillian slowly lowered himself back into his chair.

"And the question is?" asked a smiling Heinrich, doing a very passable imitation of a game show host.

"Shit, shit, shit," Pat muttered under his breath. He looked over at the telephone operators. The two with current bidders on the line were rapidly talking into the mouthpiece, their hands covering their mouths, obviously explaining what was happening to their bidders. By the looks on their faces, this was going south, and getting there quickly.

He picked up the walkie talkie and exclaimed in a low, but urgent voice, "Schafer!"

"Go for Schafer," came the immediate reply.

"Be ready to pull that asshole off the stage on my cue and not a…" Pat stopped in mid-sentence when he realized that Dave Givens was talking.

"Roger that," replied Schafer, "Asshole off the stage, on your cue."

## CHAPTER 66
# Make It Three

*Saturday – August 26 – 6:42 PM CDT*

> "Dean, go backstage and
> babysit your buddies."
> — Antoine Guidry

"Is the car, as it sits on that platform, *exactly* as you found it? Has there been *any* additions or enhancements?" asked Dave Givens.

Heinrich swayed a bit on stage. He was thinking about another vape hit, telling himself it was purely for theatrical reasons. He immediately decided against it, but a millisecond later changed his mind.

With the practiced grace of a gun fighter, he snatched his vape mod from the holster. Keeping his eyes on Givens, he inhaled deeply and blew out a massive white cloud. Little eddies in it, seemed to swirl and glow in the stage lights.

Andy stared at Heinrich from offstage with a mixture of alarmed amusement and irritation. It was, after all, his only vape cartridge! He then looked at the huge cloud streaming from Heinrich and seriously wondered how the man was still even remotely coherent. He then smiled and thought that it really was true that youth was wasted on the young, and that this young one was indeed, totally wasted.

Andy then touched the transmit button on his earpiece and asked, "Are we getting this?"

He saw the subtle nods from the Twins. They were no longer even pretending not to be shooting the scene. But for once, nobody seemed to be paying any attention to them.

"Audio is good," replied Raston. "Damn good."

"Standing by," replied a once again, sullen sounding Dean.

Andy looked up at the camera pods in the grid and noticed they had turned back around. The A/V camera ops and the Jib were also back in play. Andy pressed transmit and said, "Dean, go backstage and babysit your buddies. And make sure my little recorder is still rolling."

Heinrich was looking up at the massive cloud of vapor rising from the stage. He then looked at his vape mod as if contemplating another drag, but instead gave his head a wobbly shake and returned the device to its holster.

He then smiled at Givens and said, "Danke for your question. It is obviously most important that this magnificent automobile be represented correctly. I can truthfully say, with complete and utter certainty, that this magnificent Mercedes Grosser Tourenwagen is exactly, and I mean EXACTLY, as she was when I personally removed her from that," Heinrich paused, searching for the right word, and then continued with a smile, "Third Reich repository of riches."

Givens stared at Heinrich, whom he could easily see was totally stoned. Givens did, after all, make his home in Hollywood. He didn't know what was going on, but he certainly knew that something wasn't right. In fact, he was beginning to think that something was very, very wrong.

Givens nodded his head, as though thinking about the answer, and then looked up at auctioneer and called out, "I withdraw my bid for this car."

The room fell silent, save a few murmurs from the crowd, and then broke into pandemonium with the entire audience seeming to speculate among themselves.

On the auction platform, Pat looked over at Frank. His eyes were blazing with anger, tinged with just a bit of fear. He put his hand over the mic and hissed, "He can't do that! Set him straight and do it NOW!"

"Well," replied Frank a bit confused. "We haven't actually sold the car."

McMillian didn't even have to look to know that Hébert's eyes were drilling into him.

"Fuck it! Go back to the last bidder and sell the fucking car," replied Pat.

"But that's a quarter mill lower!" replied Frank.

Pat's eyes were blazing as he slowly enunciated each word, "Sell the fucking car. Now. If you have to, keep backing it down until you get to the last phone bidder." He then looked over at the phone ops and saw the operators were all busily screwing up that option by telling their bidders what was happening.

"It is now back to you, sir," Frank's voice boomed out of the speakers as he pointed to Hanson, referencing his last bid. "Your bid is four point one five million, that's four point one five million dollars." His arm began swinging back and forth across the crowd as he continued, "Do I hear four point two five million, do I hear four point two five million?" He paused his swinging arm gesture, and pointed directly to the phone operators with an expectant look on his face, "Do I hear four point two five million dollars?"

Mark Hanson shot a look over to Dave Givens, wondering why he retracted his bid, and why the auctioneer didn't seem to care.

As if able to read his mind, Givens turned and looked at Hanson. He just shrugged at him and then turned back to the stage.

The IMAG screens on either side of the stage had huge close-ups of Heinrich's face, obviously both confused and incredibly stoned. It was as if he couldn't make up his mind whether to look at Givens, the Tourenwagen, or Frank and Pat on the auction platform.

"Do I hear four point two five million?" pleaded Frank, still pointing and looking at the phone operators. The two that were standing up, with phones to their ears, both just shook their heads.

Frank swung his arm back to the crowd and, pointing at Hanson said, "I have four point one five million going once. I have four point one five million going…"

"I withdraw my bid," shouted Hanson. The room fell completely silent for a full three seconds before the crowd began to howl.

Joe Fontenot no longer felt sleepy as he wondered what the hell was going on with this car. He then looked over at his partner, who still hadn't moved an inch despite the pandemonium. Joe smiled and thought he really needed to figure out how to do that.

Then, as the crowd went completely wild, he thought he heard something. It was like a bass beat coming from the trunk of the car but this time it was loud enough to hear even in the current mayhem. He realized he didn't recognize the song, if it even was a song, as the yelling and screaming of the crowd finally overwhelmed the thumping.

"Quiet... QUI-et... QUIET!!!" yelled Heinrich, over-modulating his mic and causing a massive feedback howl from the speakers, but for only a fraction of a second.

"I hate when people do that," muttered Malcolm as his fingers muted the channel on the audio board in the Video Village. He watched the monitor closely and when Heinrich began to speak again he clicked the channel live, but kept his finger on the fader.

"That guy is stoned out of his gourd," said Malcolm.

"*Camera 1, get the guy that asked the question,*" said Brian Simmons into the Clear-Com.

"*Got it,*" replied the camera op. The shot on one of the monitors was now a medium close-up of Givens.

"How about this, Cool-B?" asked Malcolm as he pointed to the monitor showing the feed from a grid camera, zoomed in on Hanson.

"Good thinking," replied Simmons. "We'll need that." He then keyed the Clear-Com and transmitted, "*Everyone, stay on your toes. This is about to get interesting.*"

"Thank you," said Heinrich to the audience as he slowly, and unsteadily, looked about the room.

His wandering gaze stopped as it fell on Givens. He stared at him for full five seconds before he spoke, "And why, if I may ask, after you have seen the provenance, do you want to retract your bid?"

"The car's not right," said Givens with a shrug while he returned the stare.

"Not right," repeated Heinrich. "I assume it was something in the provenance video that has led you to this... this conclusion."

"No," replied Givens. "Not necessarily. The provenance video was beautifully made. Perhaps too beautiful, but that is *not* the reason I have retracted my bid."

Heinrich opened his arms wide and played to the crowd, as if he was already vindicated. He then stopped, smiled at the crowd and walked off the main stage.

As he made his way to the Tourenwagen platform, he repeated Given's words, one by one and carefully enunciating each word and literally shouting the last one. This time Malcolm was ready on the channel fader and pulled it down just enough so that it neither distorted nor caused any feedback.

"Malcolm's good," thought Dean as he watched the audio meters on the Blackmagic Video Assist screen surge to the top of the range but not hit the red.

"The... Car's... Not... RIGHT!" said Heinrich as he walked past the still impassive Charlie Bonet and mounted the steps to the Tourenwagen platform that led to the front of the car.

Pat's eyes had probably never been that wide in his life. His lips were moving, but nothing was coming out. It was if he knew he needed to say something but he couldn't formulate the words.

The walkie-talkie on the table in front of him crackled with Joe Fontenot asking, "Is it OK for the owner to be on the platform?"

Pat looked down at the walkie-talkie and still couldn't think of anything to say. It was like being stuck on the train tracks and seeing the locomotive headlight, way off in the distance but steadily getting bigger.

Schafer's voice came right after Fontenot and asked, "Mr. McMillian?"

"And what... EXACTLY... isn't RIGHT about this... CAR?" asked Heinrich, now standing next to the beautiful, ornate grill of the huge automobile.

Not getting an answer from McMillian, Fontenot had nevertheless decided he should at least mount the stage to be at the ready. He was now standing directly opposite Heinzburg, at the rear of the car.

Givens cocked his head and nodded it ever so slightly, as if he were thinking about the question. Finally he replied, "Do you really want to know? Right now? It is, after all, merely an *opinion* on my part."

"An *opinion*," replied Heinrich, as if not fully understanding the term. His lips were smiling but his eyes were blazing. "It is your OPINION that this car isn't RIGHT?" he said.

By this time the room was virtually silent as all eyes were on Heinrich. His face filled the IMAG screens and his red rimmed eyes gave him a manic look as he stared at Givens.

"And WHAT in your opinion, if may I be so bold to ask, is not RIGHT about this…" asked Heinrich, who suddenly stopped and looked at Joe Fontenot, who was staring at the trunk of the car. He then smiled, giggled a bit and continued with, "Other than having MC Hammer in the trunk?"

Now that the hall was virtually silent, the people nearest the stage could easily hear the muffled thump of a discordant bass line, and the barely audible "Can't Touch This!" lyrics coming from the trunk.

Heinrich smiled and turned back to Givens and said, "Is that the 'issue?' Is that what's *not right*? Well then, let's fix it." He turned back to Joe Fontenot, started walking towards him and said, "Officer, would you be so kind as to…"

Pat finally broke out of his temporary catatonia and snatched up the walkie-talkie and transmitted, "Schafer! Don't let them…," but stopped speaking when he saw that Schafer had already bounded up onto stage. Pat saw in horror that Schafer had his Glock 21 in hand, but hanging down by his side, shielding it from the crowd's view.

"Fontenot!" shouted Schafer, "Don't touch that trunk!" Heinrich turned to look at Schafer, back at Fontenot, and then back at Schafer. He opened his mouth, started to speak, but couldn't think of what to say. So he just left it open.

Joe Fontenot had been reaching down for the trunk handle, but stood back up at Schafer's command. He then saw the gun in Schafer's hand and started reaching for his own pistol.

Schafer's hand immediately came up to waist level, and pointed the gun at Fontenot. He was no longer attempting to hide the gun from the crowd, which by now had mostly risen to their feet. A few were trying to leave, but most seemed mesmerized by the scene and stood quietly watching, save for a few muttered comments like "Oh shit." and "He's got a gun."

The IMAG screens then switched to show a medium close up of Schafer with the gun at waist level and pointed directly at Fontenot. Schafer drew in a deep breath and shouted out, "Back away from the trunk."

As if on cue, the trunk started thumping. It was still playing "Hammer Time" but the thumps were not even close to being in sync.

Fontenot raised his hands just a bit, to show they were away from his gun and slowly said, "Look Schafer, I don't know what's going on here, but it stops now." Joe pointed to the trunk and said, "You're going to put that gun down and I'm going to open this trunk."

Heinrich, as if finally realizing that he was between two armed men in a serious situation, started walking to the edge of the platform. Schafer took two quick steps, grabbed Heinrich around his neck and pulled him close to act as a shield. He lifted his Glock to shoulder level and pointed it at Fontenot and "Don't be a rent-a-cop hero! Back away from the fuckin' car."

Joe looked at him, his eyes in slits and steely resolve on his face. He briefly looked past Schafer and then, with a barely perceptible smile on his lips, replied, "Rent-a-cop, sometimes. NOPD, all the time. Drop your weapon now and no one gets hurt."

"I tried…" said Schafer with a shrug and a smile. His shoulder lifted and his arm began to straighten out, his muscle memory kicking in to absorb the recoil.

Blood, bone, and brain matter then splattered the audience in sync with a mighty BOOM. The upward trajectory of the bullet caused the gore to easily reach the people closest to the platform. Some of the crowd screamed, but most still stood there, transfixed by the scene.

Schafer immediately dropped to the floor of the platform, dead before he hit it. Blood and gore continued to pour from what was left of skull. His body fell against the back of Heinzburg's knees, making them buckle and causing him to pitch to the platform as well.

The crowd in the back of the room, watching the IMAG screens, had seen Schafer's head explode. As he fell, the rig-mounted camera was at the perfect angle to revel Charlie Bonet standing at the rear of the stage. The camera zoomed in to reveal a small curl of smoke exiting the barrel of his own, outstretched Glock.

Fontenot ran over to Schafer and Heinzburg. He knelt beside Heinzburg, looked him over without touching him, and then asked, "Are you wounded?"

"No," Heinrich replied. "No, I don't think so."

Fontenot helped him to his feet, a bit more forcefully than necessary, and moved him aside. He then stared down at Schafer, moved the pistol that was lying next to his body a few feet away and then looked over at his partner. He gave Bonet a quick nod. Bonet returned it as he holstered his Glock. Fontenot reached into his pocket, pulled out his phone and paused. He had to think about how exactly to call this in.

Heinzburg, who was now in shock in addition to being stoned, wobbled his way to the back of the car. The music had stopped, but the thumping had not. He cocked his head over and looked at it. He then reached down and opened the trunk.

The IMAG screens showed a close up of the trunk lid as it opened and revealed the swollen, bloody, bruised, and battered face of Jack Calman poking out from the tarp he was wrapped in. The one eye that wasn't swollen shut by the puffy purple skin was now squinting at Heinrich, who was outlined by a halo of stage lights. In Jack's barely coherent state, he mouthed the word, "Nina?" The one arm he had managed to free from his polypropylene shroud was still moving, as if it continued to beat against the trunk lid.

Joe Fontenot, standing by Schafer's body, was talking on the phone but staring at the wide-eyed, horrified look on Heinrich's face as he stood looking down at the open trunk.

"We'll need an M.E. and a vehicle to transport the body. No hurry," he was saying as he walked towards Heinrich. As he walked to back of the trunk and saw Jack in the trunk, arm still moving feebly, he said into the phone, "Scratch that, we'll also need an ambulance and a medical team, STAT."

Suddenly a voice from the auction platform yelled "Sell the car, damn you! Sell the fucking car!"

Almost immediately, the PA system boomed as Frank's rapid-fire voice asked, pointing to Bozeman at the rear of the room, "Do I have four million? No?"

Frank's outstretched finger then swung over to the other side of the room as he implored, "Three point five million dollars, that was your last bid sir, three point five million. Do I still have three point five million dollars? Yes, I still have three point five million, going-once-going-twice-sold!"

"What the hell," screamed McMillian from the platform. "That's not enough!"

"EVIL!" screamed a voice from the back of the room. "NO BIDS FOR HITLER HATE!"

All eyes, a cameraman, and two of the robotic cams, immediately turned to Saul Wittmann. His hair was disheveled and his eyes were wide and wild as he looked about the room and again screamed, "That car is EEEEVVVVIIIILLLLL!"

He then stopped abruptly and stared across the room. One of the camera ops, swung around and the IMAG screen cut to Herman Adler. Adler, looking a bit dazed and a lot confused, was standing there, still holding up his bidding credentials.

The screen then cut to the horrified look on Saul Wittmann's face. Suddenly he looked up at the sky, clutched his chest, and fell like a stone.

"Correction," said Joe into his phone. " We need two medical teams. Possible heart attack, repeat possible heart attack in progress." He then looked over at Heinrich, calculated the distance, and realized he wasn't going to make it.

Fontenot tried anyway and came really close to catching Heinzburg as he crumpled to the platform floor, smacking his head against the bumper of the Tourenwagen as he went down. Fontenot looked down at the man, now with blood streaming from his head. He sighed, lifted the phone and said, "Make it three, repeat, three med teams to the River City Complex."

As if on cue, the crowd burst into a screaming mass of moving bodies. As people started to stream towards the exits, Joe looked up and screamed at Pat McMillian, "Secure the exits. Have your people secure the exits. Nobody leaves the building!"

McMillian leapt up from the platform and literally ran down the steps to the auction floor. But instead of rushing to the exits, he ran to Prescott Hébert, who seemed mesmerized by the scene.

"I don't know what the hell is going on," he blurted out to Hébert. "I had nothing to do with this, but we can stop it. It's not too late."

Prescott turned to look at him and asked, "Stop what? Stop this?" as he gestured to the pandemonium.

"Stop the money transfer!" said McMillian. "I, huh, we aren't going to make any money from this. You can tell the bank. They'll listen to you. Tell them to hold the transfer! We've got to stop it now!"

Prescott Hébert's eyes narrowed as he asked, "Didn't that buyer have a bid bond with us?"

"Yes, but... but... but..." stammered Pat, as he desperately tried to think of some reason other than the fact he wouldn't get a dime out of this.

In a low, controlled monotone that suggested he shouldn't have to explain this, Prescott replied, "A-Bear auctions *does not* renege on a deal. Now go do what that officer told you to do and lock this place down. We *will* talk about this later."

Guidry walked out of the wings and onto the main stage. He looked at Joe Fontenot yelling at the crowd, giving instructions, and motioning for Charlie Bonet to go over and cover the main exit.

Guidry looked over at the Twins who were busy shooting the pandemonium in visual syncopation. He then locked eyes with Raston, who had a huge smile on his face, pointed to his ears, and gave him a thumbs-up.

Andy reached up and touched the transmit button on his earpiece and asked, "Dean, do we have this?"

After a couple of very long seconds, Dean's voice replied, "We've got it. We've got it all."

Andy stood there. Considering the circumstances and the chaos, he was trying hard not to smile, but was losing the battle. Nodding his head and looking around the room he softly said a single word, "CarAlity." As his grin became so big it literally hurt his face, he added, "It fits."

# CHAPTER 67

# Nowhere Else To Go

*Saturday – August 26 – 9:12 PM CDT*

> "Malcolm, you heard the man."
> — BRIAN SIMMONS

"By the time I got back with the first aid kit, Schafer said the ambulance had already taken him away," Pat McMillian told the detective. Trying hard to sound sincere, he continued with, "I was going to check in on Jack the very moment the auction was over. He is, after all, a very close friend."

"And you didn't think it was *odd* there were no police involved. That no one was asking you any questions about the incident?" asked the detective.

"Schafer was connected. He told me he had handled it and I… well, I believed him," replied Pat. He then leaned in a bit and lowered his voice, like he was imparting something in confidence, "I was scared not to."

The detective just looked at him, shook his head, sighed and said, "Yeah, well, when Mr. Calman is more coherent, we'll very likely have more questions for you. Don't leave town."

"Or course not," said Pat, a smarmy smile plastered on his face. "Anything I can do to help the NOPD. Thankfully, I hire a lot of your fine officers for my events, and I pay them quite well." With what he considered a subtle wink and a nod, he continued with, "If you catch my drift."

The detective just shook his head, closed his notebook and walked away.

The auction hall was now nearly empty. The majority of the crowd had been briefly questioned and then released. Of course, as they left the building they were literally ambushed by various news media outlets.

Backstage, in the Video Village, Malcolm had just finished showing the lead detective the multi-cam feed of the shooting for the third time. All the various angles were playing in sync, each in their own little window on the massive flat-screen preview monitor. The program monitor was playing the live-switched recording, also in sync.

The detective looked at Brian Simmons and asked, "You were, like, editing this as it was happening?"

"We call it live switching," replied Brian. "It's what we do."

"But there was a shooting," the detective continued, a bit incredulous. "Someone died, right in front of you and you kept, huh, live switching?"

Malcolm spoke up with a big smile, "Nothing fazes Cool-B. He's the pro's pro."

"Yeah, well," replied the detective, shaking his head. "We're going to need to confiscate all the video footage you've got until the investigation is complete."

"Pull the hard drives," Simmons said to Malcolm. "And don't forget the..." he was looking at the place where the small Blackmagic video recorder had been. There was now only the SDI cable; one end lying on the console top, the other still connected to the patch panel.

"Don't forget the *what?*" asked the detective.

"The, huh, the proper shut down procedure," replied Brian. "Malcolm, you heard the man. Give him everything we've got."

Guidry and his floor team were still in the auction hall. They had already been questioned, but been told to stay until the rest of the *principles* had been cleared. And that it was verified they had permission to be there with all their equipment.

Earlier, while they had been waiting their turn with the police, Guidry had looked up and seen Dean Preston slowly walking towards them. He had wisely left his post in the Video Village before the detectives had gotten there.

Guidry, looking at Preston, had cocked his head, raised his eyebrows, and lifted his hands as if to ask a question. Preston just nodded, and slightly lifted a crumpled paper bag he had liberated from the Video Village trashcan. In it was the Blackmagic video recorder.

"Just keep walking," said Andy holding down the transmitter button on his earpiece before Dean got too close. He didn't want to call attention to the fact that Dean was with them. What he wanted was to get that footage out of the building as soon as possible.

"Go get in line to leave," Andy transmitted, "We'll meet you at the Escalade when we're done. If they ask you what that is, tell 'em it's your movie player, but the battery's dead."

Preston had stopped in his tracks. He then slowly nodded, sighed, and started towards the exit, his back to Guidry with his shoulders slumped forward. Even from a distance, his depression was easily apparent.

"Dean," Andy said into the small microphone.

Preston stopped and turned, looking at Guidry expectantly from across the auction floor.

"You done good," said Andy. "This is great TV. Incredible TV. Honest to God, Reality TV. We're not here to manipulate what's happening, we're here to document it. And we did it extremely well. You're going to be proud to have been a part of this."

"Yeah..." said Dean, pushing the transmitter button on his device. "I'm sure I will." He then turned and continued towards the exit, carrying at least a million dollars worth of programming stashed in a stained, brown paper bag.

Heinrich was now sitting on the front edge of the Tourenwagen platform. He had more or less recovered from the shock, trauma, and his inadvertent cannabis overdose. He had since been interviewed and cleared by the police. Next to him on the platform was an open, multi-compartmented box with various medical supplies. Standing beside him was a medic who was finishing the last of the stitches on his scalp. Heinrich had refused to allow him to shave the area around the wound. A shaved patch on his head would be a little too distinctive, and he was planning on shortly becoming anything but.

"I still think you should let us take you to the hospital, Mr., huh…" said the paramedic and he dug into the box for a small pair of scissors.

"Heinzburg," Heinrich replied, "but no hospital. I will be fine." Heinrich looked at his watch and once again mentally calculated when he would need to leave for the airport. The pilot had already been paid. He would land, wait for exactly ten minutes, and then take off; either with or without Heinrich on board. But there was still a while before it was time to leave. He didn't want to be waiting for the small HA-420 HondaJet for too long. The longer he was at the small Lakefront Airport, the more chance he would be noticed and remembered.

"Those should come out in about a week," said the medic as he snipped at the last suture with the scissors and started packing up his kit. "Keep it clean and keep an eye on it. If it gets red or starts to burn, go to a clinic immediately."

The medic then picked up the kit and walked away.

Heinrich pulled out his vape mod and looked ruefully at it. Even if he had wanted to take one of his massive vape hits, it was no longer an option. There was only a small drop of sticky looking liquid left in the pre-fill cartridge he had gotten from that Dean, or Andy, or whatever his name was.

He then pulled out his phone and checked it again, as he had at least ten times since he had become coherent enough to remember to do so. His Cayman account balance had indeed increased by three point five million dollars. Heinrich smile got even larger, until it pulled on the stitches and turned into a wince. He toned it down a bit, but he was still smiling.

Earlier, when McMillian was leaving the auction, reluctantly following that old man who had told him he owned the business, he had given Heinzburg the universal *call me* sign. He had pointed to his ear and mouth with his outstretched thumb and pinky. Heinzburg had smiled and nodded back. He rationalized that since the sign was also a Russian gesture meaning to drink vodka, he might just have to fulfill that request. As long as it wasn't in a Hurricane.

Now, watching the medic go, Heinrich just sighed and shrugged his shoulders. He literally had nothing to do until it was time to leave for the airport. He wasn't particularly hungry and the mere thought of vaping made his stomach flutter. He had already checked out of his hotel and deposited his suitcase into the nearest dumpster. He wouldn't need his Heinrich clothes again, at least not for the foreseeable future. And if he did, he could always buy more.

It was the classic *hurry up and wait* situation, and he literally had nowhere else to go.

# CHAPTER 68

# Something Like That

Saturday – August 26 – 10:04 PM CDT

> "They just don't realize what
> it takes to make it."
> — Antoine Guidry

"Hi, remember me?" asked Andy as he stood in front of Heinrich, who seemed lost in thought as he was sitting on the stage in front of the Tourenwagen.

"Ah, yes," said Heinrich looking up at him. "It's Dean... or Andy... someone who is *not a reporter*." Heinrich had earlier seen him sitting with the garishly dressed fat man and the Twins as they were waiting to be interviewed by the police. Now, as he glanced around the room, he noted that the Twins and fat man were nowhere to be seen.

Heinrich shook his head ruefully and held up his vape mod, "You could have warned me."

"I tried but you were very insistent. And quick," replied Andy with a mischievous grin on his face. "Way too quick for an old man like me."

Heinrich smiled back, nodded his head, and then suddenly stopped with a wince on his face. He reached up and gingerly touched the fresh stiches on his head.

"So," he said to Andy, "Are you still not a reporter or still claiming not to be? Still claiming to be here merely to sell a car?"

"I'm not a reporter," replied Andy. "I am a TV guy, but I don't do news. And I really was here to sell a car. I consigned it over a week ago."

"And were you happy with your results?" asked Heinrich.

"Yes, I believe it all came out well," said Andy. "But how about you? Were you happy with your results?" Andy asked, gesturing to the car behind Heinrich. "It's not a lot of money for one hell of a lot of car, no matter whose butt used to grace the cushions."

Heinrich nodded his head in agreement. He started to look over his shoulder at the car but stopped in mid-motion with another wince. He turned back to Andy and said, "It is a lot of car, and it should have brought more money, but..." Heinrich slowly shook his head, mindful of the stiches. "Something happened after the provenance video. Givens, the movie man from Los Angeles, didn't like something." He shrugged, looked down and muttered, "I don't know why. The video is seamless."

Andy looked at him for a long time, studying his face. "Seamless is a good word. Cinematic would be another."

Heinrich looked up. Looking into Andy's eyes, he slowly smiled and replied, "Cinematic... yes, I think so." A more thoughtful purse of the lips replaced the smile as he continued, "Do you think it is *too cinematic*?"

Andy shrugged and said, "No, not if it's supposed to be. You produce for your audience. People are used to seeing great work. They just don't realize what it takes to make it. And that's a good thing, as it would just spoil the illusion. For me personally, it was that lock-down transition when it went from 16mm film of building the wall to you sitting there, crying with your back against it. Nice touch by the way. You're an excellent actor."

"Danke," replied Heinrich, "Go on. You didn't like the shot?"

"I loved it," said Andy. " It was perfect. It was just too perfect to be real."

"Well," said Heinrich, "thank you, it certainly did take some effort. I suppose that the lovely Mandy and Brandy have told you of their involvement in the production."

"Not until late last night, and not personally. They don't seem to *share* a lot," replied Andy. "At least not with me. So, I didn't find out about it until today, and after all this happened. But to be honest, it really didn't matter and wouldn't have made a difference, one way or the other." He stopped, shook his head and continued, "Of course, I guess it mattered to Jack."

"Jack?" asked Heinrich and then quickly continued with, "Ah, yes, the man in the trunk."

Andy stared at Heinrich for a moment and then continued, "And you had nothing to do with that; with Jack getting his head bashed in and left for dead in the trunk of your car."

Heinrich sat up a little straighter and replied indignantly, "I most certainly did not. Seeing him in that trunk was... was..."

"Yeah," Andy interrupted, "I didn't think so. You're a good actor, great actually, but if you'd known about that, you'd deserve an Oscar just for the look on your face when you saw him in the trunk."

"You could see my face?" asked Heinrich.

"Everyone in the room could," replied Andy, smiling at the memory. "Your face was filling the video screen. That director on the video crew is incredible. You want to talk cinematic; those cuts were perfect."

"I have a feeling I will see what you are talking about," replied Heinrich. "And likely sooner than I'd like. Do you suppose it was the *cinematic* quality of the video that made Givens retract his bid?"

"No. At least I don't think that was all of it. While waiting for the cops to clear us, I had a quick conversation with Givens," replied Andy. "He also mentioned that the video was *too good to be real*, but said that wasn't why he pulled his bid. He said it had to do with Phillips head screws on the Nazi flags and your insistence that the car was exactly as you found it."

Heinrich just shook his head and muttered the old family motto. "Too much is too much," he said, more to himself than to Andy. "Subtlety is the mark of the master." He then smiled at Andy, sighed and said in a normal tone, "And I was so proud of those flags."

"If it's any consolation," Andy continued, "he said he withdrew his bid on impulse and was ready to continue bidding when, well, when all hell broke loose. He said before he knew what was going on, the car was sold."

"All hell did indeed break loose," said Heinrich. "But thanks to your, huh," he pulled out his vape mod, unscrewed the cartridge, and handed it to Andy. "Thanks to your little vial of vape juice, I don't seem to recall the details very clearly."

"I'm sure it will all be clear to you... eventually," replied Andy, looking somewhat incredulously at what little remained of the liquid in the cartridge. Andy took out his slender battery, screwed the cartridge onto it, and stuck it into his shirt pocket. He then studied Heinrich's face. Heinrich just stared back.

"So," asked Andy in a casual tone of voice, "Where did the car really come from and to whom does it belong?"

Heinrich smiled, paused a bit and replied, "Well, it now belongs to the man who bought it. And just because the video was *cinematic* doesn't mean it wasn't true. Although *based on a true story* might be a better description."

"Okay," replied Andy. "It's *based* on a true story. Then why not just tell the real story, without all the *embellishment*."

"Ahhh," replied Heinrich, "That would pose a bit of a problem," he said with a smile. "The Tourenwagen was in a place where its discovery would not be prudent to... to continued financial stability."

"Ok, fair enough? So you're saying you had to invent some sort of provenance because of," Andy turned and gestured to the platform, "whatever it is or wherever it's from. Okay, but even if you had to disguise its origination, why go with all this Hitler bullshit? Almost anything would have been easier to pull off, with far less chance of the truth coming out, whatever that is."

"My family, like all Jews, suffered greatly from the war, or at least during the war. We were — we are — what are sometimes referred to as *Gypsy Jews*. Traditionally, and to this day, our kind have always kept a very low profile. My ancestors sort of lived off the land, in the woods. They kept away from other people, as much as they could, but they also lived off them. During the war, my great-grandfather and our tribe were living in Czechoslovakia, near Lidice, close to Prague. It was under Nazi control, but that area wasn't a huge concern to the Third Reich. At least not near the end."

Heinrich paused, looked around, nodded to himself, and continued in a somewhat more confidential tone.

"The local Nazi command had helped themselves to most of the valuables throughout their little corner of the Reich. One night, with the war fast approaching its inevitable end, my great-grandfather was *conscripted* to help the senior German officers hide their ill-gotten gains. They came to our camp, entertained themselves by raping the women, and then took my great-grandfather to their storehouse thirty-two, along with his two brothers and his oldest son, my grandfather."

Heinrich paused, looked at Andy, smiled and continued. "It basically happened just like in the provenance video with a few *minor* differences. The main one being that when my great-grandfather found a pistol in the Tourenwagen, he immediately shot one of the guards. The other guards started shooting back. When it was all over, only my great-grandfather and his son were still alive."

"And in the first video, when you found the car," asked Andy, "was that also just based on a true story? Or was it real? Were you really seeing the Tourenwagen for the first time?" Andy smiled and continued with, "I mean *real* other than it actually being in the Hitler valley. When the drone did that great flipping maneuver at the end of the valley drop, there was the flash of nothing but blue sky. That is, of course, when you cut to the other footage, where the drone is flying to the car location. The real location."

"You are quite the TV guy," said Heinrich with smile. "Yes, that is exactly how I created the illusion that storehouse thirty two, and the Tourenwagen, were found in the Obersalzberg valley, instead of in our little, far more remote corner of the world."

"It was a great move," replied Andy. "Well planned, like everything in the video. But we were talking about whether the video of you finding the car was real?"

"It was a pre-planned reality," replied Heinrich. "It actually took a great deal of searching to find the storehouse. No one had been there in decades, and there aren't exactly road signs or GPS coordinates to go by. Some in our family didn't believe it would still be hidden, much less still have the car in it. But after a couple of months of traipsing through the woods, I finally found the lagerhaus zweiunddreißig, storehouse thirty-two. I personally knocked down enough of the hillside wall so that I could squeeze into the storehouse. I then drilled a small hole in the inner wall, and used an inspection camera to ascertain the car was still there. So, yes I did know it was there. I then repaired the hillside wall and left it at that."

Heinrich then paused and, with a shrug and a smile, continued with "That's when I began to plan the actual production. To produce something that would both enhance the vehicle value, and hide its true origination."

"Well it was an incredible presentation," asked Andy. "It was as good as anything I've seen on the big screen."

"Thank you," said Heinrich, all trace of his German accent was now gone, replaced with just the bare tinge of a Slavic tone. "My Master's degree was going to be in film. I was actually on a extended holiday, taking time off to decide on my thesis film project. That's when I decided to start looking for the car, the car my family had talked about for generations. I guess I just got too caught up in it."

"Wait a second," Andy replied incredulously. "This is your *student film*?"

"Well, sort of," replied Heinrich with a big smile. "But I don't think it would be a good idea to submit it."

"Anyway," Heinrich continued, "As luck would have it, after I found the car, I went to Cologne for Photokina, to decide on my production package. The first evening there, I met Mandy and Brandy shooting video at a market with the new Canon cameras. Of course, I had to talk to them. I am only human. And after seeing some sample video on their phones, I also knew I had to hire them. They were perfect. Not only did I think they were great shooters, I also figured that with their, as you put it, their *reluctance to share*, I wouldn't have to worry too much about undue publicity. At least I wouldn't until it was too late to matter. Later, I found out exactly how amazing they are. With what they shot, well, it was just too hard *not* to fully utilize it."

"How did you do the *provenance* video?" asked Andy. "I understand the Twins didn't work on that one and it was obviously the harder one to make."

"It most certainly was," agreed Heinrich. "Even with a very detailed script, that shoot took weeks of planning, days of rehearsal, and three takes of the money scene to get it right. It was a true directorial challenge. Plus it's damn hard to clean up stage blood and make the area look dirty again. And don't get me started on getting that damn car to look right, for both the *then* and the *now*."

"Directing is one thing, but you have to have good people to pull it off. Who did you use for that production?" asked Andy, with genuine interest in his voice. "That wasn't easy, especially not how well it blended into the HiDef footage."

"I utilized a Russian crew, both in production and in front of the camera. The drone pilot was incredible. Actually, the Russians have an amazing film community, especially in post-production and CG work," Heinrich replied. "It is, I believe, rather unappreciated."

Heinrich paused, took a deep breath and again touched the stitches on his head before he continued, "Anyway, the provenance video. What with shooting on 16mm film and the long continuous takes, it was quite a challenge to both the cast and the crew. But at four times their normal day rate, they didn't seem to mind it was a *student* project. They were also paid for their silence. I told them it needed to be kept *off-line* until its festival introduction."

"At four times my day rate, I wouldn't care either," replied Andy. "But, from one pro to another, I gotta commend you on one hell of a job! Where did you go to school?"

"I've been educated in the US since prep school. I did my undergraduate work at…" Heinrich suddenly stopped and shook his head. With the German accent back in his voice, and even more pronounced, he continued with a sly smile, "You are obviously very accomplished at interviewing, Mr. *I'm a TV guy, not a reporter*. I believe I have gone into far more detail than I should have. Likely due to the lingering effects of your vaping fluid."

Losing the accent, Heinrich continued, "After all, I'm going to need to be on the down-low for a while." Gently tilting his head towards the Tourenwagen he continued with, "Luckily, I can easily afford to do so. And, I might add, in considerable style."

"So, was it worth it?" asked Andy. "The Nazi connection kinda backfired on this. I think you could have gotten more money by just telling the real story. I'm a professional storyteller and that one is fascinating. And you wouldn't have had to spend all that money on the production."

"A lot of the *success* of my family, and its continued financial stability, is related to their acquisition of the other items that were in that warehouse," replied Heinrich with a sly smile. "Items that could be construed as not exactly falling into the *finders keepers* category. And we couldn't exactly put a car like this on the open market, with its real provenance, without calling attention to the, huh, how did that old radio commentator used to phrase it? Oh yes, to *the rest of the story*."

Heinrich sighed as the smile slowly left his face and continued, "But the money really wasn't the point. I've got money. And I always knew the subterfuge would be revealed. I really didn't care about getting anything more than what I considered a fair market value for the car, and only the car. I, we, my family… we thought, or rather, I convinced them it would be a nice *vehicle* in which to teach someone a lesson, perhaps even the entire world. I wanted to illustrate that putting a value on something, just because of its association with evil, is not a prudent thing to do; especially not *that* particular brand of evil. And what better way to teach, than through the power of film? Especially when combined with a very public loss of large amounts of money."

"Was A-Bear in on this, the subterfuge?" asked Andy.

"No. They believed what I told them," replied Heinrich. "At least I think they did. And I made it very much *worth their while* to want to believe it." He then smiled, shook his head ruefully and continued, "At least it was supposed to be worth their while."

"You say that as if it isn't; as if they aren't making any money?" asked Andy. "Ten percent commission on three and a half million dollars is still a hell of a lot of money."

"Like I said, money wasn't the point," replied Heinrich. "What I needed more than maximum profit was their complete cooperation in this consignment, as well as in every detail of the agreement. To quote a truly great movie line, *I made them an offer they couldn't refuse*. Had it been completely successful, they stood to make a lot of money, many times more than ten percent. It wasn't, so they won't. Just another lesson that one shouldn't dance with the devil."

Heinrich's phone buzzed and he looked down at it. He then hopped off the stage to his feet. He winced a bit at the pain in his head, but then stood up straight, clicked his heels together and said in his very pronounced German accent, "And if you vill now excuse me, I have un appointment to keep, und mein Uber iz here." He then briskly walked off towards the exit thinking he was really going to miss that whole heel-clicking thing.

Andy waited and watched until Heinrich left the building. He then tapped on his earpiece and asked, "Did we get it?"

"Of course," came the voice of Mandy, immediately followed by Brandy confirming, "We got it." They then ducked out from their shooting positions within two strategically placed Mardi Gras heads that flanked the room.

"How about audio?" asked Andy, tapping lightly on the pocket that held the folded up, microphone enabled glasses.

"Audio was outstanding!" replied an enthusiastic Bobby Raston who came rolling into the room atop the scissor lift. "Damn I love these mics," he said pointing to one of the Sennheisers in the grid. "They sound great, and we've got two additional video angles."

"Well then, grab your gadgets and let's get the hell out of here," said Andy. "And I don't care what anybody says. The name of this show is *CarAlity*, with a capital A." Andy paused and looked at the Tourenwagen and continued, "Make that, *CarAlity: A Tribute In New Orleans* because I'm pretty damn sure we're going to be making a bunch more of these shows. And in a lot of different places. Everyone up for that?"

"Sure," said Mandy.

"We're up for it," continued Brandy.

"Let's do it," said Bobby, as he walked off to get the scissor lift.

"I suppose so," said Dean who had been waiting in the Escalade. Even through the headset you could hear the somber tone in his voice.

Andy's phone buzzed and he took it out and looked at it. He smiled, pushed the transmit button on the earpiece and said, "I just got a text from Jack Calman. He says... huh, well he basically says we better have all of this in the can, because it's going to be one hell of a show!'"

"Really! He's texting you and he said that. Wow! That's great!" said a now enthusiastic Dean.

"Then fire up the Escalade and put the A/C on high. I want to get back to the hotel and start backing up footage. We've got one hell of a show to edit and I don't want to take any chances."

Guidry looked down at the text message from Calman. Reading between the numerous lines of the swearing and accusations, Guidry was thinking that was probably exactly what Calman had meant to say. Or, rather, likely would once the show was on the air.

Without a word, the Twins picked up their monopods and headed to the exit. Guidry stood there for a bit, watching Raston on the scissor lift as he removed the microphone pods from the grid. He was excited, elated, and invigorated. He was thinking that *CarAlity* was going to turn his career around and give him a new beginning; one he sorely needed.

Almost subconsciously Guidry's hand pulled the vape pen from his pocket. He stopped with it almost to his mouth. He then looked down at it, figured there might be a few normal size drags left in it. He then shrugged and tossed it onto the platform, where it rolled under the Tourenwagen and out of sight.

Andy suddenly remembered something that made him grin so big it hurt his face. "Hey, Bobby," he yelled up at the lift. "Thanks again for buying my car back. I appreciate that you know how much it means to me. I'm really starting to like this partner thing and that was simply a great gesture on your part."

Bobby just nodded, continued removing the audio rig and replied, more to himself than to Andy, "Yeah, it was something like that."

# EPILOGUE
# Who Knew

*Wednesday – August 26 – 12:22 PM CDT*
*(3 Years Later)*

> "I'd go get a seat now because
> it tends to fill up fast."
> — Herman Adler

"Aren't we there yet?" whined Marcus Sebastian Susskind. The thirteen-year-old boy had been grumbling about this trip since the day his parents told him about it. He had gotten so tired of the incessant pleading from Angie Susskind, his mother, to "Look out the window!" he had actually put down his Sony Vita. He was now staring sullenly at the Wisconsin landscape.

Highway 14 had just divided into two roads, as the GPS announced, "In one mile, exit right on Highway Zee Zee."

"Almost there," said Albert Susskind, Marcus' father. It had been his idea to make the four-hour trek. He had convinced himself it would be good for the boy, but, to be honest, it was he who was most looking forward to the trip.

He had first read about it in a *Hemming's Classic Car* feature. And, of course, being a car guy, he was a subscriber to NGTV ByDemand and literally loved the *CarAlity* series.

They had been seeing the occasional billboards for the last sixty miles, but this one was the biggest yet. In huge, bold letters it told them to "Visit the HEIL! Flip Off Der Führer! As Seen on CarAlity! Next Exit!"

"Here we go," said Albert as he piloted the Range Rover off Highway 14, and onto the two-lane road. The number of cars was a bit surprising, but the traffic moved along at a good pace on the rural road.

As they got closer to the HEIL, the traffic slowed as the cars pulled off the highway and were directed into the new parking lot.

After parking, they walked to the entrance instead of waiting for the shuttle. There was a single parking space next to the entrance and in it was a '76 Cosworth Vega. The car looked as though it had just rolled off the showroom floor.

In the window, next to the double glass doors, was a large sign that confirmed today was indeed the monthly presentation of *Let It Shine*. That explained both the traffic and the twenty-minute wait it took to get to the ticket counter. The ten-dollar per ticket surcharge didn't seem to be much of a deterrent, as these were always the busiest days.

"This is so BORING," whined Marcus, looking up from his iPhone. He had just been posting the exact same message to his Facebook page.

"Hush," said his mother, "We're not even inside yet. Now put away that phone."

Marcus just dropped the phone to his side and waited until his mother turned away. He immediately picked it up again and started to look through his news feed.

"Two adults and one student," Albert told the tall, muscular young man when they finally got to the counter. "We're not too late for the show, are we?"

"Nah, that'll be sixty-five dollars," replied the somewhat sullen cashier. He barely looked up as he ran the card Susskind had inserted into the reader. "You've got time."

Sunlight streamed in through the immaculate glass windows of the entryway. The walls were lined with various souvenir items. The most popular were the t-shirts with a picket sign graphic on the front proclaiming *No Bids For Hitler Hate*, although the newer *I Flipped Off Der Führer!* t-shirts were a close second.

Herman Adler was standing between the ticket counter and the entrance to the HEIL. Underneath the big letters was the full title, in initial caps, "Hitler's Evil Insidious Life."

Adler smiled as the Susskinds paid their sixty-five dollar entrance fee. His smile got even larger as he eyed the line of people behind them and began mentally tabulating the total.

Herman walked over to the counter, smiled and told the Susskinds, "*Let It Shine* begins in ten minutes. I'd go get a seat now because it tends to fill up fast. Enjoy your visit and thank you for coming."

As the Susskinds walked away, Albert and Angie's faces were lit up with expectation. Marcus' face was buried in his iPhone as he tapped furiously on the screen.

Herman then leaned over to his new employee and said in a low voice, "Steve, we've talked about you being more friendly to the customers. All these people driving out here is what pays your salary. You do like getting paid, don't you?"

"I'm sorry," replied Steve Rampart. "Of course I do. I'll try to be, huh, more, huh, friendly. I guess I just really wanted to…"

"No excuses," Herman forcefully cut in. "Just do the job."

"Yes sir, Her… I mean, Mr. Adler," said Steve through moderately clenched teeth and with what he hoped passed for a smile. He was thinking how much he hated that he really needed this job.

Herman replied, "You'll get the hang of it, Steve. I've got faith in you." His smile was genuine as he walked towards the entrance to the main hall and thought how much he loved that Steve really needed this job.

Herman walked into the hall and surveyed the scene. It was three years to the day that he'd been in the River City Complex nodding his head as the auctioneer screamed at him, "Three point five million! Do I have the three point five million?"

His face took on a somber expression as he recalled the shocked look on Saul's face after the man yelled "Sold!" and Saul had seen it was him who had bought the car. He also remembered the way the blood seemed to drain out of it as he clawed at his chest and fell like a stone. Herman closed his eyes, took a deep breath, and shook his head as if to clear the image from it.

He opened his eyes again and looked around the cavernous building. It was filled with people, crowded around the various interactive exhibits, each detailing a stage in Hitler's life. Nothing was hidden, nothing was glorified; it was like an onion with all the layers peeled back to reveal a rotten, slimy core.

There were exhibits on everything from his less-than-stellar service during WWI, his single-minded quest for power, his subsequent jailing, the writing of *Mein Kampf*, his manipulation of the German people, the war years, the sycophant generals, his drug addiction, the wanton greed for power, the decline into insanity, and, of course, the holocaust.

Easily his favorite attraction, and that of the visitors, was the *Sieggy Mobile*. It featured the Hitler statue, the one that literally started it all, as well as the main attraction, the 1940 Mercedes 770k W150 Grosser Tourenwagen. The lack of actual Hitler provenance was a non-issue. Now its provenance was that of making Internet-based video history. Herman had actually laughed out loud when, just a year after the auction, Dave Givens had called to offer him twelve million for the car.

It had been the featured car in the premiere episode of *CarAlity*, the number one automotive show on the web. Since then, the car had been featured in countless news stories, literally from around the world.

Two years ago, one of the visitors had posted a selfie of her flipping Hitler off. It had immediately gone viral on Instagram, reaching nearly ten million shares in less than three days. That little human interest story had also gotten its share of news media attention, and brought even more visitors anxious to give Hitler the one-finger salute. And to share that gesture with the world.

Herman had seen an opportunity, and capitalized on it. There was now a line of people waiting to climb the short platform that held a sidecar equipped, BMW R75 motorcycle. The motorcycle was in full WWII military trim and elevated to the same level as the Tourenwagen. It was positioned as if it was flanking it in a parade.

People depleted their debit cards by ten dollars at a kiosk at the bottom of the platform. They then climbed up and straddled the motorcycle and/or climbed into the sidecar. As they sat down, a pressure switch in the saddle triggered the video wall background to light up and start displaying the moving background. High-speed fans would complete the illusion of speed as a countdown clock started on the background screen.

At the end of the ten-second countdown, an integrated, precisely angled camera would then record fifteen seconds of UHD video, precisely framed for use on either YouTube or Instagram. The illusion of riding next to a smiling Hitler, with a background of thousands of saluting Nazis was quite realistic; even more so if you chose to have the video delivered in black and white.

By far the most common activity was *Flipping off Der Führer*. There were untold thousands of video clips floating about the Internet, as well as still photos pulled from the video clips. People came prepared with costumes, props, and carefully scripted scenarios designed to fit in the fifteen-second time frame.

After they left the platform, the patrons would go to any one of another bank of kiosks. There they would tap on an icon that represented their performance. They then had precisely ten minutes to review it, select two *stills* from the video, which were immediately delivered through a slot in the front of the kiosk, and send themselves a download link to the video clip.

This little bit of custom-made high technology had completely paid for itself in less than twelve weeks, as Herman knew it would. He had gotten very good at running numbers once the management of the HEIL had fallen to him.

Suddenly, the room lights dimmed as the sound of klaxon horns came through the overhead speakers. An intricate Dolby Atmos soundscape, complete with carefully placed sirens, machine gun fire, crowd noise, and distant bombs exploding, served as the background audio for the announcer.

"Ladies and gentlemen. Please direct your attention to the main stage where this afternoon's special presentation of *Let It Shine* is about to begin."

Herman smiled, and his head started nodding in anticipation of the music. That was still his favorite part.

The chairs in front of the stage were already filled to the tenth row. The lights in the main hall dimmed slightly, but seemed to be even darker in contrast to the brilliant lights that slowly faded up and illuminated the stage. Incredible sounds of the First Mission Baptist Church choir, recorded live in New Orleans, slowly filled the air.

> *"This little light of mine,*
> *I'm going to let it shine.*
> *Oh, this little light of mine,*
> *I'm going to let it shine.*
> *Hallelujah*
> *This little light of mine,*
> *I'm going to let it shine,*
> *Let it shine, let it shine, let it shine."*

"And I am!" came a booming voice as the music faded to a background level and a man walked out on stage. From his silk tie to his patent leather loafers, he was dressed entirely in white. He was resplendent and positively glowed from the backlights. A wild mane of pure white hair stood straight up, and looked almost like a halo.

"I am here to shine a light! And this light will not revere... but revile!" He paused for the applause and continued. "I am here to shine a light on the most concentrated depository of evil in the history of mankind!"

Herman then had an idea. He smiled at the thought and walked back into the entrance/gift shop area.

He tapped Steve Rampart on the shoulder and said, "I'll take over for a while. Go inside and watch the show." Herman smiled ruefully and continued, "I've seen it. A few times."

Steve looked up at Herman, then at the line of people that were impatiently waiting to pay the entrance fee. He then looked back at Herman with a hopeful smile on his face.

"Really," he asked, his eyes widening with anticipation. "I can really go see him?"

"Sure," said Herman. "You really can."

"Wow," replied Steve as he stood up a bit too quickly, wincing from the pain in his knee. "I've seen him on Joel Olsten twice, but to get to see Saul Wittmann testify, and in person, WOW! But he calls himself Paul now, right? Anyway, who ever knew that old man Wittmann was such an incredible speaker!"

Herman just nodded and sat down at the cash register. "Yep," he muttered to himself with a wry smile. "Who knew?"

# About The Author

J. Daniel Jones spent 8 years as a producer/director/host at a small TV station in San Diego, CA. During that time he received 7 EMMY˚ nominations and 3 EMMY˚ awards.

He spent the following eight years as a writer/producer in the corporate world working on big budget videos for hi-tech clients such as Intel, Siemens, and Motorola.

Finally, he was able to combine his television experience with his long-term love of classic cars and began working exclusively on automotive programs that aired on ESPN2 and The Outdoor Channel.

One highlight of his automotive television experience was the opportunity to shoot and field produce most of the 2005 season of *Hot Rod Magazine TV*, including two major cross country events, the "Hot Rod Power Tour" and the 1st ever "Drag Week."

He also successfully managed to avoid Montezuma's Revenge while shooting and field producing the "Carrerra La

Panamericana," a 7-day classic car race in Mexico. This made him quite a bit luckier than some of the drivers.

Jones was exposed to the collector car auction world while working as a episodic producer, and editing supervisor, for the first season of *At The Auction*, which showcased RM Auctions, now RM/Sotheby's, one of the world's premier auto auction houses.

His first car was a '64 Barracuda, followed by a '67 Comet Calienté and a '62 VW Bug, all before he graduated high school. He has a deep passion for old cars and currently owns a '64 Cutlass and '79 MGB. He has always lusted for a '68 911 Targa, and likely always will.

J. Daniel Jones lives in San Diego, CA with Cindy, his wife of 29 years, and their youngest son. They are also the proud parents of two older children, a son and daughter, who live in Los Angeles, CA and Salem, OR.

Made in the USA
San Bernardino, CA
02 March 2017